TAMING HUCK FINN

THE NEW ADVENTURES

E.E. BURKE

Cover Design by Erin Dameron-Hill

Cover image (painting) by Gary R. Lucy: THE BENTON: The Benton Steaming Past the White Cliffs in Montana, 1878. Courtesy of the Gary R. Lucy Gallery Inc., Washington, MO

Published by E.E. Burke
eBook ISBN: 978-0-9985382-4-2
Print book ISBN: 978-0-9985382-5-9
www.eeburke.com

This book is dedicated to the extraordinary man who gave America an unforgettable orphan named Huckleberry Finn.

AUTHOR'S NOTE

From an early age, I've been afflicted with a fondness for two precocious Missouri-bred boys introduced to me by Mark Twain. As I read (and reread) Tom and Huck's adventures, I hated to bid them farewell at a point where their stories were just taking off. I wanted to know what happened to them when they grew up. I wondered, *What if...?* For an author, pondering that question is a sure sign a book is about to be born.

Taming Huck Finn picks up Huck's story fifteen years after he "set out for the Territory" at the end of Twain's original novel, *The Adventures of Huckleberry Finn*. As in Mr. Twain's stories, the river is a primary character. Only in this book, it is the Missouri River, which at the time this novel is set constituted a natural border between civilization and the Western frontier. Along the way, Huck encounters surprises and challenges connected to American life and its spirit. He also sets out on his greatest adventure.

I humbly offer this historical tale with profound gratitude to the man who inspired it. Perhaps more than any other author, Mark Twain influenced my love of the written word and my belief in the power of a well-told story.

Special thanks to my editor, Jena O'Connor, for her invaluable guidance, to my friend and critique partner Sunny Cole for encouraging me to write this book, and to Missouri artist Gary R. Lucy for allowing me to use his beautiful period paintings as the perfect settings for my novels.

After you finish *Taming Huck Finn*, be sure to pick up *Tom Sawyer Returns*.

Enjoy the New Adventures!

E.E. Burke

CHAPTER ONE

JUNE 2, 1870, ATCHISON, KANSAS

"What you layin' in there for, mister?"

A high-pitched voice disturbed Huck's sleep. He screwed his eyes shut, willing his mind to return to dreams of pleasanter things than inquisitive children.

Something struck the bottom of his boot.

Huck jerked awake and his head connected with a crack against the inside of the barrel. "Ow! Blame it."

He gingerly touched a rising lump, grimacing at the painful reminder of where he'd ended up after a bout of celebrating his imminent return to the pilothouse. The abandoned barrel that smelled of a type of spirits he did not recall consuming had, in the wee hours, appeared to be the most convenient place to await the next packet steaming up the Missouri River. In the sharp light of day, sobriety declared his decision a bad idea.

Curling around, he squinted at the opening, past his legs, to where sunlight outlined the figure of a child. Huck shut his eyes. Hopefully, it was just a dream.

When he looked again, the boy had bent to peer inside the

barrel. Gap-toothed smile, snub nose, merry eyes that held the promise of mischief.

"Tom?" Huck rasped. No, couldn't possibly be. Tom would be full grown and have his own children by now.

The boy giggled. "I'm Tad."

Who? Huck rubbed his stinging eyes. He must've gotten hold of some bad brew like that Fire Rod his old man used to swig by the jug full. It made Pap see crazier things than a boy who wasn't there.

The spitting image of Tom laughed again. "Uncle Huck?"

Uncle?

Huck shook his head to clear it. By God, he'd swear off whiskey forever if it brought on these strange imaginings, and it had to be his imagination. Huck Finn was nobody's *uncle.*

He backed out of the barrel, grumbling. It wasn't just his head that ached, now his stomach joined in, churning in objection to the rank odors washed up by the river.

Surprisingly, the child didn't vanish, which meant he was annoyingly real.

Huck scowled to warn him off. "Here now. Don't you got nothin' better to do than comb a body?"

The boy—couldn't be more'n seven or eight—just grinned. From beneath the brim of a straw hat, his brown eyes gleamed with anything but repentance. Not Tom, but he could've passed for the younger version with his sorrel coloring and cocky stance.

The oddness of the moment rendered Huck speechless. Some weeks ago, when he had been out of his head from the morphine a doc had given him for pain, he dreamt of Tom and their pirate gang and the murderous Injun Joe. This pint-sized rascal showing up could be a sign. But what kind? Good or bad?

"Pardon us for disturbing you, sir. Young Thaddeus meant no offense."

Huck hadn't noticed the man standing off to one side. A

whiskered gent with a stovepipe hat and trim black coat. Undertaker or lawyer. Neither boded well.

The man tipped his hat. "We're looking for Mr. Finn. One of the gentlemen in the freight office said we might find him down by the river."

Huck scratched his head. He didn't owe anybody money, and far as he could tell, he was still among the living. Maybe it was *another* Mr. Finn they were seeking. He scanned the wharf expectantly. The only other folks out this early were dock workers and morning crews, most of whom he knew. None of them would answer to the name of Finn.

"Reckon you mean me." Huck reluctantly stuck out his hand.

"I knew it!" Tad squealed, throwing his arms around Huck's middle, which sent him staggering back and nearly toppled him over the big barrel.

He tugged at spindly arms as strong as braided hemp while his unhappy stomach flip-flopped and sweat popped out on his forehead. This had to be a prank, but he couldn't think clearly enough to work out who would be in on it and why.

At last, he pried the boy loose and set him at arm's length, and kept a wary eye on him while addressing his keeper. "Who's looking for me?"

The gentleman dipped his chin in a little bow. "Ambrose Dubois, attorney for the late Mrs. Douglas."

"The *late* Mrs. Douglas?" Huck echoed. A cold shiver passed through him, the same as when he'd been shot by that gang of thieving jackals. Only this time, it wasn't bullets that stunned him. The sweet lady who had taken him in years ago...*dead*. He barely had time to register the wave of grief when the lawyer continued.

"I'm handling matters related to her will. You have been assigned as guardian for her orphaned grandson, your nephew, Thaddeus Douglas..."

Guardian? Nephew?

Huck groped behind him for the barrel's rounded edge before his legs gave way. "Here now, what's this about the widow dying and making me this boy's—" He shook his head. "No, there has to be some mistake. You got it wrong. I've never seen this child before."

The lawyer kept on like he hadn't heard. "His father, Captain Douglas, was killed during the war, and his mother passed when he was a baby. Mrs. Douglas, his grandmother, cared for him until her death. She named you as guardian and next of kin."

Huck's mind got clear real quick. Whether this was a simple misunderstanding or an elaborate prank, he was in no mood to play along. It was time to send this gentleman and his sidekick on their way. "Well, now I'm *dead* sure you got it wrong. I'm no kin to Widow Douglas."

"Is that so?" The lawyer cocked his head in a gesture that reminded Huck of a bird examining a bit of string. "According to papers filed fifteen years ago, Mrs. Douglas adopted you."

Try as he might, Huck couldn't wrap his mind around what this lawyer was telling him. Adopted by the Widow Douglas? How was that possible? Well, she *had* claimed she was set to raise him up after his pap had died, and there wasn't ever a shortage of prim ladies wanting to civilize him. He reckoned she had given up on him after he ran off. That must've been about the time she made her move.

He drew in a deep breath and slowly released it. The Widow Douglas's son, all these years, and he never knew it. His whole life could've been different.

No. He wouldn't have stayed even if he'd known.

"Mr. Finn, you are legally this boy's uncle, and now, his guardian," the lawyer pronounced.

Huck opened his mouth, but all that came out was one word that stuck like a bone in his craw. "Guardian?"

"Yes, that's right," Dubois continued, in a tone that implied he

4

was dealing with a simpleton. "It means you have full responsibility for Thaddeus's care and education, and will be expected to act in his best interests until he is of age. That is unless you sign over guardianship to someone else."

"No!" The boy shot off like a bullet from a gun but missed his mark when Huck dodged to one side. "You won't give me up, will you, Uncle Huck? There ain't no perversions in that will what'll let you do that."

"*Provisions*, you mean, and I don't know a thing about this will." Huck sidestepped another pass and put his hand out to keep the boy from hugging him again.

He hadn't gotten this much affection since letting in an old cat from out of the cold to sleep at the foot of his bed. Stray cats he could manage. Stray boys were another matter altogether.

Mr. Dubois stepped in and scooped the child away. "Mind your manners, Thaddeus. You will make a better impression on your uncle if you use them."

This calmed the little imp right fast. He stood Sunday school still with his hat clutched in his hands. Why hadn't the widow asked this lawyer to be the guardian? He seemed right handy at it. Besides, the boy looked respectable and well brought up, even young as he was. The last thing he needed was the influence of a restless wanderer who didn't put stock in what society deemed necessary.

"What about his other family?"

Dubois shook his head. "No other family has spoken for him."

Huck met the child's anxious gaze and felt a tug on his heart. He understood that alone feeling. It wasn't something a boy outgrew like shoes and britches. Even if he could sympathize, that didn't make him a fit guardian. "Why did the widow reckon I could take care of this boy?"

The lawyer looked pleased he'd asked. "Mr. Sawyer received a letter from you several months back, and he shared it with Mrs.

Douglas. They were under the impression you had a good job and had settled down."

Huck bent and retrieved his hat from the ground to hide the shine on his face. How could a little harmless exaggeration have landed him in such a predicament?

He wasn't much for writing and had only penned the letter to Tom because of a strong urge to reconnect after coming so close to death. He'd filled the pages with memories of their youthful adventures, plus a little bragging thrown in about his "luck" in the gold fields. He hadn't mentioned being robbed and nearly killed, or that his injuries had kept him land-locked for so long that he had to seek temporary employment. Rather, he'd played up his good fortune at finding work managing the freight yard.

A job he'd quit yesterday so he could get back on the river doing what he loved best.

"They ought to know better than to take what I wrote as gospel."

Dubois frowned. "You lied?"

"It was mostly true, with a few stretchers. Truth always sounds better when it's decorated up, like this here hat." Huck rubbed his thumb over the beaded band. "If I'd known the widow was thinking of sending me this boy, I would've wrote I was broke and near dead. That was true as well, just at a different time."

Keeping his gaze lowered, Huck preoccupied himself with brushing dirt off the sleeve of his old buckskin coat. He'd planned on cleaning up before he started searching for a pilot's position. But if he put on like he was a bum, maybe this man would go back to St. Petersburg and find the child a proper family.

His stomach let loose with a rumbling growl.

Tad's eyes widened.

Dubois cleared his throat. "Mr. Finn, perhaps we could go somewhere more comfortable and discuss this further. May I buy you breakfast?"

It would be downright rude to refuse, and he had to eat. Once he'd filled his stomach, his mind would work better and he could figure out how to get rid of these two. Then he'd find a private spot where he could properly mourn the Widow Douglas. He couldn't see how taking him in all those years ago had done her much good, but she had put her heart into it, and he was grateful even if he hadn't ever showed it.

He secured his hat on his head and motioned for the two to follow. "There's a boarding house up on Commercial Street. Mae serves a fine breakfast."

Gravel crunched beneath their feet as they trod up the path to a road that led into town. The levee was quieter than usual, with lonesome freight piles scattered about, along with barrels and wood flats stacked up at the head of the dock. Fewer big boats crowded the landing than when he'd first arrived on the edge of the frontier, a shavetail with no money, no prospects, and not enough sense to care about either.

He cast a wistful glance over his shoulder at the sprawling river, swollen so high its brown water consumed the lower half of the wharf. The current ran like a racehorse, bearing along leafy limbs, broken branches, and even whole trunks that served as temporary rafts for the birds that rode them with the unblinking nerve of keelboat men.

A shrill sound pierced the air. Not the melodic chords unique to each steamboat but a railroad whistle that gave him the fantods every time he heard it. Each day, railroad crews laid track westward across unspoiled lands. Soon, the trains would follow, bringing with them society folk intent on taming the uncivilized.

Huck lengthened his stride with renewed determination. They could build all the railroads they wanted, and send a hundred orphans his way, and it still wouldn't change him. He'd escaped civilizing before and he could do it again. Nobody was going to tame Huck Finn.

CHAPTER TWO

The locomotive hissed, a sound not unlike the sigh of a weary traveler at the end of a long journey. With a tight hold on her satchel, Hallie stepped down from the dark interior of the passenger car into a bright Kansas morning and a cloud of smoke smelling of oil and dust.

She shook ashes from her cape before removing it and tucking it into her bag. How different train travel had turned out to be, as compared to gliding on a peaceful river where one could sit on the promenade, breathe in the fresh air and enjoy a gentle breeze.

A wistful sound escaped before she slammed the lid on her longing. She had not traveled all this way to daydream about steamboats. At any rate, she would never set foot on one again.

The crowd thinned as men and women and children and old folks peeled away. Most were greeted by loved ones who carted them off in the comfort of carriages or wagons.

No one came to bid Hallie welcome because no one expected her. She had no family left, except for one little boy whom she'd never met.

She blinked to vanquish the stinging behind her eyelids. She could not go back to relive the past with more wisdom. She could only go forward, find her nephew, and give Thaddeus the love and devotion she had withheld from his mother. Perhaps then she would find a measure of peace.

Hallie withdrew her spectacles from her handbag and put them on to read an address. Thaddeus would have arrived with the lawyer yesterday. She must locate them as soon as possible to present her claim as his only blood relative before the boy was turned over to his new guardian. Pray God she wasn't too late.

She walked faster, passing people in front of her on a steep dirt road that led into Atchison. The Kansas town was perched high on a bluff overlooking the river separating it from Missouri. A different river had separated her from her sister, but what kept them apart hadn't been a body of water. In order to rectify her mistakes, Hallie would cross more than two rivers. She would do whatever she must to gain custody of Caroline's son.

Upon reaching the main thoroughfare, she had to slow down to navigate through a swarm of rough-looking men in soot-covered dungarees. In addition to railroad workers, countless immigrants crossed the Missouri River each day. Wagons of every shape and size packed the streets.

How on earth would she recognize her nephew in this teeming crowd, even if she was fortunate enough to catch up with the man accompanying him? Another person she had never met.

A covered wagon rumbled past. Hallie couldn't dodge fast enough to avoid being splattered with mud.

"Bother!" she exclaimed, and shook her skirt. The offending filth clung as stubbornly as her guilt.

For once, she was glad to be wearing mourning garb. Her mother had passed more than six months ago, but Hallie had been in a constant state of bereavement for years, having buried everyone she loved.

Could she bear to open her heart to someone else she might lose? She owed it to her sister to try.

At last, she reached the hotel. Upon checking with the clerk, she discovered the dratted lawyer had already set out. If she waited around, she might miss her chance.

A porter dressed in a fine suit with white gloves approached her. "Miss, that gentlemen you's lookin' for, I seen him and a boy going into Mae's. Across the street."

What a joyful coincidence...or an answer to prayer. Although, the Almighty had not answered a single one of her petitions before now. She breathed a quick *thanks* in case the Lord thought her ungrateful.

"Thank you!" Hallie pressed a coin into the porter's hand. "I'm Miss MacBride. Will you watch my bag, please? I'll be back to check in."

Her heart pounded in anticipation as she rushed out the door. Across the street. There, the building with the word *Mae's* on a sign above the porch.

She dashed in front of a slow-moving team of oxen, across a wooden plank serving as a sidewalk, then drummed up the steps.

No children were in the parlor.

Hallie turned to the right and entered a crowded dining hall. The clatter of silver on dishes mingled with the low murmur of conversation.

In a far corner, a gentleman wearing a dark suit was seated next to a brown-haired boy with his back to her. The child appeared to be the right age.

Across from the two sat a bear of a man with an unruly mane of russet hair and a bushy beard concealing half his face. Her nephew's potential guardian? As a child, she had heard stories about Huck Finn, but she had never met him.

Quelling her nervousness, she made a beeline for their table. The unkempt man noticed her first and jerked to his feet as if he'd seen a ghost. His reaction caused the older gentleman to turn. Then the boy twisted in his seat.

Her heart tripped in her chest as she met a pair of snapping brown eyes. He looked so like his father. But that stubborn chin and tip-tilted nose, the way he widened his gaze when curiosity piqued...*Caroline*. Seeing her features on her son was like looking through a window into the past. Before everything had gone wrong.

Hallie drew her spine into a stiff column to support her melting insides. God would grant her a second chance to make things right.

She dragged her attention away from the boy to address the lawyer. "Sir, I apologize for disturbing your meal. Might you be Mr. Dubois?"

The gentleman's expression flashed confusion before breeding took over. He scraped his chair back and stood with a slight smile. "I am Ambrose Dubois. But I do not believe I have had the pleasure..."

"Miss Mahaliah MacBride." She extended her hand. "My sister called me Hallie," she added, seeking her nephew's reaction.

He stared as if her name might have been Smith.

Her straight spine nearly collapsed. "I am Thaddeus's aunt."

An expression reminiscent of a cornered animal crept across the boy's face, driving another stake through her heart. She longed to gather him into her arms and to explain that *he* wasn't the reason she stayed away.

"Miss MacBride, this is quite a surprise." The lawyer didn't sound as though he found her presence all that astonishing. His cool greeting might have stopped a less determined woman.

"Your partners were gracious enough to direct me." Hallie clasped her hands together to cease their shaking and ventured a curious glance at the other man.

His buckskin coat had seen better days. The vest hung open,

revealing red suspenders and a soiled shirt. No collar or tie. Dirty trousers tucked into thick work boots fit with what she'd been told by the other lawyers, that Mr. Finn worked as a common laborer. She had great respect for hard-working men, but this one looked —and smelled—as if he'd stumbled out of a saloon. He couldn't be prepared to take on the responsibilities of raising a child. In fact, he might be relieved to hear that someone else was willing to take the boy off his hands.

She turned a pleasant smile on the lawyer. "As I understand it, you traveled this distance to find a suitable guardian for Thaddeus."

If Mr. Finn had picked up on her not-so-subtle implication that he was *un*suitable, he didn't let on.

"Yes, Miss MacBride. I am charged with that task." Mr. Dubois didn't elaborate.

She forged ahead. "Then I'm glad I caught up with you. As this child's closest living relation, I am fully prepared to assume his guardianship."

HUCK COULDN'T TEAR HIS ATTENTION AWAY FROM THE BLACK-GARBED woman hovering over Tad. If he didn't know better, he'd swear Providence had gone and raised Miss Watson from the dead—or the spitting image of her anyway. Only younger, before she got all pruned up.

The last time he'd seen the old lady was nigh on fifteen years ago, when he'd stayed with the Widow Douglas for a few months. Mrs. Douglas had been kind. Her old maid sister had pecked the flesh off him and threatened him with hell every time he hadn't sat right or talked right or even breathed right. Nothing could have compelled him to stay in the same house as that old crow.

When he saw her ghost coming at him from across the room,

he'd nearly taken to his heels. About the time he'd realized this woman was too solid to be a *haint*, he could also see she was too young to be Miss Watson. By a couple decades at least.

Still, she gave a remarkable impression, what with her black hair scraped back and her cheeks drawn in tight like she was sucking a lemon. She even had that same slim figure covered over by a shapeless black dress and round glasses.

She blinked with disapproval like she might set into him with a spelling book or a switch.

"Miss MacBride, may I present Mr. Huckleberry Finn."

The lawyer's introduction jerked Huck out of the trance. He'd been standing there gaping like a fish when he ought to be smiling and shaking her hand. If this woman was who she claimed to be, he could be rid of the child in a jiffy.

"Folks call me Huck. Pleased to meet you, Miss, uh—"

"And you, Mr. Finn." She promptly turned her attention to the child. "Thaddeus, did you enjoy the train? Would you like to ride it home?"

Huck let his hand drop. Had she not let him finish because he spoke slowly or because she thought he was slow in general? Based on her quick dismissal, she'd already passed judgment and decided he wasn't guardian material. He knew that already, and it had nothing to do with how he looked.

The boy jutted out his jaw. "My name's Tad. I don't like trains."

Huck anticipated the response. If he'd spouted off like that, Miss Watson would've rapped his knuckles with her ruler and stuck him in a closet on his knees.

Instead, the aunt put her hand on Tad's head and stroked his hair. Her elegant fingers looked nothing like the scrawny claws Huck remembered.

"Most boys your age like trains..."

And her voice, that was different too. Not fingernails-down-a-chalkboard screechy, but low, and smooth as whiskey. Huck reckoned if she stroked his hair and talked soft like that, even *he* might be convinced to get on a train.

The direction of his thoughts stopped him cold. *What the devil?* He wasn't attracted to a buttoned-up, priggish woman, even if she did have pretty hands and a nice voice.

"Don't you want to come home with your Aunt Hallie?" she crooned.

"You're not my aunt," Tad pronounced. "I don't got one."

Her eyes brightened as tears threatened.

Miss Watson didn't weep over ornery boys—she thrashed 'em. And her eyes weren't the color of new grass on a hillside.

Huck had a hard time separating the woman in front of him from the ghost of his past. Not that it made a lick of difference. He didn't care about this woman's eyes or any other part of her.

She blinked as if the tears annoyed her. "I'm very sorry you don't know me, Thaddeus. We shall soon know each other very well."

Why wouldn't Tad know his only kin? The lawyer hadn't been expecting her either. Come to think of it, why hadn't the widow put her grandson in the care of his aunty? Any female, even a spinster, would be a better guardian than a man gone missing for fifteen years.

Huck sniffed. Something smelled here and it wasn't just him. Before he cut bait, he needed to ask a few questions. "Beg your pardon, miss."

She pointedly ignored him. "Mr. Dubois, I know my claim comes as something of a surprise. I wrote to Mrs. Douglas, but I fear she may not have received my letter before she passed on. The fact is, I am this boy's only surviving *blood* relation, therefore, his proper next of kin, and I am fully prepared to care for him."

"You are not married," the lawyer pointed out.

Neither was he, Huck thought, but didn't say it out loud. He wanted to hear Miss MacBride's excuse before he opened his mouth again.

"No, I am not married, but..." She ventured to put her hand on Tad's shoulder again. When he flinched, she withdrew it. "I have sufficient income from a modest inheritance, and my mother left me a house and property. It overlooks the Mississippi River across from the town where Thaddeus lived with his mother and grandmother. I feel certain if Mrs. Douglas had known of my interest in adopting him, she would have named me as—"

"No! I don't wanna be 'dopted by you!" Tad hopped down and rushed around the table where he crouched behind Huck. "Tell her she can't have me. She's scary."

She jerked up straight, then marched around the table after the boy. "Young man, you are behaving in a rude and ungentlemanly manner."

Now that sounded just like something Miss Watson would say. She'd pull out that ruler yet.

Huck didn't move out of her way. "You reckon on locking him in a closet and praying over him?"

"What?" Her color drained and then flushed back into her cheeks in two bright spots. "I have prayed for this child since he was born, which is more than you've done, I'm certain."

She'd missed his point.

"I meant you got no need to bullyrag him."

"Bullyrag! Why you...you..." Whatever she was about to say got sucked up in a sharp breath. "Did you even know he existed before Mr. Dubois tracked you down? You can't possibly care one whit about Thaddeus. All I can assume is that you are after something. Money, no doubt."

She flung the accusation like a startled rattler.

Forbearing a grouchy old maid for the widow's sake was one thing, but he didn't have to put up with this woman's venom.

"What are *you* after? Seems mighty strange a boy wouldn't know his aunty."

Her chin went up and those green eyes flashed. "I have proof of kinship, and I can assure you my claim is stronger than yours."

Tad tugged his sleeve. "Don't make me go with her, Uncle Huck."

The child's distressed plea tore at his innards. Having been subjected to a nasty-tempered biddy, he knew the kind of misery a boy would suffer. He had run away rather than put up with it. But he'd been out on his own beforehand and was tough enough to survive. A young fellow like Tad, who'd been reared by his granny, wouldn't know how to get along. If this crotchety woman got her way, Tad would be chained to her until he was grown. Maybe longer.

Before Huck could stop it, a promise flew out: "You don't have to go with her if you don't want to."

Tad beamed up at him.

Huck's skin crawled with the itchy sensation of approaching calamity. He had no business getting involved with this child, and he intended to pass the first chance he got. Only now he'd gone and given his word.

He turned to the lawyer, who'd been watching the exchange with the shrewdness of a raven. "You said Widow Douglas's will gives me rights over this boy."

"It does," Dubois conceded without appearing to take sides.

"That means he don't have to go with this woman lessen I say so."

The aunt's face flamed like a sunset. "Mr. Dubois. I understand you have the authority to decide who is most *capable* of caring for Thaddeus, and I assure you I am more than—"

"Miss MacBride." The old gent put a cap on her shrill objection. "I do beg your pardon, but Mr. Finn and I need to finish our business. After that, I should be delighted to meet with you to address whatever issues you might want to raise."

She sputtered out like a candle. Her countenance took on such a crushed, wounded look, Huck almost felt sorry for her. "Of course," she murmured. "I'll wait at the hotel."

With that, she turned on her heel and walked away. Her hand went to her face. It was hard to tell whether she was wiping away tears or adjusting the spectacles.

Another tug came at his sleeve. He looked down into Tad's hopeful brown eyes. "Uncle Huck, does this mean I get to stay with you forever?"

CHAPTER THREE

The full-throated whistle of a resplendent packet sent Hallie's pulse racing. A long time had passed since she'd stood at the edge of a bluff, watching a big steamer ply the river. The familiar scene made her fingers itch to capture it, but she hadn't come here this morning to paint steamboats. She was here to find the miserable cur she had to talk to, reason with, bribe, or drown—anything to get Huck Finn to release his claim on her nephew.

Earlier, Mr. Dubois had graciously consented to consider her request, if she and Mr. Finn were of one mind. She had some convincing to do. But she felt certain she could navigate a conversation with Huck Finn as capably as her father had steered his steamboat on a starless night.

The sternwheeler approached the landing, bells ringing, and the huge paddlewheel stopped. A moment later it began to turn backward, pounding the water into a frothy foam before it halted and moved forward again in a slow lap. Sunlight glinted off gilded spreaders stretched between two towering smokestacks that belched out pitch-black clouds.

Through the open window of the pilothouse, a dark figure at the wheel took on an impossible face and form. Her father's boat hadn't ventured into these waters and never would. The grand old side-wheeler was gone, along with its adventurous captain. He had been planted beneath the earth in a cemetery near his home. Years later, his wife had been laid to rest beside him. In death, Mama had finally gotten her dearest wish. A husband who wouldn't wander.

Hallie rubbed away the wetness beneath her spectacles. The painful memories served no purpose other than to remind her of why she was here—to claim her only living relative. She scrunched her eyes, attempting to locate the knave who stood in her way.

Agile roustabouts with chain hawsers snubbed the boat fast. The boom swung a broad stage over the port bow, and a mad scramble ensued as passengers, crew and freight were unloaded with shouts and curses hot enough to redden even a strumpet's ears.

A flash of white skin appeared amidst the shining dark bodies unloading cargo. Huck Finn was easy enough to spot, being a head taller than those around him, and shamelessly bare from the waist up. Few white men were willing to work the docks. Perhaps brute labor was the only thing he knew how to do. Another reason he ought not to raise a child.

A warm breeze blew against her as she threaded her way down the path. At the head of the wharf, she stopped, willing to wait, however impatiently, until the last of the freight had been loaded and the steamboat was on its way. Fifteen minutes felt like an eternity for someone whose future hung in the balance. When the man she sought turned in her direction, she waved and called out. "Mr. Finn!"

The surprise on his face quickly transformed into an expression that wasn't hard to read even through all that hair. He wasn't pleased to see her. Nor was she eager to engage him. That humiliating encounter yesterday had left her tossing and turning all night. Regardless of their mutual dislike, they must spar off the sandbar they were stuck on, and that wouldn't be accomplished by ignoring the problem.

Again, she raised her hand to let him know she wished to speak to him.

He started in her direction, albeit slowly. Her irritation increased when he made no move to clothe himself. The uncouth fellow went without a shirt often enough that his skin had taken on the ruddy tan afforded to fair-skinned men.

An odd fluttering started in her stomach. *Nerves.* She made her way to a dock post where someone had hung a shirt along with a vest and coat that looked familiar. "Are these yours?"

"If you aren't claiming them." Not a flicker of embarrassment crossed his features. Yesterday, the knave had taunted her into losing her temper. That would not happen again. She would ignore his vulgarity and steam ahead.

Hallie tossed him the shirt, making it clear she expected him to put it on.

As he buttoned it up, perspiration seeped through the light fabric, forming damp circles. Surprisingly, his body didn't have the sharp odor of a man who hadn't bathed in weeks. Or other, more offensive smells at the dock covered it up.

The day had already grown warm and humid. She fished out a handkerchief tucked beneath her sleeve and dabbed at beads of moisture on her upper lip and proceeded with civility. "What kind of work do you do at the docks?"

His eyes, a murky shade of blue like the shifting colors of the river, registered surprise before he squinted them. "Is that why you're down here? To make sure I have a job?"

He'd taken her simple question as a challenge.

"I don't care whether you have a job."

"Then how come you asked?"

He was doing it again, baiting her.

"I am attempting to make polite conversation. As you seem disinterested in proper customs, I'll get straight to the point. I came here to speak with you about Thaddeus."

"Tad? What about him?" The neutral expression worn by her opponent made it difficult to divine whether he was irritated or just indifferent. Perhaps she could appeal to his softer side if he had one. His body looked to be hewn from stone.

She jerked her gaze upward from his chest to his face as the alarming flutters started up again. "Mr. Finn, do you believe your nephew deserves a good home and an education?"

"Don't see as I could argue that."

Hallie raced ahead before he changed his mind. "Of course, as his uncle, you want what's best for him. Mr. Dubois says you'll be leaving soon. He mentioned something about you going to work on a steamboat. I'm sure you'll agree that isn't the best place for a young boy. If you're concerned about Thaddeus's education, I can assure you he will go to school. And I'm well-versed in literature and the arts, and can teach him things a gentleman needs to learn."

The annoying man stuffed the extra length of the shirt into his trousers as if she weren't standing right there in front of him. The muscles on his shoulders pulled at the fabric as he slid the suspenders into place. "How many boys did you say you'd raised, *Miss...*?"

"MacBride," she snapped, irritated that he hadn't bothered to commit her name to memory. "That is beside the point."

"Well, you just said Tad ought to have the best home, so how am I to work it out if I don't have all the facts?"

"The *facts* are, I looked after my younger sister and our bedridden mother and ran a household from the time I was fourteen. I assure you I am quite capable of caring for a child."

His regard turned speculative. "That may be, but raising a girl is different from raising a boy. You haven't raised a boy, so you might not know that."

The conniving rascal wasn't going to lure her into another argument.

"Regardless, you must admit I am in a better position than you to provide for Tad." She handed him his vest.

He put that on just as slowly. "Oh, I didn't reckon we were talking about providing for him. Mr. Dubois says there's a fund set up to be used for his care...unless you're saying you've got no use for the money."

"Stop twisting my words. This isn't about whether either of us needs his money."

"No, I don't need it. You were the one that brung it up."

She snatched his coat off the post and held it out. "I did *not* bring up money. I was trying to get you to agree that the most important thing is to give Thaddeus the best home and education."

He slipped his arms into the coat sleeves, regarding her with a puzzled expression. "Hang it, Miss MacBride, but I don't see where there's a problem. I know the boy's got to have a good home and educating, and I'll see that he gets it."

Her patience unraveled. "How could you possibly give him a home or an education when you have neither?"

A long silence stretched out, the space filled by the crunch of gravel as men trod past, casting curious glances. Hallie's conscience smote her for callously throwing Huck Finn's low situation into his face. Never had she been so deliberately cruel. But he had goaded her into it, and he needed to hear the harsh truth, if that's what it took to convince him how foolish and irresponsible it was to keep Tad with him.

"I don't recollect saying *I* would be giving him those things."

His even reply conveyed neither hurt nor shame. "You reckon the widow was a good granny?"

Mrs. Douglas's fine character could not be disputed, but what did that have to do with Mr. Finn? He wasn't even related to her by blood. Reportedly, he hadn't been back to visit or even attend her funeral. Hallie couldn't claim she had either. However, she wasn't Mrs. Douglas's adopted child.

"I am sure Mrs. Douglas did the best she could," Hallie acknowledged.

"So you agree she wanted the best for Tad."

"Yes, but—"

"Then you ought to agree she had a good reason not to give him to you in the first place."

"She didn't know I wanted him." The confession tumbled out before Hallie could stop it with her hand. *God forgive her.* Had she reached out sooner Mrs. Douglas wouldn't have given Thaddeus to this insufferable man.

Remorse bubbled up and threatened to boil over. She kept the lid on tight. Huck Finn wouldn't be moved by tears. At any rate, she was too proud to weep in front of him. "If you must know, I was estranged from my sister, something I deeply regret. The least I can do is see to it that my nephew is raised right."

Her adversary's face hardened. "Raised right? I recall old Miss Watson tried that on me. She worked hard at it, day and night. 'Bout wore me out."

"Miss Watson?" It took Hallie a moment to place the name. "What does Mrs. Douglas's spinster sister have to do with—? Are you comparing *me* to a grouchy old maid?" She fisted her hands at her sides, barely restraining an urge to shove him off the dock. "Mr. Finn, I refuse to be drawn into a pointless exchange of insults. Didn't you say you want Thaddeus to have a good home? You've as much as admitted you cannot provide that."

"I *said* I'd see to it he has those things. By putting him with the right family. One that knows how to raise a boy without pecking at him, and suffocating him, and making his life so miserable he wished he was anywhere else."

Hallie gasped in outrage. "What makes you think I am the type of person who would torment a child? I wish to raise my nephew to be a man of honor. You want to turn him over to strangers."

"Who said anything about giving him to strangers?"

Who else could he be talking about? Tad had no other family, nor did Finn, according to the lawyers. He made the threat to spite her.

Frustration crumbled her self-control, releasing a flood of anger. "Whoever you think to give him to, I'll fight you, Mr. Finn." She shook her fist in his face. "In court, in the street, if I have to, but I won't let you give him away. He belongs with his family. He belongs with *me*."

CHAPTER FOUR

Tad peeked around the edge of the counter at the hotel lobby. He'd eaten lunch and rested and Uncle Huck still hadn't come back for him. His aunt, on the other hand, had been sneaking around all day, trying to talk Mr. Dubois into siding with her.

While the two adults conversed, Tad sneaked past them and out the front door. He ran so fast, the slick soles of his new shoes skidded on the boardwalk. Dodging men's legs and women's skirts, he continued downhill.

If he didn't act quick, he might end up on that train with his aunt rather than on the river with his uncle. He knew what was best for him, and it wasn't doing what Mr. Dubois said, *trusting matters to the grownups.*

He'd go back to the river. That would be where he'd find Uncle Huck just like he had yesterday. Hadn't his uncle promised to let him choose what he wanted? Well, he already had.

Down at the levee, a steamboat had docked. Maybe his uncle had come down to look at it with all these other folks. Shading his eyes, Tad peered at the pilothouse, soaring high above the three decks. My, wouldn't it be grand to steer one of them big boats down the river? His granny had told him they wouldn't let him pilot a steamboat if he didn't go to school. He wasn't sure he believed her.

Grownups preached against lying, but they didn't mind stretching the truth. Like the time she'd told him he had an aunt who was too afraid to cross the river to come see him. Aunt Hallie didn't look like she was afraid of anything. But she sure scared *him* with her black dress and glinting glasses, and all that talk about getting on a train and taking him home with her. That was why he'd told her that he didn't have an aunt because he didn't care to have one if she planned to take him away from his uncle.

Uncle Huck wouldn't let her. He'd promised.

Men loading crates with nets on big hoists shouted to each other. They ignored two barefooted boys who'd thrown aside their jackets and rolled up their trousers and were playing chase around one of the thick ropes tethering the steamboat.

Tad envied those boys. He had to wear a coat and shoes whenever he went outside. He'd never been allowed to play at the landing back home or go down to the docks by himself. All that would change once he went to live with his uncle. Maybe those boys had seen him.

"Hey," he called out. "I'm looking for Huck Finn."

The boys moseyed over and circled him like dogs checking out a new pup. The tallest one got up close enough to sniff him but didn't. "Who?" he asked.

"Huck Finn. He lives around here."

"Lots of folks live around here," the boy replied. "Never heard of him."

"Oh." Tad assumed everyone had heard of his uncle. "He's famous."

"What for?"

"Lots of things. Stealin' off with a slave, for one."

"That ain't true."

"Yeah, it is."

"There ain't no more slaves."

"It was a long time ago."

"That don't mean he's famous."

Tad puffed his chest out to show he wasn't backing down. "Is so. He has a pirate treasure."

"Hey!" a man called out. "What are you boys doing there around those ropes?"

"He's looking for a pirate," the tall boy hollered, before he and his friend ran off, laughing.

Tad stood his ground and waited until the bearded man walked over. He'd tied a scarf 'round his head and wore a frown that wasn't a pretend one like Uncle Huck used.

"Go play elsewhere, boy. This ain't a safe place."

"I'm looking for Huck Finn"

"Ain't seen him lately."

"You know him?"

"Yeah. Everybody down here does."

At least the grownups were knowledgeable.

"He's got a raft, I think."

"If he does, it'll be down there." The man pointed to a second pier where smaller boats were tied up. "Go on now. Stay away from those ropes, lessen you want a whippin'."

Tad didn't want one of those. He ran off in the direction the man had pointed him. He'd keep looking until he found his Uncle Huck. Once he did, they could jump on a raft and sail away and live like pirates or Indians.

He whooped with joy when he saw a big raft at the end of the pier. That one had to belong to his uncle. It had an animal skin tent and everything.

Tad made it as far as the edge of the dock before he realized he'd have to jump over the water to get onto the platform. Despite his fear, he didn't slow down. If he wanted to live with his uncle, he'd have to be brave. He could make it across in one leap.

His new shoes hit the slick edge and he slipped.

UNAWARE THAT TAD WAS LOOKING FOR HIM, HUCK WENT UP TO THE hotel to attend a meeting he would rather skip. He'd been visited by Mr. Dubois about an hour after Miss MacBride had left in a huff. The lawyer made a tentative suggestion to allow Tad's aunt to raise him if her story checked out. He'd proposed getting together to discuss *final arrangements*. Like they were planning a funeral.

Removing his hat, Huck threaded his fingers through his damp hair. He'd cleaned up. Not to please Miss MacBride. He intended to go find a job steering one of those packets. Earlier, she'd mistaken him for one of the rousters. He hadn't bothered to correct her.

She stared at his chest while she kept handing him his clothes. Proper Miss MacBride would die before she confessed to being fascinated with a man's body. A spinster who squelched her desires would make a young fellow feel guilty about having normal hungers. She knew nothing about raising a boy.

If not her, then who? He couldn't take Tad along. He planned to head north, up to the rocky part of the river. From there, he might trek west. Clear to the ocean if that's what it took to cure this gnawing restlessness.

Miss MacBride had been right in saying he had no business raising a child, though he'd eat dirt before admitting as much to her face. She'd remarked on how he didn't have a home or an education. Well, who said he needed either? He'd gotten along just fine without them.

At the same time, he'd be the first to acknowledge the boy deserved better than what he could offer. As a child, he'd wished for a father who cared about him and could guide him. He'd like to help Tad find a good one, but how would he recognize such a thing, even if he saw it? Then he'd have to convince the boy to go along and wrestle Miss MacBride, who'd threatened to grapple with him in a street brawl.

Now *that* was an interesting notion. He could just imagine the startled expression in those grass-green eyes when he pressed her down beneath him.

Huck shot to his feet, alarmed at the provocative image that popped into his head. "Devil take you, Huckleberry. You've gone plum crazy if you're thinking about doing *that* with a snappish biddy." He jerked his coat into place with a sharp reminder that he didn't care for skinny women. His tastes ran more to soft and curvy —and good-natured.

He strode inside. What little he did know about women and children didn't amount to enough to make him good husband or father material. He'd let the lawyer decide what to do with the child.

In the lobby, he spotted the object of his cussed daydream in deep discussion with Dubois. She clutched a dark bonnet in one hand like she was set to use the long ribbons to whip the lawyer into submission. A small crease between her brows marred her smooth skin. Rebellious black curls poked out of a net she'd used to imprison them. Even her *hair* wanted to get away.

Huck released an amused huff. What had possessed him to entertain low thoughts about a woman who likely undressed in the dark to keep from blushing?

As he approached, he picked up a thread of strain in her voice. "We must alert the authorities."

"I'm here," he said. "No need to set the dogs on me."

She goggled at him from behind lenses that made her eyes look owlish. "What are you talking about? We weren't discussing you. Thaddeus has run away."

"What's this?" Huck looked to Dubois for confirmation.

The lawyer removed his hat and held the brim in both hands. His balding crown glistened with sweat. "When Thaddeus left the room, he said he intended to visit with the staff. He's a very sociable child, and I thought nothing of it. But I haven't been able to find him for the past two hours. It appears he's run off."

Huck rubbed his chest a spell before he recognized the achy feeling as worry. He'd never had cause to fret over a child before and didn't much like it. One more reason he had no business keeping Tad. "Don't you reckon he's just hiding?"

"We've checked all over." Miss MacBride wrung her hands. She might not be the best person to raise Tad, but it was clear enough she was worried sick over him.

Huck resisted the urge to offer a reassuring hug. Worried or not, she was pricklier than a cactus. "What about the levee?" he suggested. "Boys can't stay away from the river."

"The river?" Horror darkened her eyes. "Dear Lord. I'll fetch the sheriff or constable, someone who can round up more people for a thorough search."

She rushed out the door without waiting for agreement.

He'd meant to ease her fears not make them worse. That boy was fine, probably hiding in the hotel somewhere. But what if he wasn't? What if Tad had ventured too near the water and fallen in?

"What do you recommend, Mr. Finn?" The lawyer's grim expression set off dark and awful images.

"You stay here in case he comes back. I'll go check the wharf." Huck shot out the door at a dead run, sending up every prayer he could call to mind. Providence might listen on account of his pleading for the life of a little boy and not an old sinner like himself.

After he reached the docks, he made a quick search. Even checked his room above the freight house. He asked around. One of the deckhands had talked to a boy matching Tad's description and said the child had been looking for Huck at the other pier.

What if the little fellow had gotten stuck somewhere and couldn't get out? Or what if someone had snatched him?

Huck shuddered at the memory of being locked inside an isolated cabin for weeks on end with his crazy, drunk pap. He'd nearly chewed off his arm, he'd been so desperate to escape.

He came to an abrupt halt, arrested by the sight of a familiar flat-bottomed boat tied at the end of the pier. Durned if he weren't the stupidest man alive. The old trapper's flatboat would make a perfect hiding spot. Any boy worth his salt couldn't resist the temptation.

In two shakes, Huck was there. As he jumped over onto the platform, it bobbed beneath his weight. The simple craft had been constructed without the usual wooden shack. Instead, the trapper had built himself a domed shelter out of saplings and buffalo hides.

Holding his breath, Huck pulled back the flap.

Inside, Tad lay curled up on a bearskin rug, sleeping. His hair stuck out every which way. He must've rolled in the dirt, and he had misplaced his shoes. He was fine.

Huck removed his hat and mopped his forehead with his shirt sleeve, at once relieved and annoyed for getting all worked up over a little nonsense. He ducked inside and sat cross-legged beside the child, who didn't wake up until he was given a gentle shake.

"Uncle Huck?" Tad murmured, blinking sleepily. He sat up, gaping and stretching, without a care in the world.

For a brief moment, Huck considered drawing the boy over his lap for a good cowhiding. Pap had beat him on a regular basis just for good measure. But he'd forsworn lifting his hand against anyone smaller or weaker, so he scowled instead. "Boy, you can't just run off whenever you want."

"You're not mad at me, are you? I heard about that time you

lived on a raft and I thought you might be in here. I was waiting for you to get back. I want to live on a raft with you."

Tad's plea stirred a distant memory, and with it, a keen yearning. The same sort of feeling Huck had experienced all those years ago when he'd discovered Jim hiding on that island and realized he wasn't alone.

Hucky, you got no business even considering taking this boy just 'cause you're lonely.

His conscience didn't need to remind him. He wasn't considering any such thing, and he'd set this boy straight. "It's not a raft. It's a flatboat, and it's not mine. Now let's get you back to Mr. Dubois."

Tad's expression crumpled. "But *you* gotta take s'ponsibility for me. That's what he said."

"I *am* taking responsibility. To put you with a good family."

"Are you sending me with Aunt Hallie?"

Huck hesitated. He didn't cotton to the idea of that woman raising Tad, but he had no right to poison the boy against her. "You want to go with your Aunt Hallie?"

Tad scrunched his nose. "No. I don't know her."

"You don't know me neither."

"Sure seems like I know you. Granny used to talk about you all the time, and Mr. Sawyer tells me stories. He told me about you and him being pirates and living on a raft and setting that slave free...."

The more Tad went on, the larger the tales became. It was clear Tom Sawyer had supplied most of them. He was nuts about enlarging stories and had done it up elegant, in a way Huck couldn't begin to match, not being brought up to that kind of style.

"I did some of those things," Huck admitted. "Mostly, we pretended. You don't need to live on a raft to do that."

The boy inched over like he wanted a cuddle but wasn't about to own up to needing it.

Huck awkwardly rested his arm behind the small form that smelled vaguely of dirt and wet wool. "You been swimming?"

"No. I slipped and almost fell in. But I crawled onto the boat and only got my shoes and trousers wet up to here." He indicated his knee. The wet shoes had been discarded somewhere.

In the past, Huck would've admired the child's dexterity. Except now, he couldn't help thinking about what might've happened had the boy fallen in and not been able to get out. With children, worry came with the territory. All the more reason not to keep this one.

"Were you a soldier in the war, Uncle Huck?"

What had sparked that question? It'd been five years since the war between the states had ended, and Tad was too young to remember. Maybe it was just one of those curious questions that boys asked.

Huck pondered how to respond. Truth was, he hadn't been able to bring himself to fight beside his friends for a cause he didn't believe in, but he hadn't been willing to pick up a gun against them. Either decision would've torn him apart. So he'd lit out and gone west. He'd been labeled a coward by those whose opinions didn't matter. This wasn't a conversation he wanted to have with an eight-year-old.

"No, I didn't fight in the war. I didn't much care for following orders."

That was true enough. He had little use for authority. Men abused power the moment they got a taste of it.

"My papa was a soldier," Tad said proudly. "He was a captain and he was brave. Rode right into the fray with bullets whizzin' all around."

Riding into a *fray* of bullets didn't sound brave as much as stupid. However, Huck didn't correct his nephew's notions. Who was he to define courage? At the first sign of danger, he'd duck or run.

"Sounds like your pap was a real brash fellow, and smart, too. I'm sure he'd want you to go live with folks like him and your ma. He wouldn't want you running off by yourself."

Tad snuggled closer. "I'm not by myself. I'm with you."

Huck grappled with the weaker man inside. In some ways, Tad reminded him of the boy he'd once been, lonely and eager to befriend someone he thought might care for him. The old hope rekindled at an enticing image. He snuffed it out. He had no skills for parenting, and no wish to be tied down. "I can't keep you. There's no profit in it for either of us."

"But you said I didn't have to go with nobody I didn't want to. You said so, Uncle Huck." Tears welled in the boy's big brown eyes.

"Don't cry. T'ain't manly." Huck blinked at the moisture clouding his own eyes. He was too soft. Something his pap hadn't been able to beat out of him, unfortunately.

"Wait. I almost forgot. I need to show you something." Tad snuffled and reached into his coat pocket. He pulled out a small leather bag and loosed the strings that held it shut. After digging around inside, he held up a coin—old gold, by the look of it.

Huck took it to examine it. "Where'd you get this?"

"Mr. Sawyer gave it to me before I left. He said I should show it to you and remind you about your treasure."

Huck rubbed the coin between his fingers and his heart warmed with the memory of a childhood adventure. "Injun Joe's gold."

"Mr. Sawyer told me you and him dug up a fortune."

Six thousand dollars apiece. Money that would've come in right handy if it hadn't come with so many strings. Everybody had expected him to slick up and start behaving. His pap had gone crazy and threatened to kill him over it.

"Did he tell you I turned my half over to Judge Thatcher? Washed my hands of the troubles that come with prosperity." Huck liked how noble that sounded. He didn't mention he'd caught the gold fever again and had learned his lesson the hard way. Riches and love were things he couldn't hold onto. The lack of money and entanglements suited him just fine. Less to lose.

"Yep, Mr. Sawyer told me everything. All about the treasure, and you and him going into the cave. It sounded ever so fine, like them other adventures." Tad heaved a wistful sigh. "You can keep that dew-bloon."

Huck slipped it back into the bag. "No, you keep it safe."

Tad's little face brightened right up. "Oh, it'll be safe in here. This is where I keep all my important stuff. I got a tooth, a feather, a marble. Here's a frog, but he's all dried up." He poured the bag's contents into a grimy palm. Other than the gold coin, it was a collection of odds and ends that would be dear only to a boy.

"I climbed a tree and got this out of a nest." He held up a piece of blue eggshell. "Robin's, I wager. And I caught a spider."

Huck recalled an old superstition. "You didn't kill it, did you? That's bad luck."

The boy's eyes grew wide. "No, I didn't kill it. Only played with it a little while."

"That's all right. If it was crawling on you, it's a sign something good will happen."

"Oh, I know that's true because I caught it on my shoulder the day before we found you."

A knot formed in Huck's throat. Nobody had ever looked at him with such worshipful awe. Well, maybe a dog once, but that didn't count for a human.

"We got to get back," he said gruffly.

Tad's lip quivered. "But I don't wanna go back. I want to stay with you."

Huck fought the pull on his heartstrings. He couldn't keep Tad. A boy wasn't a pet. "Don't you want to live somewhere you got your own bed with a ma who will feed you regular and take care of you? You wouldn't have that with me."

The child's tears welled up. "What does it matter if I can't have fun? Granny never let me be a pirate or find treasure. I want adventures like you had. Livin' ain't livin' lessen you enjoy it. That's what Mr. Sawyer says."

What else had Tom said? He spun a story for just about everything. Made even crazy sound reasonable. That must be why he'd ended up being a lawyer.

An idea popped onto Huck so fast he jolted up. His old friend Tom had gotten married and settled down. Based on what he'd written, he liked children, and it was obvious he and Tad had formed an attachment. Tom Sawyer could give this boy everything he needed, and make sure his life was filled with enough adventure to keep him satisfied.

"By golly, it's brilliant," Huck said to himself.

"What's brilliant?" Tad asked.

Huck smiled down at his charge. "Reckon I can take you on one adventure *if* you'll agree to go with the family I pick out for you."

Tad's lip curled out. "You said I don't have to go with nobody I don't want to."

"I promise you'll like the folks I've got in mind. I'll tell you who it is, soon as I work things out." Huck patted the boy's shoulder. Might take a little wrangling, but hadn't he helped Jim escape a life of bondage? How could he do less for his nephew?

Tad chewed his lip. The inner struggle played itself out in his eyes. At last, he gave a sigh and a reluctant nod. "All right."

"Good." Huck started to offer his hand, then hesitated. A simple handshake wouldn't carry enough weight to prevent Tad from changing his mind later. "Let's swear to it like me and Tom did when we were kids."

He didn't much like the idea of cutting the child's finger for a blood oath, so he spit on his palm instead. Tad did the same, and they shook.

The boy's dark eyes sparkled with delight. "Are we gonna ride this raft?"

"How about a steamboat?" It would make the trip back home faster.

Tad appeared tempted by the idea. "Maybe later. Right now, I want to ride a raft."

"This isn't a raft, Tad. It's a flatboat."

"But we can *pretend* it's a raft." The child's appeal struck a chord deep inside Huck.

It had been a long time since he'd lived so free and easy as he had those days spent floating down a wide, smooth river with a friend. A whisper said it wasn't such a good idea, but a louder voice insisted this might work to his advantage.

If he took Tad on a brief adventure using this boat, he wouldn't have to deal with that tiresome Miss MacBride. They could slip off before she knew what was going on. It was a plan worthy of Tom Sawyer.

Huck lowered his voice to a conspiring level. "Look here, this is what we'll do. I know the old trapper that owns this flatboat. He won't be needing it, so we'll just borrow it for a spell."

Tad leaped up and threw his arms around Huck's neck. "Thank you, thank you, thank you. You're the best uncle in the whole world, and I won't never forget it 'til I rot."

"Let me fetch some trifles and talk to Mr. Dubois, so he won't be in a sweat over what happened to you." Huck patted Tad's back. He was beginning not to mind the hugs so much.

He crawled out of the tent. The sight and sound of the rushing river sent excitement thrumming through his veins. He'd made the right decision, felt it clear to his bones. He'd give his nephew a taste of freedom before Tad had to go back to being at least partway respectable. Every boy deserved time on a river.

"Mr. Finn, what are you doing there?"

Huck jerked his head up in alarm. That voice could belong to only one person, and here she came, flying down to the landing. It flashed through his mind that Miss MacBride didn't so much resemble a crow as a chicken hawk sighting its prey.

Her determined steps kicked her skirts out behind her. Inky strands of hair whipped across her face. "Get off that boat this instant," she commanded in a tone that would have done a riverboat pilot proud.

Huck stiffened before he realized she was talking to Tad, who'd come out of the tent behind him. His plan wasn't spoiled, but they'd have to find another way to get shy of the boy's aunt. "Hold on, now, Miss MacBride. We were just coming back to tell you—"

The boat lurched, pitching Huck to the floor. He twisted around and his heart nearly stopped. Tad had untied the ropes holding the boat to the posts and was attempting to man the massive oar and steer them into the channel.

With a curse, Huck dashed to the stern. He snatched the boy from the steersman's box. "Sit," he ordered.

Tad flopped down.

Just then the current snagged the light boat and carried it away from the wharf.

"Mr. Finn! Stop!"

Throwing her the ropes would be useless. The momentum would drag her into the water.

Huck gripped the tiller and lowered the oar.

"You must stop!" Her voice pitched up another octave.

Huck spared the woman barely a glance as he fought to right the boat so it wouldn't spin out of control or strike debris carried along by the swift current. With the river running this fiercely, he'd never be able to pole to shore. He'd take them downriver a few miles and find a safer spot to land. Their adventure would be starting slightly ahead of schedule.

After gaining control of the boat, he took another look at the wharf.

The confounded woman had hauled up her skirts and came full tilt down the pier. She couldn't catch up no matter how fast she ran.

"Stay back," he yelled. "I'll take care of him."

Tad danced from one foot to the other and waved his arms. "Hey, Aunt Hallie! Guess what? We're goin' a-raftin'!"

Her startled expression changed to one of horror as she reached the end of the pier.

The blamed fool woman *had* to stop.

But it was Huck's heart that halted when she flung herself into the air.

Her black dress flapped like wings as she took flight for less than a second—then dropped like a stone into the river.

CHAPTER FIVE

The shock of plunging into frigid water forced the breath from Hallie's lungs. She clawed her way to the surface, only to be dragged along by a determined current despite her frantic strokes. She renewed her struggle to reach the raft as it bobbed along at about the same speed.

Her nephew was on that flimsy craft in this raging torrent. If the river didn't kill him, that horrid man surely would with his ignorance.

Hallie lunged for a limb as it went whizzing by. She kicked at her skirts, which kept wrapping around her legs. The heavy layers would pull her down if she couldn't catch hold of something to help her stay afloat.

Her nose and mouth filled with water. In a panic, she kicked furiously until she broke the surface. *Help.* Her lips formed the plea, but for the life of her, she couldn't give it voice. Every ounce of her energy had to be focused on remaining above the water.

She'd lost sight of the raft or terror had blinded her. Her ears still worked well enough to hear the angry shouts coming from somewhere behind her.

"Grab the rope! Don't flap like a bird, you durn fool. Get ahold of the rope!"

Something plopped on top of the waves and a strand of brown rippled across the water's surface.

Hallie launched herself toward it, but the devilish petticoats trapped her.

The rope disappeared. A moment later, it whistled past and smacked the water right next to her head. She grabbed the thick hemp with both hands and was jerked like a fish on a line.

"Tie it 'round you! Dang it, woman, tie it quick. Knot it. I'm reelin' you in. Keep your blamed head up. Look out for that goldurn limb." The angry voice kept up a stream of instruction, liberally laced with profanities, as the rope tugged, pulling her closer.

She focused on the flatboat, intent as the Israelites gazing upon the bronze snake in the wilderness, knowing with terrified certainty she would die if she turned her eyes away. After an eternal moment, strong hands gripped her arms and hoisted her into the boat.

Seized by uncontrollable coughing, she spewed out mouthfuls of muddy water. *Too thick to drink and too thin to plow.* The well-known maxim about the Missouri River flashed through her mind an instant before someone flopped her, turtle-like, onto her back.

A furious face came within inches of hers. "What the *hell* were you thinking to jump in like that? This ain't no crick. It's a rising river that'll snatch the life right outta you." The louder he yelled, the coarser his insults grew, grating against nerves already raw. "You got to be the stupidest chucklehead I ever known or heard of. You got no more sense than a cross-eyed cat. Why I ought to..."

Her stomach roiled. She rolled over, emptying it of a nasty broth containing enough soil to start a garden. Then she was hauled back, as her rescuer splashed away the offensive sludge with a bucket of water.

"Crazy woman," he muttered, thrusting a wet rag into her hands.

He traipsed to the back of the boat and stepped up on the platform. After untying the stern tiller, he guided the vessel into the middle of the channel. "There's a towhead 'bout a half-hour's ride downriver. We'll lay up there in the dead water—if you'll keep 'til then."

Hallie rose unsteadily to her knees, her mind so jumbled she could barely surface a coherent thought.

Her nephew sat next to a crude shelter. Some sort of tent made of animal skins. He'd looped his arms around his knees and watched with a horrified expression that conveyed how much he didn't want her anywhere near him.

No wonder. She must look monstrous. The foul-smelling water poured out of her dress, her hair, and even her eyes. She reached up to wipe it away. "My spectacles..."

"Lost in the river, I reckon," came a clipped reply.

Her lip quivered. She was fortunate that was all she'd lost. She hugged her arms and hunched over to keep from shaking, but it didn't work. Fear rattled her bones. The aftermath was almost worse than drowning.

After what seemed like hours, her irate savior guided the craft out of the fast current and into slack water. A short time later, he brought the boat to rest at the end of an island bristling with slender cottonwoods.

After securing the vessel, he squatted in front of her, his scowl lessening as his gaze raked her shivering form. "You'll catch a thousand agues if you stay in them wet clothes. There's some old rags in that tent. Go put on something dry."

She wouldn't be wet if he had stopped as she'd asked.

"Why did you s-set out on the r-river?" Her teeth chattered.

Something flickered in his eyes. Doubt? Guilt? Was a man

who'd risk a child's life even capable of such emotions? "Tad wanted a little adventure. I promised I'd take him if he—"

"A little adventure?" A weak laugh gurgled out. "You deem this death-defying act a *little adventure*?"

Whatever softness she'd perceived disappeared behind a flat gaze. "The only person I see courtin' death is the one sitting in front of me."

Hallie stiffened. He'd saved her life, but that didn't give him the right to curse at her and pile insults on her head. "Where is the closest town we can put in? I am taking Thaddeus back to Atchison so we can gather our things before we return home. After this foolish stunt, I cannot imagine Mr. Dubois will hesitate to declare you unfit to care for a child."

Her adversary rested a heavy hand upon her shoulder. "I promised Tad he won't have to go with you if he don't want to— and he don't. I can't imagine why you came all this way to fetch him when you couldn't be bothered before. But I'm dead sure you got no business raisin' a boy."

She started to object, but the hard look he pinned on her stopped her cold.

"Argue all you want. There's no profit in it. Even if you convince Dubois to give him to you, he'll just run off the first chance he gets." Finn's hard expression softened slightly. "I know what I'm talking about, Miss MacBride."

Misery seeped through her chilled skin. What he hadn't said, but implied, was that Tad had run away because he didn't want to be with her.

Desperate to escape, she crawled into the tent and knelt on a fur rug. An ache spread through her chest and soon encompassed her whole being. That lively brown-eyed boy might've been her child if the two people she'd loved most in life hadn't betrayed her. But it had been her choice to hold onto bitterness until it was too late.

Tears burned behind her eyelids. She swallowed hard, but the scalding flood wouldn't be held back. It spilled over, streaming down her cheeks in a torrent of recrimination and remorse.

The boat shifted as heavy steps moved toward the tent.

Hallie bit down on her lip to prevent her anguished cries from escaping. She swiped at her damp face and bottled up her grief. God forbid that odious man see her fall apart. He'd only use it against her, as he had everything else.

"Did you find the clothes?" he called.

"Yes, I..." She looked around, spying a pile of what looked like rags. "I see them. I'll be out in a moment."

The boat bobbed as his footsteps receded, and she heaved a relieved sigh. Thank goodness he'd left her alone. She couldn't face him again. Not until she'd regained her composure.

She shook out her wet hair and tamed the frightful curls into a heavy braid. It was the best she could do under the circumstances. Sorting through the clothing, she held up each article to determine its usefulness: long underwear patched in so many places it resembled a checkerboard, stained bibbed dungarees, soiled shirt, all equally distasteful. The tattered rags would have to do until she returned to town. Mr. Finn was right about one thing if nothing else. She would catch her death if she remained cold and wet.

What had he meant when he said she wasn't fit to raise a boy? The answer came to her as she changed into men's garments. He assumed she wasn't adventurous enough. If she proved otherwise, he might change his mind and give up his claim.

It chafed that she must submit to the boorish lout, but she would do any penance if it meant gaining custody of Caroline's son. Swallowing her pride, she went back outside, dragging her wet clothes behind her.

Mr. Finn had secured the boat on the shore in a small cove that appeared deceptively peaceful. She knew better. Rivers were dangerous, especially when they were rising.

Her reluctant rescuer had started putting out fishing lines, tying them to white limbs that poked up out of the water like bleached bones. Did he plan to stay overnight on this sandy strip of land in the middle of the river?

She rolled her eyes. Of course, he did. It was part of the absurd adventure. Very well, one night on an island should give her ample opportunity to prove her mettle.

Thaddeus squatted beside the big man, watching his every move. At her approach, her nephew turned and his eyes widened. "Aunt Hallie, you look like a boy."

He hadn't meant it as an insult, though she was painfully aware of how ridiculous she looked. She ignored her discomfort and drew her lips into a smile. "I thought these clothes would be better suited for going on an adventure."

His look of surprise transformed into alarm. "*You're* coming with us? This kind of adventure ain't for girls."

It wasn't suitable for him, either. But if she wanted to win his affection, she had to pretend she was excited about the idea.

"It sounds like fun. Surely you can make an exception?"

Her nephew screwed up his face in confusion. "What's a neck-cep shun?"

His idol unfolded from a crouched position to his full height. He seemed taller than before, his shoulders broader. It had to be a matter of perspective, what with them being so close and on a small boat. He rested his hand on her nephew's shoulder and the boy beamed with pleasure.

Hallie's heart bled. She couldn't even coax a tiny smile out of him.

"What she means is, she's going with us to the next landing. We can take her that far, can't we, Tadpole?"

"Uncle Huck says you can go with us as far as the next landing," Tad pronounced.

She dipped her chin, acknowledging what he viewed as a boon granted by his river god. "Thank you...Tad."

If she were to bridge the gap between them, she had to at least address him by his preferred moniker, and he couldn't possibly prefer *Tadpole.*

Tad's smile encouraged her, until he looked up at the man standing next to him, seeking approval. Mr. Finn missed the cue because he was preoccupied with frowning at her.

"We'll put in at Weston tomorrow. You can take a carriage back to Atchison. I'll get word to Dubois that Tad is going with me on a side trip."

Not without her. She squared her shoulders. "I will be going with you. Just think of me as a crew member."

The furrow between his brows deepened. "Crew member? You got no skills for being on this or any other boat."

"You have no idea what skills I possess."

"And I don't want to know."

She wouldn't expound on her qualifications even if he demanded it. "Either you take me with you or I'll report you to the sheriff."

"The sheriff? What for?" His voice boomed so loud that a flock of birds left the shelter of the island and took to the sky.

Hallie stood her ground. "For one, taking a child without permission."

"I'm his guardian."

"Not until you sign that paper you aren't. By the way, does this boat belong to you?"

"I didn't hook it if that's what you mean. We're just borrowing it."

"Borrowing?" she scoffed. "Such a soft word for stealing."

His expression turned thunderous. "I didn't steal it. I know the fellow who owns it. He won't care if we use it, so long as he gets paid back."

Tad swiveled his head to glare at her accusingly.

She would get nowhere splitting hairs over the difference between borrowing and stealing, and Tad clearly wouldn't take her side in an argument. "If you take me along, I won't make trouble for you with Mr. Dubois. We can send word to let him know we are working out our differences."

"Forget it. You ain't goin' no further than Weston."

She braced her bare feet. "Just try to throw me off."

He flexed his hands at his sides, and for a worrisome moment, it seemed he might toss her back into the river like small fry.

"Uncle Huck?" Tad's small voice interrupted. "I don't care if she stays a little longer."

Thank heavens. Somehow, she'd broken through to him. She smiled encouragingly. "Thank you, Tad. I'd love to go with you."

"Fine. I've had my say." Mr. Finn snatched up a shovel and jumped off the boat, marching a few paces away before starting to dig.

Hallie ventured closer to her nephew, anxious to make contact, if only for a brief hug. With a startled look, he whirled away and ran after his uncle.

"Tad, go gather driftwood, as much as you can carry, and haul it over here for a fire," the captain ordered. "I'll see what supplies we got and check the lines. Then our slush cook can show us them *skills* she's so mortal proud of."

CHAPTER SIX

The sun sank out of sight about the time the fire burned down to red-hot coals. It warmed Huck's face as he positioned the skillet to heat the lard.

Fortunately, the flatboat carried plenty of truck. Besides a rifle and ammunition, he'd found a couple big knives, fishing hooks and lines, an axe, a lantern, tin cups and plates. Plus a side of bacon, a bag of corn meal, and a jug of home brew.

Once they reached Weston, he'd arrange for his pay to be turned over to the old trapper—a generous amount for goods the fellow would end up selling anyway. Contrary to what Miss MacBride thought, he wasn't a thief. Nor had he set out to steal away with Tad. That had been an accident. She'd tried to make it into a crime.

Soon, the grease began to sizzle. Huck dropped in good-sized chunks of a catfish that their slush cook had cleaned and prepared, as instructed, and without even grimacing.

The self-proclaimed *crew member* sat cross-legged on the other side of the fire pit, stirring up batter for pones. With that thick black braid and those raggedy clothes, she looked more like a squaw dressed up as a scarecrow.

Miss MacBride could act the part if she thought it would do her any good. Or she could go to perdition, for all he cared. But she wasn't tagging along on their trip.

He'd as soon catch sight of a new moon over his left shoulder than invite the kind of bad luck she would bring with her. Not to mention, she'd drive him crazy and foul up his plans in the bargain.

Their eyes met for an instant before she returned her attention to the bowl in her lap. Flustered or scared? On the boat, she'd faced him with plenty of grit.

Uncomfortable feelings sloshed around inside Huck's stomach. He hadn't treated her anywhere near considerate, and he wasn't so ignorant he didn't know how to show respect to the weaker sex. But she'd about given him heart failure when she'd heaved herself into the river. Did she know how close she'd come to drowning?

She hadn't uttered a word since Tad had broken up their argument with that unexpected offer. The boy had avoided her since. Tad didn't want her around. He was just trying to keep the peace.

Tad dragged over another chunk of driftwood. He'd gone at his task with more eagerness than any boy ought to show for the job. "Are we gonna use all this for the fire?"

"Only some of it. We can sell what's left to the steamboats once we put in at the next landing." Huck used a tin fork to turn the breaded pieces of fish. "When I was your age, I could get by a long time from what I made collecting wood scraps after the spring rise. That's when the river brought in the best treasure."

"Wood ain't treasure," Tad insisted.

"It is when you can turn it into custom."

"Who'll give us money out here?" Tad hovered over Huck's

shoulder. A moment later he wandered away, getting interested in a tangled mess of timber down by the water.

Huck watched out of the side of his eye. He didn't trust Tad not to fall into trouble. Not after he'd run off and then cut them loose.

Some sort of punishment ought to be meted out. Pap would have whipped him 'til he couldn't sit down. Huck didn't feel up to administering a beating.

He motioned to the slush cook. "Here, this fish is ready. You can fry those pones in the grease."

She came around next to him to take the skillet, squinting like she couldn't see it. He guided her fingers to the rag he'd wrapped around the handle to keep it from getting too hot. His palms slid over smooth skin and a delicate wrist.

She stared at him instead of the fish.

He let go fast and moved away. "Don't burn yourself," he muttered, rubbing his hand over his trousers to remove her warm imprint.

Without a word, she hunkered down by the fire, as if nothing had happened.

Well, nothing *had* happened. He'd just kept her from blistering her fingers.

She forked crispy pieces of fish onto a tin plate before dropping dollops of batter into the hot grease. "Did your father have a wood yard?"

Why did she care about what his old man did? Maybe she was just nosy.

"Pap didn't put much stock into work—of any kind." He didn't add that his worthless father had drunk and gambled away what little his mother made by taking in laundry. After she'd died, Pap had stolen what he needed.

Miss MacBride focused on cooking the pones, all golden brown, and smelling heavenly enough to make a body's mouth water.

Huck crouched next to her and rested his wrists on his knees. He was ready to eat.

"Why did Mrs. Douglas take you in? Did your parents pass away?"

More questions. She had to be poking around to find things lacking in his upbringing, so she could argue against his suitability as a guardian. His miserable childhood would give her a goldmine. Not that it mattered. He didn't plan on keeping the boy anyhow.

"Pap ran off after my ma died. Came around every so often to check on me." And to take anything of worth he'd managed to squirrel away. "At least, he did until he got murdered."

Her gaze flashed up, shocked. That stopped her questions.

"How come he got murdered, Uncle Huck?"

Huck jerked around in surprise. He hadn't heard Tad creep up behind them. The boy's rapt expression made him wish he hadn't blurted out that bit about his father's murder. It wasn't something a boy needed to hear about or fret over.

"Was it the robber gang?" Tad asked in an awed tone.

Robber gang?

Huck shook his head. It had been so long since he'd been a boy, he'd forgotten how their minds worked. "What gave you that idea?"

"Mr. Sawyer told me that when you joined his robber gang, you were sworn to secrecy. If you broke your vow, they got to murder somebody in your family."

Huck snorted. "That's nonsense Tom made up. I didn't put my pap at risk."

Didn't bear mentioning it was Miss Watson he'd put up as surety so Tom would accept him into the gang. He hadn't wished the old lady ill. Mostly, he just didn't want her around and hadn't been too particular about how that might be accomplished. Youthful callousness.

He glanced over to see how Miss MacBride was coming along with the pones. Intent on her task, she didn't have that anxious, pinched expression she'd worn earlier. She had her lips pursed like she was offering him a kiss.

She's concentrating, you fool.

Huck dropped his arm between his legs. Durned if he didn't have the least particular parts in the country if he found a dried-up old maid to his liking. Well, she wasn't old, probably not even thirty, but that didn't matter. She was wound tighter than a capstan.

"How far are we going tomorrow?"

There she went again, assuming she had an invitation when she didn't. He wasn't about to reveal his plans and have her underfoot for the rest of the journey.

"Me and Tad might lay in somewhere around Kansas City."

"Surely you don't intend to take a child that far on such a flimsy craft?"

Truth be told, he hadn't planned on traveling that far on a flatboat. A steamboat would be faster, not to mention safer. But he couldn't resist baiting her.

"Why, that boat ain't flimsy. It's sturdier than a raft, and I been on all kinds of rafts."

"You were a raftsman?" She shook her head and made a little ticking sound with her tongue. "That explains a great deal."

The reputation of raftsmen for being coarse and brutal as the devil was known far and wide. But like most things, it was only part true. As was his claim. He'd rafted timber down the Mississippi River for less than a year before joining a crew on a steamboat. But he didn't owe her an explanation in light of the fact she had her mind made up.

"It explains why I'm so good at navigating a river that's got more temperaments than a woman."

She spooned pones onto a plate along with the fish and handed him a fork. "Are you making a point, Mr. Finn?"

The only point he cared to make wasn't fit for tender ears. Uppity folks like her had always looked down their noses at him like he was nothing more than an ignorant creature, not deserving of having a family or a home.

Out of pure spite, he shoveled the fish into his mouth with his fingers.

Tad grinned and mimicked his bad manners.

Sure enough, Miss MacBride's lips turned down in disapproval. But instead of fussing at them, she gripped a bent fork and went to work on her victuals.

The boy's antics and her reaction didn't improve Huck's mood. He felt downright childish. He had given into mean habits, something he didn't typically do, and had got Tad to go along with him, which made it worse.

After finishing the last bite, he resisted the urge to lick his fingers and cleaned his hands with a rag. He shook it off and held it out to Tad, who followed suit.

While the aunt cleaned up the dishes in a bucket, Huck secured their boat to sturdier trees for the night. The clouds were bunched together in dark masses and the wind had picked up. Those birds flapping around earlier hadn't lied. A big storm was brewing.

He lit the lanterns onboard and then checked the tent to make sure the sides were lashed down. Depending on how much it rained, water might seep in, and he'd have to stack their food stores on crates and cover everything with an oilcloth to keep it dry.

So, the starched and proper Miss MacBride thought she wanted to travel with them, did she? Well, this would be the first test of her resolve.

Huck stretched and yawned like he was all tuckered out.

"Think I'll turn in early. Tad, you too. Storm's a-comin'. That means more wood to collect come morning."

She jerked to her feet. "Where should I—?"

"You can sleep with us in the tent," he offered. "We'll strip down and put our clothes under an oilcloth in case the rain seeps in. That way, we got dry things to wear tomorrow."

She followed them as far as the tent. Even bent down to look inside at where he'd spread out blankets over the buffalo rug. "Could you give me one of those blankets so I can make a bedroll?"

He had to give her credit for having the courage to take it this far. "There aren't enough to go around. Why don't we just clump up together? Body heat will keep us warm."

She took a step back. "We can't sleep under the same blanket. It's not...respectable."

He wouldn't make her do it, but she didn't need to know that. She would rather curl up next to a rattlesnake, so she'd be pleading to go ashore in no time.

Turning to Tad, he shrugged and lifted his hands. "She said she wanted to join the crew."

With a huff, she hooked one of the lanterns onboard then nabbed the axe he'd left outside the tent.

"Where do you think you're going?" he asked, as she stepped off the boat and headed toward the trees.

"To build a shelter," she called over her shoulder.

A loud clap split the air. Thunder went rumbling and grumbling down the river.

He frowned as she vanished into a thicket of cottonwoods. She couldn't find her way through there, especially without her glasses. But if he went after her, she'd know he wasn't prepared to stick to his guns.

"Well, reckon we ought to turn in." He pulled back the tent

flap while fishing for the pipe he kept in his coat pocket. A smoke would soothe him while they waited for her to return.

Tad, who'd remained near the edge of the platform, turned with worry etched on his face. "You think she'll be all right?"

"Sure she will." Huck patted his nephew's shoulder and smiled to cover his unease. "Women are like cats. Being out in the wet don't suit 'em. She'll be back soon enough, and begging us to put ashore at the next landing."

The boy's fretful expression transformed into worshipful awe. "You're uncommon smart about women, Uncle Huck."

HALLIE APPLIED THE AXE TO THE BASE OF A COTTONWOOD SAPLING, hearing it crack with a satisfying split. A sound she would dearly love to hear when she whacked Huck Finn's head.

Thwack. "Uncouth brute." *Thwack.* "Red-headed by-blow of a mud cat." There weren't names bad enough for that low-down, ornery mule's hind end. Well, there might be, but she had no business thinking about them, much less saying them.

She leaned the cut poles against a thick tree trunk lodged sideways in a tangle of brush and vines. The dead tree had probably washed up in a flood, as none of the saplings on the island were anywhere near that big around. It made a convenient frame for her shelter.

The scheming reprobate knew full well she wouldn't sleep next to him. He thought she would give up her plan to go along with them.

Ha! She would show him. Hallie MacBride was made of sterner stuff. She could swim better and run faster than her male cousins and had spent many a summer night outdoors, sleeping under the stars. Although after she turned twelve, her mother put down her foot and insisted her daughter behave like a lady. Hallie had been forced to grow up.

She leaned on the axe to rest. How deeply she'd resented the constraints put on girls. Then again, setting up a lean-to in the middle of a bug-infested island wasn't exactly how she pictured enjoying freedom.

Fat raindrops struck her cheek just as she laid the last leafy branch across slender limbs forming the top of her makeshift lean-to. As she crawled beneath the shelter, the skies opened. She had to crouch on her knees and scoot as far back as she could to stay out of the downpour.

The shelter would hold until the storm passed. Then she would go steal a blanket and find a spot on the boat to curl up, as far away from Huck Finn as possible.

Rain pattered, then hammered against the sloping roof of the lean-to. Water seeped through the leafy cover and then began to pour in. She cried out as a cold stream cascaded down her back.

Within minutes, she was soaked clear through. Suffering unnecessarily because Huck Finn was a louse. Had he been reasonable, they could've shared the tent while maintaining a respectable distance.

She fought against an urge to return to the flatboat and bargain with him. That would only prove his point—that she wasn't tough enough to raise a boy.

Shivering, she cupped her hands around the lantern to keep the wind from passing through the holes in the tin. A gust extinguished the tiny flame.

"No!"

Hallie called down curses on the self-appointed Pharaoh of the Flatboat. *Frogs in his bed. No, locusts. Better yet, snakes. Spiders. Ants. Fleas.*

Wait. Tad was sleeping with him.

Spare the firstborn.

Lightning flashed, white-hot and blinding, lighting the inside of the shelter. Crackling energy lifted every hair on her body. Then a thunderous clap resounded, shaking the ground.

Hallie put her hands over her head. "Don't strike me down, Lord! I didn't mean those bad things."

Something crashed against the front of the shelter and she shrieked. Whatever it was—a large branch or a downed tree—trapped her inside.

The rain set up a vicious pounding.

Given the intensity of the storm, the whole island would soon be flooded. She'd be swept away in a tangled ball of debris, never to be found.

She laced her fingers and prayed for deliverance.

"Miss MacBride? Are you out there?"

She lifted her head. Was that Huck? It sounded like him. But why would he come out in the storm after her? He'd been the one who let her walk away without so much as an oilcloth.

"Dad durn it, I swear I'm gonna—ouch!" A crashing noise ended the angry tirade abruptly. "Dangnation Hallie! I can't see through the rain. Call out!"

"Over here! I'm trapped behind a limb or a tree or something."

She heard him traipse closer and then he tore into the blockade. He hauled the downed branches away from the front of the shelter. Another lightning strike illuminated his broad shoulders as he thrust his face inside.

In a burst of gratitude, she grabbed his head and pressed her lips to his, which parted with a soft grunt of surprise. He tasted like cool rain and warm tobacco.

Her galloping heart thundered and her skin prickled as it had when the lightning struck.

She jerked back, horrified at her impetuous behavior.

"I-I didn't mean—" Her stammering explanation was cut short as he dragged her out of the shelter.

He slung her over his shoulder as he would a grain sack and set off in the direction of the flatboat. His heavy strides jostled her so hard that her teeth snapped together.

"Put me down, you blatherskite. I'm going to be sick."

He jerked to a stop long enough set her on her feet, then enveloped her hand in a calloused grip. "You can cuss me all you want after we get back to the boat."

"I did not cuss—" She gasped when he yanked her arm nearly out of the socket. He dragged her behind him at such a pace she thought she might take flight. They raced pell-mell through the sheeting rain, which didn't let up until they were near to the boat.

Huck had braved a storm to rescue her, even after taking such pains to drive her away. His actions would indicate he did have a conscience after all.

She stepped onto the platform and stopped to catch her breath. "I appreciate—"

"Get inside." He shoved her through the tent flap, causing her to stumble.

One display of chivalry did not a knight make. And to think she'd *kissed* the knave. Fear had stolen her wits.

"I was trying to thank you," she muttered.

Her surly rescuer turned his back and made fast the opening.

Inside, it was cozy and dry. An oil lamp hung from a hook attached to a branch forming the backbone of the tent. The light illuminated a small boy seated on the furry rug.

Hallie longed to gather him into her arms. However, her experience of late cautioned against the motherly display.

His anxious gaze fixed on the man behind her. "I was praying real hard you wouldn't die."

"Nobody's dying," Huck grumbled.

How could he be so unfeeling? She would give her right arm to be the recipient of Tad's admiration and concern. "You needn't bite the child's head off for being worried."

Huck answered with a scowl.

She stepped closer and dropped her voice to a whisper. "Why are you so angry? You were the one to stage this little drama, knowing full well I wouldn't concede to sleeping next to you."

Water flowed out of his clothes, forming a puddle on the floor. Droplets clung to his hair and beard. A glistening bead dripped off the end of his nose. They both looked like a pair of drowned cats.

"This whole episode could have been avoided if you had just given me a blanket," she pointed out in an even tone.

He went to where Tad sat and snatched a quilt rolled up beside him. Somehow, he'd managed to *find* another covering. "Here. Now, stop yappin' and get out of them wet clothes before you get sick."

Without missing a beat, he proceeded to peel off his dripping coat. He unbuttoned his shirt and drew it over his head. His hands went to the closure on his trousers.

Hallie jerked herself out of her daze and whirled around. She hefted one crate on top of another to separate the space then sat behind the barrier with her quilt. "I will remain behind here."

"I don't care where you stay," came a low-pitched response. "But if I don't see them wet clothes in two shakes, I'll drag you out here and strip you down myself."

"You wouldn't *dare*."

From the other side of the crates came a muffled curse. The boxes shifted.

With a shriek, she dodged his arm as he reached around to grab her. "You miscreant. Keep your filthy hands off me! There's an innocent child in here."

"Wrap up in that quilt then, if you don't want him to see you."

With jerky movements, she shed the soaked garments and tucked the quilt around her. Still fearful he might engage in other mischiefs, she ventured a peek around the side of a box.

Flickering shadows danced on the hide walls.

Huck had tucked one of the two ragged blankets around his waist, leaving his upper half bare. Fierce and savage were two words that came to mind. The thrill she couldn't explain. She didn't understand her attraction to the brute but was determined to ignore it.

He sat next to Tad and said something in a low whisper. When Tad scooted up next to him, he rested his hand on the boy's shoulder in a protective gesture. It appeared Huck had a soft side after all. He just didn't show it very often.

Hallie withdrew behind the crates before he caught her spying on them. She guarded her heart, too. Therefore, he must've assumed she didn't have one. How could she change his mind about her without becoming vulnerable? She couldn't. Getting through his barriers required she first put her own aside. Not literally, of course. She would keep the crates in place.

"Thank you for coming after me." She forged ahead to take the first step in making peace. "I made several wrong assumptions when I met you, and said some things I shouldn't have."

A steady rain drummed on the tent. Her heart thudded nearly as loudly as she waited for his response.

From across the room came a rustling sound and a low murmur. "Go on to sleep, Tad. I'll sit up long enough to make sure we don't get washed away."

"Are we going back on the river tomorrow, Uncle Huck?"

"Maybe. Leastwise, long enough to put your aunt back on dry land where she belongs."

Hallie closed her eyes and fought the urge to cry. He continued to be rude because he wanted her to break down and give up.

Never.

She would find a way to win this war if it was the last thing she ever did.

CHAPTER SEVEN

By morning, the storm had spent itself after breaking up trees and tossing limbs around. One had landed on the boat, busting up the stern and snapping the tiller in two.

Huck bent over to pick up the broken halves and stood with a weary sigh. He'd have to make repairs before they set out, which meant another day stuck on an island with that aggravating woman.

He hadn't known what to say to her last night. He didn't deserve thanks and hadn't asked for an apology.

Sighing again, he picked up the soggy pile of clothes she'd shed and spread them over a bush. The sun would dry them soon enough. He'd rescued her dress and underclothes before the rain, but they still needed a little extra drying.

Miss MacBride would have to stay put for a little while longer. He ought to lock her up until they made land so he wouldn't expire from worry. She gave him worse trouble than Tad. What had possessed her to set out on her own with bad weather coming in?

You sent her packing, Hucky.

Not exactly. He'd offered her a place to sleep. Next to him. She was supposed to get faint and beg to be taken to town. How was he to know she'd haul off into the woods?

He picked up a stick and raked wet debris out of the fire pit and arranged the kindling, along with some of the driftwood he'd managed to keep dry.

His nephew had gathered every stick in sight. Obedience weren't a steady thing in a boy that young. Tad was out to prove he would make a good ship's mate.

Huck didn't have the heart to let on that nothing would change his mind. His nephew deserved better than the life he could give him.

"Uncle Huck! Looky here. I found another lantern." Tad ran up with the dented tin treasure. "I dug it out of a pile of lumber that washed up. Wonder where it came from?

"An unlucky steamer would be my guess."

Boats expired on these waters with alarming regularity, mostly due to the abundance of snags.

Tad dropped the useless lantern by Huck's feet. "Can I go see what else I can find?"

"Keep an eye out for snakes. They'll drop right out of the trees after a heavy rain."

"Oh." His nephew eyed the branches of a nearby cottonwood. "Maybe I'll stay here and help you with breakfast."

"Suit yourself." Huck tossed another piece of driftwood onto the fire. "I'll make us corncakes and fry up some bacon. Looks like our cook won't be stirring anytime soon."

Last night, the poor woman had stayed cramped up behind those crates into the wee hours. He'd finally gotten tired of fretting and fetched her. When he'd scooped her up in his arms, it shocked him to discover she wasn't a bit bony or even thin. Rather, her body felt lithe and firm like she was used to doing work, but still soft in all the right places.

She'd been so tuckered out she hadn't woken when he lifted her, or when he put her on the bearskin rug beside Tad, or even after he laid down beside her. He, on the other hand, hadn't slept a wink.

"Suppose I ought to check on her."

"Suppose so," Tad echoed. He picked up a stick and poked at the fire.

The boy's mimicking didn't annoy Huck like he figured it might. Back in the day, some of the younger boys who'd followed him around liked to copycat to put on airs. Tad just seemed anxious to please him.

He ruffled his nephew's hair.

Tad grinned. If he had a tail, it would've been wagging.

Huck felt a mite awkward showing affection, having not been brought up with it. Though it was a dang sight easier to pat Tad on the head than it was to put up with the inconvenient reaction he had to the boy's aunt.

It couldn't be that Hallie MacBride had him stoked hot as a boiler. It was just the *idea* of a warm, naked woman.

He opened the flap and slipped inside to get the makings for breakfast.

She'd burrowed beneath the quilt and hadn't budged an inch.

Had she taken sick? Concerned, he knelt beside her and lifted the corner of the cover.

She lay curled up on her side with one arm tucked under her head. Her breathing seemed regular enough, though he ought to make a closer inspection, just in case.

He drew aside a heavy mass of curls. No wonder she was always fighting to tame them. It must annoy Miss MacBride to no end to have such wild hair.

A strand curled around his finger, soft as a feather.

Desire streaked through him, startling in its intensity, and he shook off the curl. He'd come over here to check on her condition not fondle her hair.

Her face looked softer in slumber, and her skin shone with the rosy glow of good health. Dark lashes rested like fans above her cheekbones. How had he ever thought she resembled old Miss Watson? Personality aside, there was no comparison. Hallie was downright pretty, and as delicate as a piece of china, though that weren't the case.

By jingo, she'd built herself a shelter and had planned to stick it out the whole night. She hadn't even hollered for help when that storm wound up.

Huck couldn't help but admire such a hardy woman, especially one so well put together.

He stared at her mouth, recalling how it felt when she pressed her lips against his. Like catching a fever, only more exciting and less tiring. She jerked away before he could react. Even in a ripper of a storm, it had taken every ounce of willpower not to drag her against him to finish what she'd started. Instead, he'd thrown her over his shoulder.

Idiot.

She rolled onto her back with a sigh and blinked in sleepy confusion.

Huck froze. He'd never hear the end of it if she caught him gawking at her. Hopefully, she'd go on back to sleep.

Her eyes drifted shut, but her lips curved up in a welcoming smile.

His heart jumped in his chest. Was that smile meant for him? The quick taste he'd got last night had left him hungry for more. Perhaps she felt the same. If so, he'd be all for it.

He leaned over and heard her murmur something that sounded like *yes*. That was all the encouragement he needed. Gently, he brushed his lips over hers until they opened like a rose unfurling its petals.

"Uncle Huck?"

Huck moved so fast he lost his balance and toppled onto his backside, sending a tin cup spinning and rattling across the floor. He glanced over his shoulder, meeting his nephew's puzzled gaze.

"What are you doing in here!" Hallie's shrill voice whipped Huck's head around.

She had bolted up with the quilt clutched to her neck. Her cheeks glowed and her eyes blazed. Not with desire.

The heat in his body went straight to his face and scrambled his brain. He came to his feet, pushed Tad to one side, and clawed at the flap, stumbling, nearly falling in his haste to get out of that tent and away from temptation in a tattered quilt.

Halfway across the island, Huck stopped running. He bent over, braced his hands on his knees, and sucked in deep breaths, as his heart flopped wildly in his chest. He hadn't fled from a girl since he was twelve.

Damn fool.

Why had he kissed the blasted woman anyhow? He wanted nothing to do with Hallie MacBride. Didn't want her around. Didn't want her, period.

He rested his back against a tree and huffed a dark laugh. At least his mind had got things straight. His body, on the other hand, was rarin' to go.

"Uncle Huck? Whatcha doin'?"

Huck straightened. He could explain. Then again, maybe not. He had no idea what had just happened in there, other than he'd lost his mind. It would be best to change the subject.

He peered up into the tree. "Thought I'd fetch us some eggs. For breakfast." He pointed upward. "There's a nest up there. Maybe you can see it."

The boy tilted his head back. "I don't see anything. But I sure am hungry."

Huck winced, as guilt flayed what little conscience remained after years of neglect. He'd pushed Tad out of the way and taken off without even considering the boy's needs.

He clapped a hand on his nephew's shoulder. "C'mon. Let's fry up some of that bacon, then I'll show you how to make corncakes. They're tolerable good with a little grease."

Tad took two quick steps and a skip for every one of Huck's strides. "What were you doing to Aunt Hallie? She seemed awful mad, worse than usual. And she fussed at me for spying on her. I wasn't spying, honest."

"'Course you weren't."

"What were *you* doin'?"

"Checking to see if she was sick after getting rained on."

"But you said she was like a cat."

"Yeah, that's what I said. How could I know she don't have sense enough to sneak in out of the wet? Tell you what. You help me make a new oar then we'll go swimming and play pirates."

"That's bully, Uncle Huck." Tad lunged and parried with an invisible weapon. "Can you show me how to sword fight?"

"Sure, I'll learn you everything I know." Huck smiled, relieved to get off the hook so easily.

Between now and when they got rid of their unwanted tagalong, he would spend all his time with Tad. Teach him how to survive on the river. Show him everything he needed to know to make it on his own. Not that the boy would ever be on his own, but it wouldn't hurt him to know how to take care of himself, and it would give them both a good reason to steer clear of Hallie MacBride.

She stirred things up worse than a nest of hornets.

CHAPTER EIGHT

The boat swayed when Hallie stood up from where she'd been sitting on a crate. She adjusted the quilt, tucking the edge under her arm to keep it from slipping off.

Where had Huck gone with her nephew? The dratted man had left her inside a stifling tent for what seemed like hours with nothing to wear. She'd checked every nook and cranny for her dress or those soiled rags. He had removed them.

Sweat trickled down her temple and she itched from the heat and frustration. This had to be another one of his ploys to break her. It wouldn't work. If necessary, she would turn the quilt into a toga.

A thump came from outside. "Aunt Hallie, I brung your breakfast."

With a tight grip on the quilt, she opened the flap and poked her head out just in time to see Tad run off to follow his uncle into the woods.

"Wait! Come back! Where are you going?"

"To make a new oar. Then we're going swimming, and Uncle

Huck is gonna teach me how to sword fight..." Tad's voice faded as they disappeared.

Huck never looked back.

She didn't call for help. That's what Huck wanted her to do. He probably thought she'd break down and cry and beg him to take her ashore. Not in a thousand years.

A savory smell drew her attention to the plate of food that Tad had placed next to the tent. Alongside it, her dress, petticoats and underclothing were neatly folded and stacked. Those hadn't been there when she'd checked before.

She lifted the pile in her hands. Dry and warm from the sun. Had Tad...? No, he wouldn't think of it. Huck must've retrieved her damp clothing and put it out to finish drying, which showed he did have the ability to act like a gentleman when he chose to do so.

He might even regret his earlier prank and horrid rudeness.

In a lighter mood, she polished off the food and got dressed in a hurry, tying on only one petticoat. Fewer layers made more sense out here, and she could be practical.

As she twisted her hair into a knot, she mulled over the odd encounter earlier. If Huck had intended to return her dry clothing, why hadn't he brought it in with him? For some reason, he'd fallen down and then stormed off, leaving Tad standing there wide-eyed with curiosity and her wondering.

She hadn't been at her best—startled awake and naked, except for the quilt—and had scolded the child, who didn't deserve it. His only crime had been interrupting a provocative dream. James Douglas had come to her, swearing he'd loved only her. His kiss had been strangely tentative. Oh, and something had tickled her face that felt like hair, or...

A beard?

Hallie put her hands over her mouth. Oh no. He wouldn't.

Oh yes, he would. Huck Finn would go to any lengths to drive her away. No other explanation would make sense, given his antipathy toward her.

She finished buttoning the dress with shaking hands. Did he expect her to remain hidden, cowering in fear? She wouldn't give him the satisfaction.

Hallie grabbed the rifle propped against the crates. If they would fish, she would hunt. This island was bound to be teeming with game and fowl. She would show Huck Finn she was up to this adventure.

SUNLIGHT STREAMING THROUGH THE LEAVES SPECKLED THE SOFT, spongy ground. Between forked ends of a low-hanging branch, an enterprising spider had spun an intricate web, and the delicate threads glistened like silver.

Hallie wished she had paint brush rather than a gun.

Clank, clank.

On second thought, a gun might be more useful.

She crept toward the bushes from where the sound originated. Another clank was accompanied by a mournful bleat and the rustling of leaves.

From between two shrubs, a nanny goat stepped out.

Hallie released a weak laugh. "Oh my, you gave me a scare."

The clanking came from a bell attached to a collar around the goat's neck, from which also hung the frayed end of a rope. Filth coated its coarse white coat.

"Where did you come from? Poor thing." Moving slowly to avoid startling the animal she took hold of the rope. She plucked burrs from around the goat's floppy ears, earning an affectionate butt.

The miserable creature let out another bleat and shook its head to remonstrate against its situation.

"Grumbling, are we? You got yourself into this fix."

Hadn't she done the same? That scene in the tent might've been avoided if she hadn't thrown herself at Huck in a frenzy of gratitude.

"I understand, perfectly," Hallie said, patting the goat's shaggy head. "We'll make good company, you and I, both of us stubborn and unsatisfied with our lot."

She wrapped the rope around her hand and set off back to the boat as fast as the goat would allow. Tad would be delighted with a new playmate, and fresh milk would make a healthful supplement to their meals. Even better, Huck would be forced to admit that she had proven valuable to this expedition.

No mention of the kiss need be made. At best, he had presumed she wanted it. Worse case, he meant to torment her. She would pretend it never happened.

Closer to the river, laughter came from the direction of the boat. Huck's lower tone along with Tad's giggling. That didn't sound like serious fishing. As she reached the edge of the woods, the flatboat came into view—along with the naked backsides of two males.

Hallie halted abruptly. She'd caught them unawares. Or, more likely, Huck expected her to arrive and be outraged. If so, he would be disappointed. Having grown up on a river, she'd seen plenty of boys taking skinny dips.

Only—her gaze moved up Huck's long, muscular legs to his pale, tight buttocks and narrow hips—that was no boy. Mesmerized, she watched the play of muscles as he crouched and shot off the edge of the boat.

Lands, she couldn't be attracted to the heathen brute. This warm, shivery feeling was nothing more than the appreciation of an artist for a fine form.

Liar.

Very well, her earlier behavior had been a fluke. She would

never willingly kiss him again.

Nanny bleated, as if to call her bluff, then jerked the rope out of her hand and scurried toward the flatboat. The reason for its haste became clear—the wrapped side of bacon on an upside-down crate near the fire pit.

"No!" Hallie took off in pursuit. They couldn't afford to lose their precious food stores. The dashed creature could graze or eat leftovers.

"Hey, Aunt Hallie, is that a goat?"

She kept her eyes fastened on the hungry nanny. "Yes, it is. You stay in the water until I catch it."

Splashing followed Tad's incredulous inquiry. No need to look to know he was crawling back into the boat, unclothed.

She grabbed the rope and dragged the protesting goat away from the food. "Mr. Finn! Could you please get out of the water and see if you can find a sturdy rope?"

Hallie didn't look to see whether Huck responded to her plea for assistance. God forbid she would catch an eyeful of the *front* of him.

The goat bucked, wresting free of her grasp, and made a second charge for the bacon. Hallie fell to her knees in a desperate lunge. Just then, Huck's large hand gripped the rope around the goat's neck, and he yanked the determined creature away from the food.

Water coursed in rivulets through the reddish-brown hair on his shins. His knee-length drawers clung to corded muscles in his thighs, the wet cloth outlining every aspect of his admirable anatomy.

For a second, she forgot how to breathe.

"Don't sit there gawkin'. Fetch a chain!"

Hallie scrambled to her feet and darted into the tent. In a crate filled with odds and ends, she found a length of chain and a padlock.

She gave herself a firm talking-to. Huck Finn would not intimidate her, would not fluster her, would not make her knees turn to jelly.

He'd dragged the goat to a tree a safe distance away from their food.

She shuffled in that direction, trying without success to keep her eyes averted from his near-naked form. Gracious, he was powerful large—all over.

"Dash it, woman, you drag your feathers slower than a killdeer," he grumbled. "Tad, bring that chain over here."

Hallie gratefully turned the chain and lock over to the first mate before taking a seat on the crate next to the fire pit, keeping her back to them while guarding the bacon.

Her traitorous mind kept replaying the scene. The tantalizing glimpse of pale flanks, his tanned arms and broad back, the fascinating color of the hair on his body and face, which perfectly complemented his river-hued eyes.

She exhaled a shaky breath. *Ridiculous.* Her tastes ran to mahogany and chocolate, not russet and blue.

From behind her, clanking chains, pathetic bleating, and a child's laughter mingled with gruff praise. "You did real good finding this goat."

Was Huck's compliment intended for her? Wonders never ceased.

"Might've got washed down here from one of the farms along the river. Lucky it didn't drown."

"Hey, let's name her Lucky!" Tad exclaimed. "I'll milk her."

The boy's buoyant eagerness brought a smile to Hallie's face. In light of everything he'd lost in his short life, perhaps a little adventure wasn't such a bad idea. As long as he was kept safe and it didn't last more than a few days. Afterward, they could return to civilization.

An instant later, Tad appeared at her side and grabbed a bucket near her feet. She shot her hand out and caught his wrist. Time to introduce discipline to counterbalance the primitive behaviors encouraged by his obliging uncle. "Put your clothes on, young man."

Tad flushed, appearing startled and embarrassed at the same time. How could he *not* realize he was stark naked?

Fighting the urge to laugh, Hallie averted her gaze. Their clothing was scattered from the fire pit to the water's edge, as if they'd undressed as they ran. "While you're at it, please give Mr. Finn his garments. Gentlemen don't parade about unclothed in front of ladies."

"They don't like it," Tad said with authority, hopping about as he pulled on his trousers.

"Some don't object as much as others," came the gruff reply.

Hallie twisted around and the heat wave struck again. Good Lord, the man stood right next to her, shirtless and buttoning up his pants. She dragged her gaze from his hands to his face. "How can you utter such a low remark in the presence of an impressionable boy?"

"Haven't uttered a low remark for at least an hour." He drew on his shirt but didn't bother with the buttons. "Besides, it's a fact he ought to know."

"Not when he's eight."

Tad slipped on his shirt, leaving it hanging open in deference to his idol.

"Button up," she directed.

"What does it matter if his shirt's unbuttoned? Just us crew members out here."

She bristled at the snide remark. "It wouldn't kill you to set a good example. Manners aside, you may not have noticed his skin is unused to the sun. If he doesn't cover up, he may burn."

Huck turned the boy around and opened his shirt, examining

the pink flesh. "Button up, Tadpole. Don't want the sun to fry you like a fish."

"When are we going to play pirates?" Tad lunged, wielding an imaginary sword.

"I thought you offered to milk our goat?" She took note of a downed sapling stripped of its branches. "Mr. Finn isn't finished making us another oar. You may play after he's done with his work."

Tad opened his mouth to object. He closed it when his uncle gripped his shoulder.

"No use arguing, Tadpole. Starchy women like your aunt are bound and determined to turn boys into lap dogs."

"Better than allowing them to grow up to be tom cats," she shot back.

Huck's eyes opened wide. Then he let loose with a boisterous laugh.

She put her hands over her face. Why had she blurted out that inappropriate remark? Being around him was turning her into a hoyden.

Following Huck's lead, Tad chortled. He couldn't possibly understand the underlying meaning, but he found humor in his uncle's amusement. She couldn't help but smile at their merriment, even if it was at her expense.

Where had Huck gotten such a warped view of respectability?

Tales about a beggar boy named Huck Finn had crossed the river with the gossipers. She hadn't paid much attention to what went on in St. Petersburg until she'd met James Douglas. He'd known Huck when they were children and had recounted how the homeless boy slept on stoops in the summer and in hogshead barrels in the winter.

Huck hadn't admitted to being abandoned, but what else could one call it? His father hadn't even cared enough to shelter him.

Sadness flowed through her, bringing with it a deep ache that settled in her chest. How terrible not to have the security of a loving family. Was it any wonder that Huck drank in Tad's adoration like a desert soaking up rain? He might even be thinking about keeping the boy as an antidote to loneliness and had made up a *good family* so she would go away.

Huck came up beside her with amusement flickering in his eyes. He'd buttoned his shirt halfway, ceding partly to her wishes. "Why don't *you* milk the goat? Tad can help me with repairs. Then him and me are going to play pirates."

"I don't gotta rest?" Tad asked his uncle.

"You can rest tonight." Huck held her gaze.

Challenging her authority at every turn.

"We shan't agree on anything, shall we?" she said softly.

Tad looked between them and his smile wavered. A crease between his brows signaled distress. Their constant bickering had to be upsetting him. She didn't want her nephew to feel insecure. He'd been through too much already.

"We shan't agree on anything except for how we feel about Tad," she amended. "We're in complete agreement on that, wouldn't you say?"

Tad looked with anxious hope at his uncle.

Huck kept his eyes averted and drew his suspenders over his shoulders. He picked up two branches cut from the sapling.

Surely the man wasn't so dense he couldn't see how important it was for him to acknowledge his feelings, even if it meant he had to agree with her.

The reason struck like a well-placed blow, leaving her breathless.

He didn't want Tad to think he cared because he hadn't lied when he said he wouldn't keep Tad. He fully intended to give her nephew away, and he'd already decided on someone.

Hallie knew without asking that *someone* wasn't her.

CHAPTER NINE

Tad shifted from one foot to the other and tried to be patient while his uncle finished *scouring up the swords*. A fancy phrase for whittling away at a cottonwood branch until it suited.

"When I was a boy, we used laths and broomsticks. They were easier to slick up." He put his thumb against the back of a big knife and carefully peeled away another strip of bark.

When he held up the sword, Tad sighed with admiration. It looked just like a rapier. Or what he thought a rapier ought to look like, with a handle to hold it and a long blade.

"You didn't sharpen the point. Ain't swords s'posed to be sharp?"

The pirate king smiled. "Only if you plan on tangling with a wild pig. We'll leave the ends blunt so we don't get hurt while we're playing. Don't want to kill the fun."

It would be more fun to have a sharp sword, and he was big enough to be careful with it. But he wouldn't argue. He wouldn't do nothing to give his uncle a reason to get rid of him. Not when things were so uncertain.

Tad chewed his lip, wanting to ask a question but afraid the answer might make him cry.

His uncle removed his shirt and tied a red rag around his head that matched the one Tad wore. "Tom called himself The Black Avenger. I'm Finn the Red-Handed. What's your pirate name?"

Tad hefted his sword without much excitement. He couldn't stop worrying about what his uncle planned to do with him after they left the island. "I dunno. Can you pick one for me?"

"How about Tad the Terrible?" His uncle held out his hand. "Here, give me your shirt so you don't dirty it up. Your aunt's excitable, and that'll send her into fits."

Tad reckoned a fellow mean enough to be called *Terrible* shouldn't have to worry about an excitable aunt. But he handed his shirt over because his uncle said so.

They walked along the edge of the water to where a stretch of sand extended into the river.

"This'll suit for learning you how to fight. Our pirate gang used to set up ambuscades for bloodthirsty outlaws. We were always attacking Sunday school picnics and other such places where Tom reckoned they'd be." The pirate king harrumphed. "I'm sure *we* can do better. Maybe those gulls over there. They look like a beady-eyed bunch."

He swung his sword in preparation, holding his weapon high like he was ready to chop wood.

"Uncle Huck, do you like me?" The question just blurted itself out. Tad waited in an agony of uncertainty for the reply.

Finn the Red-Handed dropped his sword to his side. "'Course I like you, Tadpole. Whatever made you doubt it?"

Tad swallowed to clear the burning in his throat. "Aunt Hallie asked if you agreed with her about liking me. But you didn't answer, and it looked like you were mad."

"Come here." His uncle knelt and laid his sword across his knee. He took Tad's arm in a firm grip, not so firm it hurt, and gave him a smile. "What I recall is your aunt asking me if we agreed on how we feel. But if I don't know how she feels, how can I agree with her?"

"She says she wants to take me home, so I reckon she likes me. But you want to give me away." Tad wiped away tears that came out despite his best effort to hold them in.

His uncle blinked hard. Maybe some sand had blown into his eyes. He peered out at the river where there weren't nothing except for birds perched on a forest of bleached trees poking out of the water. After a moment, he cleared his throat. "I like you real well, Tadpole. Better than any fellow I ever traveled with, including Jim. And he was the best friend I ever had, except for Tom."

Tad's spirits lifted. "I like you, too, Uncle Huck. Better than my bestest friend. That's why I want to stay with you. I won't cry or be no trouble. And I can help, now that you taught me how to set fishing lines and gather up driftwood and how to make pones and—"

"Look here." His uncle squeezed his arm. "Taking you with me isn't a measure of how much I like you. I'm set in my habits. I don't have a wife to help raise a child. Dontcha see? It wouldn't be right to keep you for my own selfish sake. I'm finding you a good home because I like you so much."

Tad's heart plummeted to the ground. No matter how much his uncle liked him, he still wouldn't keep him.

Unless he's got a wife.

Tad got so excited he could hardly contain himself. By golly, he could find a wife for Uncle Huck, and everything would work out just the way he wanted.

His uncle sighed real deep. "Now you gave me your vow if we took this adventure, you'd go with the family I picked out."

Tad nodded, keeping his lips sealed so he wouldn't blurt out the grand plan. It might take some doing, considering his uncle didn't put much stock in women, particularly Aunt Hallie. But there had to be some way to get them to like each other, seeing as she was the only wife available.

"You ready to learn how to fight like a pirate?" His uncle used his sword to point to a flock of gulls resting on their bellies on the sand bar. "Let's *get* them varmints."

"Yaaaaa!" Tad ran at the birds, swinging his sword. He'd show them rascally outlaws how terrible he could be.

The birds lifted as a single being—screeching, cawing, and flapping their wings in a fury.

Tad skidded to a stop and his heart nearly jumped out of his throat as a monstrous cloud of beaks and talons headed straight for him. With a scream, he turned and ran, launching himself into his uncle's arms.

His sword *thunked* hard against the pirate king's mouth.

CHAPTER TEN

Dusk drifted in, bringing with it a heavy fog that hovered over the water like a river ghost. Stepping back to the stern, Huck attached the steering oar he'd fashioned from a slender cottonwood tree. It would suit until they got to where they were headed tomorrow.

He stood and stretched. All he cared about tonight was getting some sleep without the distraction of a womanly body or a wiggly child. He'd be shy of the woman tomorrow, but he'd have to bear with Tad another couple weeks until he reached St. Petersburg and arranged for Tom Sawyer to adopt the boy.

Huck wandered over to one of the wooden boxes he'd lugged ashore. He sank with a weary sigh and rested his arms on his knees. From behind came a plaintive bleat. The goat couldn't chew through that chain.

A few feet away, water lapped softly against the hull of the boat. Tad's heels drummed on the gunwale where he was seated, drinking a cup of milk, while his aunt finished washing the dishes they'd used for supper. The scene was so ordinary, so peaceful.

Huck's heart hurt almost as bad as his swollen lip. He tested the tender spot with his tongue. Blamed thing hurt like the dickens, but he had to smile when he thought about how he'd got it. Funniest thing he'd seen in a long time. Tad hadn't meant to whack him with that sword, but the boy had leapt up all in a fright after those crazy birds had come after him.

A dull ache pressed against the inside of Huck's chest. Whatever it was, the dad-blamed feeling seemed to be growing, made worse by how low down he'd felt ever since coming back from playing pirates. He had been dead certain this adventure was a grand idea. But the past few days had him all confused. He had to get the boy to Tom Sawyer as soon as possible, and in the meantime not allow his nephew to entertain any illusions about staying with him.

Huck rubbed his neck and sighed. He didn't know how to parent a child. All his pap had taught him was how to be mean enough to survive. Tad needed equal parts discipline and adventure, with plenty of affection thrown in. He was desperate for a role model, and Tom would be a fine one.

"Are we leaving tomorrow, Uncle Huck?" Tad rubbed his eyes with his fists. Tuckered out. Perhaps he should've rested earlier, though it rasped to admit the aunt had it right.

She settled onto a crate opposite the fire and pulled Tad into her lap. The boy didn't utter a peep in protest. Seeing as how he'd avoided her up until now, he must be too tired to care.

Hallie had cooked them dinner and she'd done a fine job. Since they'd been on the island, she had been intent on proving her grit and getting along, no matter what. Trying to show she'd be a good ma. Wouldn't make no difference. What that boy needed, she'd never be able to give him, having accepted the life of an old maid.

Huck stroked his hand over his beard, purely puzzled. What had happened to that pretty woman to make her so scared that she hid behind spectacles and ugly clothes? Wasn't any of his business. He couldn't let his heart soften to her pleas, for Tad's sake. He straightened up, determined to stay the course. "We'll set out, come dawn. If the fog moves off."

"Why do we got to wait for the fog to leave?" Tad squirmed out of Hallie's lap. She scooted over, making room for him to sit next to her on the box.

"The lantern we got doesn't give off enough light to let the steamboats know we're coming. They might plow right through us," Huck explained.

The boy's worried gaze shifted to his aunt.

"Most pilots are good, honorable men who wouldn't purposely hurt anybody," She slipped her arm around his waist in a comforting gesture. "You don't need to worry, though. Your uncle won't let anything bad happen to you."

Huck almost fell off his seat at her unexpected declaration. Not to mention this being the first time she'd referred to him directly as Tad's uncle. Could it mean she'd not fight his efforts to get Tad adopted by his boyhood friend?

Not likely. There weren't no backdown to Miss MacBride.

"I'll keep us away from the steamers," he assured his nephew. "I've worked on the big boats for fifteen years. I know their habits."

"You worked on a steamboat?" Tad's awed tone implied he held his uncle in higher esteem than ever.

Huck relaxed into one of his favorite subjects. "Oh, I worked on heaps of 'em. Mostly chugging up and down this big muddy river."

"What kind of work have you done?" Hallie appeared less inclined to be impressed.

"Started on freight boats doing odd jobs. Then got on as a mate. Worked my way up from the boiler room to the pilot house."

"You piloted steamboats?" Her face reflected disbelief.

Pilots were respected men. If Hallie respected him, she might honor his wishes where Tad was concerned, or at least not fight him so hard.

"You're looking at one of the best steersmen on this here river." Huck wasn't lying or bragging, just stating a fact.

She shook her head as if *she* knew better. "But the lawyers I spoke with in St. Petersburg said you were working on the docks."

Huck wished he'd never written that stupid letter to Tom. "I wasn't working the docks. I managed them for a time, and I only did that because I got laid up. It's a long story."

"I like stories," Tad declared. "Especially ones about finding treasure!"

Huck leaned forward on his knees. He'd set the boy straight, just so the aunt would know he wasn't entirely irresponsible. "Treasure hunting ain't what it's cracked up to be. I traded piloting for a year to be a miner up in Montana. Never worked so hard in my life."

"Did you strike it rich, Uncle Huck?" In the firelight, Tad's eyes glistened like gold.

"Oh, I made a little dust off my claim, but..." Huck noticed that Hallie watched him intently. He didn't have to explain anything. Unless he wanted her to believe he was telling the truth about being a pilot, which meant being truthful about why he'd been off work. "I got robbed last winter when I stopped off at Atchison."

Tad looked equal parts horrified and enthralled. "Was it thieves like Robin Hood?"

"Reckon you could call them thieves. But they weren't helping the poor. They were helping themselves—after they shot me."

"That's dreadful," Hallie put her hand to her chest and her eyes rounded. "Thank heavens you weren't killed."

Was she thankful? Right about about now she ought to be wishing him dead.

"Got laid up a spell, recuperating. Had to earn a little money, so I took a job managing the freight yard until I got well enough to go back on the river."

His audience appeared spellbound, waiting for more. Huck was too ashamed to admit it was his foolishness that had nearly cost him his life.

"How did it happen?" Tad again. Being a boy, he'd want the gory details.

"I went down an alley to check on a hurt pup..." Huck stared into the fire and his mind returned to the scene of the crime. His partner had cautioned him against going after it, but the dog had been whining like it was hurt. In hindsight, it made sense that the attackers were the same men his partner had fleeced in a game of cards. "A couple fellows ambushed me."

Amidst the smoke and the shock from being hit by three bullets, Huck couldn't recall what happened after that. Later, a gal at the saloon told him she'd seen them thieves taking Dan away. They'd likely shot the gambler and pitched his body into the river for no one had seen him since.

Tad inched over to Huck's side. Not touching him, but coming close enough for a hug if one were allowed. Huck fought against an urge to gather his nephew into his arms. Pap had always said it wasn't manly for fellows to be hugging each other. He'd also said not to spare the rod. Cowhiding seemed a sight less manly than giving a boy a hug.

"Do you remember your pa, Uncle Huck?"

Another odd question or Tad had some powerful mind-reading skills

"My pap? Sure I remember him." There were things he'd rather not remember and would never tell Tad. "You recall your'n?"

Tad shook his head. "No. I don't remember my ma either. Granny said she liked to rock me when I was a baby."

Yearning sank a hook into Huck's heart. "Sounds like

something a good ma would do. Mine died when I was your age or thereabouts. I recollect sitting in her lap, her clutching me like a piece of driftwood."

He had no other good memories to share. His father had beaten his ma and thrashed them both when the old man got drunk. They'd lived in mortal fear of him. After he'd been murdered, it had felt like being on a downriver steamer drafting high in the water with nothing to weigh it down.

Huck noticed the boy's drooping eyes. "Go on to bed, Tad."

His nephew blinked sleepily. "Will you be coming along, Uncle Huck?"

A rustling of skirts came closer. Hallie had been awful quiet. He was too tired to work out what that meant, and in no mood to annoy her. Just the opposite.

"You two hole up in the tent," he offered. "I'll get a blanket and sleep outside."

As she reached for Tad's shoulder, the boy sidled away. "I'll stay out here."

"No," Huck said firmly. "You'll do as I say."

When his nephew started to object, he took hold of Tad's arms and gave him a stern frown. It had to be this way. He didn't want Tad to keep looking at him like he was the Father, Son, and Holy Ghost all rolled into one.

The child's lower lip quivered. "I won't be a bother. I'll keep real still."

Tenderness squeezed Huck's heart and a sigh came out. "You ain't a bother, Tadpole."

No, it weren't hard to put up with a child like Tad. It was easy... too easy.

Huck cast around for a way to soften the blow. "Your aunt needs protecting. She'll feel better if you're the one seeing to it."

With a reluctant nod, Tad walked off to the boat, followed by Miss MacBride, who looked relieved.

Huck stood and stretched. Durn, he should have retrieved his coat where he kept his pipe and tobacco. He could use a smoke and maybe a swig of that brew, just enough to help him get to sleep.

He squatted in front of the fire and used a stick to stir the embers. It wasn't cold, but for some reason, a chill had seeped clear down to his bones. Enough to make his shoulder ache. The lingering bother served as a reminder of his stupidity. How his attackers had managed to put three bullets in him and still not kill him was some kind of miracle.

Old Jim had prophesied his future right all those years ago, saying he'd get hurt a-plenty but always get better. He wasn't sure that hairball prophecy applied to this pain in his heart.

HALLIE TUCKED THE BLANKET AROUND HER SLEEPING NEPHEW AND tenderly combed her fingers through the silky hair on Tad's forehead. The poor child had become so exhausted she'd feared he might topple into the fire, even with his uncle seated right beside him.

The man was oblivious sometimes, but tonight he'd woken up. He had also, thank the Lord, given her the tent. He had dropped his attempts to frustrate her and acted willing to build a bridge, however rickety.

She sat back on her heels and considered what might be behind Huck's pensive mood and odd behavior. He'd revealed things about himself tonight which had shocked and surprised her. Not the part about being robbed and nearly killed for his gold, as awful as that was. Too many men who'd gone off in pursuit of riches ended up in a sorry situation. The real surprise was how wrong she'd been to assume that he was shiftless and poor. Pilots were neither. If Huck had done what he'd said and ascended to the top of the steamboat aristocracy, then he was cleverer and more capable than he'd let on. She could not take for granted his ability to outwit her.

He had returned from their pirate outing with a bleeding lip and a worried expression. Something had happened out there that had nothing to do with the injury. The way he'd looked at Tad tonight—with longing and frustration written all over his face—it was clear he was wrestling with some deep uncertainty. Perhaps questioning his decision.

She grabbed a blanket and Huck's coat. He had a guardian in mind. If she could find out who, she could make her case while he might be swayed.

It was cold outside and she shivered in the night air.

Over on the bank, Huck sat by the fire, appearing lost in thought. He hadn't completely buttoned up his shirt and he wasn't wearing shoes. His trousers were rolled up like a deckhand's. It would be a miracle if he didn't come down ill.

"I thought you might want these." She laid the blanket beside him along with his coat.

He shot her a look of surprise before returning his attention to the fire. "Reckon you didn't think to bring that jug with you."

"Do you mean that foul-smelling brew? That stuff would cure leather. You can't be serious about drinking it."

She eased onto her knees and studied his solemn expression, which was a far cry from the look of mocking amusement he'd worn earlier in the day. A word of affirmation might be a good place to start. "It was very gentlemanly of you to let us have the tent."

"Weren't trying to be gentlemanly," he muttered. "I need a good night's sleep without Tad flopping like a fish or you gettin' laid out by a tree." He eyed her as if he expected her to dress him down.

Like old Miss Watson.

She winced at the prick to her vanity. Was that the image he saw when he looked at her, a shriveled-up old maid? Admittedly, she wasn't beautiful, and she must look an absolute fright after a dunk in the river and a night of roughing it in the woods. She brushed uncombed curls away from her face. They'd become a permanent fixture ever since she'd given up attempting anything more elaborate than a braid.

Huck lifted his hand. For a heart-stopping moment, she imagined he might cup her cheek, and let her rub her face cat-like against his calloused palm.

He dropped his hand and picked up the coat. After rummaging through the pockets, he withdrew a pipe and a small tin. Then he made a great show of tamping the tobacco although a good portion spilled onto his trousers. Using a glowing stick he pulled from the fire, he lit his pipe, puffing out clouds of smoke that didn't quite cover the sheen of perspiration on his forehead.

An awkward moment passed before she realized he was purposely avoiding looking at her.

Surprise rendered her speechless. Was Huck attracted to her? It would certainly shed a different light on his earlier actions, and might even present an opportunity. When men were susceptible to women, they could be influenced. Look at what her sister had accomplished.

Hallie's whole being recoiled at the thought of using womanly wiles to gain Huck's agreement. Desperate times called for desperate measures. Huck would drop her ashore tomorrow and then it would be too late. She wasn't out to seduce him, only to apply a small amount of pressure.

Galvanizing her courage, she touched his sleeve. Hard muscles flexed beneath her palm and a tremor went through her. "I-I meant to tell you how much I admire your...swimming ability," she stammered.

"My swimming ability?"

She closed her eyes and suppressed a groan. If she didn't do better than that, this would be a short conversation. "Not just that. These past two days, you have shown me that you are a decent man and a caring uncle. I believe you mean to do what is best for Tad."

He removed the pipe from his lips and pointedly stared at where she gripped his forearm. "Is that so?"

She snatched her hand away. Huck had called her bluff. What would she have done if he had responded? Her heart fluttered upward and she had to swallow to force it back down.

Lord above, she was ten times a fool to even consider exploiting this unwanted passion, given her moral weakness. No more touching. A heartfelt appeal would be the best course.

She rested on her legs with her skirt tucked underneath and curled her hands in her lap. "Please consider what you will do about Tad. You know I'd never hurt him, never let him go hungry or without shelter. I'd take good care of him and provide him with everything he needs."

"Why?" Huck's voice had an odd rasping quality. Not anger, exactly, frustration, perhaps. "Why are you so all-fired anxious to have that boy now, when you couldn't be bothered with him before?"

Hallie moistened her dry lips. She clasped and unclasped her ice-cold fingers. If she told him the whole truth, he'd never grant her guardianship. "It isn't that I couldn't be bothered. My sister moved across the river after she got married. My mother was bedfast for years, and I had to care for her day and night."

As Huck puffed on his pipe, the smell stirred Hallie's memory. Sometimes when she would go into her mother's room, she'd smell a similar fragrance. Her mother had kept her father's pipe beside her bed. Waiting. For years.

"Mama took to her bed a few weeks after my father died. I do believe her spirit perished with him, but it took her body another decade to catch up. Every day I'd go in her room and open the curtains to let in light and fresh air, and it seemed she'd faded a little more, become smaller, more shriveled up. I half expected to one day walk in and she would be gone. Vanished."

Hallie released a deep sigh. She hadn't shared with her ailing mother any details about what Caroline had done, other than to say her sister had eloped and moved away. "I couldn't leave her. Not until she passed on. That was only a month before Mrs. Douglas died."

Huck removed the pipe and gave her a doubtful eye. "Tad's eight years old. You're telling me, in all that time, you couldn't even slip away for a visit?"

He made it sound as bad as it was.

"I had reasons." She couldn't go into them or he would never grant her request. "I did write to Mrs. Douglas to ask if I might come to visit Tad, but she never responded. Based on what I learned from Mr. Dubois's partners, the letter I sent must've arrived a few weeks before she passed away. Perhaps she never read it or she was too ill to respond."

"Or she reckoned it was a little late for making introductions." Huck didn't hold back on the sarcasm. He must believe she was ten times worse than that old spinster lady he despised.

Hallie rubbed her icy hands together to generate warmth. "I... it isn't what you think."

"What do I think?"

"That I'm heartless and cruel."

"Are you?"

She winced at the pointed question. "You believe so, even though you haven't given me a chance."

"If you want a chance, tell me the truth." The firelight and smoke from the pipe cast his face in shadows.

He puffed and waited. It struck her; he wasn't slow, he was patient...with most people. He hadn't been patient with her.

If she laid bare her soul, he might give her the second chance she sought. Then again, she hadn't trusted anyone with the truth and didn't know Huck well enough to be sure he wouldn't use it against her. She had no choice if she expected him to trust her with Tad.

Hallie looked down at her tightly clasped hands, unable to face him. "My sister and I...fell in love with the same man."

"Tad's pap?"

She nodded.

Huck let out a soft huff, a sound of disbelief. "You kept away from your nephew all this time because of *jealousy*?"

She bit her lip at a stab of pain. Jealousy didn't begin to describe the emotions that had torn her apart. "It isn't," she caught her breath, "what you think."

"Tarnation, Hallie, stop saying that and explain why you weren't a proper aunt to that boy before now. I got two good eyes and can see for myself that you care for him. But you haven't told me why you never got to know him."

"Because I feared I couldn't bear to look at him!" She clapped her hand over her mouth. Too late. The ugly truth was out. Now she had to repair the damage she'd done.

"That's not how I feel now. I can explain." She wrung her hands. Nothing would work short of letting go of her pride and telling him the whole shameful story. "How well did you know Mrs. Douglas's son, James?"

Huck knocked the ashes from his pipe into the fire pit. "Hardly knew him. I recall he was off at military school most of the time I lived with the widow."

James hadn't spoken well of Huck, so she was glad he hadn't been fooled into thinking they were friends.

Hallie took a deep breath and forged ahead. "I met Captain James Douglas when his company was stationed in Quincy, early in the war. There was a dance. He was...well, quite handsome and very charming. Every girl had her eye on him, including my younger sister, Caroline. She was so lovely and gay, and completely foolish about men. I worried about her."

But she hadn't seen it coming.

"Surprisingly enough, Captain Douglas showed a special interest in me. Afterward, he came around to visit. I fell madly in love and believed those feelings were mutual. Threw caution to the wind and gave myself to him." Her voice warbled. She swallowed until she'd regained her composure. Confession was humiliating enough without breaking down. "James indicated we would marry, but a few days later, I..."

She stared into the fire's center, the flames growing indistinct as the past came rushing back with vivid clarity.

Her sister had gone missing—again. Caroline's faded calico dress lay in a heap on the bed, as if the previous occupant hadn't the time or inclination to hang it up. Hallie checked the clothes in their wardrobe. Her good gown was missing. She stormed down the stairs and out the door, headed for the barn.

No doubt, Caroline thought she could sneak away to another party in the company of those soldiers. With her fair beauty and vivacious personality, she had more than her share of admiring swains, but she knew better than to go out unaccompanied.

The buggy was still in the yard, even though the barn door stood ajar. Low moans issued from within. A sound not of pain but of pleasure. Hallie knew this because she'd made those sounds. Her skin crawled with a sense of impending disaster. Caroline could be in there with a bounder who was taking advantage of her innocence. The thought turned Hallie's stomach. The man who'd taken her virginity at least was honorable. He loved her and had asked to marry her. She was fortunate. Her sister, on the other hand, might not be.

Hallie refused to stand by and let Caroline be ruined. She opened the door and strode inside—then jerked to a halt, shocked and speechless by the sight of a couple copulating on the straw. The man, his uniform pants pulled down to his knees, worked over her sister, who had Hallie's best dress balled up around her waist, and her legs wrapped around him. Like a harlot.

"Caroline." Hallie tried to shout, but all that came out was a hoarse whisper.

The man twisted around. His familiar dark eyes widened with surprise.

"I caught him with my sister." Hallie rubbed her stinging eyes. "They were in the barn and they were..." The words stuck in her throat. She couldn't get them out. Her body shook like she had palsy.

She scrambled to her feet, intending to flee, but Huck was up in a flash and caught her arm. He hauled her to him and flattened her face against his chest. She knotted her fists in his shirt even though she knew she ought to push him away. But, dear God, she was sinking and had to have something to hold onto or she would drown. "I-I can't..." her voice cracked.

"Hush now, it's all right. Don't say no more about it." Huck stroked her hair with awkward gentleness, as if comforting wasn't a skill he'd developed. His simple kindness wrenched her heart open.

She burrowed into his shoulder and breathed in the smell of wood smoke and tobacco, so warm and familiar that she yearned to curl up against him. The hurt festering for years began to drain as her tears flowed, wetting her cheeks, eventually soaking his shirt. He didn't seem to care and kept holding her, petting her.

"I know I did wrong in giving myself to him," she choked out. "If I hadn't encouraged him...if I'd watched over my sister better, none of this would have happened."

"Ah, Hallie." Huck's breath stirred the hair by her ear. "The only thing you did wrong was to trust a man who wasn't worth trusting."

His absolution stunned her. She knew of no man who would

blame another for a woman's fall from grace. His compassion acted like a balm to her soul. For the first time, she felt able to share her hurt and allow another to ease her pain.

"Even so, I made things worse by not letting go of my bitterness until it was too late. I was afraid to see Tad. I feared he would be a constant reminder of everything I'd lost, all my mistakes. I'll regret not reaching out sooner until the day I die. I know I'm selfish and sinful, but...I'm not cruel and heartless."

Huck's hand moved in soothing circles on her back. "No, you're not. That's why you got to let me give Tad to a good family."

She stiffened at his words and then jerked out of his arms. The wretch might as well have stabbed her in the back. How could he be so kind one minute and callous the next?

"He belongs with *his* family. With me." She struck her hand against her breastbone. "*I* can give him a good home. With someone who won't leave him."

The firelight cast light and shadows over a face that appeared to be carved from stone. "You might be well-intended, but you got no husband. Tad needs a father. Mine was worthless. That's how I know it's important for a boy to have a good one. If he's got a fine pap, he'll turn out better than me."

"He needs a mother, too!" Becoming desperate wouldn't sway him if her tears hadn't. She clenched her hands at her sides and forced a calm she didn't feel. "I'll see to it that he's around men who can be good examples for him."

Huck shook his head. "That ain't the same."

What else could she offer as a bargaining chip? Perchance the opportunity to maintain a connection? She'd rather navigate blindfolded up the Mississippi than have Huck Finn in her life, but she would put up with Lucifer himself if it meant she could keep Tad. "You can come to visit whenever you want."

Her offer had caught him off guard based on his stunned expression. He turned to toss more wood on the fire. "I won't be coming around. It'll just make things worse. It's best if he forgets about me."

Shock rooted her to the ground. Even Huck couldn't be that unfeeling. "You would lure Tad out on this-this *mis*adventure so you can have your fun and then toss him aside when he becomes inconvenient? Is that what you're saying?"

Huck swung around with a scowl. "You know that's not what I'm sayin'. I got a good family picked out, the best. He and Tom are already chums—"

"Tom?" Hallie's heart seized with dread. "Tom Sawyer?"

Huck gave a reluctant nod.

Her heart drummed a frantic beat. He had selected a trusted friend who'd gone on to become a war hero and a state senator. Short of blood kinship, she had no advantage when pitted against such a formidable foe. "Do you even know if Mr. Sawyer wants him?"

Huck glowered at the mere suggestion that his plan could have a flaw. "Tom's married and settled down, so nothing's standing in the way. Besides, him and Tad are already fast friends. The boy is always spouting off stories Mr. Sawyer told him."

"Stories about you, no doubt." Hallie heaved a frustrated sigh. Pushing Huck to acknowledge his feelings wouldn't help her cause, but for Tad's sake, she had to try to make him see that he couldn't simply end their relationship like he'd snip a loose thread. "You know that child idolizes you. It will devastate him when he learns you don't want to be part of his life."

"I can't be that boy's pap. Ain't cut out for it." Huck crossed his arms over his chest and lifted his chin. The belligerent stance was at odds with the anguished look on his face. "I don't stay anywhere long afore I get an itch to move on. That's why I can't have him counting on me."

Hallie longed to pummel the mule-headed wanderer and knock some sense into that thick skull. "You insist on controlling

Tad's future, yet you aren't willing to remain part of it. That isn't right, and it isn't fair to him. You are easing your conscience by giving him to Mr. Sawyer. You might as well give him to me. That way he will know at least one person truly wants him."

The muscles in Huck's jaw tightened. Holding in some profane comment, perhaps. What held him back from voicing it when he'd never spared her before? Finally, he spoke in a cold, bloodless tone. "I understand you might be lonesome and reckon a child can fill the empty spaces, but that's not what Tad needs."

Hallie took a step back, feeling the slap as surely as if he'd struck her.

"He deserves folks that won't draft him down with loads that aren't his to bear. If I keep him, or you keep him, it'd be out of pure selfishness."

How dare he twist her words and use a confidence to gain her agreement?

"Don't shake your head at me," he scolded. "You know I'm right."

Oh no, he would not defeat her by playing on her guilt.

She raised her hand and pointed a shaking finger at him. "Mr. Finn, you are wrong. You are wrong about me, and about what Tad needs. But I assure you, before we are quit of each other, we shall be in complete agreement on what is best for our nephew—and it won't entail *abandoning* him as your father did you."

Huck spun away, blowing out a loud breath in a great show of irritation. When he swung back around, he braced his hands on his hips and planted his feet. "Nobody's *abandoning* Tad. He'll get a good home with a nice family."

Trying to force Huck to embrace softer feelings was a waste of time, and nothing she did would gain his acceptance because he'd already made up his mind. "I won't let you see this ridiculous plan through. I will go with you and fight it."

"You ain't a-going one peg further than the next landing."

Her furious gaze roved over his unruly hair and bearded face, the half-open shirt and bare feet. In the flickering light, he did indeed look like a pirate—primal, fierce, and merciless.

She jerked up her chin, gathering courage enough to face Blackbeard himself. "I'm going wherever you take him—to hell if I have to."

CHAPTER ELEVEN

A shaft of sunlight pierced the clouds, striking the water with a silver gleam as Huck poled the flatboat over to the quiet wharf. As the bow bumped against the dock, he jumped out and secured the lines to a sturdy post.

Just up that sloping levee, past the tarpaulins that protected bales of tobacco and hemp, wound a rutted path that led into Weston, Missouri—and freedom.

He rolled his shoulders and exhaled with relief. Lands, he was glad to be parting company with the tight-lipped Miss MacBride. The sooner he sent her on her way, the better. After they'd locked horns last night, he'd tossed and turned so much he'd tied his innards into knots. She was bad for his health, not to mention his peace of mind.

When he turned to offer his hand, she'd already clambered off the boat. She stood to one side, clad in that ugly black dress with her hair covered with a raggedy bonnet that looked like it belonged to her granny.

Devil take him. He wished he had never pressed her into explaining why she'd kept away from her nephew. Now he couldn't look at her without hearing that tortured confession. Her sad story didn't make him think poorly of her, as she feared. Rather, it made her all too human and easy to care for—and he didn't want to care.

Tad tugged the bleating goat to the edge of the gunwale. Huck lifted them out.

His nephew bent to grab the rope dangling from the goat's neck and had to yank his straw hat away from the critter's busy lips. "Come on, Lucky. When we get back to St. Petersburg, I'm taking you and Uncle Huck to meet all my friends."

Huck's chest grew tight at Hallie's accusing glare. He'd cut off his tongue before admitting she was right. Tad would be devastated once he learned his uncle wasn't sticking around.

It couldn't be helped, and parting was best done quickly. That way, the hurt wouldn't fester. His conscience reminded him that he'd been cleaved in two when his pap had deserted him, despite having to put up with welts all over whenever the old drunk came around. But he wasn't deserting Tad. He was getting him a good home, and the boy would thank him for it one day—if they ever saw each other again.

He ruffled his nephew's hair, giving in to the need to touch him, yet not wanting to appear too affectionate. "Hate to say it, Tadpole, but we can't take that goat. We need the cash, and a nice goat like that ought to be worth at least five dollars."

Tad's cheerful countenance fell. "Aw, can't we keep her, Uncle Huck? Lucky ain't no trouble and I'll take care of her."

Huck rubbed his chin. It couldn't be a good sign if Tad hung onto every stray that came along. But if a goat would keep him happy, maybe he wouldn't object so much to getting rid of the aunt. "Let's unload this driftwood so we can offer it to the steamers. I'll sell the flatboat and see what it fetches. Then we'll know if we can afford to keep Lucky."

His nephew grinned with delight and threw his arms around

Huck's waist, hugging him so tightly he had to shift onto the balls of his feet to keep his balance. "See Aunt Hallie? Ain't Uncle Huck the bestest uncle in the whole world?"

Huck awkwardly patted Tad's back. He wasn't used to such enthusiastic displays of affection, but it came as natural as breathing to the boy, so he couldn't push him away.

While the two of them unloaded driftwood, Hallie kept a firm hold on the nanny goat. "I thought you said you were *borrowing* that flatboat."

The blasted woman still thought he was a thief.

"I did borrow it. But that's a *downriver* boat," he explained, reminding himself to be patient with her ignorance. "Nobody bothers with taking flatboats and mackinaws back upriver. It's just as easy to build one the next time you need it. That old trader was looking to sell this boat anyhow. I'll arrange to have the last of my pay turned over to him. We'll be more than squared up."

His explanation seemed to settle it, or at least she didn't appear inclined to chew on the matter. That was a blessed relief.

Tad removed the last of the driftwood and set it next to Huck's stack. He pointed to the only packet docked at the levee. "Are we gonna ride that boat?"

Huck shaded his eyes. "*Hesperia.*" The name was familiar, but it couldn't be the boat he remembered. That one was at least five years old. This steamer looked brand new. White as a starched collar from the hull up to the pilothouse. "Perhaps. I'll talk to the captain."

"A *steamboat?*"

Huck drew up his shoulders at the shrill cry.

"Absolutely *not.*" Hallie swung her head back and forth so hard he was surprised it didn't fly off. "I will not allow you to take this child on a steamboat."

Who did she think she was, ordering him around?

"I don't recollect asking your permission."

"What if that boat explodes or catches fire? Tad could die." The agony in her eyes tugged at Huck's heart, even as he tried to harden it.

"Look here, I been on these steamers for more than fifteen years, and in all that time I never got hurt." He kept his voice low and even, like he did when he was soothing a fretful passenger.

She gripped the goat's rope in a white-knuckled fist. "Don't you patronize me. My father knew these boats inside and out, and his engineer was a smart, competent man."

"Your father?" Huck wasn't sure he'd heard right.

Her lashes dropped, concealing her eyes but not the tightness around her mouth. "He was a steamboat pilot. Killed thirteen years ago when the boilers on his boat exploded. I swore I'd never again set foot on a steamboat."

Huck's mind whirred back to the first time he'd seen a boat after its boilers exploded. What was left of the main deck resembled a pig slaughter, with scalded, naked bodies scattered about, half buried beneath goods blown to bits. He couldn't forget the screams and groans, the cries for water and prayers for help, though little could be done. He wasn't about to mention that, though. It would send her into fits.

"Hallie, I'm awful sorry about your pap, but you can't go around thinking every boat is going to blow up. I only saw it once, and that was because they ran the pressure too high. Since the war, boilers have better safety valves, temperature gauges are more accurate. It's safe as anything."

She didn't look convinced.

He'd waste his time trying to argue with fear. But now his nephew stared up at him with wide, anxious eyes. He knelt and offered a reassuring smile. "I'll keep you safe, Tadpole."

"What about the train?" Hallie issued the suggestion like a

command. "It will be faster, and you said yourself you're in a hurry to take him to St. Petersburg."

"But..." Tad squared his shoulders. "I want to go with Uncle Huck. On a steamboat."

Pride swelled in Huck's chest. His nephew was full of sand, brash as any man.

He stood up, challenging the aunt with a look. Best be firm or she'd never give way. "I promised him an adventure. We're taking the steamboat. Ride on the railroad, if it pleases you. You won't be going with us anyhow."

Her eyes widened and two patches of color appeared on her cheeks. "You cannot force me to leave or keep me off that boat."

"You said yourself you'd never set foot on a steamboat again." He hoped fear would overcome her insistence on dogging their heels.

Her chest heaved. Then she started blinking. Most women loved dissolving into tears and watching men fall all over themselves to soothe them. Not Hallie. She'd remain dry-eyed. But the look on her face as she gazed at Tad was so raw and filled with longing it would touch the hardest heart.

Huck yanked down the brim of his hat so she wouldn't see that she'd touched his heart. Over the past two days, he'd caught a glimpse of a fascinating, caring woman, and had to admit his first impression had been wrong.

Even if she wasn't a pruned-up harpy, he couldn't let her raise Tad alone. His nephew needed something she couldn't give him— a good father to help him grow up and know how to fit in. He had to stick to his guns and take the boy to Tom Sawyer.

She lifted her chin in a stubborn tilt he'd come to recognize. "I am going with you."

"Don't reckon you are, considering you got no way to pay for passage." He paused, letting his words sink in.

Her face turned white as milk. Made him feel like he'd kicked a puppy. Then her expression shifted, hardening into that brittle mask she'd worn when he'd first met her. "You, sir, are the most *loathsome* man I have ever had the misfortune to meet."

The hateful remark struck him square in the chest, hurting him worse than he thought possible.

Well, there weren't any question about where Miss MacBride stood on the matter. And he *was* a bastard for treating her so mean. It had to be that way. She wasn't about to let go unless he made it clear nothing would change his mind. "I been telling you all along, but you ain't been listening. And I won't have you gnawing my ear the whole way back about giving you this boy."

His nephew tugged at his sleeve, looking mighty shaken. "Uncle Huck?" he paused, his brown eyes pleading. "Can't Aunt Hallie go with us a little further? If she promises to be good?"

First the goat and now the aunt. Had to be the child's tender nature. Tad felt sorry for her after hearing that terrible story about her father. Nevertheless, they couldn't take her along. She'd cause no end of trouble. They had to slip their lines right here on this wharf.

Huck put his hand on Tad's shoulder. "Even if your aunt promises to be extra good, this wood here won't fetch enough to pay for one passage, much less three."

Hallie's eyes fastened on him, unblinking as an owl. "Sell the goat to cover my passage."

Tad's hopeful expression melted into grief. "But Aunt Hallie..."

Huck ignored a prick of conscience. This could work to his advantage. That goat wouldn't fetch enough to get her a stall on the main deck, much less a cabin, but it would keep her out of his hair while he made his arrangements. He heaved a big sigh and put on a sorrowful face. "No. Your aunt has got the right. It's her goat. She found it, so she can sell it."

Hallie shot him a withering look. He adopted an expression of feigned innocence. Unfortunately, he couldn't quite shake the guilt.

He was low down and ornery. It was the way he'd been raised and he couldn't change it. Besides, with what the goat fetched, she could afford a room at the hotel and stagecoach fare back to Atchison. Either way, she wouldn't be his problem anymore.

CHAPTER TWELVE

Hallie tugged the goat up the cobbled street, muttering curses every step of the way. Tad's last memory of his aunt would be of her taking away a beloved pet. Huck knew this, the cur. That's why he'd so easily given in to her desperate suggestion.

One day he would get his comeuppance. God willing, she would be there to witness it. In the meantime, she had to find a way to get on that boat before it left.

She approached a row of tidy brick buildings housing shops and offices. The hungry nanny tugged at a strip of lace hanging from her sleeve. Even the goat was intent on reducing her to a beggar by devouring what was left of her dress.

Perhaps someone at the mercantile would want to purchase the insatiable creature. She might also discover why the *Hesperia* had remained at the landing instead of leaving at dawn, as was the custom. They might've encountered mechanical problems. If so, she could demand they stop the boat from setting out.

After she secured Lucky to a hitching post, she stepped inside the store.

Rich fragrances of tobacco and coffee teased her senses,

conjuring memories of her father seated by the fire with his pipe and a steaming cup, telling her stories of the river. Always the river. He had no other interests. At least none he loved so well.

At the counter, a woman with titian hair and a queenly aura chatted with the bewhiskered proprietor. Her dress, made from watery silk dyed a vibrant aqua blue, flowed naturally over her slender form without the stiff underlayers. It was quite unconventional, yet thoroughly lovely on the wearer.

"We'll delay another day if necessary, but be sure and send word if you hear of a pilot in need of a job," the woman said, giving the shopkeeper her card.

Piloting was a job Huck had claimed he could do. He didn't fit the idealized image of a steamboat pilot—responsible, committed, and devoted to his craft. But in some ways, Huck served as a perfect specimen of those independent, egotistical lords of the river.

Hallie eased closer. "Pardon me, I couldn't help overhearing. You are looking for a pilot?"

The woman turned in surprise and gave Hallie a quick once over.

She flushed with embarrassment. Given her bedraggled state, it would do little good to profess she was not a bum, so she repeated the question. "You said something about needing to hire a pilot."

"I am Kate Kinney," the stately woman offered. "My husband is Captain Kinney, owner of the *Hesperia*, and yes, we need a second pilot. Do you know of one?"

"I might."

If Huck had made contact with the ship's captain, he'd undoubtedly convinced the man to hire him. He had an uncanny way of manipulating situations to his advantage. If he could do it, she should be able to talk her way aboard, without outright lying.

"My companion, Mr. Finn, has piloting skills. I am traveling with him. and at present don't have the means to cover the fare. Would you know of anything I might do to offset the cost of passage?"

Curiosity sparked in the woman's china-blue eyes. "We have a full staff, or all the staff we require, except for a second pilot. Our man took ill."

Drat. There had to be *some* way to get on that boat.

"Oh, that is too bad. Mr. Finn and I were accompanying our nephew home, and we ran into a bit of misfortune. We require additional funds."

"You and your nephew could travel with your husband if he is hired on. I am certain we could include your meals as part of his salary."

Hallie's hopes plummeted. Huck wouldn't hesitate to repudiate her if she tried to pose as his wife. *Now what?*

Her father would have said honesty remained the best policy.

"We are not married. Mr. Finn and I would not be traveling together if not for our nephew." Desperation urged her on. "Mrs. Kinney, I am willing to cook or clean."

"Call me Kate, Miss...?"

"Mahaliah MacBride. But please, call me Hallie."

"MacBride?" Kate lifted a finger as if a thought had struck her. "Are you kin to Captain Matthew MacBride? He was a pilot on the Mississippi some years back."

"Yes, he was my father."

"Your father?" The captain's wife beamed. "My dear, I am delighted to make your acquaintance. Captain MacBride was the most charming man—next to my husband, of course. We met your father once on a trip we made down to Memphis. My, that was a long time ago."

Hallie forced herself to speak past the lump in her throat. "He died."

The woman's gaze filled with sympathy. "I heard. I am so sorry."

Hallie still couldn't speak of her father's death without getting choked up. Sad stories wouldn't buy her passage, however. She had to keep the conversation going until an idea came to her. "You have a beautiful boat. Is it new?"

"Not new, exactly. We refurbished her after she ran aground on a sandbar last summer. We had a prosperous season, so I talked my husband into adding some extra features. I want the *Hesperia* to be known as the finest packet on the Missouri River."

Kate's wish sparked an idea. Steamboats were regularly ornamented with paintings on walls and above doors, along with other lavish adornments that made the spacious main cabin as fancy as any first-class hotel.

"Have you any murals?" Hallie asked.

"No, alas, we haven't found someone to paint them."

Hallie drew her shoulders back to appear as dignified as possible. "I would be pleased to offer my services as a painter in exchange for passage to St. Louis."

"You are an artist?" Kate sounded as if she doubted it.

How could one prove such a bold claim without producing a single painting?

But wait. There was one Kate might have seen.

"Do you recall the mural in the main cabin on my father's boat?"

Kate's smile turned dreamy. "Oh yes, that lovely river scene. It looked so real I thought my fingers would get wet just by touching it."

"I painted that."

The older woman's mouth dropped open. "You? But you would have been a child, surely."

"Fourteen," Hallie conceded. "My mother was an artist. Her name is not well known, but she was quite skilled. She taught me from the time I could hold a brush. I would sketch and paint whenever I traveled with my father. One year, Mr. Bingham joined us on the *Evening Star*. He taught me some of his techniques, and that mural was a result of his tutelage."

"Are you talking about the Missouri artist, George Caleb Bingham?"

"The very same. He saw some of my work and said I showed promise. He told me he had been assisted as a boy by Chester Harding. Mr. Bingham said because Mr. Harding had aided him, he would teach me, as a way of passing along the favor."

Hallie prayed Kate would take a chance on her because she had no other ideas.

"Oh my." Kate's smile returned. "Then you *are* an authentic artist. Perhaps you could paint a mural in the ladies' salon. A river scene like the one you did on your father's boat, only featuring the *Hesperia* on the Missouri."

"Yes, I can do that." Hallie nodded eagerly before dread struck. She needed her glasses to do close work, as well as the proper supplies. Dash it all, she couldn't get this far and fail. "I lost my spectacles and left my paints and brushes at home. I have a goat tied outside. My nephew is very attached to it, but I am willing to sell it."

Kate's lips twitched. "For heaven's sake, don't sell his pet. I can purchase what you require. Your work will cover your passage." She threaded their arms together with a frank appraisal. "Perhaps we'll have time for you to freshen up before we leave."

Hallie blushed at the frank suggestion. However, no amount of embarrassment could hold back her excitement. She had done it. Found her way onto the steamboat despite Huck's efforts to keep her off.

As she stepped outside with her newfound friend, she grappled with the last of her jitters. Getting back on a steamboat was the first step in what promised to be a difficult journey.

Regardless, she would do whatever was necessary to stay on that boat and use the time to win Tad's affection and wean him away from his loyalty to Huck.

In the meantime, she would build her case. Once they reached St. Petersburg, she was certain she would have more than enough evidence to convince Mr. Dubois that Huck Finn was incapable of deciding her nephew's future.

After Hallie had wandered off with the *Lucky* goat in tow, Huck got busy. He sent a telegraph to Dubois, and a second one to Tom, explaining the dilemma and setting it up so the adoption idea would be his. Everything got put into motion with no interference from the aunt. Within an hour, he'd taken care of all the necessary arrangements, except for one.

Huck needed a little money, and for that, he needed a job.

The first mate who purchased their driftwood mentioned the *Hesperia* needed a second pilot. While he and Huck spoke, Tad toppled off a stack of wobbly crates. Five minutes later. the boy got stuck shimmying up a spar, and nearly hove himself off the boat swinging from a hog chain.

Huck corralled the scamp and headed up to the top deck to speak with the captain. As soon as he started a conversation, his nephew ventured too close to the edge. That fancy molding weren't high enough to trim a garden path, much less keep a child safe.

"Get back here, Tadpole." Huck dodged a burly deckhand and grabbed the back of Tad's coat. He squatted down and pinned the boy with the meanest glare he'd given him yet. "It's more than fifty feet down to the water, and that's no swimming hole. You need to stay put while I finish my business with the old man."

"Is he old? He don't look a lot older than you."

Ten years older, at least. Huck smoothed the hair on his face. Had to be the beard that aged him. "It's just a phrase. What the crew calls their captain. His age doesn't matter. Never mind, you call him Captain Kinney."

Tad cast his eyes downward. "Yes, Uncle Huck."

Huck glanced over his shoulder and smiled as the captain approached them. "The boy won't be a bit of trouble," he assured the older man with more confidence than he felt.

"Of course not." Captain Kinney stood erect with his hands folded behind his back, keeping an eye on his crew as they loaded cargo in preparation for departure. Tall and spare with a trim gray beard, he looked like a king and had a calm that quieted even the air around him.

"Your first mate said you're ascending as far as Sioux City, then going back downriver?" Huck confirmed.

The captain gave an affirmative nod. "Our usual trade is with St. Joe, but there's a load of freight in Sioux City taken off a rescued steamer. Goods that need to get to St. Louis. It's a fair amount. Worth the time and effort."

It wasn't unusual for an independent boat to take advantage of hauling freight when another steamer met with disaster. A detour north didn't fit with Huck's plans, but they couldn't afford to wait around if they wanted to break free from the tenacious Miss MacBride.

He gestured at a set of antlers mounted in a conspicuous spot above the front window of the pilothouse. "She's a fast boat, I see."

Captain Kinney's chest swelled so big it nearly busted his buttons. "Fastest in these parts."

If speed impressed him, Huck could do one better. "I took my training under one of the fastest, cleverest pilots on the upper river."

"Don't say? Which one would that be?"

"Grant Marsh."

The old man's eyes gleamed with interest. "I could use a fast pilot."

Huck released a sigh of relief. He was as good as hired, and with a boat as sleek as this one, they wouldn't lose much time. It'd take maybe four days to Sioux City, then another couple of weeks to return to St. Louis. He could still make St. Petersburg before the end of June, as he'd committed in a telegram to Dubois.

With an impatient little shuffle, Tad pulled away. He didn't get far before Huck caught him by the scruff.

"Told you to stay put."

Tad hung his head. "I was just lookin'."

What was wrong with the boy? He was always a handful, to be sure, but he hadn't ever carried on like this.

Huck heaved a sigh of pure frustration. How could he pilot a steamboat while fretting over his nephew's safety? He'd worn himself out already just keeping the child out of trouble. "I don't care if you look around, but you can't keep doing things that'll get you hurt."

Tad curled out his lip in a belligerent pout. "I want Lucky."

At the mulish demand, Huck's patience snapped. He grabbed the boy's arms, ready to shake some sense into him. The hurt in his nephew's eyes stopped him cold. Durned if he weren't just like his pap if a little bit of nonsense could send him into a fit of violence.

"No changing what's done," he muttered, releasing his hold.

Why had he let Hallie go off with that dad-blamed goat anyhow?

That's what you wanted her to do.

Just so Tad wouldn't hate him.

What's it matter, if you're giving him up?

Huck cursed his conscience. It'd been clattering away ever since Tad had come into his life. Weren't nothing more tiresome. He longed for peace, having only himself to consider.

But you weren't peaceful, Hucky. You was lonesome.

Oh, shut yer hole.

Huck put a hand on Tad's shoulder to keep him in one place. Maybe he'd fashion a leash like he'd done for that goat. "Let me finish talking to Captain Kinney about the job. If you stay out of trouble, I'll let you help me steer this old boat up the river."

Tad's eyes got round as buttons. "Can I touch the pilot wheel?"

Finally, something to distract from the missing goat.

"Sure you can. Once we reach easy water."

The captain strolled up beside them. Surprisingly, he didn't appear annoyed by Tad's antics. Instead, he clasped his hands behind his back and leaned forward with a slight smile, addressing the boy. "Young man, you see that black-haired fellow over there? That's my first mate, Mr. Sullivan. He could use an extra hand to help stack cargo. Do a good job and I'll give you a penny."

Tad nodded vigorously. "Oh, I can do that easy." He swaggered off after the first mate.

"Wish I'd thought of putting him to work," Huck said. "Could've saved myself a heap of trouble."

The captain's dark eyes gleamed with amusement. "Boys can't help being curious."

"Maybe so, but he normally don't have so many ants in his britches."

Tad happily lugged a box to a location indicated by the first mate. The simple task of moving small items from one place to another could keep him busy for at least a half hour, judging by the cargo scattered about.

"Is this the first time he's been with you on a steamboat?" the captain asked.

"First—and only."

That elicited a sage nod. The captain stared out over the water, seemingly lost in thought. "We raised three sons on the river. Put them to work as soon as they could walk."

The captain's situation boded well for Huck's chances of getting a job and would make the trip go easier. "You got your family on this boat?"

"Not anymore. It's just me and my wife now. Our youngest son is a clerk on the *Robert E. Lee*. Our two older boys died in the war." The captain's face crumpled for an instant before he smoothed it out again.

"Condolences to you and your missus." Huck couldn't imagine his pap grieving over him. He'd gotten better sleep after Pap was gone, so he had nothing more to offer.

Captain Kinney turned and waved to the first mate. "Shin, ready her quick and we're off. Bring the boy to my office after you're finished here."

"Ay, cap'n," the mate returned.

"Now, Mr. Finn, shall we go finalize our agreement?"

Huck wanted to kick up his heels. The captain would hire him despite his nephew's ornery behavior. He took one last look to make sure Tad was still following orders.

The child lifted a chicken crate and then set it down, staring off in the direction of the wharf. His surprised expression transformed into delight before he took off at a dead run right toward the picketed edge.

"Oh no, you don't." Huck dashed after him, nabbing his coat before he got to a foot-high barrier that wouldn't even break his fall.

"Looky, Uncle Huck," Tad squealed. "It's Aunt Hallie. And she's got Lucky."

Huck jerked his head around. His mouth dropped open.

Sure enough, there was the aunt, striding onto the stage plank, pulling along that gol-durn goat like it was a prize bull at the county fair.

Blast it. She wasn't supposed to be here. If she hadn't sold the goat, how did she figure on getting passage?

"Aunt Hallie! Aunt Hallie!" Tad waved his arms like he was signaling a warship. "We're up here."

She tipped her chin. Shiny glass glinted in the noonday sun. How had a woman who didn't have two pennies to rub together come by a pair of spectacles?

"Ah, I see your wife has arrived," the captain commented.

A spurt of alarm shot through Huck. He'd said his nephew was traveling with him but made no mention of a wife. The captain must have assumed he'd bring one along rather than try to mind a youngster while steering a ship. If he didn't produce a wife, did that mean he wasn't getting the job?

His nephew lit out for the stairs like his tail feathers had caught fire.

"Tad, wait!" Huck went after the boy and caught him by the wrist.

"Lemme go. I want to see Lucky." Tad tugged, straining to get free.

Huck's anxiety soared. *Now what?* He couldn't make out like he was married to Hallie. He didn't trust her further than the next bend in the river. No, there weren't any way he'd let that conniving woman on this boat.

"Looks like your missus has met my wife," the captain commented.

Huck stared in horror at the two women walking side by side. How in tarnation had Hallie found the captain's *wife?* And what sorry tale had she spun to wheedle her way onto their steamboat? He could only imagine.

"Oh, my uncle ain't married to my aunt." Tad twaddled on, spilling the beans.

The old man's brow furrowed. "Don't know as I quite understand—"

"Oh, it's not what you're thinking. I'm kin on his pap's side. She's his ma's sister."

That appeared to provide some relief, but the captain still looked mighty confused. "Here now, are you saying she's coming along to watch the boy?"

Tad jerked away.

"I'll be back soon as I have a chat with his aunt," Huck called over his shoulder, taking off in hot pursuit. He rattled down two sets of stairs and sprinted over to the stage plank, where Hallie and her new *friend* stood chatting, seemingly oblivious to the smells of scorched oil, pitch pine, and escaping steam.

The engines started up, rumbling the platform beneath his feet. The boat was being readied to leave. It still wasn't too late to concoct a reason to have Hallie thrown off. After he found out what deal—if any—she'd struck with the captain's wife.

Tad dropped to his knees and hugged the goat, which promptly began chewing on his straw hat. He laughed and looked up at his aunt. "I'm awful glad you didn't sell Lucky."

Hallie smiled, sweet as the Virgin Mary. "I couldn't part with her, knowing how much she means to you."

She turned to Huck with a smile that weren't so innocent. "Good afternoon, Mr. Finn. May I present my new friend, Mrs. Kinney?"

The captain's wife dipped her chin. A wide-brimmed hat concealed her expression, but not that flaming red hair—a worrisome sign if there ever was one.

Huck jerked off his hat. No doubt Miss MacBride had made him out to be the very devil. He'd have to do some fancy talking to worm his way into Mrs. Kinney's good graces. "It sure is a privilege to meet you, ma'am. Captain Kinney told me he had a fine-looking wife, but he didn't say you were pretty as a sunset."

She cocked her head and the brim tipped up, revealing eyes as sharp as a hawk's. "And Miss MacBride failed to mention what a glib-tongued flatterer you are, Mr. Finn."

His innards twisted. No easy mark, this one, and not likely to take his side in the matter.

Lucky butted his leg, sending Tad into a fit of giggles.

Even the goat had turned against him.

Huck cast about for another angle. "Are you well acquainted with Miss MacBride?"

From behind the glass lenses, Hallie's eyes shot flaming arrows. "Mrs. Kinney has offered me a position."

Huck stared at her, purely confused. No well-bred lady would sign on as a chambermaid. Nothing else came to mind. "What sorta position?"

"Painting."

"Painting?" Well, that had to be a lie. There wasn't a square inch of this boat that hadn't been slathered with a new coat of paint.

"Oh, Mr. Finn, you cannot imagine how thrilled I was to discover that Miss MacBride trained under the illustrious Mr. Bingham." Mrs. Kinney went on blathering. "You've seen his work, no doubt."

Who the hell was Bingham, and how much training did it take to slap on a coat of paint?

Huck's face burned with embarrassment for being ignorant of some important bit of information everyone else seemed to know. For the first time since he'd met her, Miss MacBride held the ace and he couldn't think of a single bluff.

The triumph in Hallie's gaze softened ever so slightly. "Of course, you've heard of Mr. Bingham. Who from Missouri doesn't know our most famous artist?"

She'd realized right off he didn't know Bingham from Adam, but for some reason, she'd saved him from looking like a complete ass.

"Ah! You're painting pictures."

She nodded, excitedly. "A mural, actually."

"A mural like what Mr. Bingham paints." Huck raised his eyebrows, putting on like he was impressed. "Well, that is something."

Hallie held onto her pleased smile, although he detected a little strain around her eyes and mouth, which set off his suspicions.

Was she truly an artist or just coloring the truth, as he was wont to do when the situation called for it? If so, he might yet have a bargaining chip.

His conscience poked him. She'd done him a good turn.

But if she was a fraud, he couldn't very well let her take advantage of these good people. Where had she got that Bingham story anyhow? It rated right up there with one of Tom Sawyer's stretchers.

The departure bell clanged, shaking Huck out of his reverie. He had to find the captain and smooth over this mess. "Come on, Tad, we got to get up to the pilothouse."

His nephew's face screwed up with pained indecision. "Can we come back and check on Lucky?"

"I'll see to her," Hallie interjected. "Go with your uncle and we can meet up later."

Huck gave Tad a little push toward the stairs. He couldn't very well get Mrs. Kinney's *artist* thrown off the boat without proof of her duplicity. She'd show her true colors soon enough. In the meantime, he'd have to work out another way to deal with her unexpected presence. Like a bad penny, she kept turning up.

CHAPTER THIRTEEN

Tad dug a finger into his ear to clear the water inside. He'd managed to avoid a bath for two whole days before his aunt had fetched him and put down her foot.

The tall lady with red hair had led them to the captain's quarters where there was a big copper tub filled with water. Aunt Hallie said she'd used it already and now it was his turn. He didn't want a turn, but she didn't care. She'd ordered him into the tub, took up a sliver of soap, and scrubbed and scrubbed 'til his skin was almost scraped off.

If his uncle hadn't been so busy steering the boat, he wouldn't have stood for it. But if it took regular baths to keep Aunt Hallie around long enough to marry Uncle Huck, he'd best suffer through it.

After Tad finished dressing, he followed his aunt downstairs into the main cabin, the very opposite direction he wanted to go. Having her on the same boat as his uncle wasn't enough. He had to get them together so they could kiss again and get hitched.

He caught her wrist. "Hey, ain't we going back up to the pilothouse?"

"No, we *are not*." She took his hand and shook her head. "I declare, you sound more like your uncle every day."

"Good. I want to sound like him and look like him. If'n I could, I'd *be* Huck Finn."

She wrinkled her nose like something smelled bad.

He didn't smell anything. He glanced around but didn't see nothing except the kitchen help setting up tables, and they were dressed in white looking cleaner than he was.

His aunt led him past a silver water cooler where a handful of grownups had gathered around. The passengers on the boat for the upriver trip were mostly men. His uncle had explained there weren't many women who went north into the Indian Territory unless they were married to the soldiers stationed there. Aunt Hallie being the exception.

"You should aspire to emulate great men who have made a difference," his aunt said. "Men like Mr. Lincoln."

"Uncle Huck is different, and he's a great man too. He knows everything. He's learning me to read the river so I can pilot a boat when I grow up."

"Teaching," she responded. "He is teaching you."

"Uh-huh. He's teached me lots already. Like how a ripple in the river means a reef. And them little dimples you see on the surface that don't look like nuthin' are snags, hiding under the water."

Her breath came out a long sigh. "Yes, he does seem to know quite a lot about the river. But there is so much more to learn. Books I can show you that will take you all over the world."

Why, he'd never heard of such a book.

"Like a magic carpet?"

"I see you have met Aladdin."

"No, I never met him, but Granny told me a story about him once." Tad hopped along to keep up with her. They passed by a row of doors that opened into the big room where people ate their meals. This wasn't the way to the pilot house.

"Hey, where are we going?"

"I want to show you my stateroom. Perhaps you would like to stay with me? It would help your uncle if you're not always underfoot."

He didn't want to spend time alone with his aunt. He wanted her to spend time alone with his uncle so they could get married. Then Uncle Huck would have a wife and could keep him.

"After we see your room, will you come back to the pilothouse with me? You can watch Uncle Huck. He's piloted mountain steamers all the way to Montana, and seen Indians and buffalo."

"That is exciting."

"You don't sound excited."

"Look up there, Tad. Isn't that the prettiest skylight?" She pointed to a colorful glass oval in the roof in between curly-cue beams stretching across the ceiling. Shiny brass lamps mounted on the white walls trembled with the boat's chugging movement.

"This sure is a fancy steamer," he agreed. Maybe she wanted one like it. "Uncle Huck says he's going to get his own steamboat one day."

"He told you that, did he? Well, he will have to work long and hard to afford a boat even half as nice as this one."

"Nu-uh. He's rich."

His aunt rolled her eyes like she didn't believe him.

"Mr. Sawyer says he is."

"Didn't Mr. Sawyer also tell you they were robbers? You know, of course, that was just pretending."

Tad huffed. He wasn't *stupid*. "But the treasure ain't pretend."

"Is not."

"He *is not* poor like you think."

"What I think doesn't matter. Besides, there is no shame in being poor."

The preacher was always blessing poor folks, but nobody ever wanted to marry them.

"I got proof." Tad dug deep into an empty pocket and frowned. "I left my pouch on my bed. Can we go get it?"

His aunt gripped his hand. "You can show me later."

"If Uncle Huck does buy a steamboat, I bet he'd take us with him."

"I have no interest in getting on another steamboat."

Aunt Hallie *had* to get on another steamboat if she was going to marry the pilot.

"Don't be scared, Aunt Hallie. Uncle Huck says—"

"I am not interested in what your uncle says." She stopped in front of a door and started fiddling with a key. It didn't work right away and she huffed. "My concern is not for myself. I objected to taking a steamboat because I could not bear it if anything should happen to you."

So, she didn't mind steamboats. She was just afraid he might get hurt.

Tad patted her arm in a gesture he'd seen grownups use to comfort each other. "It's all right. Uncle Huck promised he won't let nothing happen to me."

"Did he?" When she looked down, her eyes seemed a little sad. "We shall pray he is able to keep that promise."

After she got the door opened, Tad rushed inside to look around. He stepped up onto the lower berth so he could peek at the top bunk. He liked his cabin better, but he ought to say something nice to please her. "This is like the beds in the officers' quarters on the Texas deck."

He hopped down and did a quick inspection of the washstand, the only other furniture besides a chair. Clambering onto that, he still wasn't tall enough to look out the narrow window below the ceiling. He rose onto his toes and reached upwards.

His aunt put her hands on his waist. "Tad, get off that chair before you fall."

"I won't fall," he assured her, but he got down anyway.

He wasn't trying to be a bother. He had only acted bad earlier because he'd wanted Uncle Huck to go fetch her. Then she got back on the boat all by herself. Aunt Hallie was smart. For a girl.

She dragged the chair over to the washstand and caught his arm to draw him over. Did she want to hug him? Granny had always hugged him, even after he got too big for such show. It had embarrassed him then. Now he sorely missed burrowing into her softness. If his aunt married his uncle, maybe he would let her give him hugs every so often.

Her hand slid to his wrist and she gave a little tug. "Come sit here, sir. I want to trim your hair. How do you see with it hanging in your eyes like that?"

"I can see." He didn't care to have his hair cut, but to please her he kept still while she set to her task with a pair of shears.

Snip. Snip. Snip.

Wet lengths of hair fell to the floor, curling up like baby snakes. His uncle had told him that touching snakes brought bad luck. Hair probably didn't count, but he wouldn't touch it, just to be safe.

For some reason, his aunt wasn't impressed with how much his uncle knew, or with the treasure, or with living on a steamboat. She had to like something.

He swung his legs back and forth while he thought about it. "Aunt Hallie, do you like Uncle Huck?"

She pursed her lips and kept cutting. "Hm...I think he is an interesting man."

Interesting? That was a good word. Like *great* and *different*.

"So, you'd marry him if he asked you?"

The hand holding the shears slowly lowered. He caught his lip between his teeth and held his breath. Please let the answer be *yes*.

She slid her fingers through his hair, smoothing it. "There. Now you look like a gentleman."

"Like Uncle Huck?"

She set the scissors aside and took his hands. Hers were cool and smooth, not warm and buttery like Granny's. "Are you hoping your uncle and I will get married?"

Gosh, he was glad she'd figured it out. He had a hard time keeping secrets. "Uncle Huck needs a wife."

"I see." She stood straight and stared at the wall for some reason. "And you believe if you find him a wife, he will keep you with him?"

My, she *was* smart.

Tad nodded again, nearly bursting with excitement to tell her his plan. "He said he didn't have a wife so he couldn't keep me. But if he gets one, then he won't have to give me away."

His aunt gave a big sigh. "Dearest, I'm afraid your uncle has no interest in being wed—certainly not to me."

He shook his head at her. That wasn't what he wanted to hear. His uncle *had* to get married before they got home, and there was no time to find him another wife. "You could talk to him. If he thought you was interested, he might change his mind."

"A lady does not seek a gentleman's attention, but that is beside the fact. Mr. Finn has made it very clear he intends to leave as soon as he settles you in a new home. I am trying to convince him to let you live with me."

"But if you and him got married, I wouldn't need a new home." His voice cracked and his eyes burned. He was about to cry, and worse, in front of a girl. He jumped off the chair and hugged her instead. "Please, Aunt Hallie."

She didn't respond right off, yet she put her arms around him. Was she considering it? He wished harder than he ever had in his whole life.

"Tad, you must not pin your hopes on this. Your uncle and I don't suit."

He looked up at her, confused. "You want him to wear different clothes?"

Her lips twitched and she didn't look so sad anymore. "What I mean is, he is not the type of man I would marry."

"What type do you want?"

She made a little sound, similar to what his granny had done when she got impatient with him, but then she stroked his hair. "If I were to marry, my husband would have to be a gentleman."

Her answer worked itself around in Tad's head. Why, he could figure out how to get his uncle fixed up to look like a gentleman. Then Aunt Hallie would marry him.

He pulled away before she got it into her head that he needed to be petted. "I understand."

"Good." She gave his hand a gentle squeeze. "Now, we shan't speak of this anymore, and you mustn't mention anything to your uncle. It will only upset him."

AN HOUR LATER, HALLIE GAVE IN AND ACCOMPANIED TAD TO THE uppermost deck where they could access the pilot house. Her hold on his hand tightened. Entering that door would open a room in her heart she hadn't visited for years, and she wasn't sure she was ready.

Tad beamed with obvious glee. He would not be placated until he had brought her to gaze upon the object of his admiration, the man he wanted her to marry. The scoundrel she must discredit.

Her heart pounded as she ascended the last step and entered the sanctuary of the riverboat pilot.

Cool air flowed through a large rectangular window, which afforded an unobstructed view of the sprawling river. Framed in bright light was the upper half of a massive wheel that reached the height of the man standing next to it.

After throwing a glance over his shoulder, Huck returned his attention to the river.

Steamboat pilots were the most respected of men, the vast majority being responsible and steady. There were a few rogues amongst them. Huck Finn would fit that category. If she could collect enough evidence of his unsuitability as a guardian, she could convince Mr. Dubois to transfer custody.

She hugged her sketchbook to her chest and hardened her resolve. Tad deserved to be with his family and she was all he had left. It was for his sake she must build a case against Huck, not because she held a personal grudge.

"Good afternoon, Miss MacBride." Captain Kinney stood from where he was seated on a high-back bench reserved for visiting pilots. "Please, join us."

He gestured opposite to a comfortable-looking sofa bracketed with gleaming cuspidors. Passengers frequently came by to chat with the pilot. The visitors were generally men. However, the captain didn't seem to mind her presence or that of her nephew.

As she took a seat, the captain sat down and resumed puffing on a curved pipe with an etched ivory bowl, similar to the one her father had favored. It stirred up sweet memories of the hours she had spent with him as he'd guided his boat up and down the Mississippi River. Those had been among the happiest moments of her life.

As Huck had assured her, boilers didn't blow up with as much frequency anymore. It didn't ease her worry. The one on this boat might. More likely, a snag would pierce the hull and they'd sink. Or a careless smoker could set the boat afire. She would never forgive herself—or Huck—if anything happened to Tad.

A kind smile creased the captain's leathered face. "We were

just wondering when you and Master Tad might drop in for a visit, weren't we, Mr. Finn?"

The mumbled "aye" from the pilot indicated his agreement with the statement, but not his frame of mind.

Huck had been downright irascible ever since she had bested him by working out an arrangement for passage. He'd be apoplectic if he realized she was mounting an offensive.

Tad wiggled on the seat. "Uncle Huck, can I help you steer?"

"Sure. Grab a root on that wheel and let's take her through the channel."

Her nephew ran over to *help*.

The delight on his face wrenched Hallie's heart. She couldn't shield him from the pain he would suffer when Huck abandoned him. However, she could be there to provide comfort. After she thwarted Huck's scheme to foist Tad off on a family that wasn't his.

"I see you got shorn," Huck commented.

"Aunt Hallie cut my hair. She said it makes me a gentleman."

Huck barked a laugh.

The poor child's face flushed crimson, spurring her to rush to his aid.

"You, sir, could stand to befriend a pair of shears, along with a razor and a large quantity of soap and hot water."

The captain chortled. "She has a point there, Mr. Finn. I know a good barber in Sioux City, should you be looking for one."

"If you get your hair cut, you can be a gentleman, too," Tad said with confidence.

Huck turned an interesting shade of red and mumbled some excuse about not having time before turning his attention back to the wheel. He shouted orders into the speaking tube, and pulled on a cord, sounding a gong that echoed from below.

Steam wheezed through the pipes, signaling that the engineer had fired up the boilers. Huck didn't act as if he sensed anything amiss. But the pilot was often the last to know, fully realizing the danger only after the floor lifted beneath his feet and he was catapulted into the air.

The boat surged forward. Fear sang through her veins, urging her to leap up, snatch her nephew, and run for her life. If she did, Huck might use it to show she was prone to irrational behavior and thus unfit to raise a child. She took a deep breath and released the pent-up pressure with a sigh.

The captain rested the pipe on his knee. "My Kate tells me you painted that fine mural on the *Evening Star*."

"Yes, I did." Hallie opened the sketchbook on her lap and smoothed the pages to busy her shaking hands.

The older man eyed one of the sketches she'd drawn while wandering around the boat. "You apprenticed with Mr. Bingham?"

Heavens, that story got better with each telling.

"He made several trips on my father's boat. Once, while I was along, he took time to teach me some of his techniques."

Captain Kinney nodded agreeably. "You are likely an old hand at traveling the river."

So, he wanted to chitchat. She could manage light conversation, and that might put Huck at ease enough to lower his guard and let something slip that could prove useful. "I did travel with my father when I was old enough to be of assistance."

"I'm old enough to be of insistence," Tad crowed.

"You certainly will be a fine assistant if you keep learning from your uncle." The captain used the pipe to punctuate his words. He leaned back and gave her a knowing smile. "The *Evening Star* was a fine vessel, as I recall. You must miss traveling on her."

Her fondness for that lovely boat did not hold a candle to how much she'd loved its captain. "I choose not to travel by steamboat anymore."

Captain Kinney's shock spread across his face and animated his pipe. "MacBride's daughter not taking steamers? Why on earth not?"

"They are dangerous. You never know when one might—" She stopped her tongue. Talking about disasters in front of her nephew would only frighten him. Besides, she had no desire to recount the horrible details surrounding her father's death.

Compassion filled the captain's dark eyes. "The world is a dangerous place, Miss MacBride. But we shouldn't allow our lives to be directed by a fear of things we cannot know. What we know for certain is enough to worry over, don't you agree?"

Her throat seized and she could only nod. When had fear taken such a firm hold? It hadn't always been this way. As a child, she would race her younger sister down to the wharf to be the first one to greet her father on his infrequent visits home. Unlike her mother, he had never minded if her feet were bare or if she was brown as a walnut from being outside so much. He'd even given in to her pleas to take her with him on the river. Until her mother had convinced him she needed her daughter at home.

Hallie absently drew a rough shape of the man at the wheel. She was no longer that heedless young woman, having learned the painful consequences of taking risks.

The captain stood abruptly. "Master Tad, why don't you come with me? We'll see if the cook has any sweets we can bring back for your aunt and uncle."

Tad's face lit with interest, but he held to his post.

"You heard the captain." Huck nodded at the door. "Run on now."

Hallie kept her head bowed to hide her distress. Captain Kinney hadn't been fooled. He might've whisked her nephew away because he sensed she was on the verge of tears. Whatever the reason, she was thankful the perceptive gentleman had not continued with that uncomfortable conversation.

Her biggest problem at the moment wasn't a hazard posed by the river. She eyed the broad back of her adversary and considered how she might gain information without letting on as to her intentions. "You don't mind if I sketch awhile, do you?"

Huck grunted something she took to be acknowledgment.

Taking up her pencil, she began to draw. First, she would finish his overall form and then fill in the detail.

He gripped a spoke and leaned forward to get a better look at something. With the movement, his wide shoulders stretched the worn shirt. It had the yellowish tinge of an old garment.

How long had it been since he'd purchased new clothes? Not that it mattered. If being unfashionably dressed were a crime, the streets would be emptied of men.

Nor could she disparage his physical attributes. He had a fine form, and stood straight and proud, not slouched like someone who lacked confidence. On the waistband of his trousers, a notch at the small of his back served to emphasize his firm buttocks.

She jerked her attention to her drawing, which had already taken shape. Faith, she wasn't here to ogle him, or even sketch him, for at matter.

What had Huck said a few nights ago when they were on the island? That he'd made his way up to the pilothouse. He hadn't claimed to be a pilot. Perhaps he'd gotten some training in steering a boat but had never taken the test. Anyone caught piloting a steamboat without a license, no matter how skilled, would face a stiff fine and time in jail.

A framed certificate hung on the wall next to him. The captain's license. Huck hadn't put one up, as required. He might not have one.

"Where did you take your training to be a pilot?" she asked in a casual tone.

Huck gave the wheel a slow turn. "I started on the Mississippi as a cub. Worked under a pilot named Clemens. Samuel Clemens. Ever heard of him?"

"I recall the name. Did you complete your training?"

"Not with him. After the war broke out, I came west on the Missouri. Finished my training with an upper river pilot."

"And received your license?"

"Got a certificate back in Atchison."

Perhaps what he said was true and he did have a license tucked away somewhere. He was supposed to keep it with him. Even if a regulatory agent caught him without it, he would only be fined. It wasn't enough to discredit him as a guardian.

She sighed with disappointment. "You would not be so foolish as to pilot a boat without a license."

"'Course not." He rang more bells and tilted the wheel in the other direction.

She rubbed her finger on the paper, shading a spot to emphasize the curve of a muscle. "Was there a reason you took a boat headed upriver?"

"It was the fastest way to get rid of unwanted baggage."

Baggage, was she?

"Too bad for you that did not work out," she replied tartly.

Hallie set down her sketchbook. This conversation was going nowhere. She left the sofa to venture closer to the wheel and peered anxiously through the pilot's window.

The Missouri had the appearance of a flooded prairie more than a river. Braided channels wound through stands of cottonwood and willows, hiding the most advantageous route. A pilot without a great deal of training would ground a boat in no time.

"The water is very shallow," she remarked.

Huck's gaze remained fastened on the river. "This is deep water compared to upriver. The shoalest point is past Dauphin Rapids. When I was a green steersman back in sixty-four, we about took our hull off scraping over them rapids in seventeen inches of water."

"Seventeen inches? Why that's less than two feet. The paddle wheel reaches three feet into the water."

"Only if the boat's loaded. We set everything on the shore that wasn't attached. Carted freight halfway to Yankton. That's not accounting for the Indians."

"Indians?"

"Well, I'll own that was on another trip."

She turned to hide a smile. It would only encourage him to continue his inflated recollections, the same as every pilot she'd ever known. Next, he'd be declaring he could navigate on a heavy dew.

Huck stopped talking as he took the boat through an intricate channel. He dodged a rippled tail of water, indicating a bluff reef, and gave wide berth to a forest of sawyers bobbing near the opposite shore.

She heard a rushing noise before she spotted the whirlpool.

He reached for a cord and pulled, setting off a clanging cacophony of signals, many of which she had memorized as a child.

Half steam. Slow. Stop and back. Go ahead...

The jangling orders came thick and fast, punctuated with colorful expletives, which appeared to help, as he deftly guided the *Hesperia* away from danger.

Hallie dropped her hand from where it had been stuck to her chest over her swiftly beating heart. Fortunate for all concerned, no case could be made against his piloting ability. "Tad mentioned you plan to purchase a boat."

"I was considering it. Until I got robbed."

An angle worth pursuing. Robbery was common among thieves, and the lowest of that species ran rampant through the gold fields.

"I recall you mentioned being attacked. Who did it?"

He shook his head. "Don't know for sure."

"But you saw them?"

"Right before they shot me. Then I didn't see anything for a while. I reckon they were after my gold. They took the belt I had under my shirt."

The mental image of Huck sprawled out, bloody and helpless, as a pack of animals descended on him brought on a shudder. No one, not even a thief, deserved such inhuman treatment.

"It's a miracle you survived."

"Pure meanness, I reckon. It took a while to get my strength back. That was why I was holed up in Atchison for the past few months."

"Did the sheriff investigate?"

Huck leveled a look that set off warning bells in her head. "You sure are curious today."

She'd gotten so caught up in the horrifying story she had not chosen her words carefully. "We didn't start on the best foot, so I thought we should get to know each other better."

He raked her with his gaze and her body tingled in response. Oh heavens, he didn't think—

"What I mean is, I would like to know how your plans might affect Tad."

"They won't." He turned the wheel, starting another crossing. "Like I told you, I'm settling him in a proper home. One with a good pap."

A *good pap*. Unlike the man who'd sired him and provided a sorry example.

Hallie resisted the pressure against a tender spot in her heart. Showing weakness would not help Tad. If she couldn't discredit Huck, she must disabuse him of his conviction.

"And you believe you are the person best suited to judge what constitutes a good father?"

The muscles in his jaw tightened. Whether from anger or hurt, she couldn't tell and mustn't care. He didn't look at her when he finally spoke.

"Whatever schemes you're hatching behind them green eyes, you'd best give it up. Unless you want me to let out your little secret, and get you hove off this boat."

CHAPTER FOURTEEN

The trip north from Atchison to Sioux City took four days. Heading downriver would go faster. With any luck, they'd arrive in St. Louis ahead of schedule. In the meantime, why not enjoy a night off?

Huck stepped out of the barber's shop and rubbed his bare chin. The cool evening air felt good on his skin, and so had that hot bath. He didn't care what Miss MacBride thought about his shaggy hair and beard, but when Tad had started complaining, he reckoned it had better come off.

Now he was ready for some entertainment, thanks to a generous advance on his salary.

He propped his hands on his hips and smiled down at his charge. "Well, Tad, you ready to explore this old town? Sioux City has lots of interesting, uh..."

Brothels? Saloons?

"Things. Lots of interesting things."

With a boy in tow, he couldn't pursue his usual distractions. Yet another reason he wasn't cut out to be a father.

His nephew regarded him with an expression that could've been awe or horror. "Geeminy, you look different, Uncle Huck."

"Different? You didn't say better. Reckon a haircut and shave didn't improve me."

"Different is good."

"S'at so?" Huck let out a laugh. "Well, I never claimed to be part of the tribe of normal."

It pleased him that his nephew would compliment him for his uniqueness. Miss MacBride didn't think much of his differences.

His pride still smarted from her snide insinuation about his worthlessness as a guardian. It stung all the more because he hadn't expected cruelty. Though perhaps he should have, as desperate as she was to get control of the boy. He understood her reasons, and even felt bad for her. But that didn't mean he was giving Tad over to be raised by a woman with no husband. His nephew needed a father, and he was going to see to it that Tad got a good one.

He started down a boardwalk, past freshly painted buildings that overlooked a wide street. The air smelled of mud and manure, both having been churned into a gooey slime by wagon wheels and countless oxen.

Sioux City no longer resembled the quaint frontier outpost from a few years back. With the coming of the railroad, the town overflowed with people—walking, on horseback, in wagons—and everybody appeared to be in a hurry.

Tad jerked on Huck's sleeve. "Can we go in there?"

Huck spotted a mercantile across the street, just beyond a caravan of wagons lined up for supplies. Not on the top of his list of fun places to visit, but he might as well purchase some respectable clothes, a shaving kit, toothpowder, and a few other things they needed. "Well, what do you know? You found just the place I was looking for."

He caught Tad's arm before they stepped out into the street.

After that odd spate of misbehaving, his nephew had been good as gold. But the boy had more pent-up steam than the *Hesperia*, and he might inadvertently run out in front of a horse or wagon.

Tad veered off before they reached the door. "No, I don't mean in there. I mean *there*."

He pulled Huck toward a small store next to the mercantile.

Huck tipped his head back to read the sign overhead. "Why do we need a tailor? We can buy readymade."

"Can't we just talk to him? Please?"

Talking to tailor. About as much fun as watching clothes dry on a line.

"All right, but we got things to buy, and I'm getting hungry. You got ten minutes. Then we're leaving."

A bell tinkled as they opened the door. The little shop, no bigger than a pilothouse, smelled of new wool and fine shoe leather. A small scale for weighing gold dust sat on the counter, the same as every other business in town. Miners coming downriver from Montana didn't use paper money.

Tad wandered over to a collection of advertisements pinned to the wall. Huck peered over his nephew's shoulder at what had caught the boy's interest. Drawings of men dressed in *the latest fashions*, according to what the paper said.

When had Tad started to care about what he wore? He'd seemed more interested in shedding his clothes when they were on the island.

They both turned at a shuffling sound.

A wrinkled-up gnome of a man emerged from the darkened doorway behind the counter. His lips drew back to reveal a mouthful of gleaming dental work. "What can I do for you gentlemen?"

Tad stepped up to the counter. "Oh, we ain't gentlemen. Not yet."

Huck choked back a laugh. Whatever Tad was up to it was worth the price of a show.

"You got any clothes that look like that?" Tad pointed at the pictures.

The old man kept a-smiling like he had eight-year-old customers walk in his door every day. "I can make whatever you want, young man."

"Oh, it's not for me. It's for my uncle. He needs the right suit, so he can be a gentleman."

The proprietor started chuckling. It wasn't so funny as all that.

"Tad, I told you we don't have time to get clothes made," Huck reminded him.

His nephew's shoulders drooped. "But you can't be a gentleman without the right clothes. Says so right there on that picture."

The aunt was to blame for this foolishness.

Huck clamped a hand around Tad's arm and firmly ushered him out the door. Once outside, he turned him by the shoulders in the direction of the mercantile and gave him a push. "I don't mind a little nonsense now and then, but you were wasting that man's time."

Tad's heels scraped the ground. "No, I wasn't. You got to look like a gentleman, and that tailor can help you."

This nonsense was going to end here and now.

Huck guided Tad closer to the building to avoid getting walloped by sacks of flour being loaded into a wagon. He knelt and looked his nephew straight in the eye. "Has your Aunt Hallie been filling your head with notions?"

Tad's lips parted and his face flushed. He shook his head. "No. She didn't say nuthin'. I just reckoned steamboat pilots are s'posed to look like gentlemen."

"Boy, you'd best learn to lie better than that if you plan on making it a regular practice."

His nephew's face twisted into an expression of profound repentance.

Huck's irritation dissolved. It weren't Tad's fault. His starchy aunt was determined to make him into a *gentleman*, and no doubt had set into him every minute they were together. She still hadn't figured out all that polishing only produced men who were shiny and smooth on the outside, so you couldn't see how rotten and wormy they were on the inside.

"Clothes don't make a gentleman, Tad. I learnt that a long time ago." Huck patted his nephew's shoulder and rose to his feet. "Let's get going—"

The hair on his scalp prickled and he tensed. He'd gotten this feeling before when he was being watched. Moving slowly to appear casual, he looked back and forth, up and down the boardwalk.

A woman in a dark dress ducked behind a wagon. No mistaking that slender form. Miss MacBride was tailing him.

Huck pressed his lips together to stop an oath. Did she not trust him with Tad's safety or was there another reason for her to be skulking about?

His instincts warned him she was up to something. He'd known it as soon as she'd started asking him all those questions. She couldn't have made her motivations clearer. She hoped to catch him doing something that would prove he was unfit to be Tad's guardian.

Anger stoked him hotter than a boiler. Nothing worse than a sneak, except a devious woman bent on getting her way at all costs. By God, he'd call her bluff.

But wait. He could do one better, and teach her a lesson in the process.

~

DAYLIGHT FADED INTO DARKNESS IN THE ALLEY. FORTUNATELY, THE outdoor lamps along the street had been lit. Otherwise, Hallie might have lost sight of Huck and Tad.

She'd seen him slip away with her nephew in tow only moments after landing the boat. It was impossible to predict what the irritating man would do next. Thus far they'd visited a barber shop and several stores. Huck had made purchases as if planning an escape.

Hallie peeked around the corner of the building just in time to see him lead his young charge across the street and through the door of what looked like a saloon.

Had he lost his mind? She'd feared he might take her nephew, hop on another boat and leave her behind. But this? Well, this beat all. Huck Finn wasn't just a poor example. He was a complete reprobate.

He didn't *look* wicked. Heavens no. She'd nearly swooned when he'd emerged from that barber's shop. Huck possessed a boyishly handsome face that perfectly complemented his strapping physique. Even from a distance, she could see well enough to get the shivers. If only his fair visage didn't conceal such a black soul.

She watched the front of the establishment. An occasional shadow crossed in front of the frosted window, which was decorated with etchings of cards and dance hall girls.

Should she go in after them? No decent woman would be caught dead in a place like that. But her nephew was in there. By Jove, she would not stand idly by while Huck subjected a child to a bout of sinful carousing.

Gathering her courage, she marched across the street, pushed open the door, and stepped inside.

The pungent odor of cigars assaulted her senses. She squinted to see through the smoky haze, attempting to locate Huck in the open room.

A tinkling piano drew her attention to an area where customers were gathered around tables, drinking and playing cards. Scantily clad women pranced about serving the patrons, who dragged the laughing servers into their laps.

Disgraceful. How dare Huck subject Tad to such a lewd display.

A woman stepped in front of Hallie. Her jiggling bosom came dangerously close to spilling out of a low-cut crimson gown. She stretched her rouged lips into the semblance of a smile. "Ladies ain't allowed, dearie. This here is a gent's club."

"I...I..." Hallie forced out her request. "I am seeking a man."

The woman's thinned eyebrows arched.

"No! Not that. What I mean is, a man just came in with a boy. My nephew. I need to find him." Peering over the woman's shoulder, Hallie scanned the room. There were so many men it was hard to tell whether Huck was one of them.

"No boys in here," the woman stated. "Just men."

"But I saw my nephew enter." Hallie drew herself up, knowing how to appear imposing even with her less-than-average height. "Direct me to him this instant."

The proprietress lifted her double chin and glared. "If I wasn't a lady, I'd have you thrown out."

"If you are, you aren't behaving like one ."

The woman stepped back with a wave that shook the loose flesh beneath her armpit. "Look around if you like, but then you got to leave. Unless you want a job."

Hallie's face grew hot enough to steam her glasses. "I shall look around, and if I find my nephew I will be reporting you to the authorities."

The woman gave a harsh laugh. She swayed her hips over to an ornately carved bar and engaged in whispered conversation with a burly man who had on a white shirt with red garters on his upper arms. Their images were reflected in a large mirror behind them. The odious woman was laughing.

Fuming, Hallie began to search the room. Soldiers. Railroad workers. A table of well-dressed men who avoided showing their faces. Although some of them gave her startled looks, most seemed engrossed in their games or titillations. Huck wasn't down here. He surely wouldn't take Tad upstairs.

Her heart rapped a frantic beat when the barkeeper approached. Did he intend to toss her out?

"Ma'am, why don't you try back at the boat?" His humorless expression didn't hide the glint of amusement in his eyes.

"Back at the...?" How did he know where she'd come from?

Heat flooded her face. Huck had played a trick on her! He must've spotted her earlier, and she had walked right into his trap. He'd gone out the back after recruiting the doxy and barkeeper for his obscene jest.

"Thank you," she ground out, then fled as fast as she could. Huck had no doubt returned to the boat to tell the captain of her whereabouts and shred her reputation. She never should've trusted him.

In the time it took her to return, she'd devised a dozen methods of torture along with a few choice words to let Mr. Finn know what she thought of him.

The lights on the boat blazed. She tromped up the gangplank, past deckhands loading freight, and glanced down the wide promenade. Dozens of chairs were stacked up along the outside wall, but one had been unfolded and was occupied by a man.

He'd leaned back and propped his feet on the rail. The hissing lanterns mounted on the guards illuminated his beardless profile. Huck had waited around to taunt her rather than engage in evasive tactics, as was his usual way.

With a furious huff, she started towards him.

He scraped the chair back and stood as she approached. His smile revealed twin dimples. Sakes, why had God given him the face of an angel when he had the heart of a devil?

"Miss MacBride," he greeted in an agreeable tone. "Sure is a nice evening for a stroll."

It took every ounce of self-control not to slap him. "You cad. Have you spoken to the captain?"

"The captain?" He crinkled his forehead like he was confused. The oaf was toying with her.

"Where is Tad?" she demanded.

He gave a casual wave. "In bed. Asleep. Where'd you think he'd be?"

She fired the first salvo. "You know very well. You were the one who dragged him through that bawdy house. Left to your own devices, you would turn him into a tramp. Even a low-born dog-in-a-manger would know better than to—"

He placed two fingers over her mouth, shocking and silencing her. Her body tingled in a shameful response to his touch.

"Hush now," he scolded lightly. "You want everybody to know what a bad temper you got?"

She jerked his hand away. "I do *not* have a bad temper. Any God-fearing lady—or gentleman—would be appalled by your disrespectful behavior tonight."

"*My* behavior?" His smile hardened. "What about yours? You were the one skulking around. That's not behavior befitting a *lady*."

"You miscreant. How dare you." As she lifted her hand, he raised his arm to block a blow she never delivered. With his other hand, he caught her jaw in a firm grip.

"Don't spew vinegar all over me because you got what was coming to you. You trailed after us like a bloodhound."

His counterattack took the wind out of her sails. She couldn't refute the accusation, but she could defend herself.

"My actions were warranted, given your deceitful nature."

"Since when is spying considered respectable behavior?" He threw her condemnation back at her without raising his voice.

Hallie's righteous anger withered. He'd tricked her, true enough, but she occupied no higher ground. Despite not trusting him, at some point she should've revealed her presence and demanded to know what he intended to do with Tad.

"Why did you follow us?" Huck asked in a softer tone. He turned loose of her jaw and curled his fingers beneath her chin. A light touch that made her insides quiver.

God help her. She was cursed with some pathetic weakness for fickle men.

Intending to push him away, she splayed her fingers against his chest, encountering the smooth wool of a new coat. The faint fragrance of soap and spicy cologne confirmed the truth. He hadn't left the boat for some nefarious purpose. He'd gone into town to get cleaned up and buy new clothes.

She dropped her arms as the last of her pride drained away. "I followed you because I feared…"

"What do you fear, Hallie? That somebody might see you?" Huck cupped her cheek in an oddly tender gesture. He didn't seem to be referring to catching her spying on him. Rather, he regarded her with a wholly different kind of intensity. "You're a pretty woman," he said in a rough whisper. "You got no reason to be afraid of it."

He thought she was pretty?

The brush of his thumb over her lip drew her closer. His nearness was a force as inescapable as the pull of the moon on the tide. Shouts and grunts of workmen loading freight on the deck below faded as in a dream. In the distance, a clock chimed the hour, but time had ceased to matter.

"For God's sake, push me away," he whispered, right before he pressed his lips to hers. Warm and firm. Masterful in coaxing a response.

Colors burst behind her cloaked vision, brilliant rainbow hues that swept away the drab grays of her cloistered life. Startling sensations stripped away her reserve, and with a moan of pleasure, she wound her arms around his neck and let him plunder her mouth.

A groan rumbled up from his chest, the tortured sound of someone fighting a battle...and losing.

Some rational part of her mind asserted itself, questioning her sanity, and she broke away with a gasp.

When Huck tried to keep kissing her, she dropped her hands to his chest and averted her face. In the space of a heartbeat, he released her and stepped back. The labored cadence of his breathing and her shallow panting was the only sound between them.

Hallie spun away, awash in feelings too confusing to name much less sort out. Never had she experienced such passion, not even in the arms of a man she had thought she'd loved with all her heart. Perhaps that heart was malformed, unable to hold anything good and pure enough to last. Or it had never known love at all.

Hunching her shoulders, she groaned in agony from a kind of pain that touched her everywhere.

"Hallie?" Huck's voice, right behind her, sounded different, less sure. He curled his hands around her arms, his warmth penetrating the wool sleeves of her dress.

Oh God, why did he have to be so warm? Pretending that he cared or that the kiss meant anything to him. Nothing penetrated that hard shell he lived in. Although he certainly had destroyed *her* defenses without a great deal of effort. He'd only kissed her to prove a point. She was soiled. Sinful. Unworthy to raise a child.

"Do not touch me." She stiffened and turned on him. "I will not allow you to use your advantage to further humiliate me."

After surprise came the glower. "You know good and well I didn't do any such thing. I might not fit with your idea of a gentleman, but I gave you a chance to push me away."

Curse the man for pointing out her weakness. Frustrated tears welled up. "Are you implying I *want* your attention?"

"Yes...I mean, no." He threw his hands up in a show of exasperation. "Blame it, woman, I don't know what you want."

She dug her nails into her palms, punishing herself with pain as she glared at him through a watery haze. "What I want is for my nephew to be safe from the likes of you."

CHAPTER FIFTEEN

Huck wound his way through the main cabin, nodding to the remaining guests who lingered over their coffee. As a pilot, he was expected to stop and chat with the passengers when he wasn't working. This morning, however, he had to find Tad before the time came to set off. The boy had gone to Hallie's room while the crew made ready to leave. By now they ought to be where she was supposed to be, painting that mural.

He reached the etched glass separating the ladies' salon from the main hall and pushed one door open a crack to peek inside. His gaze skittered over a plush settee and fancy chairs, none of them occupied.

She wasn't so crazy she'd run off in a wild place she knew nothing about. No, they were likely with the captain's wife. The older woman had all but adopted her painter. She bought Hallie supplies and gave her clean clothes to wear. Miss MacBride fancied herself too much of a lady to shine out and leave her friend high and dry. She was around here somewhere, stirring up trouble.

Huck scratched the back of his neck where it itched. Other

itches he couldn't do a thing about. He hadn't slept a wink last night after he'd given into temptation and kissed her.

Blame it, he *knew* better. But when she'd put her hands on his chest, with her face so soft and vulnerable, her eyes pleading and her lips trembling. he just hadn't been able to stop himself.

Then she'd hauled off and accused him of taking advantage. He'd wanted to shake her. Then kiss her again. Except that might be what she wanted, and her eager response to the kiss had been a ploy to trip him up. Although it hadn't seemed that way last night. That's why he had to find her and apologize. Not just because he felt bad about tricking her into going into that gaming hall, but because he'd wounded her somehow and hadn't meant to.

He let out a frustrated sigh. After last night, he would never convince her of his good intentions. She'd be laying for him every chance she got. As much as it pained him, he had to find a way to get her put off the boat. He hadn't worked out how, considering Mrs. Kinney adored having an artist on board, even if that *artist* hadn't produced a single painting.

Or had she?

Huck tossed a cautious glance over his shoulder before he slipped through the doors. Men weren't supposed to enter the female sanctuary without being asked, but with no women around, it shouldn't matter.

The room smelled of paint and turpentine. He surveyed the white paneled walls and noticed a shiny area across from the sofa. So, she had cleaned that spot and even gotten as far as slapping on another coat of white paint. Still, no mural.

Huck harrumphed. He had it right. She was just a-going to whitewash that wall for days, talking about how she'd start her painting when it was just so. Hallie weren't no more an artist than he was an opry singer.

But how could he prove it? They'd believe her as long as she kept up the ruse.

Something on a side table caught his eye. Hallie's sketchbook. The one she'd been scratching in these past few days.

Huck tucked the book into his coat and shot out the door. This ought to give him all the evidence he needed to get rid of her. He'd track down the captain and present the scribblings. Once Captain Kinney realized he'd hired a fraud, he wouldn't have any option but to put her off the boat. She'd have no one to blame but herself for making up such a whopper of a story.

With his conscience quieted, he rattled down the stairs to the main deck and approached the first mate, who was hollering at the dockhands loading freight. Those fellows had been busy last night and were still going at it this morning. Maybe the *Hesperia* had a pokey crew.

"Shin." Huck interrupted when there was a lapse in swearing. "You seen Captain Kinney?"

"Him and the clerk left early this morning," the burly officer answered curtly. "Don't let her drop!" He ripped out at two deckhands struggling with a hogshead barrel. "Blamed mud cats. Hump it now! Stop dragging yer feet like you're at yer granny's funeral. We don't got the whole dang week to get this boat loaded."

The hands appeared to be lugging boxes and barrels aboard plenty fast. Must be the load was more than expected. Likely, the captain had gone to meet with the transfer agent to make sure they weren't getting cheated.

Huck left Shin at his job. With nothing to do but wait for the old man to return, he sat on a crate and pulled the sketchbook out of his coat. Wouldn't hurt to take a look and see what the *artist* had been scrawling these past few days.

His hopes for an easy solution to his problem faded with each page he turned. Filling Hallie's sketchbook were all sorts of amazing drawings. The sprawling river. Towheads thick with cottonwoods. Snags poking up out of the water like bleached bones.

"I'll be danged," Huck whispered, impressed in spite of his disappointment. These pictures were good. No, they were more than good. Hallie had real talent.

He examined a drawing that featured a slice of the bow where a mate had let down a long pole to feel for the bottom of the river. He half expected the dark leadsman to rise up and sing out.

The drawings appeared to end. Except, there was a bent corner near the back. He slipped his thumbnail beneath it and flipped past the blank pages. More drawings...

Surprise snatched his breath. She'd drawn pictures of him. One sketch showed his face, turned to the side, looking out like he was thinking deep thoughts. She'd done this one before he'd gotten shorn.

Another drawing featured a man at the pilot's wheel with his back to her. She'd used her pencil to shade parts of his shirt to show how the fabric stretched across his shoulders and wrinkled up beneath the crisscrossed straps of his suspenders. Had to be him, considering the old man wore his coat while he was on duty.

And here was a drawing of him with Tad and that blamed goat chained up, pulling to get to the bacon.

Huck chuckled as turned the page, then busted out laughing. The next sketch showed a man and a boy, naked as jaybirds, poised on the edge of a flatboat, about to jump. Danged if she hadn't drawn him and Tad skinny-dipping. This just proved she wasn't as prudish as what she put on.

He puzzled over why she'd put these drawings in the back when they were as good as the others. Probably because she didn't want anybody to see them and make more of her interest in him than was warranted. It was clear enough by all these sketches that she scribbled whatever caught her fancy.

Only, she didn't fancy him. Or if she had, she didn't anymore.

She had no use for him. No matter how many pictures she'd drawn—even the naked one.

He heaved a weary sigh. Hallie wasn't a charlatan. Not like those characters he'd taken up with in the past. With drawings as good as these, he couldn't very well call her out as a fraud. The captain wouldn't care about one naughty picture in a notebook.

Now what? She had flat owned up to the fact that she'd fight tooth and nail to thwart his plan, and she wasn't beneath being devious, as evidenced by her sneaking around after them. He couldn't watch his back every moment. He'd have to find another way to convince her to leave.

Huck tucked the sketchbook inside his coat. She'd be missing it soon, so he'd best return it. He wouldn't chance going back to the ladies' salon. He'd slip into her room after the bell rang for dinner.

As he started up the stairs, his steps grew heavy. The extra weight bearing down on him didn't come from carrying around a little notebook.

THE BELL CLANGED, CALLING PASSENGERS TO THE DINING HALL FOR the noontime meal.

Hallie stood in front of a small mirror mounted on the wall in her room, fiddling with a mess of ringlets arranged in a coiffure that was *all the rage*. Her hair was too curly for the style to look right.

She sighed with disappointment at not being able to see more than a small portion of her evening attire. Kate's stylish dress, with its loose-fitting bodice and flowing lines, appeared to complement her figure, but it was hard to tell. She'd always been too thin for popular styles to flatter her, yet hadn't cared enough to add extra stuffing.

With a sigh, she turned away from the mirror. Who was she trying to impress, anyway? She wouldn't have accepted the gown if it hadn't been for Kate's comments about her black dress being more appropriate for funerals than dinners. She didn't want to embarrass her new friend.

Tad sat on the top bunk with his legs dangling. "Geeminy, Aunt Hallie. You look real pretty."

His compliment warmed her heart because the boy came out with precisely what he thought, not having perfected the art of flattery.

"Thank you, Tad."

"That Mrs. Kinney sure is nice. I bet she'd ask the captain if we could eat with the officers."

Sadly, he had picked up his uncle's unfortunate talent for manipulation.

Hallie gripped her nephew's swinging ankle before his foot came into contact with her head. "I want you to stop that."

His legs stilled.

"Thank you, but I meant I want you to stop talking about eating with the officers. You and I are not part of the staff, therefore we will dine with the other passengers. Come down and let me comb your hair."

He scrambled off the berth wearing an aggrieved expression. Lands, but he was wearing her out with his continued pestering about dining with his uncle, and his tireless efforts to match them up. The last person she should consider was an unprincipled schemer, who, for some unfathomable reason, she found irresistible.

Heavens, all it had taken was a kiss, and she had been clamoring for more. She should've learned her lesson when she'd fallen for a faithless charmer.

She ran a damp comb through Tad's hair to smooth it into

place. He had none of his father's guile, thank goodness. "You look nice in your new clothes."

He shrugged and wandered away from the washstand.

Just beyond the door, the main cabin bustled with the dinner crowd. The knob jiggled, then Huck peeked in. Surprise lit on his face before he jerked back. "Sorry, Hallie...I mean, Miss MacBride."

What on earth?

She marched over and yanked the door open. "Do you know how to knock?"

Tad slipped around her and grabbed his uncle's hand. "Hey, Uncle Huck. Look at Aunt Hallie. Isn't she pretty?" As Tad dragged Huck inside, she took a quick step back to avoid having her foot stomped on.

"Sorry," Huck muttered and shook off Tad's hold. His other hand remained tucked inside his coat as his gaze moved over her in a slow appraisal.

She clamped down on a rise of eager anticipation. The uncivilized lout had burst into her room, and all she could think about was whether he liked the way she looked.

"You did something to your hair," he started.

Her hand flew to her head and her face heated. No doubt, she looked like a frowsy old biddy trying to primp for a suitor. "What do you mean by barging in uninvited?"

"Didn't think you were here. Wanted to drop off, um..." He pulled something from beneath his coat and thrust it out. "I found this."

She stared at what he held—her sketchbook—and her eyes flew to his with a silent question. Had he looked at the drawings she'd done of him?

Of course, he had.

She snatched it away. "Where did you find this?"

His expression turned guarded. "I didn't hook it if that's what you're thinking. I found it laying out where anybody might pick it up."

She didn't leave her sketchbook *laying out*. The last place she'd been was the ladies' salon. Perhaps she had left it behind. But why would he go in there? Unless he sought to undermine her in some way. After that incident yesterday, she didn't trust him an inch.

"Uncle Huck, it's not just her hair. She's got a new dress," Tad crowed. "*Now* can we eat at the officers' table?"

"No," she said firmly. "We are not eating with the officers."

Huck's stance shifted from uncertain to challenging. "You got no call to rip out at him. He can eat with me if he wants."

She glared at the impudent intruder. "How dare you barge in here and then act as if *I* am the one in the wrong?"

"I didn't barge in. Told you, I found that blamed book. I was bringing it here to leave for you. How was I to know you were in here? You have been avoiding me all day—"

A jarring bang was followed by rattling and a loud click.

Hallie stared with disbelief at the closed door, then at the empty keyhole where she'd left—

"The key!" She rushed over and twisted the knob. "My God, Tad has taken it and locked us in here."

With the flat of her hand, she banged furiously on the door. "Thaddeus Douglas! Unlock the door this very instant."

Huck clamped his fingers around her wrist and stopped her frantic pounding. "You want everybody on the boat to hear you?"

Good Lord, no.

She pushed at his chest to make him move. "Get away from me."

With a snort, he set her aside and addressed the door. "Tad, stop fooling around. Let us out right now."

The only sounds from the other side were the tinkling of glass and silverware.

She tugged at a wayward curl. "Tad wouldn't run off. He's playing a joke."

"Some joke," Huck muttered. "You got another key?"

"Of course not. There is no reason for two when one will do."

Turning back, he thundered, "Unlock the door, Tad! You got one minute or I'll give you such a cowhiding you won't sit down for a week."

"Oh, good grief, do something useful!"

"I did. That threat always got me hopping when I was his age. Give him a minute to think about it. He'll open the door soon enough."

"I suppose if you beat him on a regular basis, he might take you seriously," she said dryly.

Huck appeared downright horrified at the thought. She wouldn't strike the child, either, but that was beside the point. More effective threats were available.

Pushing her way past him, she pressed her cheek against the door and pitched her voice just loud enough to penetrate the wood. "Tad, you will not be allowed into the pilothouse if you don't let us out this instant."

"Here now." Huck pulled her back. "You got no say over who goes into the pilothouse."

"Get your hands off me." She struggled to escape his grasp, but he held her tight. Her anxiety spiraled into full-fledged panic.

He'd already threatened to reveal her secret. Being caught in an improper situation would certainly give validity to what he might've told the captain about her wanton behavior.

She pummeled his chest with her free fist. "If you think to ruin me, I'll deny everything."

He responded by imprisoning her against him with one powerful arm wrapped around her waist and his fingers splayed across the back of her head. "Hallie, calm down."

She moaned. Things couldn't get worse.

"I'm not going to hurt you." His breath stirred her hair, setting off a shiver of longing.

Oh yes, things could get worse.

She turned her face into his shoulder. How could she explain she didn't fear *he* would lose control? Although it was reputed that men could be thrown into a sexual frenzy at just the sight of a table leg. Huck did not appear so unstable. But the passion he roused in her was something no decent woman should feel.

"Huck, please. Don't do this."

He grasped her shoulders and made her look at him. "What sort of man do you think I am?"

Her heart thrummed a frantic beat. She had thought him an uncouth bum when she first met him. After spending time in his company, she'd seen a different man—intelligent, if uncultured, at times even coarse, but with a deep core of kindness. Then he had crushed her nascent trust with his unending pranks.

What sort of man was he? She wished she knew.

WHEN HALLIE DIDN'T ANSWER HIS QUESTION, HUCK REMOVED HER gold-rimmed spectacles, wanting to see what her eyes were saying. She hid her emotions behind the glass, so if he wanted the truth, he had to remove the barrier.

He wasn't sure why it mattered what she thought of him, but it did. It mattered a great deal.

"Give me those," she demanded.

He held the spectacles out of reach. "Not until you answer my question."

Her efforts to reach the dangling prize brought her closer and the air between them heated up like it had the night before. Her eyes widened. He had the strangest notion that he could lose himself in that green forest.

When she'd first yanked open the door, he almost hadn't

recognized the beautiful woman staring back at him. She'd crawled out of that black cocoon and transformed into a beautiful butterfly.

The devil on his shoulder tempted him to suggest an exchange. The new goggles ought to be worth at least a kiss.

Her anxious expression became fearful.

No. He wouldn't do what she expected, take advantage when he had the advantage. That would make him no better than the man who'd used her and cast her away.

He folded her spectacles and slipped them into his pocket.

Confusion crossed her face, followed by a spark of ire. "If you are a gentleman, you will return my spectacles, then help me find a way out of this mess."

If he was a gentleman? Well, he'd never claimed to be. But he didn't wish her harm. On the contrary, he had a strong urge to protect her. He wasn't certain what sort of man that made him, but if she saw a speck of goodness in him, perhaps he weren't such a bad sort after all.

"I know a way out, but first you got to answer my question."

Her mouth formed an O. "Are you saying you had a key all this time?"

They didn't need a key. She must've forgotten. Every door and window on a steamboat was hung with gravity hinges. He could remove one and they'd be out in no time.

"You haven't answered me yet."

The spunk drained out of her. "Should we be found in here together, I will be ruined. If that is what you want then I think you are the lowest of men."

"Hang it, Hallie, that's not my intention."

"But you threatened that very thing."

"What? I never did."

She stepped back, crossing her arms over her chest, and eyed him with obvious disbelief. "You said you would reveal my secret."

"Your secret? You mean about you not being an artist?" He laughed at his stupidity. "I reckoned you wouldn't do a thing but whitewash that wall and scratch on paper until you could slide off once we got to St. Louis. But that sketchbook proved me wrong."

"That's what you meant?" Surprise flickered across her face and then she closed her eyes, looking mighty relieved.

"What secret did you think I was talking about?"

Her eyes snapped open and her cheeks turned pink. He studied her face, searching for a clue. The only other secret she'd told him was—

Why, he'd be a *dog* to let out that she'd been bedded by Tad's father. It hadn't even occurred to him to betray a confidence like that.

But it had occurred to her. Now he knew for certain what sort of man she thought he was, and it just confirmed what he'd known about himself all along.

He dipped his hand into his pocket and handed her the spectacles.

Even if he wouldn't betray her most embarrassing secret, he'd been looking for ways to get her off the boat. He was lowdown and ornery, not the kind of man a well-bred woman like Hallie could respect. Nor the sort a boy like Tad needed as a father. Just as well, they'd both hate him anyway once he accomplished what he'd set out to do.

From behind him came the click of a lock. The door eased open and Tad stuck his head inside, grinning like he'd landed his first fish. "Ain't you two kissed yet?"

CHAPTER SIXTEEN

"Mr. Finn!"

Huck peered out the side window of the pilothouse. The captain waved from the stage plank. Muttering curses, Huck pounded down three flights of stairs, out of sorts and out of patience. They'd lost the better part of a day sitting at the dock in Sioux City for a little extra freight, and the old man hadn't seen fit to let him know when they were leaving.

Didn't he have enough to worry about, what with Tad acting up and Hallie still smoldering over getting locked in that room with him?

She'd thrown him out as soon as Tad returned with the key. Hadn't even given him a chance to apologize for the trick he'd played on her the night before, for looking at her sketchbook, or for barging into her room. The list of offenses was getting so long that he was losing track.

If she would just meet him halfway, they might reach an agreement they both could live with. He'd be content to put up with her for the remainder of the trip if she'd agreed not to fight him over Tad. He'd even be willing to set it up so she could visit the boy anytime she wanted.

But no, she wouldn't give him a chance. She'd fired the first shot and hadn't stopped loading since.

Captain Kinney met him at the bottom of the stairs. "Mr. Finn, we need to talk."

"What about? Is there a problem?"

"Everything is fine. I had to meet with Lieutenant Colson to finalize our arrangements, and that took a little longer than I expected."

"Who's Lieutenant Colson?"

"He's in charge of the army's contract with the Northwest Transportation Company. The outfit is short on boats. The lieutenant is looking for someone to transport troops and supplies to Fort Sully."

That army outpost was another three hundred miles *upriver* in the Dakota Territory. They were supposed to be headed in the opposite direction.

"That'll add another couple of weeks," Huck pointed out. "We already have goods that need to get to St. Louis."

The old man folded his hands behind him like he didn't care. "We can afford two weeks' delay, given what the army is willing to pay us for our trouble."

Huck lifted his hat and raked his fingers through his hair. Under normal circumstances, he would consider it a boon, as well. Not in this case. "I reckon I told you I need to get back. Got some important business to take care of."

The captain's face rearranged itself into an agreeable expression. "Look here, Huck, I need a pilot who knows the upper river. I'll pay you well if you stay on. Four hundred fifty a week."

"Four hundred fifty?" Huck echoed. That was twice what he normally made for a run like this.

"You heard right, and it's worth it to me," the captain continued. "If we help the army now, it increases my chance of securing a government contract for the next season. You know business is drying up downriver. The money is up here, transporting goods for the army, the miners and the railroads."

Huck forced his mind to reason. The captain was right, and maintaining a reputation as a dependable pilot meant not leaving them high and dry. He could manage Tad for another couple weeks, but he dead sure couldn't remain on a boat with Hallie for a whole month. He had to get shy of the aggravating woman before he went and did something more foolish than kissing her.

An idea came to him for how he might get rid of her. It was so underhanded, so unprincipled, it offended even him. On the other hand, Hallie wouldn't hesitate to do the same if it meant she could get control of Tad. He wrestled his conscience into a chokehold. "I'll make you a deal, sir. I'll stay...if Miss MacBride goes."

That startled the old man. "Why on earth would you want her gone? You need her to watch over your nephew."

Now came the negotiating. "Reckon I can manage with a little help from your wife, and she ought to be willing, seeing as how this extra trip means so much to you."

The captain's brows slashed down and Huck started to sweat. This scheme could explode in his face like one of those homemade handguns. "My Kate has become fond of Miss MacBride. She has her heart set on having that mural painted."

He's right, Hucky. Hallie did strike a deal. She'll be mighty hurt if you do this.

Huck hooked his thumbs in his waistband, refusing to listen to his better self. The captain needed a pilot more than he needed an artist, which meant this was a perfect opportunity to get rid of the problem. "I made my offer. You decide."

A SHORT TIME LATER, THE CLERK CALLED HALLIE TO HIS OFFICE. SHE couldn't imagine what he might want unless he meant to reassign her to make room for the new passengers.

Instead, he informed her she would have to disembark.

She remained in front of his desk and tried not to panic. "The captain agreed that I could paint a mural in exchange for passage to St. Louis. Have you spoken to him?"

The young clerk shifted nervously in his chair. "Yes, I've spoken with him. He is truly sorry. We need every available room for the soldiers we have to transport to Fort Sully. The army pays us well. We can't afford to give up a stateroom to a non-paying passenger."

With a hesitant smile, he slid an envelope across the desk. "The captain instructed me to give you this. It's enough for train fare to St. Louis."

Hallie flushed with embarrassment. What a horrible turn of events, being put off the boat so far from home with nothing more than a pity payment. "What of Mr. Finn?"

"He has agreed to stay on as the second pilot."

Of course. What else should she expect? Huck would take her nephew and head off into the wildest country imaginable without anyone to look after the mischievous boy.

"I cannot believe this," she muttered.

The clerk leaned back as if he feared she might strike him. "Miss MacBride, I am very sorry we could not accommodate you."

Ignoring the envelope, Hallie paced in the small space between the desk and the door. She cared not a whit for money or apologies. What she needed was a place on this boat.

Appealing to the captain, or even Kate, would be pointless. It was a business decision, not a personal rejection. But she could not leave Tad alone with Huck. Her nephew could meet with an accident or Huck might disappear with him.

She halted her pacing. "I will work for deck passage."

The junior officer appeared horrified at the suggestion. "The main deck is no place for a genteel woman traveling alone."

Yes, she knew that. Not only were deck passengers required to provide their own food, they had to jostle for a place to sleep amongst the freight and the rough deckhands.

She gave a sharp nod. "I will make do."

"No, no, I'm sorry." The clerk fumbled with his pencil and his face turned red. He pulled a ledger in front of him. "There is not enough room even on the main deck. It's filled up with freight."

A bell sounded, alerting passengers that the boat was readying to leave.

God help her. She would appeal to Huck, and beg him to reconsider sending their nephew home with her. Promise to take no action against him until they could work things out face-to-face.

Snatching the envelope from the table, she fled out the door— and slammed into a man. The envelope flew from her hand and greenbacks fluttered to the parquet floor.

"Oh! Oh dear, I'm so sorry..." She dropped to her knees to collect the scattered money. *What a wretched day.*

"Good heavens, ma'am. Allow me to help you." The stranger squatted next to her. "I hope you'll forgive me. I didn't realize anyone would be coming out that door."

The man scooped up the last of the bills and offered them to her. He wore a fashionable day coat, not a uniform. He took her hand and helped her to her feet. "It was my fault entirely, Miss...?"

"MacBride," she said, distractedly. She had to find her nephew. Earlier, Tad had been playing by the silver water cooler, but she didn't see him there now. Huck might've rounded him up, knowing this was coming.

"Dan Devol, at your service." The man doffed his hat, revealing straight brown hair slicked into place. His waxed mustache lifted as he smiled. "Are you a passenger? I heard there would be soldiers aboard, not lovely ladies."

Lands, she didn't have time to make small talk with a dandy. She had to find Tad. "I am...I was." She looked down to where he still held her fingers in a light grip and pulled her hand away. "Excuse me, Mr. Devol. There is something that requires my immediate attention. I do thank you for your assistance."

"Aunt Hallie!"

She twisted around at Tad's voice.

He came running through the doors leading into the main cabin with tears streaming down his face, and Huck fast on his heels.

"Aunt Hallie, you can't leave. You got to stay. Please."

She enveloped her nephew in her arms and her heart melted. "I have no intention of leaving you, dearest."

Pinning his pursuer with a hard look, she braced herself for the coming battle. Huck, however, wasn't looking at her.

Surprised flickered briefly over Mr. Devol's face, followed by a broad smile. "Huck Finn! Great Jupiter! As I live and breathe, it *is* you!"

He grabbed Huck's hand, pumping it, then jerked him forward to embrace him with exuberance. "You are a veritable Lazarus, my friend."

Huck appeared dazed after Mr. Devol released him, beaming with obvious delight. "How on earth did you—?"

"Aunt Hallie, tell Uncle Huck you ain't leaving," Tad urged in a loud whisper.

She nodded. This touching reunion could wait. "Pardon us, sir. Mr. Finn and I have important business to discuss. Perhaps you two could visit later?"

The gentleman's pleased expression turned contrite. "Of course. I do apologize if I've interrupted." He eyed Tad with curiosity before he dipped his chin in Huck's direction. "I will be at the bar if you have a moment later. Good to see you alive and well."

As the man strode away, she noted Huck's frown. He seemed less enthusiastic about renewing the acquaintance. He reached for Tad without making eye contact with her. "Let's go, Tadpole. Your aunt has to gather up her belongings. You'll see her later. After we get back."

"No." She hauled her nephew up against her. "Tad will return with me. On the train."

Tad twisted out of her embrace. She tried to catch his arm, but he skittered out of reach and shook his head. "I don't wanna go on the train."

He turned to his uncle and the tears started up again. "I want Aunt Hallie to stay with us. Please, Uncle Huck."

He wasn't crying because he wanted to be with her. He still held out hope that he could match up two of the most mismatched adults on the face of the planet.

"There's no extra room, Tad." Huck rubbed his palms against his trousers in a telling gesture.

Why was he nervous? He wasn't getting thrown off the boat.

Her nephew's lower lip curled out. "She can sleep in your room with me."

Hallie gasped and met Huck's horrified gaze.

"She can't sleep in a room with me," he muttered.

"You ain't even trying!" Tad cried.

Emotions played over Huck's face, as clear as if written on paper—anxiety, then regret, and finally, guilt.

Hallie narrowed her eyes. The clerk's twisted truth, Kate's absence through all of it, and now this scene with Tad. It all added up to one conclusion. Huck had somehow engineered her dismissal. She didn't know how he'd done it, but she would not leave this boat. She might, however, heave Mr. Finn overboard.

She thrust her finger in the direction of a leather chair next to a brass woodstove. "Tad, sit there and wait for me. I need to speak with your uncle. Privately."

Hallie grabbed Huck's coat sleeve. "Come with me—unless you want your nephew to find out how truly *despicable* you are."

CHAPTER SEVENTEEN

Huck grudgingly followed Hallie outside to the crowded promenade deck, fighting a full-fledged headache.

Confound it. He'd arranged things perfectly with Captain Kinney, and it wasn't even a lie, mostly. There were too many soldiers and too few rooms. Everything had worked out all neat and tidy. But then his nephew had melted into tears and wouldn't stop crying, and Hallie had figured it out and blown a gasket. His dead partner showing up out of the blue had thrown another wrench into the gears.

She stopped near an isolated spot along the rail and set into him. "I don't know how you managed it—nor do I want to—but if I am forced off this boat, I will go straightaway and hire a lawyer to begin proceedings against you. I do not doubt once I present my evidence to a judge, he will not hesitate to revoke your rights over that child."

Huck's head felt like a flue being pounded to dislodge built-up sediment. He had trouble concentrating on her tirade. "What are you clattering on about?"

"Need I spell it out?" She held up a finger. "One, you stole a flatboat."

Was she back to that old news?

"I borrowed it, and already arranged for the man to be paid."

"Your distinction will not be appreciated in court." A second finger went up. "You put Tad in danger by keeping him on an island in the middle of a rising river."

"He wasn't in danger and you know it."

"Three. You lied about your ability to pay for my passage, yet failed to provide proper care for a child when you agreed to pilot this craft."

"I did *not* lie, and he never needed—hang it, I can take care of him as well as you."

Once again, she played the self-righteous savior and painted him to be the very devil.

The engines kicked and the platform rumbled beneath his feet. Or was it his temper heating up?

He pointed a finger in her face. "You'd steal away with Tad in a second if you got half a chance. I was willing to talk things over and come to some sort of agreement, but you won't give me the time of day, and I'm tired of dealing with you."

With how red her face turned, he expected she might start breathing fire. "You have never negotiated in good faith."

"Ha! You don't want to negotiate. You want it your way."

"I want what's best for Tad. You seem to have forgotten that." She gripped his lapels and her eyes burned with fury. "No judge in his right mind will support you. You have flouted the law, disregarded your responsibilities, and flagrantly risked a child's safety and well-being."

She was dead set on discrediting him, and now she'd threatened to bring a judge into it. He should've seen that coming. The worst thing for Tad would be a court battle. For the boy's sake, he had to calm down and make her see reason.

He gathered her hands. "Take it easy, now. I want what's best for Tad too, and I'm willing to work things out. But first, you got to promise—"

"Stop it!" She jerked free. "Stop trying to manipulate me and every other person who will not dance to your tune."

Huck's head swelled up like a boiler about to explode. He grabbed her arms and gave her a firm shake. "You're no better than me! Sneaking around, scheming. So you can make me out to be an ignorant, snake-bellied varmint who don't give a damn about anybody but himself."

Behind the round lenses, her green eyes widened. She didn't say a word, just stared at him like she'd been struck dumb—or scared speechless.

What the hell was he doing? He could crush her like nothing without even trying. He was bad as Pap, putting angry hands on a woman like that.

His anger dissolved beneath a flood of regret. He grazed her slender arms with his fingers, needing somehow to communicate that he hadn't intended to hurt her, and would never harm her.

She gazed up at him with sorrow swimming in her eyes.

For the life of him, he couldn't think of a single thing to say. No amount of apologizing would erase what he'd done, mostly because she was inconvenient and troublesome, and made him question his judgment where his nephew was concerned. Even if she was a harpy, she was a woman, and he had no business handling her roughly.

"For God's sake, Hallie," he rasped.

She rested a hand over his pounding heart and her expression softened and became pleading. "Huck, we must call a truce. For *Tad's* sake."

"A truce," he echoed wearily.

"Mr. Finn! Miss MacBride! May I speak with you?" The captain came striding up with Tad in tow.

The boy's eyes were wide and fearful. What trouble had the imp gotten into now?

"Miss MacBride." Captain Kinney dipped his chin. "I've given some thought to our arrangement, and I believe it will be best for all concerned if you take your nephew with you."

What the hell? This wasn't the deal.

She let out a breath, which might've been a laugh or something between between relief and triumph. "Thank you, Captain. I agree."

"Well, I don't agree," Huck said firmly. "Tad's staying with me."

The captain's face darkened in a thundercloud of disapproval. "Mr. Finn, you cannot pilot a boat and mind a child at the same time—and we have no help to spare."

The old man had him over a barrel. He could walk away and ruin his reputation as a trustworthy pilot. Or let Hallie leave with Tad. In which case, he might as well sign over guardianship here and now.

"I won't give up my nephew, but..." He had to give a little. "I reckon Miss MacBride ought to stay aboard."

Captain Kinney shook his head. "Her room is already occupied by another passenger."

Her soft gasp buried itself like a knife in Huck's heart.

"I see. Well then." He curled his hand around her arm and swallowed his pride. "She and Tad can take my room."

CHAPTER EIGHTEEN

The sun had crawled across the sky before Huck turned the wheel over to the captain, grateful as anything to be off his watch even for a few hours. It had plum worn him out trying to focus his attention on the river while his mind kept backing and filling over every mistake he'd made since he'd first clapped eyes on Hallie MacBride.

"Five feet," Huck muttered, giving the captain the last measurement of the water's depth. Normally, he'd know the difference from the previous year, but he had been in the gold fields all last summer. He rubbed his temples, fighting a headache that had persisted through the previous night and into the morning.

The captain tossed him a sympathetic glance. "Ask Mr. Lacey to make up one of his juleps. It always puts me right, especially after an argument with the missus."

"It ain't that," Huck grumbled.

"Of course not," the old man said smoothly. "You did right, letting Miss MacBride stay. Better for the boy, you know. And my steward will keep the young lad too busy to get into more trouble."

Why hadn't Captain Kinney thought of this solution before he demanded that Tad leave with Hallie?

Huck didn't ask because he already knew the answer. It had to do with being a gentleman, something he hadn't shown himself to be by any stretch of the imagination. He owed Hallie a proper apology.

First, he had to sort out something else that was bothering him. Dapper Dan showing up like Jesus. Looking mighty fit and awful surprised to see his old partner.

The reason the gambler might've faked his death stuck like a bone in Huck's craw. He didn't want to believe Dan would've betrayed him, but he wouldn't rest easy until he'd resolved the matter.

Huck trotted down the stairs and ducked into the clerk's deserted office where he found the log book with passengers' names. He ran his finger down the entries until he found the right name next to a number—Hallie's old room.

He heaved an aggrieved sigh. Was God getting back at him for treating her so poorly? More likely, it was the devil's doing, considering who got the room.

He headed across the main cabin and rapped on the door, hard. After a moment, it opened a notch, revealing a slice of the occupant's face.

"Ah, come in," Dan greeted, opening the door and stepping back to allow Huck to enter. "Wasn't expecting you."

"That so?" Huck strolled inside. "I reckoned you would be since you asked me to stop by and visit."

"Yes, I did, didn't I? I suppose I'm still in shock. To be honest, I never thought to see you again. Not on this side of eternity." Devol's face reflected not a flicker of guilt.

Huck had seen his former partner wear that same honest look when he fleeced a miner out of a week's worth of diggings. Then he'd turned around and given the money to a poor woman whose husband had died in a cave-in. Dan had always lived by his own code. Something they both had in common.

"It took me months to get strong enough to come back to work after the attack," Huck informed his former partner.

"Mm, I can imagine. It's a miracle you survived." Dan clapped him on the shoulder and his solemn demeanor gave way to a crooked smile. "Let's not dwell on morbid thoughts. Take a seat and tell me what you've been up to. Have you recouped your losses?"

Huck sank onto a chair with a weary sigh. The stolen money was all Dan cared to talk about. Getting rich had always been high on the gambler's agenda. That didn't necessarily make him a Judas. "I'm doing all right."

Devol crossed to a small mirror hanging above the washstand. He smoothed the mustache that didn't need more smoothing, and fiddled with a winged tie before turning down his collar. Then he slipped his arms through silk suspenders and gave the starched shirtfront a final tug.

Last October, the fellow hadn't had enough yellow dust to buy breakfast, much less a suit of new clothes, after he'd made the mistake of trying to outwit a pack of jackals. That foolishness had cost them their gold and got them both chased out of Montana Territory. Then Dan had gone right back to the tables after they'd reached Kansas.

"Looks like you improved your lot considerable since we laid in at Atchison last fall." Huck offered another opportunity for Dan to explain where he'd gone and why.

"Well enough to get by." Dan sat on the lower bunk and pawed through packages of playing cards. He ruffled a deck then slipped it back into a box.

On the bed lay tin plates the exact size of playing cards, except for being curved in a hair on each side to allow for certain cards to be shaved. Not enough for anyone to notice except a gambler with sensitive fingers. That explained the newfound wealth.

"You're back in the business of marking cards," Huck said.

Dan scooped up the incriminating evidence. "I am in the business of making money. Same as every other red-blooded capitalist in this country."

"Like those frauds selling worthless railroad stock."

"Exactly."

The liquor bottle on the washstand, along with the packs of cards, formed part of a familiar scene. Out in the men's area, the barkeep would carry doctored decks. He'd ply the guests with plenty of liquor while keeping Dan's glass filled with his *favorite* whiskey—flavored water.

"Is that barkeep your new partner?"

"We have an agreeable arrangement. It's not an exclusive one if you're interested in working out your own." Dan tucked the tin plates into a bag and slipped it beneath his bed. Didn't act a bit worried.

"I lost my appetite for gambling." Huck fisted his hand on his knee, annoyed with Dan for treating what happened as if it was no more than a bump in the road. "I thought you were giving up this nonsense after you got haltered by those boys in Montana."

"They didn't succeed in hanging me." Dan shrugged. "Cards are what I know best."

"Cheating is what you know best."

The gambler smiled. "We all have our talents. I like to think Providence gave me mine to teach an important lesson to imprudent men."

Huck let out a huff. Dan's talents were nowhere near divine, but setting a crooked man straight wasn't why he was here. He came up out of the chair and started to pace, too restless to sit still. His old partner hadn't taken the hint, so he'd come right out and ask. "Why did you run off and leave me draining blood like a sieve?"

"Those thieves emptied their guns. I was certain you were a dead man, and I feared they would come after me next." Dan gripped Huck's arm, stopping him in mid-stride. "Finn, I'm sorry. I never would have fled had I thought you lived."

Huck shrugged off the restraining hand. "You could've come back and made sure or gone for help instead of paying that woman to make up a story so you could disappear."

"You were riddled with bullets. Hanging around wouldn't have improved matters. Going after the law would have gotten me killed." Dan's expression was open, regretful, but without a trace of true remorse. "You know as well as I, there are times we must cut our losses."

His *friend* had cut him loose like a trotline caught on a snag.

Huck's face heated. Only a damn fool would've expected loyalty from a cheater. He ought to have known better, having traveled with shady characters before. But he'd thought Dan was different somehow, more like him. Low down and ornery perhaps, but not the kind of man who'd abandon a friend in need.

"I hope you'll accept my apology and we can be friends." Dan extended his hand. "I've missed you."

Taking that hand meant trusting again. Even if Dan hadn't set him up, at best, the gambler was a coward. Not someone who could be counted on.

Huck stuffed his hurt into the box with all the other disappointments in his life and kept his arms at his sides.

Dan dropped his hand with a sigh. He pivoted and reached for his coat, obviously headed to the tables to hunt for easy pickings. "You haven't mentioned anything about that woman, Miss MacBride, and the boy. What's his name?"

"Tad."

Dan slipped his coat on. "Are you traveling with them?"

It was a simple enough question, but the answer was complicated and none of his business anyway. "I'm taking my nephew home. She chose to tag along."

"You don't want her along?"

"No, but I don't see how that matters to you." Huck started for the door.

"It doesn't...unless you would like some assistance with distracting her?"

The unexpected offer stopped Huck in his tracks. "Why do you want to get involved? There's no profit in it for you."

Dan returned a rueful smile. "It's the least I can do."

Huck didn't cotton to the idea of Dan snooping in his business, and he sure as hell didn't want him anywhere near Hallie. "I don't reckon you can help me."

"With a problem involving a woman? Come now, next to cards, distracting ladies is my forte."

Huck snatched the rascal by his lapels. "You don't go nowhere near her."

Dan jerked his coat out of Huck's grip and brushed it off, looking mighty offended. "What was that for? I was only offering to help."

Huck grasped the doorknob rather than Dan's necktie. He wasn't normally so quick to flare up. Lately, he'd been like a powder keg, waiting for somebody to light a match. "Just leave her be. I can manage without your help."

Tad's day hadn't started out good and it wasn't getting any better. He rubbed a polishing cloth over the brass foot rail at the bar, working slowly because he didn't want to get sent back to the kitchen before supper. He'd cleaned plenty of fish and didn't want to clean no more. The steward told him moping weren't helping, but he couldn't stop.

Locking his aunt and uncle in that room should've worked. They were supposed to kiss and get married. Instead, they'd gotten mad at him and yelled at each other, and the captain had tried to send him off with his aunt.

He sniffed and wiped his nose. Uncle Huck would give him away now, for sure.

A gentleman strolled up and asked for a deck of cards from the barkeep. It was the same man who'd hugged Uncle Huck and called him a "Laz'rus"—whatever that was.

His uncle's friend was dressed like he'd walked right out of one of those advertisements in the tailor's shop, right down to the tie with a pin stuck through it. He even had one of them mustaches slicked up at the ends.

He caught sight of Tad watching him and came over. "Hello, young fellow. Tad, is it?"

Tad nodded.

"Name's Devol. Dan Devol. Perhaps your uncle has mentioned me?"

"No sir, he hasn't." Tad swallowed his misery rather than let on that his uncle wasn't talking to him much these days.

Mr. Devol pulled out a chair from one of the empty tables and sat down. As he shuffled a deck of cards, he smiled. "Would you like to see a trick?"

Sure he would, but... Tad shook his head and went back to work. "I can't. I got to polish this 'til it shines."

The gentleman turned sideways in the chair and leaned forward, bracing his arms on his knees so he could study the brass footrest. "Looks shiny enough to me."

Tad got to his feet. "But if I stop, I have to go back to cleaning fish."

"Sounds awful." Mr. Devol wrinkled his nose. Exactly how Tad felt about the matter. "Are they so short on cabin help they need to employ children?"

"I got into trouble. Uncle Huck says I have to work off my punishment if I don't want a cowhiding." Tad hung his head and stared at the floor, not wanting the man to see him tear up. Not for pie would he break down and cry like a baby. He'd done that yesterday and look where it got him.

"What would warrant such a heinous punishment?"

Tad didn't know what *hay-nus* meant. It sounded bad, though. "I locked Uncle Huck and Aunt Hallie in a room together."

The gentleman gave a little cough. "And why did you do that?"

"I wanted them to kiss and get married."

"Didn't work, eh?"

Tad shook his head. "I even tried turning Uncle Huck into a gentleman, like you, but that didn't work neither."

"I imagine not. Tell me, why are you so intent on seeing them married off?"

"Uncle Huck says he can't keep me because he don't have a wife."

Mr. Devol leaned back in his chair, fiddling with the deck of cards. "So you reasoned you would find him one. Miss MacBride being the obvious choice."

Tad nodded eagerly. This man sure figured it out easy enough. Why couldn't his aunt and uncle? "I reckon if they marry then Uncle Huck won't give me away. We can all stay together."

Mr. Devol turned over one of the cards. A joker. "You might as well know, my boy, there are some men who leave no matter what you say or do. Believe me, your uncle knows this as well as I do."

Fear squeezed Tad's chest. That made it sound like there wasn't any hope.

The man fiddled awhile longer with the deck of cards and finally set them aside. "Come closer," he said in a nicer voice. He reached up and tweaked Tad's ear. "Look what I found."

He held up a penny between his thumb and forefinger.

Tad gasped. "Where'd you get that?"

"It was right there, in your ear." The man handed him the penny.

Nobody had pulled money out of his ear before.

"Can you get more?" Tad asked hopefully.

"I wish it were that easy. That's all I have at the moment."

"Hey, I got more'n a penny." Tad dug into his pocket to retrieve the leather pouch, eager to show off a real treasure. He tugged open the strings and felt inside until he found the gold coin. "This here is a real dew-bloon. It's gold!"

He proudly displayed the coin on his palm so his new friend could see.

Mr. Devol took it and turned it over in his fingers to give it a good look. "I've never seen one of these before. It's very old. Where did you find it?"

"Well, it ain't mine, exactly. I'm keeping it for my uncle. It's his treasure."

Mr. Devol chuckled. "*This* is Finn's treasure?"

"It used to be pirate treasure. Then Injun Joe found it and hid it in McDougal's Cave after he kilt his partner. Then he starved to death when he got stuck inside." Shifting from one foot to the other, Tad recited the familiar story he'd been told many times. "Uncle Huck and Mr. Sawyer dug up the treasure, but they was just boys, so the judge had to put it in the bank 'til they got older. Mr. Sawyer collected his half, but Uncle Huck hasn't been back to get his."

Mr. Devol rubbed the coin between his fingers. "Maybe it isn't worth his trouble. A few coins, perhaps?"

"Oh, it's heaps more than a few. They dug up a whole box of them dew-bloons. Mr. Sawyer said it started out to be six thousand but it growed somehow. He told me all Uncle Huck has to do is come home and claim it, and he'll be rich as minus."

"You mean King Midas. He had a great deal of gold."

"Yeah, that's who I meant."

Mr. Devol returned the coin. "I do recall your uncle mentioning this adventure, but the way you tell it is a little different. Are you making this up?"

Tad bounced on his toes, too excited to stand still. "Nuh uh, it's true."

"Does your uncle know his money is still there in the bank?"

"I reminded him, like Mr. Sawyer told me, but he didn't say nuthin' except I should keep this coin safe."

"Some men don't appreciate wealth," Mr. Devol spoke like he was talking to himself. "What happens if Finn doesn't come back to claim it?"

Tad shrugged. "Mr. Sawyer said I get it 'cause I'm his next-akin. But I don't want his treasure. I want to find my own."

"Of course you do. Who wouldn't?" The gentleman cuffed Tad's shoulder in a friendly manner before he leaned forward like he wanted to say something nobody else could hear. "Does your aunt know about the treasure?"

Tad thought for a minute. "I tried to tell her once. She wouldn't listen. Do you think I should tell her again?"

"I suspect your uncle would prefer for you to keep this knowledge to yourself if he instructed you to ensure the treasure's safety."

Uh oh.

Tad put his fingers over his mouth. "Maybe I shouldn't a-told you either. Uncle Huck might get mad at me again."

"Never fear. Your uncle needn't find out, for I won't breathe a word." Mr. Devol winked. "It shall be our secret."

CHAPTER NINETEEN

Music seeped through the thin wall separating the main cabin from the ladies' salon. Lively and uplifting, though not distracting. Just what Hallie needed to keep her mind focused on the mural. She painted with feverish haste, intent on capturing the exquisite image before it faded from her mind.

Just yesterday, a spectacular sunset on the western shore had reminded her of another she'd seen from the banks of the Mississippi years ago. One she'd tried without success to capture on canvas. The sun's fiery breath striking the surface of the water, making it gleam like molten gold.

She used her brush to smear red and yellow together on the palette. Too bright. The newest invention of paint in tubes proved more convenient, but it didn't give her the full range of colors she needed. She would have to experiment with the plants and flowers she'd seen growing along the riverbank.

The real challenge would be depicting the luminescence of the water, and how the light struck it just so. For that, she would use a technique Mr. Bingham had shown her. He was the master at creating luminous river scenes. She, on the other hand, had a long way to go.

"Miss MacBride, may I join you?"

Hallie jerked the brush back, startled by a man's voice. She'd been so focused on painting, she hadn't heard the door open.

The man she had quite literally run into outside the clerk's office poked his head inside the ladies' salon. "Would you enjoy company this afternoon?"

Painting was a task best done alone. Not only that, she didn't wish to encourage Mr. Devol in light of his repeated greetings whenever they passed each other.

She asked a rhetorical question to avoid being rude. "Do gentlemen typically come into rooms reserved for ladies?"

"Not unless we're invited." His hopeful expression made it clear he desired an invitation, and good manners dictated she extend one.

Hallie gave a negligent wave of her brush. "Come in, then. However, I warn you the smell of paint has driven everyone else away. I won't mind if you decide you can't abide it."

There, a polite offer followed by the clear hint she would prefer he not accept.

With a pleased smile, he entered the room. Either he was dense or undeterred, or both.

He gestured to the sofa. "Do you mind if I sit?"

"Do as you please." She turned her attention back to the painting. If she ignored him, he would lose interest and leave.

Huck had denied having any intention of ruining her, but it was clear by his actions he wasn't above using whatever advantage he could find—in this case, an old friend.

"You've captured the river very well. That sunset is magnificent." Mr. Devol's voice came from directly behind her.

She frowned, keeping her gaze on the wall. Should she demand he leave? If her suspicions were unfounded, it would be unforgivably rude. "Thank you, but I have barely started and haven't painted enough of a picture to deem interesting, much less magnificent."

Mr. Devol continued to examine the wall. "Where did you take your training?"

Perhaps if she humored him she would learn his purpose in seeking her out.

Hallie dipped her brush into a cup of turpentine to clean it. "My mother taught me, and I was fortunate enough to receive a few weeks of tutelage under Mr. Bingham."

"George Caleb Bingham?"

She nodded.

"Impressive."

"You are familiar with his work?"

"I should say so. He is quite well known amongst people of quality."

Huck hadn't heard of him before, although one could never accuse him of being *amongst people of quality*. However, he had other admirable traits—most of which he kept to himself when she was around.

"Did you grow up in St. Petersburg? Is that where you met Mr. Finn?"

"No, we met in the gold fields and struck up a friendship, after discovering we had a few things in common."

They couldn't appear more different.

"Pray tell, what would that be?" she asked.

"You wonder, do you?" Mr. Devol crossed his arms as if quite serious, yet his eyes twinkled with humor. "For one, we were both orphaned. We both grew up in small towns along the Mississippi River. And we have a shared appreciation for steamboats. However, he wants to pilot them, whilst I prefer to enjoy the ride."

"Now that you've explained it, your friendship makes perfect sense. A kindred bond exists amongst those who've grown up on the river. My father used to say river water runs through our veins."

"Your father sounds like a wise man."

"He was. He was also a riverboat pilot."

"Ah, that's why you're able to capture the feeling of the river so well." Mr. Devol went back to studying the painting, although it seemed less like an examination of her work than a strategy to continue to engage her in conversation. "I suppose, like you, the river is bred in me. When I was a boy, my father purchased a two-boiler sternwheeler to explore the western rivers. We spent many enjoyable hours hunting and fishing."

"You lived on the steamboat?"

"From time to time." An emotion flickered across his face, but it was gone so quickly she couldn't decide if it was pain or anger or something else entirely. "The *Intrepid* wasn't a large boat, but the cabin was big enough for two."

She knew few men wealthy enough to buy a steamboat—even a smaller one—for leisurely pursuits. "It doesn't sound as though he operated his steamboat for profit."

"A tactful way of putting it. He was rich enough, I suppose. For an English nobleman."

Hallie swallowed a laugh. Mr. Devol had to be embellishing this story for the purpose of impressing a woman who was gullible enough to bite. "Your father was a member of the British aristocracy?"

"Sounds absurd, doesn't it?" He twisted off a ring on his right hand and held it out to her. "My mother gave this to me. It bears his signet."

Hallie examined the ring—it certainly looked authentic—and gave it back. Huck could care less what she thought about his pedigree, which upon reflection, she found refreshing. "What was a British aristocrat doing in America?"

"He was the youngest son of an earl. With three brothers

ahead of him, he had little chance of attaining the title. His father wanted him to go into the church. That didn't suit him, so he collected his inheritance and left home."

"Like the prodigal son?"

"Yes, only this one never fed among the swine. He only rubbed elbows with them." The storyteller's cerulean eyes gleamed as he delivered the witty rejoinder.

Bright, urbane, possessed of a quick wit, as well as fine features, Mr. Devol would set many a lady's heart a-swoon. As for her, she might as well be gazing at a portrait, admiring its qualities but not drawn to its warmth. Unlike her reaction to Huck.

Her enjoyment of the moment fled. Any warmth she sensed in Huck was an illusion. The dratted man was intent on getting rid of her. Now, it was clear he'd sent a Lothario to shred her reputation and get her thrown off the boat.

"Your father doesn't sound like a very responsible gentleman to drag along a wife and child on his adventure." She figured a rude question ought to insult the charmer sufficiently to send him back to Huck.

Mr. Devol picked up her paintbrush and examined it as if she hadn't just insulted him to his face. "He had a peculiar sense of responsibility, that's true. He built a small cottage for my mother on a bluff overlooking the river. That's where I was born and where I lived, except for the times I convinced him to take me along."

This part of the tale seemed too like her own. But Huck couldn't have known enough to tell it because she hadn't shared those details about her childhood. "You said you were orphaned. What happened?"

"When I was eleven, my mother became ill. Shortly after her death, my father returned to England."

"But you were just a boy. Why would he leave you?"

Mr. Devol carefully placed her brush on the table and moved

the cup of turpentine away from the edge. "He had other matters to attend to, and I would have been...inconvenient."

At once his meaning became clear. He hadn't said his parents were married. He wasn't an orphaned heir. Rather, he was an illegitimate son whose father had cast him away like refuse. The story was too wretched to be something he would share to impress a woman.

"Why are you telling me this?"

"This morning, I had a chance to meet your nephew. He's a delightful child. Although I understand he's been causing some trouble. It seems he fears his uncle plans to give him away. Is this true?"

Mr. Devol had sought her out and offered intimate revelations as a way to lead up to a conversation about her nephew. This came as a complete surprise. "You...you are concerned about Tad?"

"I am. My own painful past makes it impossible for me to ignore his tender feelings."

The gentleman's compassion touched her. "To answer your question, yes, it's true. Mr. Finn is Tad's legal guardian, but he has decided to place him with another family."

Mr. Devol shook his head with a rueful twist on his lips. "I am sorry to hear that. I suppose you, as his aunt, will be taking him in?"

"That is my dearest wish, but Mr. Finn will not consent."

"I cannot imagine why." The gentleman appeared genuinely puzzled. "You appear to be an upstanding young woman, and you obviously care for the boy. How could Finn object?"

Given Mr. Devol's childhood, he sympathized with Tad's feelings of abandonment. On the other hand, being a man, he might agree with Huck's reasoning.

"He insists Tad must be in a home with a father as well as a mother."

"Ah, I see. Now it makes sense why Tad believes a marriage between the two of you would solve his problem."

Her cheeks warmed. Heavens, what else had Tad shared?

"That will never happen," she said firmly.

Dan drew his coat back and braced his hands on his hips. His gold brocade vest complemented an immaculate white shirtfront. "I can't say your reaction surprises me. You two don't appear to be well-matched."

"No, not at all." Her traitorous mind recalled the kiss she'd shared with Huck and how she longed for another. Any sane woman would be daydreaming about the attractive gentleman in front of her instead of swooning over a scoundrel. How she wished she could erase her yen for Huck as easily as he could banish her from the boat.

"I can understand why Finn would want Tad to have a father. But a child shouldn't have to be separated from his relations in order to get one," Dan observed.

Enlightened, as well as gentlemanly.

"That is exactly what I've been saying. Tad must remain with his family. I am the only living relative who shares his blood. He needs a mother as much as he needs a father."

"Of course. Every boy needs a mother, and there is nothing to hold you back from marrying, should you find a man worthy of your respect and love." Mr. Devol held her gaze until she grew uneasy.

"Sir, I—"

"Please, call me Dan."

Unease made her shy away. "We are not so well acquainted."

"I hope we shall be." His voice came out low and smooth, not rough and halting, as Huck's became whenever emotions ran high between them.

Why was she making comparisons? She wasn't interested in either man.

Hallie picked up her brush and palette. "Thank you for bringing your concern to my attention. I do appreciate it, but I must get back to work."

"Yes, of course. I'll remain quiet as a mouse." He went to the sofa and took a seat.

She turned her back to him and focused on her work. He'd get the message eventually.

"Miss MacBride, have no fear that I will force my attention on you. You have my utmost respect. I do sincerely hope you will accept my friendship on your nephew's behalf."

For Tad's sake, she would make a deal with the devil. Mr. Devol didn't strike her as having nefarious intent. In fact, if he could influence Huck, she'd be a fool to spurn his assistance.

"Sir, if you truly care about Tad then go to your friend, Mr. Finn. Plead with him to let me have the child. Perhaps he will listen to you."

"Be assured I shall. What will you do if he is not swayed?"

Despite his assurances, Mr. Devol had declared himself Huck's friend, and anything she said might be shared. She would remain cautious and reveal no more than what she'd already made clear.

"That will be for the courts to decide."

WHILE HALLIE PAINTED, HUCK LINGERED OUTSIDE THE DOOR TO THE kitchen galley where his nephew leaned over a basin, up to his elbows in fish guts.

The poor little fellow had been cleaning the day's catch, as well as scouring pots, lugging wood, peeling potatoes, and every unpleasant task the boat's steward could dream up.

"I can't stand this much longer," he muttered under his breath. "Especially if he keeps looking at me with them big brown eyes a-pleading for mercy."

Mr. Lacey didn't crack a smile, but his black eyes sparkled with amusement. "Don't fret, Mr. Finn. A little hard work ain't yet killed a boy."

That remained to be seen. This sure wasn't the kind of adventure Tad had been promised.

Huck rubbed his chin, debating the wisdom behind such a harsh punishment. His pap had whipped him regular but had never worked him this hard.

The weary child lugged the basin out the back door. He'd dump the smelly pile of fish parts into the river and then come back for more. Cook was hard-pressed to keep up with meals for a boatful of hungry soldiers, so the fish-cleaning job would be unending.

"Ease up on him a little," Huck instructed the steward. "I'll be back to fetch him later."

He strode away, determined to return soon and rescue the poor child. In the meantime, he'd put off his apology to Hallie long enough. Besides, she had asked for a truce and they needed to spell out the terms—other than him giving up his bed.

Upon entering the main cabin, he passed the men's domain, marked off with swags of velvet-cased rope. The area brimmed with soldiers who were drinking and smoking and playing cards. Surprisingly, Dan wasn't around. Was he waiting 'til those boys in blue got drunk enough not to notice his shenanigans?

Huck shook his head and kept on going. Every riverboat had its gamblers. A sign posted over the bar warned patrons to play cards at their own risk. He wasn't getting paid to pass judgment or warn heedless fools. He had bigger fish to fry.

He moved closer to the wall to avoid disrupting a group of musicians who had set up to play for the afternoon's entertainment. The few women on board, mostly wives of officers, had gathered in chairs to listen to the fiddlers. They'd probably been run out of the ladies' salon while Hallie painted.

As he reached the glass doors, he pulled up at a familiar drawl coming from inside.

"I do admire you, Miss MacBride."

By God, he'd told that rascal Dan to stay away from Hallie. Why was he bothering her?

Huck shoved the door open and entered without waiting for an invitation.

Hallie stood in front of the mural, holding her artist's tools. Her face reddened like she'd been caught doing something naughty. Just how much trouble could she get into with a brush in her hand?

"What's wrong?" she asked. "Is Tad all right?"

"He's fine. Mr. Lacey is keeping him busy." Huck shot a glare at Dan, who lounged lazily on the sofa as if he had the right. "What are *you* doing here?"

The gambler returned an unconcerned smile. "Miss MacBride and I were having a conversation. It's refreshing to find a lady well-versed in literature and the arts."

Huck gave a disbelieving snort. The only *art* he'd ever heard the gambler comment on was a picture of a naked woman hanging over a bar. "I didn't reckon you appreciated culture. You never mentioned it before."

"There are a great many things I didn't mention, knowing you had no interest in them."

And Dan didn't have no interest in spinsters, so what was he doing in here? Sticking his nose where it didn't belong.

"Gentlemen, please." Hallie motioned to the partly painted wall. "I have work to do."

"I need to talk to you." Huck pointed at Dan then jerked this thumb over his shoulder. "Outside."

"Very well." The gambler rolled to his feet and sallied out the door with a straight face. "I'll see you at dinner, Miss MacBride."

Hallie had already gone back to painting. Whether she heard him or not, he wouldn't be seeing her at dinner or any other time.

Huck stalked him through the main cabin outside to the promenade deck. They passed clumps of soldiers standing around, smoking and talking.

Dan continued on to an unoccupied spot at the rail. He rested his arms and set his sights on the endless prairie rolling by, the same scenery that would stretch on for days until they reached the fort. "Was there some greater purpose behind your rudeness?" he asked coolly.

Huck adjusted the brim of his hat to shade his eyes from the setting sun. "She's not out here, so you can quit acting like lord of the manor."

"Ah. You were trying to reinforce her low opinion of you."

"Don't get uppity on me. I don't want you sniffing around after Hallie."

"Sniffing around?" With a chuckle, Dan straightened and soft-punched Huck's arm. "Finn, have I told you how much I've missed your earthy repartee?"

Huck returned a stony stare.

Dan didn't stop smiling. "Aren't you the least bit interested in what she confided?"

Hallie had confided in him already?

Dad-blamed womanizer.

Huck gripped the rail. It was that or fling the snake overboard. "What did she say?"

"She's determined to gain custody of your nephew, and plans to take you to court."

"I know that."

"Then I assume you are also aware that Tad has been playing matchmaker, which is why he locked you in that room."

"Hallie said all that?" Huck couldn't believe she'd reveal something she was so keen to keep secret.

"She didn't have to. Your nephew told me."

What was the sneaky devil doing cozying up to Tad?

Huck fisted his hands at his side. He'd give this rascal one more chance. "I already told you I don't want your help. Leave 'em both alone."

Dan slid his arms across his chest and leaned against the rail with a posture that conveyed unconcern. "My friend, you may not need my help, but it seems your nephew does."

"So you reckon you ought to attach yourself like tick?" Huck forced himself to calm down. He didn't think straight when he got riled up. Maybe Dan did feel sorry for Tad. It was easy enough to like the boy. He'd soften even the hardest heart. "Just so you know, I got a good family picked out. Tad'll be better off with them."

"Why not let Miss MacBride raise him?"

Shouldn't come as any surprise that Hallie would recruit even Beelzebub to her cause rather than deal fairly with him.

"Tad needs a pap, not some prickly woman set on civilizing him like a lap dog."

"She doesn't strike me to be as bad as you make her out to be."

"No, she ain't bad, that's not what I'm saying." Actually, he had said something like that. "Miss MacBride is a good woman, don't get me wrong, and I know she means well, But Tad needs more than just a ma."

"If she finds a husband, your problem is solved. Tad will have a father and a mother."

"A husband? Who's she going to...?"

Dan's smile broadened.

Huck's temper soared. "*You're* not thinking of marrying her."

"Why not?"

"*Why not?*" Huck started counting to ten but made it only to three. "Why, you're no better than me. You lie and cheat and run off when things get tough. You said yourself you've never stayed with a woman more than two weeks."

"A man can change."

It didn't make a lick of sense why Dan, all of the sudden, got it into his head he wanted to settle down—and with Hallie and Tad no less. The two of them together didn't have enough custom to keep a gambler flush for a year, much less a lifetime. And he'd quickly relieve them of what they did have.

"A man like you can't change that much," Huck insisted.

"He can if he's got a good enough reason." Dan once again rested his arms on the rail. He'd lost the smile. "Finn, I know you consider me a coward for not coming to your aid. And I'll admit I wasn't the kind of friend I should've been. But that business in Atchison shook me up."

"You went right back to gambling."

"Because that's what I know, and I didn't see another option." Dan stared out at the western horizon as if the answer might be found out there. "Truth be told, I've grown weary of this constant wandering. Meeting your nephew and Miss MacBride made me realize I still have a chance to turn my life around. Settle down. Find a wife, have a family. I understand you might not feel the same, and I commend you for recognizing your limitations, but don't tar me with the same brush."

A yearning pulled at Huck from a place deep down inside. For as long as he could remember, he'd never had a proper family, never felt like he belonged anywhere. He'd been told he was born bad. It was in his blood and there weren't a thing he could do about it. But if a scamp like Dan could change his ways, why couldn't he?

If he chose to keep Tad, he'd have to marry and settle down. Give up his freedom. The restlessness that gnawed at him would get worse and eventually turn him mean. Just like his pap. Then he'd run off, leaving behind the human wreckage that came from destroying hopes and dreams.

"You look like you could use a smoke." Dan slid his hand into his pocket. "Cigar?"

Huck shook his head. He preferred his pipe, and his former friend knew it.

The tip of the cigar burned bright orange as Dan lit it and gave a few puffs. "I've heard news of another gold strike in Montana, up near that place we staked out. Would you consider going back?"

"You trying to get rid of me?"

"Of course not." Dan blew a smoke ring into the air. "I just thought it might interest you. You always were up for an adventure, as I recall."

"This pilot's job is adventure enough." No sooner were the words out of Huck's mouth than he realized it was true. Maybe it was his age, or coming close to dying, but he had no desire to set off on another treasure hunt.

Hearty laughter drew his attention to a group of soldiers who'd come out onto the deck. They called, waving Dan over, eager for a game with the friendly but inept, Mr. Devol, whose money now lined their pockets. Dan's age-old strategy, lose enough to boost a fool's confidence.

"I am being summoned." Dan smiled and returned the wave. "You give some thought to what I said. Miss MacBride would make a good mother, and it would save you from having to stick around for months, battling her in court."

Dan sallied off in the direction of the soldiers. Those fellows wouldn't be so pleased when the *unlucky* gent suddenly developed an astonishing winning streak—just as they were due to reach Fort Sully.

No, Dan would never change. He was a born swindler, and yellow to boot. Despite what he said, he wouldn't settle down, especially with a woman who couldn't bankroll him for the rest of his life. However, he wouldn't think twice about seducing her and taking whatever she had.

Hallie might not know this. But she might believe if she snagged herself a husband, she would have a stronger case to make for custody of Tad.

Huck jerked off his hat and fanned his face. Blast it, she was smarter than that. She'd been betrayed by Tad's rascally pap, and ought to be able to see past Dan's fine clothes and dandy manners. Had to be because she was getting desperate.

What could be done?

The answer settled on Huck's soul with the weight of an anchor. He didn't have to trick or elude her or even distract her to win this battle. All he had to do was stay out of the way. If Hallie weren't careful, she'd find her reputation ruined and her hoped-for husband long gone. Then, no judge in the land would consider her fit to raise a child.

CHAPTER TWENTY

Hallie applied a careful brushstroke to shade a section of water she'd been working on. She paused to roll her shoulders and ease the tightness.

For the past two days, she'd been painting every moment she wasn't with her nephew. She'd declined Mr. Devol's invitation to join him for the evening's entertainment so she could work on the mural while Tad stayed with his uncle.

Tad had begged to go up to the pilothouse before bedtime. Huck declared he didn't mind the child's company even when he was still on duty. For a man who claimed to have no paternal instincts, he exhibited surprising patience and tenderness with their nephew.

Unfortunately, those same qualities didn't extend to his dealings with her. Except for when they'd been locked in that room together. His gentleness had surprised her. Then, he'd tried to get her thrown off the boat. When that didn't work, he'd called out the only man who'd shown an interest in her.

She rinsed her brush with angry swirls. Lands, he was difficult to decipher. She might've guessed jealousy if it were anyone other than Huck. Besides, she had no intention of becoming romantically involved and had told both men as much.

Dan respected her wishes and agreed to friendly companionship for the duration of the journey. She enjoyed their conversations, and, even better, she didn't have to deal with Huck. He left every time Dan showed up.

On the other hand, he hadn't given an inch when it came to Tad. He would be a formidable adversary if they ended up in court, and her friendship with a riverboat gambler wouldn't be much help. She needed a trusted ally.

Taking a step back, she eyed her progress with satisfaction. The painting was coming along nicely, and she would finish well before they docked in St. Louis in two weeks. Hopefully, Kate and Captain Kinney would be pleased.

The sounds of music and laughter drifted in from the main cabin as the glassed doors opened and the captain's wife slipped in.

Kate wrinkled her nose. "Whew."

"The smell is strong, I know." Hallie gestured at the transom windows along the ceiling. "I've opened them for ventilation."

"Never mind. I'll get used to it." Kate approached and examined the panel. "I love what you've done so far."

This splendid room, with its bright Brussels carpet and ornate rosewood furniture, served as a perfect setting for the scene Hallie had chosen. The *Hesperia* wending its way past towering bluffs on a watery mirror that reflected the glorious bronzes and vivid reds of a setting sun.

"How do you make the water look so...well, like water?" Kate asked.

"Translucent darks and opaque lights."

"You make it sound easy."

"It's a simple enough concept. Difficult to execute." Hallie finished rinsing her brushes and wiped them off.

She'd sketched a collection of images for inspiration, but the mural had come mostly from her imagination. Hearing Kate's praise went a long way toward easing her doubts about her ability to bring her vision to life. "I didn't have all the colors I needed, so I mixed up a few of my own."

Kate eyed Hallie's palette. "How do you manage that?"

"Using whatever is at hand: flowers, plants, even a bit of rust off the boiler. That gave me a nice russet tone, close to the shade of Huck's hair." Oh, that was unfortunate slip of the tongue. "Or your hair."

Her sponsor's titian brows formed an inquisitive arch. "My hair isn't brown."

"I was just giving you an example. I'm not painting anyone's hair."

The captain's wife was gracious enough to let it pass. Actually, she was more than gracious. She'd been encouraging and caring. Also, she'd raised children. Who would understand better than a mother?

Hallie warmed to the idea of recruiting Kate's help. "Do you have a moment? There is something I would like to discuss of a delicate nature. I'm certain you'll understand."

Kate took a seat on the sofa, her eyes bright with curiosity. "You can trust me to keep your confidence."

"I know." Hallie sat in a bolstered chair. "You are aware of Mr. Finn's attempt to have me removed from the boat?"

The captain's wife appeared chagrined. Offending her hadn't been the plan.

"I'm sorry, that's not what I meant to—"

"No, don't apologize." Kate waved it off. "You have every right to call me out. I am ashamed of what my husband agreed to, but... We'll talk more later. Go on with what you were saying."

Thank goodness. Now, to proceed with more tact.

"What you may not know is that Huck and I are at odds over

our nephew's future. He wants to give Tad away to friends of his whilst I believe my nephew should remain with me."

"Yes, of course, that child should be with you. Why would Mr. Finn think otherwise?"

Hallie leaned forward, encouraged by Kate's reaction. "Huck was named as Tad's legal guardian, but he doesn't want him."

Untrue. Despite his insistence to the contrary, Huck showed every indication of becoming increasingly attached to Tad. Another reason to act fast and decisively.

"He's decided he isn't fit to raise a child," she restated. "But he took an immediate dislike to me. I have tried everything to convince him that I am the right person to raise Tad, but he will not be swayed. I fear he may attempt to discredit me if we go to court."

"I did wonder why he was so anxious to see you leave."

Hallie rubbed her hands together to warm them. "Will you help me come up with a strategy?"

"A strategy? You make it sound as if you are waging war."

"I might as well be. Huck has turned it into one."

"He has, has he?" Kate reached toward the coffee table and picked up a caste miniature of a steamship. "I agree that he treated you abominably in his attempt to have you removed from the boat. However, I have never heard of a pilot giving up his berth."

"He had no choice, once your husband told him I would be leaving with Tad."

"But if he had a cruel nature, he would not have offered his own bed, nor would he be moved by a weeping child."

Kate's observations unsettled Hallie. True enough, Huck had a soft spot when it came to Tad, but he cared nothing for her comfort. Perhaps he'd offered his berth out of guilt. Or more likely... "Worry moved him," she said firmly. "Especially after I threatened to start proceedings against him. He cannot decide the bigger threat. Keeping me close or sending me away."

"I suspect you are formidable, regardless," Kate said in a teasing tone.

"I could be more formidable if I had someone willing to stand beside me," Hallie returned, in all seriousness. "Even with the evidence I've amassed of Huck's negligence, I am still vulnerable. He may twist things I shared with him to show me in the worst possible light. I would be most grateful if you would be willing to testify to how I have comported myself whilst in your employ."

Kate returned the tiny boat to the table. "Hallie, dear, tell me something. Do you want what is best for Tad?"

"Of course I do. How could you doubt it?"

"So does Mr. Finn, I believe."

Hadn't her friend just said that Huck had behaved abominably, and now she was defending the wretch? "I don't deny that he *thinks* he knows what is best."

The older woman gave Hallie a look of sympathy. "It is obvious to me that you *both* want what is best for Tad. Why not consider what a future might look like together?"

Her suggestion was so preposterous, it rendered Hallie mute. Tad would certainly approve, but...a future with Huck? Was such a thing possible or even desirable?

Shivers danced across her skin. Hallie gripped the arms of the chair, alarmed at her body's assent. Despite her attraction to him, he was the worst match in every way she could conceive—ill-mannered, uneducated, not to mention unconventional in the extreme. Even if she could look past his rough edges, he wasn't the type to settle down.

"No," she stated emphatically.

Kate shifted forward on the sofa with a determined set to her jaw. "Hear me out before you rush off to continue your private war. That child is reason enough to consider the possibility of becoming a family. Anyone can see Tad loves both of you and wants you all to be together."

Tears stung behind Hallie's eyelids. She desperately needed Kate's support, yet she had to be honest and forthright about the situation. "You are right in saying Tad adores his uncle, but he doesn't harbor the same tender feelings for me. I am merely a convenient mother."

"How can you say that?" Kate's voice conveyed disbelief.

Only because she didn't know the whole story.

"His uncle cried off on keeping him by saying something about not being married. Tad believes if he can find Huck a wife—any wife—then all will be well." Lands, it hurt to admit she had made so little progress with Tad. Perhaps Kate would know what to do. "What is wrong with me, that I cannot win the heart of such a sweet, loving child?"

The compassion in her friend's eyes made Hallie feel worse than ever. "But don't you see? Tad chose *you*."

"Not because he loves me. He chose me because he thinks he needs a mother."

"My dear, in a little boy's mind, they are the *same*."

Hallie's heart trembled with hope. If what Kate said was true, she might yet have something to build on beyond Tad's desire to see his uncle wed.

"Believe me, I have raised three sons," Kate continued confidently. "I know how boys think, and it's not complicated. If you love that child, he will love you back."

"I hope you are right. That will help my cause considerably."

Kate frowned. "I am not saying this to aid you in some campaign against Mr. Finn. Your continued fighting will tear the poor child apart. And you must consider, Tad needs a mother *and* a father."

Advice from a *married* woman.

"You don't understand. Huck despises me. He thinks I am a calculating shrew, a cold-hearted, dried-up old maid." Her voice cracked on the last two words.

God help her, she didn't feel old and dried up. She'd never felt so alive and young as when she was with Huck. When his lips had moved over hers, hungry and seeking, something inside her came alive. But he had only kissed her to humiliate her, even if it hadn't felt that way.

"Mr. Finn doesn't look at you as if he believes those terrible things." Kate's expression softened. "Perhaps he is afraid. Men have a hard time showing their feelings."

"Huck isn't afraid—" Hallie stopped short of admitting she was the one who was terrified of being vulnerable.

Kate clasped her hands together. "Listen to me, Hallie. You and Mr. Finn have more in common than you want to admit. Both of you are river born and bred. You both love Tad. I truly believe you could make a life together. If you want it."

Hallie started shaking her head before Kate finished. While the idea of marrying Huck held some appeal. It also scared her to death. "I know you mean well. But I'm not willing to risk putting our lives into his hands."

She rose from her seat and took up her brush and palette. As she stared at the mural, she was tortured by how incomplete it looked. Something was missing in the painting. In her life, as well.

"You said you want what is best for Tad," Kate reminded her.

Hallie touched up a spot she'd been working on. Maybe she was being too stubborn and letting fear rule her. Tad would benefit from having a father, and if marrying Huck was the best she could do, she had to at least consider it.

Would Huck? She sensed he was lonely and hungry for love. Yet, he avoided intimacy and denied he wanted a family. Instead, he ran after freedom, adventure, and even danger. Like her father.

Her hand trembled. She yanked the brush away before she ruined the painting. Her poor mother had fooled herself into believing a man afflicted with wanderlust would make a reliable partner. "I'm not certain Huck would support a family."

"He certainly makes enough as a pilot to support one," Kate countered. "How rich does he need to be?"

Hallie dipped the tip of her brush in the russet tone she'd mixed. "What I mean is, he never stays long in one place. He's a wanderer. An adventurer. And he readily admits he would not be a good father."

"Maybe no one has ever told him he can be." A rustling of skirts came from behind, and a moment later, Kate rested her hand on Hallie's shoulder. "All I am saying is, consider the possibility. Mr. Finn could be a good husband and father—with a little help."

Hallie's heart trembled. "I might believe it, if he hadn't betrayed me."

"If you made mistakes you regretted, wouldn't you want to be given a second chance?"

Perhaps Huck deserved a second chance. She wasn't sure she did. She'd dreamed of finding a husband who was as good a man as her father, except without his itchy feet. Instead, she'd trusted a rogue, and look where that had gotten her.

CHAPTER TWENTY-ONE

Flickering lanterns on poles mounted to the bow cast long shadows from three men doing business on the shore. Huck watched from the pilothouse window as the hawkers were paid for the wood.

Fortunately, he'd remembered this spot where an old Indian and his son sold fuel to passing steamboats. Otherwise, the crew would've had to forage. Not a smart thing to do in what the Sioux considered to be their territory. But this stretch of beach was a safe enough place to put in for the night.

"Mr. Finn." The oil lamp hanging from the ceiling illuminated a man's face and uniform. Lieutenant Colson, the officer in charge of all these soldiers.

"Yes, sir?" Huck said politely. "What can I do for you?"

"Why are we stopping here? Those men out there, the ones who brought the wood. They're Indians."

"You're right," Huck drawled. "They are."

The officer's frown deepened. "I've been told that one of their tricks is to send someone out with wood to lure steamboats to shore so they can attack."

"It's happened a few times," Huck conceded. "But as I told your men, I know these two fellows. Done business with 'em before. And this stretch of shore is wide open. There's nowhere for a group of warriors to hide. If we do happen to encounter unfriendly natives, we've got artillery on board, and your boys have plenty firepower. We can defend this boat."

"Why can't you keep going? Your captain said the fort is only a few hours away. It would make more sense to dock there."

"It's dark, sir," Huck explained patiently.

"You can't steer this boat at night? Other pilots don't seem to have that problem." The lieutenant stood so stiff and straight he might have a steel rod down the back of his coat. Or maybe that rod was shoved up his ass. Ever since they'd left Sioux City, he'd been annoying the crew with an unending list of demands, as if the army owned the boat.

Huck kept his tone friendly. "Which pilots would you be talking about, the ones on the Mississippi?"

"Aren't they the best?"

"They'll suit well enough for *that* river. This one's not the same. A Missouri River pilot has to be able to see to navigate around obstacles that change by the hour. Sandbars, snags, whirlpools. Can't see 'em at night."

"If we remain here, we risk being attacked by one of those bands of Sioux."

"Frankly, sir, I prefer to take my chances with them."

The officer gave a curt nod. "I'll speak with your captain. Good evening, Mr. Finn."

Captain Kinney wouldn't give a damn about Colson's opinion. He didn't pilot the boat.

"Good evening to you, sir," Huck said pleasantly. "Come back anytime."

He heaved an irritated sigh after the officer had left. The officer's concern wasn't unfounded, given the army's problems with the natives. What was more annoying was the man's assumption that the pilot was so ignorant and irresponsible that he'd risk the boat and its passengers without reason.

But you're plenty willing to put Hallie at risk with a rat.

Blamed conscience. It had been chewing on him ever since he'd overhead Dan ask Hallie to a dance at the fort. So what if she went with him?

She needs to be enlightened.

By gum, Hallie was a grown woman and ought to know better than to let that scoundrel put his hands on her, even if it was just to dance. She was so anxious to get married and gain custody of Tad, she let it blind her to what Dan was after.

Huck grabbed his coat and hat and headed out the door. He didn't have time to debate himself. He had to fetch Tad while they were docked.

Tromping down the stairs, he passed the officers' quarters on his way to the aft section where the cabin help bunked. After he'd given up his space to Hallie, the captain had told him he could share a room with the steward. Maybe the old man thought to punish him for treating Hallie so poorly. If so, it wasn't much of a punishment. He didn't give a damn where he slept, as long as he had a clean bed, and the steward had been good-natured about it.

Huck opened the door to the room and snuck his head inside. Tad lay curled up on his bunk, sound asleep. Waiting for him, no doubt.

On the lower bunk, the steward sat hunched over buffing his boots in the candlelight. He'd taken a shine to Tad, which wasn't surprising considering how friendly the boy was to everybody. What was more astonishing was how much Tad liked the old fellow, regardless of how hard the man worked him. It was worth remembering, a firm hand on the reins applied with kindness wouldn't rasp on a boy but instead, earn his respect.

"You mind watching him awhile longer?" Huck whispered. "I need to see if his aunt's ready to take him."

Mr. Lacey gave a wave. "Go on. He's no trouble when he's sleepin.'"

Weren't that the truth? Tad could be downright angelic with his eyes closed.

Huck shut the door as quietly as he could. If he could hire the old steward to watch his nephew for the remainder of the journey, he wouldn't need Hallie's help.

She might need yours.

That stubborn woman didn't need his help, and she didn't want his advice or anything else he might offer. She wouldn't ask for his assistance if the boat caught fire.

But he wouldn't sleep a wink if he didn't warn her about the dangers of trusting a swindler in a starchy suit.

He rattled down the stairs to the second level and strode through the doors leading into the main cabin. The bar was packed with soldiers. As expected, Dan had commandeered a table where the chips were piling up. Huck hardly spared the game a glance and continued through the cabin to the glass doors, where he heard Mrs. Kinney's voice.

No telling how long the captain's wife might be in there.

Huck heaved a sigh, resigned to being rude and annoying both of them. He had to talk to Hallie before Dan made his next move. He pushed the door open a crack. "Excuse me, ladies."

"Do come in," Mrs. Kinney called out.

Huck snatched his hat off and stepped inside.

The captain's wife, who occupied the sofa, turned a smile on him. "Mr. Finn, what a nice surprise."

Hallie bolted up out of a cushioned chair like she was the one surprised. Smudges of yellow, brown and red marred her fingers and stained her apron.

"Are you off your watch already?" She nabbed a shawl draped over the back of the chair. "I should get Tad to bed."

He snagged her arm as she barreled past. "Hold your horses. Tad's fine. He's tucked into my bunk, and Mr. Lacey is watching him. I want a word with you."

Behind the glass lenses, her eyes widened. "What about?"

"It's a private matter." He caught a whiff of linseed oil. He'd never thought of the smell as particularly arousing, until now. Startled by his reaction, he released his grip on her arm.

Mrs. Kinney stood and shook out her skirts. "I believe I need to check with the cook about tomorrow's menu." She whisked past them, pausing at the door. "Miss MacBride, you will give some thought to my advice, won't you?"

The blood drained right out of Hallie's face.

Had the captain's wife suggested Hallie shoot him and throw him overboard? Mrs. Kinney had been none too pleased when he'd tried to get her artist put off the boat. Though she didn't seem angry anymore.

Hallie twisted the end of her shawl like it was a washrag. Something had her all worked up and it wasn't because she'd lost track of time.

"You all right?"

"I'm fine." She wouldn't meet his eyes.

He hesitated, uncertain. He hadn't thought through how he was going to get her to trust him enough to listen to his warning. He couldn't just up and tell her to be careful not to get seduced. She'd slap him silly. "You want to step outside for some fresh air?"

Her chin jerked up. "No, I do not."

Huck clamped down on a rush of impatience. They hadn't been on speaking terms for days, so he couldn't expect her to step out with him on command.

Maybe complimenting her on that mural would loosen her up.

He strolled over, prepared to feign interest. He didn't have to pretend. "Hey, this is good."

"Thank you," she replied in a tone that told him she didn't give a hoot what he thought.

Restraining a smile, he returned his attention to the mural. The paint shone wet where she'd been working on a rocky bluff. The dark, silky river glided along beneath. She'd caught the reflection of the sunset on the water just right, only…

"This here looks like the Mississippi, near where I grew up."

Hallie came up beside him. "What makes you say that?"

He was sorry he'd said anything when he saw how worried she looked. "No reason. It's a good painting."

True enough, it was magnificent, even if it did resemble the wrong river.

"I mean, it's not supposed to look just like the thing, right? It's more an improvement." He was digging himself a deeper hole, if her frown was any indication.

"I am not attempting to improve on nature, only reflect it as it is meant to be seen. Tell me what I'm doing wrong." Her tone and expression became anxious.

He could say he was mistaken and be done with it. But she'd know he was lying and wouldn't listen to anything else he had to say. Turning back to the painting, he studied it.

The difference between the two rivers was clear enough to him, but how did he explain it?

"Well, there's times the Missouri is still and quiet, like what you painted here, but that's not a steady thing." He struggled for the right words. "This big muddy river ain't shiny and still. It's always a-churning with dirt and debris from chewing up the land and spitting it out. Just when you think you got it mastered, it'll sneak up on you. Poke a snag in your hull, or suck you into a whirlpool, or lure you into shoal water. It's more unpredictable than a wild donkey. And where the two rivers meet up, the mighty

Mo tumbles into the Mississip', kicking up such a fuss it changes the Old Man. Turns him into a different river all the way down to N'Orleans."

Huck straightened up and waited for her to respond.

She didn't say a word, just kept looking at him and back at that picture.

His spirits sank into his boots. He'd made a fool of himself or offended her, neither of which he'd come here to do. "Don't pay me any mind. You're doing a fine job. The smell in here is giving me a headache. Can we step outside?"

Her face paled a little, but she nodded and slipped past him when he opened the door. Once outside, he led her up the stairs to the uppermost deck. Here, they'd have more privacy, but not so much as to start tongues a-wagging.

He stopped alongside the pilothouse and pulled off his hat to let the breeze dry the sweat on his scalp. Hang it, she hadn't stopped looking at him like she was studying some strange creature. Why had he opened his mouth and commented on that painting anyhow? He'd been hunting easy water and got saddle-bagged instead.

The clouds cleared and a full moon turned the prairie silver, setting the coyotes to yipping and yapping like miners who'd struck a new vein. The old slaves had claimed that a full moon worked magic. If so, he could use a little right now.

"Hallie, I didn't mean to...what I was trying to say in there... Well, you're no slouch when it comes to painting."

The light glinting off her glass lenses made it impossible to see her eyes. He could see her mouth, though, and her lips weren't pressed tight like she was aggravated. They curved up just a little.

"I had no idea you were so poetic."

Poetic? Him?

"You ought to hear me sing."

Her soft laugh relieved him. Now that he'd mounted this first reef, the rest would go easier.

She stood still as anything and gazed out over the water. "What you said about the river, I want to capture that. The ferocity and restlessness of this river, and its untamable nature."

"Was that what I said?"

"Oh yes, and you said it beautifully."

Her response triggered a warm glow inside and made him want to do more than just tell her about the river. "There's plenty of things you can learn once you get to know it better."

He wasn't just talking about a river, and she was going to figure that out right quick if he weren't careful. What had gotten into him anyhow? One little word of praise, and he was panting to please her.

Moonlight whitewashed her face and shimmered on her dark hair. She glowed like one of those bright fairies his ma had told him stories about. Drawn by a fascination he couldn't resist, he lifted a stray curl off her cheek and fondled its silky texture. "You got the handsomest hair," he murmured. "Never seen the like."

Her lips parted in an expression somewhere between surprise and anticipation. The look of a woman who wanted to be kissed.

He grappled with a feverish urge to haul her up and cover that soft mouth with his. He yearned to touch her, but he'd promised not to do anything that would stain her reputation. Reining in his hunger, he stepped back—and bumped up against the outer wall of the pilothouse.

The way she took to studying him made his skin go shivery, as though she'd trailed her fingers over his body.

No other woman had affected him like this one. He longed to take her into his arms and cart her off to some place they could shut out the rest of the world. That would be a mistake. The world would crowd in eventually, and she'd figure out he didn't belong.

She up and closed the space between them, placing her

fingertip to his breastbone, leaning in so close he could feel her soft breath on his chin. "Why did you bring me out here?"

A SURGE OF FEMININE POWER FLOWED THROUGH HALLIE AS SHE HELD Huck in thrall with the tip of her finger. Perhaps Kate had been right and he was simply having a hard time expressing what was in his heart. She wasn't quite ready to consider a proposal, but they would get nowhere if he refused to acknowledge his interest in her.

"The truth," she demanded.

"I been telling the truth," he rasped. "You got to be careful around Devol."

"Dan?" She backed away, confused. This moonlight interlude had nothing to do with Dan Devol. Huck had been about to kiss her. The sensual heat rolled off him in waves.

Then again, if he'd brought her up here to woo her, why was he inching along the wall of the pilothouse like a trapped animal? He stepped over a piece of trim work, as if putting that short partition between them would somehow keep him safe.

The big lout. He'd lured her up here, not the other way around.

"You're saying you brought me up here to warn me about another man."

"That's right. You need to steer clear of Dapper Dan. He's not what he's putting on to be, no matter what he says."

"Not what he—" She realized with a shock what Huck was saying—or not saying—and her confusion evaporated in a rush of anger. He was up to his old tricks again. "You *sent* that man after me, didn't you?"

Even with only the moon for light, she could see his face

darken. "I vow I never did. He offered to help me, but I told him I didn't need his help."

Once again, she'd let this irrational attraction turn her into a fool. That pretty speech, the compliments, how he'd looked at her, touched her, it was all an act. Except for his stunning description of the river. That vivid image he'd painted with his words was the purest truth she'd ever heard him speak. If only he could be as honest in his dealings with her.

"I see. Then you brought me up here to ruin me."

"No!" He muttered an oath and thrust his fingers through his hair, pacing in the small space between the skylight and the edge of the deck. "You're doing it again. Misreading my intentions."

"Which are?"

He faced her and held his hands out in a pacifying gesture that she was certain he'd practiced in front of a mirror. "Look here now, I never asked Dan to do anything. It's him that's acting crazy, saying he wants to court you."

Hallie stiffened at the insult. Could he possibly offend her more? And she had almost let him kiss her again because she'd convinced herself there was something in his eyes beyond mere lust. Thrusting hurt aside, she crossed her arms and pinned him with a glare. "Let me see if I have this right. Mr. Devol is perfectly sane so long as he intends to ruin me. But he is crazy for wanting to court me?"

Huck's horrified expression was almost comical. "That's not what I meant. Devol is pure trouble. He's not the kind of man you need."

She gripped her skirts. It was either that or smack him. The wretch had some nerve to warn her off another man when he so thoroughly represented the worst of them. "Just what kind of a man do you think I need?"

He crossed his arms over his chest. "Well, I reckon a quality gent is fine, far as it goes. But you got to see beyond starchy clothes and good manners."

And past a boyishly handsome visage.

"Is that all?" she said dryly.

"No." Huck rubbed his chin, giving the inquiry serious consideration. "You need a man that's good as wheat about taking care of his family. Respectable, but middling fun. So you don't get bored. A fellow that'll let you rip out every so often when you want to speak your mind. But he's got to have enough gumption not to let you walk all over him. He ought to be truthful, and kind. Not the sort who would...hurt you."

Curse him. How did he do it? They were hardly close, barely civil, yet he knew her well enough to describe exactly the kind of man she'd looked for all her life. "Why are you telling me this?" she choked out.

Huck gestured with a weak shrug. "My pap, he was a cheat who didn't care about nobody but himself. Dan's the same. He won't make you a good husband."

Husband?

At last, Huck's motive for seeking her out became clear. He feared she might battle him in court as a married woman. Coupled with whatever evidence he thought she had, it would have spurred him to act. And this was just an act, another attempt to manipulate her.

She turned away rather than allow him to see her tears. Disappointment drenched a tiny flame she'd nurtured without realizing it. "You needn't worry that my hopes will be dashed. They already have been."

"Hallie, I'm telling you God's truth. I don't want to see you get hurt." Huck's voice dropped to a rough drawl. Was he sincere or a conniving actor who would stoop to any lengths to trip her up? Doubt tipped the scale against him.

"If you truly cared about my welfare, you wouldn't have

brought me out here where you could take advantage of me in the sight of witnesses."

He let out a long sigh. "Ain't you tired of fighting? You said yourself we ought to call a truce."

She wiped the dampness off her cheeks before facing him. "A truce is generally entered into with a small degree of trust on both sides. If you don't trust me, I can't trust you."

CHAPTER TWENTY-TWO

Close to dusk, a wagonload of revelers started up the road leading to Fort Sully. Everyone on the boat had been invited to a dance welcoming the new soldiers. Most of the crew was going, other than those who'd volunteered to stay behind to watch over the boat.

Huck looked out the pilothouse window and blew an aggravated puff around the stem of his pipe. He hadn't wanted to remain on board, but he wasn't keen on watching Hallie get herself seduced. It wasn't that he didn't trust her, as she'd accused him, along with a lot of other things. He didn't trust Dan Devol. The gambler had charmed the drawers off many a *good* woman.

With a curse, Huck knocked the hot ashes from his pipe into a box filled with sand. He slipped the warm pipe into his coat pocket. It hadn't calmed him as usual.

For days, Hallie had holed up in that room where she was painting, ignoring him, except for when they had to work out who was going to mind Tad. Between piloting the boat and watching his nephew, he hadn't had time to deal with her moods. To make matters worse, Dan hadn't fleeced those army boys and lit out. The gambler had meant it when he said he was going straight. It wasn't likely to last, though. An honest gambler was as rare as a virtuous whore.

From the back stairs came a thundering sound. A second later, Tad bounded into the pilothouse. "Hey, Uncle Huck."

"Hey, yourself. Where've you been?"

"Oh, around. I was with Aunt Hallie before Mr. Devol came to fetch her. He said he'd teach me some card tricks later. Do you know any card tricks?"

Huck's mood soured further. "You don't need to learn card tricks."

"But I want to learn 'em." Tad jumped up on the *lazy bench* and peered out the window. "How come you didn't go with Aunt Hallie to the dance?"

"She doesn't care anything about going with me."

He hadn't asked her. Even if he had, she wouldn't have accepted. Besides, he had no business dancing with her or doing anything else that might confuse him more. He was confused enough already.

He was still trying to figure out what he'd done lately to set her off. Maybe she'd realized how badly he wanted to kiss her—an idea he couldn't seem to put out of his head—but that didn't explain why she'd go off and ignore his warnings about Dan.

"You need to sweeten her up," Tad announced. He dug inside his coat and produced a clump of wildflowers tied with a dirty ribbon.

"Where'd you get those? And who told you about sweetening up women?" Huck suspected the answer. "Was it Devol?"

"No, Mr. Lacey told me. He said flowers are sure to win a woman's heart. He took me out to that field this morning so I could pick some."

"Now, why would Mr. Lacey care about helping you win a woman's heart?"

Tad looked at him like he was too stupid to live. "Not *me*. I reckoned *you* could give 'em to Aunt Hallie, so she'll stop frowning at you so much."

Huck heaved a heavy sigh. A bunch of flowers wouldn't fix what was wrong between him and Hallie, but he didn't want to hurt Tad's feelings. He took the limp little flower bundle, tucked it into his coat pocket, and pasted on a smile. "I'll give it a try when she gets back. If you think it'll make her feel better."

Tad's face brightened with so much hope it dang near broke Huck's heart. He couldn't stand talking about this anymore. "Hey, why don't we go visit the engineer? You can see how they drain off the boilers and clean the flues."

"That don't sound like fun."

Huck chuckled at the natural response. He hadn't thought things like that sounded fun either when he was Tad's age, and his pap had never pushed him, being the king of laziness. But somewhere along the way, he'd changed. Working on these boats had grown him up. Just like it would Tad, once he was old enough to take to the water. "If you're going to captain a steamboat one day, you got to learn all about 'em. Not just how to steer the pilot wheel."

From his perch on the bench, Tad looked out the window. Something else had caught his attention. Could be the fort up on the plateau or the valley that swept out into a sea of grass. It was probably the Indians trudging single-file into the wilderness. The band of Sioux, mostly women and children, had been camped outside the stockade when the boat arrived. Now they were leaving with the supplies they'd been waiting on for weeks.

Huck joined his nephew at the window. "Looks like they got their annuities and are headed back to the reservation."

Tad craned his neck around. "What's a 'nuity?"

Huck nudged back the brim of his hat as he tried to come up with a simple definition. "I suppose it's a fancy word for *bribe*."

"What's a bribe?"

Did Tad think he was a dictionary?

"It's when you make a deal to give somebody something so they'll do what you want."

His nephew looked back out the window. "The Indians don't look very happy. Don't they like the bribe they got?"

Now the boy wanted him to explain *politics*?

"No, I reckon they don't."

"How come?"

Huck released an exasperated sigh. What did he know about such things? He'd rubbed elbows with plenty of Indians and knew enough to appreciate what a raw deal they'd gotten. But how did he explain that to a child?

"Sit down here a minute, this might take a while. Especially the way you keep asking another question every time I answer one."

Tad hopped to the floor and sat on the bench beside him.

Huck braced his hands on his knees. "Let's see if I can expound...that's another word for *explain*," he said before Tad could ask. "The Indians agreed to move off their lands to make room for the white folks, who keep moving out here. Our government—those fellows in Washington mostly—promised to give them food and clothes and books and such. Best I understand, a whole heap of supplies arrived late or didn't show up or it wasn't what they were told. But I reckon their biggest problem is, they want to go home and they can't."

Tad's expression turned glum. "That's sad."

"Yeah, it is."

His nephew kept quiet. Were the questions done? Huck sure hoped so, because he was out of answers, especially when it came to Indians. There wasn't a thing he could do, but it still bothered him that white folks who ought to know better could be so blamed ignorant.

"Uncle Huck, I don't like my bribe neither."

"You ain't an Indian, Tad. Nobody's bribing you."

The boy's chin went up. "You said you'd give me an adventure if I went with that family you picked out. Ain't that a bribe?"

Huck opened his mouth, then closed it, then opened it again. This boy was sure enough related to Hallie, with the way he twisted words around. "It's not the same thing. Besides, haven't I made good on my promise?"

Tad nodded, but his eyes welled up. "But I'd ruther go home. With you."

Huck jerked to his feet and crossed to the opposite window to hide his tears. Like an unsuspecting steamer, his hull had got pierced by what he knew was out there but couldn't avoid.

Hallie had warned him his nephew would be devastated to be left behind, but she hadn't said anything about the damage done to his own heart when he had to let go. He honestly believed the best thing was to walk away and not look back. God help him, he couldn't do it.

He unknotted the kerchief around his neck to wipe his eyes and hoped Tad wouldn't notice. After taking a firm grip on his emotions, he faced his nephew. "Tell you what, Tadpole, I'll make you a deal."

"Another bribe?" Tad looked mighty shaky.

Huck shoved the handkerchief in his pocket and knelt in front of his nephew. "No. No more bribes. What I mean is, I want to offer you something, and you don't have to do anything to get it."

That cheered Tad up. "Like a present?"

"Something like that." Huck swallowed to clear the lump from his throat. "First off, you got to accept that I can't keep you with me all the time. You're too young, and the kind of life I lead isn't proper for a child."

Tad's eager expression faded.

"But I could come back and get you for a few weeks every

summer and take you on a trip with me. As long as your folks agree, and I'm sure they will." Huck had no idea what Becky might think, but Tom would be all up for an adventure and might even come along. "How does that deal sound?"

His nephew's eyes slid away like he was thinking about it. After a minute, he looked back. "When I'm growed up, will you let me stay with you all the time?"

"If you want to, I don't see why not."

The boy whooped to Jericho. He jumped up and ran over to the big wheel, pretending like he was steering. "That's bully, Uncle Huck. We'll get us a big old boat like this one, and I'll be a pilot just like you."

Huck laughed, breathing easier after a heavy weight was lifted off him. This new plan would work out fine. One day, he might even have a new traveling partner. In the meantime, his nephew would be in a good home, and he'd get to see him regular, even if it were only once a year. He sure would look forward to those few weeks.

But what about Hallie and that compromise?

Well, why shouldn't Tad's aunt have the same deal? If he put it to her nicely, he might even gain her agreement not to marry Dan. She didn't need that varmint for a husband, anyhow.

Huck rubbed his chin. Would she accuse him of manipulating her? He wasn't doing anything of the sort, and it weren't a bribe— mostly. He was just offering terms for a truce. She ought to appreciate his generosity, not to mention he'd be saving her from a scoundrel.

He got excited thinking about it and didn't want to wait until she got back to tell her. She ought to be feeling better by now, with all that dancing, so this might be the best time to present his idea.

He cupped his nephew's shoulder. "Let's go find Mr. Lacey and see if he'll take you to the engine room. I got to go talk to your aunt."

THE MUSIC STARTED UP AGAIN. WITH A RESIGNED SIGH, HALLIE HELD out her hand and let Dan lead her onto the dance floor. After painting all day, exhaustion had set in. Now she had a pounding headache due to the cloying odors in the hot, crowded room.

Why had she agreed to come to this dance? Because Huck had goaded her into it with his dire warnings. Issued only after he'd become alarmed that she might find a husband and thwart his plan. Dan had no expectations about marriage. He'd offered to accompany her so she wouldn't have to put up with Huck.

He swept her into a waltz. "You're a marvelous dancer, Miss MacBride."

"You are too kind," she murmured.

Her form was far from *marvelous*, and his flattery only made her feel awkward. It had been years since she'd danced, and tonight she had danced with every man in the room. Or if she hadn't, her feet certainly felt like it. Thank heavens she didn't have to dance with Huck. If she did, her problems would extend to more than her feet.

He had acted surprised and aggravated when she'd informed him that Dan would be accompanying her to the dance. She ought to feel victorious. Instead, she wrestled with unmerited guilt.

"I spoke with Finn again about releasing his claim on your nephew," Dan said, taking her on another turn.

"What did he say?"

"He still isn't agreeable. Give him another week with a boy underfoot, and I'm certain he'll be begging you to take the child off his hands. He isn't cut out for parenting. I wouldn't be surprised if he pulls heel before we reach St. Louis."

She regarded her partner with skepticism. "It seems to me he is taking his responsibility as an uncle quite seriously. And he's stubborn as a mule about his plan to give Tad to his friend, Mr. Sawyer."

"Keep your chin up, Hallie. Things could change."

The remark, rather than encouraging her, left her feeling unsettled, though it made no sense. She was just worn out, what with trying to spend time with Tad and painting every spare minute in between. Not only that, her nights had been interrupted by indecent dreams. Huck plagued her even in her sleep.

The room whirled by in a blur of plastered walls and pastel gowns. She silently counted the three-quarter beat, too unsure to simply follow her partner's lead.

The musicians were every bit as good as those she'd heard in Quincy. Heavens, it had been ages since she'd danced the waltz. More than eight years ago, at a ball where she'd met the dashing Captain James Douglas. His warm brown eyes and ready smile had taken her breath away. But now his face seemed a fuzzy memory and another image formed in its place, one with russet hair and eyes reminiscent of restless waters.

She stumbled.

Dan gripped her tight. He'd tromped on her instep because she had missed the beat.

"I-I beg your pardon," she stammered.

"The fault is mine." He led her off the dance floor. "I imagine we've danced your feet off. Would you like to rest?"

"Yes, please."

He guided her through the crowd to a row of chairs lined up against the wall. She took a seat next to some of the officers' wives, who were managing snatches of conversation in between rounds of dancing. With men far outnumbering women in this remote army post, there could be no wallflowers at this gathering.

Dan hovered beside her chair, nodding his head in time to the beat.

She cringed at the thought of more dancing. "I believe I will sit out the next few rounds. I am more tired than I realized."

"Shall I take you back to the boat?"

That sounded like a grand idea. "No need, I don't want to spoil your fun."

He bestowed an indulgent smile. "Let me fetch you some punch. That will revive you."

Hallie curled her toes in her shoes, biting back a moan. *Oh no, no more dancing.* Her feet ached, fatigue weighed her down, and heavens, it was hot in here.

After a few minutes, she stretched her neck to see over the crowd and noticed Dan was engaged in a conversation with one of the officers. Perhaps she could escape, at least long enough to get some fresh air or until the dancing was done.

She slipped out the door and took a right turn through the dark sally port. The breeze coming off the river would be more refreshing on the far side of the building.

The shape of a man materialized in the passageway in front of her. He caught her about the waist a moment before they collided, and her body quivered like a witching rod.

"Huck?"

"Hallie? S'at you?"

God help her. She knew his touch in the dark, but he wasn't certain of her identity even after he'd put his hands on her.

She wrenched out of his grasp. "I thought you were staying on the boat. Where's Tad?"

"With Mr. Lacey."

"Why did you come here?"

"Why did you?"

Blast the man for answering her question with another question. She sidestepped him and hurried out of the passageway then headed across the moonlit parade grounds. If Huck intended to go to the dance, she would leave. She'd make her apologies later. Dan would understand.

Huck caught up and matched her pace. "Where are you going?"

"Back to the boat. I'm tired."

"You're walking the whole way back?"

Flying, if she could. She gripped her skirt and set off at a fast walk down a winding, rutted road that led to the landing.

Huck kept pace beside her. The moon shone bright enough for her to make out what he was wearing, the new suit he'd purchased. He had applied a razor to his face, something that wasn't a daily occurrence.

Had he intended to dance with her?

A delicious shiver raced across her skin. If the mere *thought* of dancing with him affected her like this, what would happen if he held her in the close embrace of a waltz?

She lifted her skirts higher and ran. Before she'd gone ten paces, he snagged her arm. The momentum swung her around into his chest. He caught her and held her close.

The smell of his spicy cologne and the press of his body against hers triggered a host of sensual sensations. Alarmed, she struggled to get away. "Let me go."

He latched onto her arms. "Did that varmint insult you?"

"Varmint?"

"Devol. Did he touch you? Is that why you're running?"

"Is that why you came up here? To hound me about Dan? Mr. Devol has been a perfect gentleman, unlike you." She pulled out of Huck's clutches and fled down the path. Her only thought to escape before he turned her into a trembling mass of want.

"Hallie, hold on." Huck pounded up behind her. "You can't run back just because you don't want to talk to me."

"Leave me alone." Becoming winded, she slowed to a fast walk. The boat was another mile down the dirt road. She couldn't run that far without ruining Kate's dress in the process. However, she was determined to reach the boat as quickly as possible and take refuge in her room. Being alone with Huck was far too disturbing.

He strode alongside her. "You're not falling for that act, are you? Dan's done it up elegant, I admit, but he's not the gentleman you think he is. I don't know what he's up to, exactly, but—"

"Stop!" She halted with her hand pressed against a catch in her side. He couldn't possibly care if she fell prey to a rogue. Straightening, she looked him in the eye. "You fear I will fight you in court as a married woman. That's what this is about, isn't it?"

The frown on his face conveyed his frustration, even if he didn't admit she'd guessed right. In one smooth motion, he scooped her into his arms, cradled her like a child, and began to walk.

"What are you doing?" She twisted in a frantic attempt to escape, causing him to stumble.

His grip tightened as he righted himself. "Stop squirming or we'll both end up in the dirt. I'm not molesting you. I'm trying to keep you from ruining that dress."

No man held a woman this close on account of a dress. She held her body rigid. He would tire soon enough and release her.

After several minutes of plodding silence, she could bear it no more. "This display of concern is not about protecting my dress."

"If you say so."

"Now that you know I am wise to your intentions I would appreciate it if you would put me down and stop badgering me about whom I choose to spend time with."

He continued without slowing his pace. "I don't care who you spend time with, so long as you know what you're getting yourself into."

"Why are you being so agreeable?"

"Because I'm plum worn out with being disagreeable."

His sincerity seemed unlikely. He'd fooled her before with a show of concern.

She studied his face. Nothing in his expression gave away his intent. He simply looked...well, determined.

Heavens, he would have to be determined if he intended to carry her down the hill to the boat. She wasn't a large woman, but she would feel twice as heavy in a matter of minutes.

His burden would be eased if she held onto him. She looped her arms around his neck but refrained from combing her fingers through his hair. That would give him the wrong idea.

"I would like to be more agreeable, as well. It's not in my nature to be difficult."

"I suspect you were born difficult," Huck said, cheerfully.

"No more than you."

"I'm just ornery. If you look the words up in a dictionary, you'll see there's a difference."

Hallie smiled at the retort. "Yes, there is. Just as there is a difference between confident and conceited."

"You got a point?"

"You are not conceited. You didn't even balk at bunking with the cabin help."

"Mr. Lacey is a friendly sort."

"So are you. All the people on the boat took to you right away."

"Except for you."

"Perhaps I bring out your worst traits."

He laughed. She found it less amusing, more humbling.

The curved path swung around, and the *Hesperia* came into view. He stepped carefully over a deep rut in the road. He'd been right. She would've ruined her dress if she'd walked back. He could also be kind, upon occasion.

"Do you mean to carry me the whole way?"

"It's not much further. You only got to put up with me holding you a little while longer." He shifted her in his arms and brought her closer. Almost as if he cherished her.

She hadn't felt cherished in such a long time, and it wasn't something she ever imagined feeling with Huck. But he'd surprised her in other ways.

What if she'd misjudged his intentions and he was sincerely trying to protect her? Come to think of it, his continued warnings about Dan smacked of jealousy.

Huck, jealous?

If so, she had misconstrued his actions. She ought to give him a chance to explain, once he decided he'd carried her far enough.

A cool breeze tickled her cheek. The drone of insects and the sound of water lapping softly against the hull of the boat lulled her into a dreamy state.

Huck held her securely, yet gently. Strength and tenderness in equal parts. Something she'd never thought to find in a man. Too soon, he reached the stage plank and set her down. So carefully she was hardly aware her feet touched the ground.

"Your tie is crooked." She reached up to straighten the silk bow, fussing over him like a wife. Kate had put that thought into her head. Not Huck. "Why did you come after me tonight? What did you want?"

"If I tell you, will you believe me?"

She sensed he wasn't simply inquiring as to whether she would believe his answer to her question. He was asking for her trust.

The air felt charged with importance. Her response would shift the future as mightily as an earthquake changed the landscape.

A strident voice warned her not to believe a word he said, but a softer one reminded her that she had become bitter and miserable when she'd closed her mind and locked away her heart.

She adjusted lapels that didn't need adjusting as an excuse to touch him and then rested her hands on his chest. "I choose to believe you."

Surprise was evident on his face. "Well, all right, then. I came looking for you to offer you something. It's, um…"

"Yes?"

He seemed nervous. Perhaps Kate had it right and he was afraid to speak his feelings. Her friend would advise her to encourage him.

She slid her hands up to his shoulders. "What is it? What do you want?"

"I want," he repeated in a rough whisper. His tongue came out to moisten his lips and his throat worked like he was swallowing. The uncertainty in his eyes flared into something hotter. He took her in his arms and she lifted onto her toes at the same moment he bent his head, slanting his mouth over hers in a perfect…

Kiss.

Hallie sighed with pleasure. Oh yes, she wanted this, too.

His lips quested in an urgent exploration. He sampled her mouth as if it were the most delicious treat. The sensation set off shock waves, making her tremble and hunger for…

More.

She kissed him back with the same inquisitive fervor. Combing her fingers through his hair, she discovered the thick strands were neither straight nor curly, rather somewhere in between.

What else might she discover about him? She drew his head down so she could kiss his ear, and his breathing grew labored. So much sensitivity in such a small part.

"Hallie." He gasped her name before grabbing a handful of her hair to pull her head back and seal his lips over hers in another heated kiss.

Joy erupted from a latent spring deep inside. What Huck

wanted was her, and he desired her as ferociously as she desired him.

Her mind telegraphed an urgent warning, but her heart refused to heed it. He'd asked her to trust him, and she desperately needed to believe how he was making her feel—beautiful, adored, desired.

It had seemed right before he kissed her that he was trying to ask her something. If he was getting used to the idea of settling down, it would solve everything in the most wonderful way imaginable.

He tore his mouth away and pressed frantic kisses across her cheek. Trembling beneath the onslaught, she let her head fall back so he could forge a hot, damp trail down her neck. She gripped his shoulders, needing an anchor for fear she would simply float away.

The warning bell in her head clanged louder. She might not be innocent, but the decent reputation she'd worked hard to establish would be destroyed should they be seen in a passionate embrace. Reluctantly, she forced herself back to earth before someone spotted them.

She splayed her hands over his heaving chest and hammering heartbeat. "I want this, too," she murmured, peeking up at him through her lashes. "But we should wait for the proper time and place after we're...you know."

He blinked at her with a puzzled expression, then released her and jumped back, as if someone had doused him with cold water. "You thought I meant..." His head moved back and forth and his eyes filled with something that looked frighteningly like horror. "I, um...no, didn't mean *that*."

She struggled to assimilate his words and the anxiety on his face. He didn't mean *what*? The kiss? His desire? No, he couldn't hide that. He was saying there was nothing to it except pure lust.

Her body trembled, alternately cold and hot. Her throat closed up and she couldn't breathe. She had done it again. Allowed common sense to be swept away in a flood of foolish dreams and wicked desires.

Humiliation clawed at her chest and tore at her insides. She shut her eyes. Couldn't look at him, *wouldn't* look at him.

"Hallie. I-I'm sorry. You're awful pretty, and that soft way you were lookin' at me, just... Heck, I shouldn't have done what I did. I mean, I did *like* kissing you, don't get me wrong, but I won't do it again. The reason I came looking for you, I wanted to offer up a-a compromise. Terms. For a truce."

She floated along on the stammering stream of his explanation, listening, yet not comprehending until she ran aground on the last word.

Truce.

He hadn't meant the sweetest kiss she had ever experienced. That had been a mistake, an unfortunate detour. She'd only imagined he wanted that kiss, maybe even her love, but all he truly wanted was a temporary ceasefire.

It was too funny when she thought about it. The best joke he'd played on her yet.

A giggle escaped, an entirely inappropriate response, given the devastation occurring in her heart, but she couldn't help it. Choking, hysterical laughter erupted out of her, along with a hot rush of tears.

"Hallie?" He sounded anxious.

She fought to control her emotions. Loathing welled up, pressing against her heart, the pain excruciating.

James had taken her innocence before he destroyed her trust. Huck had only kissed her, and he was trying to apologize, but it didn't matter. Because the truth was, he didn't want her either, other than for a tumble in bed. Perhaps that was all she was good for and she was simply the last one to realize it.

Hallie dashed away tears with the back of her hand and forced her features into a hard expression. It was easier and less painful when she faced the world through that mask.

Huck held out his hands as though he had something useful to offer her. "I know I'm a low-down dog for taking advantage of you like that, and you don't have to forgive me, but I swear I won't ever—"

"Stop talking." She cut off whatever useless promise he had been about to make. "I wish to never speak of this again."

His mouth closed and his head moved in energetic assent.

"If you have terms to propose, I want to see them in writing. I will let you know if they are acceptable. In the meantime, we will keep our interactions limited to necessary conversations about Tad."

Another nod, this one slower and less certain.

"Do you understand what I am saying, Mr. Finn? I want nothing to do with you other than what is required to ensure Tad's well-being. Beyond that, I expect you to stay away from me for the remainder of this detestable journey."

CHAPTER TWENTY-THREE

The *Hesperia* had left Fort Sully eighty miles behind and now winged its way downriver on a fast current, aided by a strong westerly wind. At this pace, they would reach St. Louis ahead of schedule.

Huck could hardly wait.

He took Tad's hand in a firm grip as they walked across the forecastle toward the edge of the bow. His nephew bounced alongside him, humming like there weren't a glum cloud in the sky. Huck recalled a time he'd felt that way. Before life had taught him not to expect too much. Especially when it came to dealing with women.

Hallie hadn't spoken a dozen words to him since the previous evening, not even to acknowledge the apology he'd given her, and in writing no less.

Why the dickens had he hauled off and kissed her instead of just offering up that compromise? He'd confused her without meaning it. Hang it, maybe *he* was the confused one. A black-haired siren haunted his dreams at night. He couldn't stop wondering what it might be like sharing a bed and a life with a woman like Hallie.

Huck jerked to a stop. That was dangerous thinking, considering he wasn't the marrying type. Not to mention, if she didn't hate him before, she sure did now.

More's the pity, Hucky.

Well, he couldn't do a durn thing about it. All that mattered was getting her to sign the terms he'd drawn up, just like she asked. Everything would work out fine if she would agree not to take him to court in exchange for getting two weeks with Tad each year. It was a generous offer, no less than what he was getting.

Forcing the troublesome thoughts out of his mind, he guided Tad over next to a man who knelt at the edge. He hadn't told Hallie where they'd be. She'd have a fit if she thought the boy was out on the bow without a rail for protection. But if Tad intended to get on a boat every summer, he needed to know more than what he picked up in a pilothouse or galley. This was a good place to begin his lessons.

"Hank is the leadsman. You see that pole he's putting down into the water? He uses it to check how deep it is. We got to have at least four feet, so the paddlewheel can clear the bottom. I recollect here it ought to be about six feet, give or take."

"Six feet, two inches," the leadsman called out.

Tad twisted around with a gasp. "Geeminy, Uncle Huck, how did you know without looking at the pole?"

Huck tapped his head. "It's facts you got to store up. I remembered what the leadsman called at this spot last time we were here."

A low rumble sounded like distant thunder. He peered up at a crystal clear sky.

"How do you know you're at the same spot?" Tad persisted.

"By landmarks and such." Huck pointed at the western bank.

"You see how the bank drops down, not much higher than a man? The land gets flatter, and the grass looks different, and..."

Clods of clay tumbled down the embankment, splashing into the river. Along the horizon, a dark cloud appeared. The low rumble became an earth-shaking pounding that sent ripples across the water, as a massive herd began to take shape.

"Well, I'll be, that's—"

"Buffalo!" The cry went up like a chorus, sung out by crewmen on the forecastle.

"Look, Uncle Huck, look!" Tad grabbed his sleeve, hopping around like a frog.

"I see 'em, Tadpole." He put a hand on his nephew's shoulder to ground him. This close to the edge of the boat, he could fall off if he got too excited.

"They're coming right at us," Tad squealed.

"Sure looks like it. Ain't that a sight? I reckon they'll cross the river before we can get by. You'll get to see 'em up close."

Deckhands charged the boom, hurriedly rigging rope into a makeshift noose in expectation of snagging a prize.

Easterners couldn't get enough of the shaggy critters—the steaks, the hides, even little calves to collect and show off as a spectacle in the circus. Any crew worth its salt would jump at the chance for easy money like that.

Moments later, rifles appeared, seemingly out of nowhere, in the hands of officers, crew, and the few remaining passengers. Keeping a child out on the bow when the men started shooting didn't seem like a good idea.

"Let's go see Captain Kinney. He might need help once this herd starts fording the river. The dimwitted devils generally go around a big steamer. But they might give her a few shoves." He pulled Tad's hand.

The boy pulled back. "I wanna stay down here."

"You can see better from above." Huck gave a firm tug.

Tad dug in his heels. "But Uncle Huck…"

Fed up with arguing, Huck dragged the ornery little mule behind him. It was the only time he could recall Tad *not* wanting to be in the pilothouse.

The herd reached the river and poured over the embankment in a solid mass of brown, then the huge beasts went leaping and sliding into the water. As it reached their necks, they set off swimming, coming at the boat in a solid dark line.

Huck's heart started to pound. Any time now, they'd split up and veer off. But just in case. He gave Tad a shove toward the stairs. "Come on, we'll watch from the pilothouse."

They met Hallie as she came thundering down the steps with her eyes wild. Maybe she'd never seen a buffalo stampede. That would scare even the bravest soldier.

"Fearsome sight, eh? But don't you worry, those furry beasts are going to swim right around—"

"Give him to me!" She took a firm hold of Tad's coat. "You, of all people, ought to know better than to bring a boy out here where there's danger."

Her sharp reprimand was equivalent to a slap in the face and had the same effect. If she would just trust him for once and stop treating him like he didn't have any sense.

"What the blazes, woman?" he roared. "I ain't going to let him get killed."

She gaped at him.

Huck clamped his teeth together. He needed a safety valve on his temper.

"Tad, come with me," she said stiffly. "I'm sure your uncle is too busy to be bothered."

"I'm not bothered." *Except by you.* No, he couldn't say that. She'd take it wrong, and he didn't have the patience to explain. "I was taking him to the pilothouse. He'll be safe enough there."

"He would be safer in the main cabin." She narrowed her eyes and held her ground, or in this case, her stair. He wasn't getting past her unless he lifted her out of the way.

It was his own dang fault for how bad things were between them. If he'd just kept his claws off her...

"Right, we'll let him choose."

Tad's head swiveled back and forth. His eyes got big and round like a little critter caught in a trap.

Huck's stomach knotted. Pap had always put him in the middle of arguments and he'd hated having to choose sides. He thrust the child at Hallie. "Here, take him, I need to go."

The boat lurched and she screamed. He grabbed her, quick as lightning, and at the same time tightened his grip on Tad's arm, barely keeping the three of them from toppling backward down the stairs.

The boat rocked and bounced like some giant had taken a ball and drummed it on the deck.

"What the hell?" Huck backed down the stairs with one arm wrapped around a terrified woman and the other latched onto a squirming child. Dropping off the last step, he let go.

Bells sounded in a frenzied ringing, followed by the hiss of steam being released. The wheel had stopped moving. The *Hesperia* was adrift in the current.

Half a dozen deckhands raced past. "Damn thing's stuck in the buckets!" one called out.

A buffalo caught in the paddlewheel could do considerable damage. They would need every hand to get it free.

"Take Tad inside," Huck hollered and didn't look back as he dashed off in the direction of the stern.

~

No sooner had Uncle Huck run off than Aunt Hallie started dragging him back to the stairs. Tad twisted his wrist and escaped her grip.

He took off running after his uncle, mindless of her angry shouts following him. He wasn't about to go with her and miss out on everything. Even if he got a thrashing later, it would be worth it.

Tad burrowed into the crowd and wound his way through a forest of trouser legs. Where had Uncle Huck got off to? Had he gone to check on the *damn thing* that got stuck?

It might be buffalo. Tad knew he'd never find out if Aunt Hallie hauled him inside.

He didn't blame her for being fearful, what with her being a woman. But he weren't no scared little girl. If he let her take him inside, his uncle would never believe he was growed up enough to stay on a boat.

Tad raced past the engine room and headed for the stern. His heart pounded as he dodged people who'd come out onto the deck.

Uncle Huck wouldn't be angry. He'd only said to go inside because he was trying to please Aunt Hallie. The last couple days she'd gone back to wearing that ugly dress and a mean look to hide the fact that she was upset. She'd even cried a time or two. This adventure weren't nearly as much fun no more, except for now.

He stood on his tiptoes trying to see around the grownups.

"Tad!"

Uh oh. Aunt Hallie, getting closer. He'd catch it for sure.

If he couldn't squeeze through the crowd, he'd go around them. He slipped between the bull rails and inched along the edge of the guard toward the stern.

Tad twisted to look down at the water, and gasped. By golly, them buffalo was BIG. Lots bigger than the cows at home, and meaner looking too, with their eyes rolling around like they were crazed. They held their noses up in the air as they paddled and bumped into each other and set up an awful commotion.

Smelly brown water sloshed over Tad's shoes. He clung to the rail and scooted faster.

He could see his uncle now. Down near one of the big beams that turned the paddlewheel.

"Uncle Huck!" he yelled.

Maybe his uncle couldn't hear him over all the bawling.

He lifted a hand to wave and hollered louder. "Uncle Huck!"

The boat jumped.

"Unc...aaaaah!" Tad's call became a scream as the rail ripped right out of his fingers and he went flying.

CHAPTER TWENTY-FOUR

A child's scream jerked Huck's head around. Something splashed into the river and disappeared. In a split second, his startled mind registered what he'd seen.

"Tad!"

Panic sent him scrambling, over people, past the engine room. He grabbed hold of a stationary, vaulted over the bull rail, and crouched on the guard, frantically searching the muddy water where his nephew had disappeared.

Damnation. All he could see was buffalo. Had the shaggy devils dragged Tad under?

Hallie's screams lifted over the hubbub. "Huck! Look! There he is!"

He tracked a line from her finger to where she pointed downriver. Amidst the herd, Tad's head appeared along with his flailing arms.

Huck launched himself in that direction. He hit the water with a loud splash and struck out with all his might, shoving his way past the bawling demons, determined to reach Tad before the boy got smothered in wet fur or ground into the riverbed by churning hooves.

He got to Tad just in time and snatched him by the coat, coughing and sputtering, up out of the water. Holding the child high as he could, he paddled awkwardly with one hand toward the boat. He had to fight to keep the ignorant beasts from crushing them.

Tad shook so hard Huck felt the child's trembles down his arm. He wanted to soothe him and promise him they'd get shy of this mess, but all his energy and attention had to be focused on swimming.

He shifted Tad around to his back and pulled the boy's slender arms around his neck. "Hold on tight!"

He struck out with powerful strokes.

After a short time, it became clear he wasn't getting anywhere. The relentless current pulled them downriver, along with the brown devils and the boat. They'd soon be swept past the bow into the thickest mass of the herd. They'd die for sure if that happened.

Huck's mouth filled with the coppery tang of fear. With a burst of energy, he kicked harder.

Tad started clawing like he was trying to climb a tree.

Huck winced as his nephew's nails ripped into his cheek. "I gotcha, Tadpole. Don't fight me. I'll get us back to the boat."

Regret squeezed Huck's straining heart. Why had he brought a little boy out to this wild place? He should've sent Tad back with that lawyer straightaway or given him to Hallie. Anything would've been better than this.

As the massive bodies clumped around them, he sent up a prayer. He would gladly spend eternity in hell if God would let him save this boy.

Huck could barely see the crowded deck over the bobbing heads of the buffalo. Men were running and hollering, waving frantically toward something on the bow.

The boom! They'd swung it out over the water. Dangling from the tackle, a thick rope, and at the end of it, the noose they'd fashioned to halter a calf.

With renewed hope, Huck struck out for the rope.

He could make it.

It wasn't far, just a few more feet.

He lunged and grabbed hold of the noose, kicking free of the clamoring beasts. Now, if he could just get it over him and—

Tad's arms slipped from around his neck.

Huck twisted and caught his nephew. He couldn't wrap this rope around him with one hand while trying to hold onto a weary child with the other.

He swung Tad in front of him, pulling the noose over the boy's head and torso, tightening it beneath his arms. After securing Tad, Huck took a two-handed grip above the slipknot and ripped out a hoarse command: "Bring us in!"

The men raced to the capstan. Soon the boom began to move, lifting them, dragging them over the heads of the buffalo.

Huck's arms burned with the effort it took to hold onto the rope above Tad, who dangled like a lassoed prize.

"Hang on, Tadpole," he gasped. "Almost there."

He tightened his hold but his grip kept slipping. He tried to climb up. His hands were slick with mud. If he tried to hang on and slid down onto Tad, his weight would pull the rope too tight and crush the boy's chest.

Huck's whole body began to quake. He squelched his fear with a darkly humorous thought. Might be that Providence had answered his prayer exactly as he'd asked, and now he had to hold up his end of the bargain.

With an agonized groan, he let go.

"No!" Hallie shrieked, as Huck fell into the seething mass of buffalo. He'd lost his hold on the rope just before he and Tad reached the safety of the guard.

The crew on the bow appeared frozen.

Was nobody going to act?

Frantic, she lunged forward.

Dan grabbed her arms from behind. "What are you doing? You can't go out there."

"Let me go!" She twisted out of his grip and ran to the front of the boat, unwound a mooring line, then stepped to the edge and heaved the thick rope out to where Huck was fighting for his life.

The first mate nabbed her arm and dragged her away. "Get back, lessen you wanna fall in and join him."

More ropes were thrown.

Deckhands crowded the bow, blocking her view.

Dan circled his arm around her waist. "You heard the man, you're too close. There's nothing more you can do. At least they have Tad."

Thanks to Huck. He'd gone into the river without hesitation.

A huddle of men surrounded her nephew, untangling him from the tackle they'd used to rescue him. His hoarse cries for his uncle tore at her heart.

Breaking free of Dan, she ran to Tad and pulled the wet child into her arms. The fetid odor of mud, manure, and every other foul thing those beasts had churned up, clung to him. A terrifying numbness took her to her knees.

Had Huck saved their nephew only to die?

The rope she'd thrown jerked taut against the bits.

She caught a sharp breath.

Two burly mates took hold and pulled hand-over-hand while she held onto Tad and held her breath. It took forever before the top of Huck's head appeared above the edge of the guard.

The deckhands caught him by his wet coat and hoisted him

onto the platform. He crawled a few soggy feet before flopping over, gasping like a landed fish.

Hallie sagged with relief. "Thank God."

"I wanna see Uncle Huck." Tad squirmed out of her arms.

In a flash, she caught hold of his sleeve. Fear rushed back—the same as when she'd seen him fall into that murky water—and she dropped to her knees, fisting his soaked coat. "Never run away from me again! Do you hear me? *Never* run away." She yanked him into a fierce hug and burst into tears. "My God. I thought I'd lost you."

Tad stilled. After a moment, his small hands brushed over her hair. "I'm sorry, Aunt Hallie." Tears slid in silvery tracks down his dirty cheeks and his eyes brimmed with tears.

She cupped his face with her hands. "Oh, Tad. I'm not angry with you, dearest. What happened scared me. I don't want to see you get hurt."

The captain's wife appeared next to them. "If you'd like, I'll take him and get him cleaned up."

As much as Hallie appreciated the kind gesture, she couldn't bear to let her nephew out of her sight. "Thank you. I'll take care of him."

"I thought you might want to..." Kate gestured with her chin to where two men were helping Huck to his feet.

Soaking wet and covered with a thick coat of slime, he started in their direction with halting steps.

Her heart urged her to go to him. Her feet wouldn't move. He would blame her for what had happened. After all, he'd left her in charge.

"Uncle Huck!"

She released her squirming nephew, who ran and flung his arms around his uncle's waist.

The child's forward momentum propelled Huck backward a few steps, and his grunt of pain shook her out of her daze.

"Easy, Tadpole," he rasped.

"Easy, Tad. You're hurting him." Hallie pried the boy's arms from around Huck's waist. "Are you injured?"

Huck cradled his ribs. "Just a bruise. After I let go, I fell on top of a big bull. He butted me out of the way."

His stunning remark, made as an offhand comment, chilled her. "What do you mean you let go? Why?"

He shifted his gaze downward and awkwardly stroked Tad's wet head. "The rope got muddy and slippery. I didn't want to hurt Tad by hanging onto him."

Hallie stared at him, stunned. He'd risked death rather than the take the chance he would injure Tad. She'd once accused him of being self-centered, but a selfish man would not have made such a sacrifice. And to think, she'd flung insults at him moments before he'd gone to Tad's rescue. While she stood on the deck, watching.

"How badly are you hurt?" She reached out, intending to pull aside the ruined shirt so she could see the extent of his injuries.

He knocked her hand out of the way. "Leave it be. I'm fine."

Regret constricted her throat. He didn't want her concern, and most certainly not a show of affection. He wanted nothing more from her than her signature on a piece of paper.

"I'm not hurt either," Tad chirped. "Did you see Uncle Huck? He came after me!"

"Yes. Thank goodness your uncle was able to reach you." She curled an arm around Tad's shoulders and tucked him against her like a mother hen with her chick.

"Go on with your aunt. She'll take good care of you. I got to get cleaned off." Huck's gaze lingered on their nephew even though he'd backed away.

He might not have room in his heart for her, but it appeared he'd forgiven her for her lapse. It would not happen again. After nearly losing Tad, even Huck seemed to know what was best for their nephew.

THAT EVENING, HALLIE GATHERED UP MEDICINE AND BANDAGES AND set off down a narrow hallway to the aft section of the Texas deck. Huck had refused to let anyone help him, other than the mate who'd hosed him down before he went inside to finish cleaning up. Several hours later, he hadn't returned and she'd become concerned. Hopefully, he wouldn't send her away.

She rapped softly at the door to the room he shared with the steward. "It's Hallie. May I come in?"

At Huck's muffled "aye," she entered.

Huck lay stretched out on the lower berth. He had bathed and put on a clean shirt that came to his knees. His lower legs were bare. He'd taken to bed. Earlier, he'd brushed her off, saying his ribs were only bruised.

"How's Tad?" he asked.

"He's fine. Very tired, and worried about you. Kate offered to sit with him while I checked on you." Hallie twisted up the flickering wick in the lamp hanging from the ceiling. Light flared, bathing the room with a soft glow.

"Tell him not to worry," Huck said in a hoarse voice.

"He's not the only one who's worried." She set the small tin canister and bandages on the side of the bed. "I brought this salve for your ribs. Kate swears it will ease the pain and help with healing. If you remove your shirt, I'll apply it."

He sat up slowly and reached for the shirttails.

Good heavens. Not in front of her.

She moved over to the washstand, keeping her back to him. From behind her came the soft shush of cloth and a grunt.

"You can turn around."

He'd scooted up to a sitting position and had a blanket drawn over his lap, along with the shirt.

Her skin tingled and grew warm. If seeing him unclothed had this effect on her, she couldn't imagine what she'd feel like if she were actually in bed with him. Well, she could, but she had no business letting her thoughts run off in that direction. She was here to nurse him.

Without comment, she went and sat beside him, opened the tin, and scooped out a glob of the pungent salve.

A raised ridge across his bicep and a pitted indention in the crook of his shoulder appeared to be old scars, perhaps from bullets. The vicious attack he'd told her about. Seeing the marks on his body roused a fierce desire to soothe him.

"Where are you injured?"

"Around here, mostly." He carefully raised his arm.

Dark bruises mottled his skin and angry scrapes marred his ribcage.

"Mercy," she whispered. As gently as she could, she smeared the oily medicine over his injured flesh. "I'm sorry if this causes you pain."

"Don't hurt," he rasped.

"Of course it does. You needn't be so stalwart."

His guarded expression shifted, and in that naked moment, she saw the depth of his agony, the wretched guilt, the pain that went beyond physical. She couldn't apply medicine to those hurts. However, she could try to ease them with kind, encouraging words.

"You did a very brave thing, going after Tad."

"Weren't brave so much as scared out of my wits."

"Even the bravest of men experience fear in the face of death."

"It wasn't my death that scared me so bad. There for a minute, I feared—" His eyes grew bright and his throat worked as he swallowed.

"Yes, I know." Hallie held back tears. She'd come here to give comfort, not to seek it. "But our nephew is in bed and safe, thanks to you."

She gently laid her hand over Huck's larger one. Even his poor knuckles were bruised. "You saved him, Huck, at great risk to your own life. You are a courageous man. The fact that you were afraid doesn't alter or diminish that."

Huck shook his head. He doubted her or himself.

She continued, determined to get through to him. "Not only that, you are caring and compassionate. You would've sacrificed yourself rather than harm Tad. There may be braver men, but few would choose death over the possibility of hurting a child. That takes a special kind of courage."

He regarded her silently, not moving, not even blinking.

It wrenched her heart that he seemed to be unwilling to accept her praise. He couldn't have received much encouragement while growing up. Perhaps self-doubt had taken root in his unhappy childhood.

"Don't you believe what I'm telling you?"

"I'm just surprised."

"Surprised?"

"That *you* believe it." He turned his hand to clasp hers, a simple gesture that set off a cascade of complicated emotions. "I haven't been any of those things when it comes to my dealings with you."

While his statement might be technically true, honesty demanded she not lay the blame entirely at his door. She'd made a host of wrong assumptions, had treated him with disdain, and criticized him repeatedly. "Perhaps we are, each of us, guilty of mistreating the other."

"Ah, Hallie, you haven't mistreated me."

"I've said some terrible things."

"Most of 'em true. Just because we can't agree on what's best

for Tad doesn't change the fact that you're a good, decent woman."
He spoke with such fervor it made his words sound like the
highest compliment he could pay her.

"You must be careful not to swell my head. I might begin to
think you like me."

He regarded her with a puzzled look. "I reckon I do."

The rush of elation unnerved her. She couldn't take too much
from what he said, having done that before with disastrous results.
Perhaps forging a friendly relationship would be good for both of
them, as long as she kept things light.

"Well, I reckon I like you, too."

His relieved smile made her unaccountably giddy.

Without thinking, she leaned forward and pressed a kiss on his
bristly cheek. He curled his hand around the nape of her neck and
held her face next to his. The scent of his skin mingled with the
smell of the tangy salve, acting as a powerful aphrodisiac.

"Hallie." The way his voice rasped over her name made her
shiver. "About last night..."

Her heart constricted with painful longing. "We don't have to
speak of it."

"Yes, we do. I made a mess of things, and I—"

A soft knock sent her scrambling to her feet. She became so
flustered at being caught in a moment of intimacy she just stood
there like a statue.

"Come in," Huck rumbled.

Kate peeked inside, gripping the edge of the door. "I'm sorry to
bother you. Tad woke up. He's upset. I think he feels a little warm."

Hallie tensed with worry. "He's feverish?"

"Most likely he's in a sweat because I haven't been to see him."
Huck picked up his shirt.

Kate shook her head. "He's not asking for you, Huck. He's
asking for Hallie."

CHAPTER TWENTY-FIVE

Three days had passed since Tad had fallen into the river. Shouldn't a brash little fellow like him be up and rarin' to go by now, instead of lying around in a dark room?

Huck eased onto a chair next to the bed and grimaced. His ribs still hurt like the dickens, but he was healing. The same couldn't be said for his nephew.

He touched Tad's flushed cheeks and forehead. Fearful hot. Maybe all these covers made him too warm.

After pulling back the blankets, Huck went to open the window to let a cool breeze slip in.

Tad's lashes fluttered and his eyes opened. He seemed confused at first, but then he smiled. "Hey, Uncle Huck." His voice came out raspy, and his breathing sounded odd, like rusty pipes.

Huck tried to smile as he sat down. "Hey yourself, Tadpole. You've been lying in here missing all the fun. We had to fix the paddlewheel after that buffalo took to dancing with it. The captain says we'll be on our way tomorrow. You got to get to feeling better so you can help me steer this big old boat."

Tad's eyes darted, searching the room. "Where's Aunt Hallie?"

Poor thing. He was awful sick if he was pining for his aunt after being cooped up with her for three days.

Huck reckoned he would've been pulling his hair out—for an entirely different reason. He wanted Hallie something fierce, and that wanting only got worse after she'd come to tend him the other night.

Understanding *those* kinds of feelings wasn't what had him so confused, it was how they could start *liking* each other while still being at odds. That seemed unnatural somehow, but he wasn't philosophical enough to work it out.

"Your aunt needed to get something to eat. I came to spell her for a while."

Tad passed his tongue over lips that resembled old parchment. "Can I have a drink?"

"Sure you can. I got some fresh water from the cooler." Huck fetched the silver teacup he'd placed on the washstand. "Even put it in one of them fancy cups you like."

Tad propped up on an elbow, took a long drink, then flopped back down like the effort had drained all the steam out of him. Hang it, there had to be something that would bring the light back into his eyes.

"Hey, there's a sight you ought to see. A whole band of Sioux is gathered on that ruined bank. I'll bet they followed the buffalo."

Tad stared over Huck's shoulder like he was looking at something, except there was nothing on that wall.

"Tadpole?" Huck leaned in. "You feel up to going to see the Indians? I'll carry you if you'd like." He searched Tad's slack features for any sign of interest.

"I'll go later," his nephew murmured. "After I talk to Mama."

"You mean your Aunt Hallie. I imagine she looks like your ma, seeing as she's her sister."

"No, Mama has light hair and blue eyes. She's standing right there. Don't you see her?"

He swiveled his head around. No one was there. Tad was seeing things. Or—a cold finger trailed down his spine—that poor dead woman had come to fetch her son.

Huck jerked back around. Had he saved his nephew from drowning only to lose him to a fever? That wasn't the bargain he'd struck with God.

But Hucky, you snatched hold of that rope Hallie threw so you could save yourself. Reckon that means the deal is off.

Durn if he weren't an awful sinner. He hadn't even thought about that.

Tad let out a sigh and closed his eyes. Poor little mite, he was sleepy.

Or dying.

Alarmed, Huck grabbed Tad's shoulders and shook him gently. "Wake up, Tad. You can't go with your ma. She's up in heaven. You ain't old enough to get in."

Tad's eyelids fluttered. "I don't wanna go to heaven. I want to stay with you."

"That's right, we made a deal. Don't you recall? I'll be back to get you a couple weeks every summer, and we'll have heaps of fun."

His nephew's eyes grew sad. "But if you leave, you might not come back. Papa never came back. Then Mama left, and then Granny."

The pitiful words tore at Huck's heart. This was why he'd never let himself get too close to anybody, so when they left it didn't hurt as much. "I'll come back. I swear it. And you'll have a good pap in the meantime. I can tell you who he is because I'm sure he won't mind. You know him. It's Mr. Sawyer."

The news didn't cheer Tad up. If anything, it seemed to increase his sorrow. "But I want *you* to be my pap. Mr. Sawyer told me you'd take to me right off. Don't you want me?"

"'Course I do." Huck's throat closed around a knot of anguish.

He'd never meant to hurt Tad, but that was exactly what he'd done. He'd let his nephew get attached and had given him false hope by taking him on this ill-fated adventure. Now the child might die because he hadn't known enough to keep him out of danger. Why did Tad want an ignorant man like him for a father anyhow?

"I love you, Uncle Huck. Please don't give me away."

Tears blurred Huck's vision. Pretty soon, he'd be bawling like a baby.

Back when he'd been about Tad's age, he had begged his father not to leave. He'd reckoned even a mean bastard was better than no pap at all. The old man had left anyway, only coming back from time to time when it suited him. Huck took it to mean he wasn't worth loving. Now, he knew it was his pap who wasn't worth a damn, and he would be just as worthless if he did the same thing to a child who loved him.

Hallie had admitted she liked him, and had called him courageous and lots of other good things. If she believed he could be that kind of man then he could believe it too.

He leaned over and stroked back a fringe of hair. The heat radiating from Tad's forehead burned his fingers.

If Tad died thinking his uncle didn't care enough to bend his life around to make room for one small boy, well, he'd never forgive himself. "Get better, now, you hear me? You're my best hand. I can't do without you."

Tad gazed at him with bright, feverish eyes. "Does that mean I'm growed up enough for you to keep?"

"Sure you are. You're plenty big enough to keep."

HALLIE FOLDED HER NAPKIN AND LAID IT BESIDE A PLATE OF untouched food. Huck had taken over by Tad's bedside, insisting that she get something to eat and then rest. She knew she required sustenance, but felt disconnected from the need, as though she inhabited someone else's body. The strange sensation had persisted since Tad had fallen ill. She couldn't force down a bite. She couldn't sleep either.

She had treated him with willow bark tea for the fever, kept him warm and dry when chills set in, and spooned meat broth down his throat to strengthen him. Nothing seemed to help. She'd tried to pray, but that wasn't working either. God had turned his back. Was this her punishment for being so unforgiving? Surely the Almighty wouldn't be so cruel as to make Tad pay the price for her sins.

Her breath hitched on a dry sob.

"Miss MacBride?" Dan showed up beside the table holding his hat.

She dipped her head and used the napkin to wipe the damp corners of her eyes. "Mr. Devol, good—"

Was it morning or afternoon? While she'd held a vigil at Tad's side, one day had folded over onto the next one and she'd lost track of time.

Dan wore a morning coat so it had to be before noon. Some men didn't pay attention to proper attire, but he wasn't one of them.

He offered a hesitant smile. "It is a lovely morning. I couldn't bear to leave you sitting over here all by yourself in this gloomy corner. Most of the passengers are out on the promenade taking the air."

She had holed up over here to be alone, but she couldn't say so without being rude. "I am glad the day is nice, even if I am not free to enjoy it."

He gestured to a chair at the table. "May I join you for a moment?"

Hallie bit back a *no*. She didn't want to converse—with anyone.

On the other hand, she had no cause to spurn his kindness. After Tad had fallen ill, he'd inquired of several passengers and had brought her suggested home remedies. None seemed particularly effective, but at least he was trying to help. She forced a smile. "By all means, please sit down."

As he sat, he straightened his coat and gray silk vest. The striped tie with a four-in-hand knot was a nice touch. His dark hair had been smoothed back and his mustache carefully groomed.

This morning, Huck had shown up at her door, his hair mussed and whiskers on his face, in the same clothes he'd worn for two days. He'd taken no time to see to his own needs in between helping the crew make repairs to the boat and hovering at Tad's bedside.

She had done little more to make herself presentable. "Pardon me for not being at my best."

"It would be difficult for anyone to be at their best, given what you are facing." Dan's expression reflected concern. "I hear Tad hasn't improved."

"He took a fever. I'd guess from being in the dirty water for so long."

"I suspect you are right. It is a shame."

The tears she'd tried to hold in spilled out. She brought the napkin to her eyes. "The real shame is that he got away from me. I should've held onto him."

"Don't torture yourself. It's difficult to hold onto a boy that size when he wants to get away. I'm surprised the crew allowed him out on the bow."

"His uncle took him outside to show him something."

"That explains it."

"Explains what?"

"Finn gave no thought to the child's safety. I suppose it's to be expected. He's never dealt with children."

Huck had little in the way of parenting skills, but he wasn't heedless of Tad's safety. They'd been on their way inside when she'd encountered him on the stairs. "I can hardly condemn him when he risked his life to save Tad."

"I'm not condemning him. He showed great valor by going after Tad. But you agree he exercised poor judgment when he took him to an unprotected area where he could easily fall in."

What Dan said might be true, and she had made the same accusation, but she had no desire to pile coals of recrimination on Huck's head. "I believe he realizes that now."

"It's too bad he didn't listen to you before when you warned him about the dangers."

"Yes, well, we have buried the axe, and he is listening now. He gave me his permission to take Tad home to recuperate. After we land in Sioux City and a doctor declares him well enough to travel."

Dan leaned forward, his gaze sharpening. "Finn has agreed to let you have Tad?"

If only. They had come to a truce, of sorts.

"Not yet. I only convinced him that Tad needs a quiet place to rest and get well, and Huck can't leave until he's completed his contract."

"This is encouraging news." Dan leaned back and stroked his mustache as she'd seen him do when he was deep in thought. "Once you have Tad, it will be easier for you to prove you are best suited to provide for him. And if you contact the lawyer and explain what happened, they may sign over guardianship to you before Finn returns."

It would be wrong to go behind Huck's back when he'd taken an initial step of trust.

"I hope to avoid a legal battle. Now that Huck and I have come to an understanding, he may yet change his mind about giving Tad away. After he sees that Tad is happy to be with me."

Dan's frown wasn't encouraging. "You believe he'll keep his word to let Tad leave with you once we reach Sioux City?"

"Why would I doubt it?"

"He means well, but...he can be inconsistent."

"What makes you so quick to impugn his character?" The challenge that popped out of her mouth surprised her, as did the surge of anger on Huck's behalf. He'd lied to her and tried to manipulate her. Yet, she wasn't the one questioning his honor. "Do you hold a grudge against him for some wrong he did you?"

Dan's expression remained neutral. "No. I don't believe in holding a grudge. But I know you want the best for Tad, and I would be remiss if I didn't warn you not to place your trust in Mr. Finn. I fear he will disappoint you."

Removing her spectacles, she polished the dirty lenses with her sleeve. Dan seemed almost eager to cast aside a past friendship to aid a woman he barely knew. Of course, Huck seemed equally interested in discrediting Dan. Which man was telling the truth?

She desperately wanted to believe Huck.

Hallie replaced the glasses and smoothed her hair. "I will give some thought to what you've said. But you must excuse me. I need to check on my nephew."

Dan shot to his feet. "Of course. Let me know if there is anything I can do."

After thanking him, she hurried away, driven by a sense of urgency. What if Tad had worsened in the time she'd been away?

As she entered the door to the officers' quarters, her nostrils flared at a strong odor. It smelled like cigars. It seemed every man on board enjoyed smoking them. She sniffed again. No, this was different, more pungent, and it seemed to be coming from...

Smoke drifted out of the transom window above her room.

"My God!" She rushed down the hallway and jerked open the door. More smoke billowed out, stinging her eyes. She coughed and waved her hand in front of her face, squinting, trying to locate her nephew.

She could see no sign of fire, but Tad sat up in bed, gripped in a fit of coughing. His whole body shook and his face had turned beet red.

The old steward was beside him and held a long pipe. Wisps of smoke curled upward from the bowl to join the pungent cloud hovering near the ceiling.

"What are you doing?" she yelled.

Huck came up out of the chair. He grabbed her arms before she could reach Tad. "It's all right, Hallie. Don't get excited."

"Leave him alone!" She struggled to break free of Huck's firm grip, but instead of releasing her, he backed her into the hallway and slammed the door.

Then he planted himself in front of it.

She stared at him for an incredulous moment before fury and fear overwhelmed her, and she struck at him with her fists. "You will not keep me from Tad! Get out of my way."

Huck's fingers locked around her wrists and he lifted her onto her toes. She twisted to no avail. Amid breathing curses, she noticed a red spot near his eye where her fist had connected. Strangely enough, he didn't look angry with her. Instead, he wore an annoyingly patient expression. "Stop spittin' and clawin'. I can explain."

"Make it quick before Tad chokes to death on that foul smoke."

Huck finally released her but didn't budge from his defensive position. "T'ain't foul, it's mullein. An old Indian remedy. Tad's got to get that poison out of his lungs. Taking the smoke will help him do that."

What nonsense. She attempted to get around, but Huck moved in front of her with every dodge. From inside the cabin, the sound of Tad's coughing subsided. Her doubts, however, did not. "Where did you learn of this?"

"Mr. Lacey's got a Pawnee wife who taught him all sorts of remedies. He brought by that lung medicine, along with some goldenrod tea to help bring down the fever."

If Huck had resorted to Indian medicine, the situation must've deteriorated.

"Is Tad getting worse?"

"He's getting better." Huck spoke with such certainty she would've believed him. The anguish in his reddened eyes told a different story.

She gripped his arms. "Tell me you're not lying. Swear it. Swear to me he's getting better."

He hesitated before gathering her into a tight embrace. She wrapped her arms around him, needing just as desperately to hold someone. Regrettably, he was the only person she wanted to hold.

When she drew back, he maintained a loose grasp on her arms, as if he were loath to let go. Or perhaps he feared she might try to bolt past him. His thumbs brushed the insides of her wrists and her pulse took off at a gallop. She was powerless to stop it.

Why? Why did he affect her like this? His clothes were always rumpled, his hair perpetually mussed, his face usually sprouted a few days' growth before he got around to shaving. Nor did he care for the social graces, unless he was forced into it. He'd deceived and rejected her. Yet, something drew her to him like a moth testing a flame.

An answering heat built in his eyes. That he lusted after her was a far cry from loving her, but it seemed her body didn't know the difference. If she would listen to common sense, she would never again confuse the two.

She pulled away. "Let me see for myself whether this treatment is helpful."

He remained planted. "You got to trust me, Hallie."

Oh no. She was not twice a fool. "How can you ask for my trust while you're trying to keep me away from him?"

"You know I won't let him get hurt."

"You already have! You put him in harm's way when you decided to take him with you." She sucked in a ragged breath. God forgive her. She hadn't meant to blurt that out.

Pain flickered in his eyes. Knowing she'd caused it drove a knife through her heart. Ever since the night she'd gone to tend to him, he'd acted differently toward her. Kinder. More thoughtful. He'd gone out of his way to see to her comfort, and to reassure her that he would do what was best for Tad. She wanted to believe him. But she kept thinking about Dan's warning.

"If you truly love Tad, get us back to Sioux City as quickly as possible so we can seek out a proper doctor. Then let me take him home on the train."

CHAPTER TWENTY-SIX

Tad's fever broke later in the night. That Pawnee medicine had done the trick. By the time they reached Sioux City two days later, the boy felt well enough to beg to get out of bed.

Huck reckoned a little fresh air wouldn't hurt, but didn't argue the point with Hallie. They'd butt heads again soon enough.

He flanked the boat with a hard turn, allowing the current to swing the stern around so he could nose up to the wharf. Guiding a steamboat into a dock was a far sight easier than bringing the aunt around to his point of view.

With a tug of the cord, he sounded the landing bell.

A frenzy of activity erupted. Deckhands snubbed the mooring lines to thick posts as the engine sighed, heaving just enough steam to turn the buckets in a slow lap. Once the boat had been secured, the stage plank swung over the bow. The few passengers who'd boarded at Fort Sully departed, most of them headed for the eastbound train—the same one Hallie planned on taking home after a doctor declared Tad fit for travel. Except, Tad wasn't leaving.

Huck drew on his coat and groped in his pocket for his pipe.

Hallie had wrung an agreement out of him to let her take the boy home to rest. He'd promised Tad he could stay. Weren't worth pondering which was the *right* promise to honor. His conscience would gnaw no matter what he decided. How on earth could he explain things so Hallie wouldn't pick up a gun and shoot him for a liar?

He'd been so afraid Tad would die, he would've lassoed the moon had the child asked for it. It wasn't just that. In those dire moments when Tad had begged to stay with him, he had realized his nephew was the only soul on this old earth who loved him. Like a fish to bait, he couldn't resist the lure.

He took a few puffs, letting the sweet tobacco soothe him.

It was an odd feeling to be loved by a child. Tad didn't pass judgment or expect him to be somebody different than what he was. Instead, the boy looked up to him, and it made him want to be a better man. Now he just had to figure out how he ought to bring up a child when he had no idea how to be a parent. Men didn't raise youngsters on their own. Or if they tried, like Pap, they did a durn poor job of it.

You need a wife, Hucky.

He sucked in such a sharp breath he nearly swallowed the pipe. He was just getting used to the idea of having a child, and now he had to take on a wife. No, he wasn't the marrying type.

What else are you gonna do?

Hire a woman to take care of Tad.

That's not the same as a ma.

The sound of boots on the stairs jerked him out of the debate going on in his head and saved him from having to answer.

"Fortune is smiling on us, Mr. Finn," Captain Kinney announced as he entered the pilothouse. "I've just learned that a doctor has come aboard as a passenger. I've told the clerk to send him straightaway to check on your nephew."

Huck heaved a sigh of relief. Having a doctor on board made it a sight easier to defend his decision to keep Tad on the boat. "I'll have to thank that Fortune fellow when I see him."

The captain chuckled. "Give him thanks for me while you're at it. We'll set off again as soon as we're loaded. Can't afford to waste any time."

Huck lifted his hat from a hook on the wall. "I'd best go tell Miss MacBride we're leaving. She was giving some thought to staying here and taking the train home."

Captain Kinney frowned. "Why would she do that?"

"She's fretful about Tad's health." That was an understatement. When it came to their nephew, Hallie was like a she-wolf with a pup. There was no question she loved that boy, and Tad had grown mighty fond of her, as well.

She'd make a good ma, doncha think?

The blood left Huck's face and his heart pounded faster, sending it rushing right back.

"You feeling all right?" the captain inquired.

"Got a few things on my mind, is all." He could debate himself all he wanted, but there was no way around it. Tad deserved *two* parents. If he was going to keep his nephew, he had to get married. Somehow, the idea didn't seem quite so dreadful now that he thought about it. There were advantages to having a wife, especially one as pretty as Hallie.

The captain had been married for years and had raised three sons on this river. He ought to be an expert by now.

Huck took the pipe out of his mouth and tried to act casual. "I bet you had a few scares when your boys were young."

"We certainly did. I don't recall any of them jumping into the river to go swimming with buffalo." The captain's eyes crinkled.

Huck didn't find the incident amusing, though he might by the time Tad was his age. That scare had taught him a few things, though. The first being, he couldn't handle a young boy on his own. Hallie not only had to marry him, she also had to come along with them—on a steamboat.

She'd rather live in a teepee.

"How did you convince Mrs. Kinney to travel with you?" he asked the captain.

"I didn't. Kate was the one who insisted on coming along and bringing our boys. Took me a while to get used to the idea. Now I couldn't get by without her." The old man eyed him curiously. "Any particular reason you asked?"

"Never knew any folks who raised a family on the river, is all."

Captain Kinney didn't look a bit fooled. "It takes a special woman to put up with the likes of us river men. I suspect Miss MacBride might be one."

"This isn't about—" Huck took another puff on his pipe and wrestled the devilish part of him that wanted to lie. He had no idea how to convince Hallie to marry him. Heck, he'd never even wooed a woman, having little need to keep one around before now. He'd be a fool not to accept the advice of someone more experienced. "Hallie's not too keen on steamboats—or pilots."

The captain's clever smile turned kind. "She might overcome her fear of one if she loves the other."

Love?

The idea teased him, like flecks of gold winking beneath the water. Convincing Hallie to marry him for Tad's sake was one thing, but getting her to love him? Why, he'd sprout wings and fly before that happened.

"Right now I need her to marry me. We can work out the rest later."

The captain clapped a hand on Huck's shoulder. "I'm afraid you have the process turned around, Mr. Finn. First, you must win her, then you won't have such a hard time with the rest."

But he had bungled things—badly.

"You don't understand. She thinks I lied to her. Tricked her. Ruined her."

The old man's friendliness vanished. He crossed his arms over his chest and gave Huck a hard stare. "Did you?"

Saying *no* would be a lie, admitting to it made him a villain, and it wasn't quite so black and white. "I did some of those things, but I had good reasons at the time. I can explain."

He'd better hurry. The captain was working up to a full head of steam.

"The same day I found out I was Tad's guardian, Hallie came after him all in a bluster, putting on like I weren't fit to raise a hog, saying the child was coming with her whether he wanted to or not. I didn't see any profit in Tad being raised by a woman like that, so we lit out. Then she followed us..." He could go on for days about how she'd dogged his heels, but what was the point?

"After a while, I realized she weren't so bad, except for her being a spinster woman, and that isn't what Tad needs. He deserves a whole family. I didn't have one, but I sure wanted one. That's why I decided to give him to my good friend Tom. He's a man I trust to be the kind of father Tad needs. But Hallie 'most blew her boilers when I told her that. And Tad, he just kept begging to stay with me. Then, after he nearly died..." Huck's heart jerked around at the thought of how close he'd come to losing his nephew. "Well, I couldn't refuse him. I promised I'd keep him with me and raise him on the river. While he's little, he needs a ma to watch over him. So, I reckon I ought to marry his aunt."

The captain's color wasn't quite so red now. He rubbed his hand over his face like he'd got confused. "When in all this carrying on did you ruin her?"

"I didn't *ruin* her. Only kissed her twice. Well, maybe three times. I didn't mean anything by it. Not anything bad. She mistook my intentions."

What were your intentions, Hucky?

Hell if he knew. When it came to Hallie, his mind didn't work right, his body betrayed him, and his heart got all twisted around.

He knocked the ashes from his pipe into the box of sand. "Thank you for the advice, sir. I'd better go catch Hallie before she gets off the boat."

CHAPTER TWENTY-SEVEN

The doctor pressed what looked like a little horn against Tad's chest then cocked his head like he was listening to something in the tubes he'd stuck in his ears. "Take another deep breath, young man."

Tad sucked in a breath—and started coughing. Although it didn't hurt as bad as it had earlier.

He grabbed the handkerchief Aunt Hallie offered and spit out a mouthful of thick gooey stuff, then wadded the cloth in a ball and handed it back to her.

She smiled like he'd given her a present. He didn't know why she would want *that*, but Uncle Huck had said there was no accounting for what pleased her. His uncle wouldn't want to give her a dirty handkerchief. There had to be something else she'd want.

"Aunt Hallie..."

"No talking, keep breathing," the doctor ordered.

Tad took another deep breath while the doctor moved the little cone on his chest around to his back. He didn't remember much from when he'd been sick, but he did remember his uncle saying he was big enough to keep. That made him so happy he hadn't thought about anything else, not even how bad he felt.

A little while ago, before his aunt and the doctor showed up, his uncle had come by to see him and told him they had to put their heads together and figure out how to convince Aunt Hallie not to leave.

"Wish I knew how to please her." That's what Uncle Huck needed to know. So that's what Tad would find out.

"Very good," the doctor declared. He put the listening tubes into a black satchel on the floor and turned to Aunt Hallie. "His lungs sound clear and his fever is gone, so I don't think we're dealing with pneumonia. However, he should stay quiet and rest for another week." He smiled at Tad. "You're a fortunate young man."

"Yes sir, I do got a fortune my granny left me, but I'm not filthy rich like Uncle Huck." With a gasp, he slapped his hand over his mouth. He'd forgotten he wasn't supposed to tell anybody else the secret.

"Not quite the same," the doctor said with a smile. "Fortunate means you are lucky."

Oh, he hadn't understood right. Well then. Maybe they didn't know what he was talking about either. But he knew exactly what had given him good luck. "I reckon it was because of that baby spider crawling on me."

"You have spiders in your bed?" Aunt Hallie's eyes got big behind the glasses. She was impressed.

"Just one. But it left yesterday."

The doctor wiped his hand over his beard like he was rubbing off a smile. "Very well. I will leave you two to debate the beneficial qualities of arachnids."

"What's a rack-nid?"

"It's Latin for *spider*." The doctor stood up. Aunt Hallie followed him outside the door.

Curious, Tad leaned over to listen. He could hear them talking but couldn't make out what they were saying. It sounded like something about the railroad. She sure did like talking about trains. Uncle Huck wouldn't want to give her a train ride. He wanted her to stay with them on the steamboat.

The door creaked and his aunt stepped back inside. She came and sat on the edge of the bed and hugged him. It stirred up good feelings inside like he'd just eaten a fresh-baked pie.

He snuggled against her warmth. He didn't mind her hugs so much, not anymore. She had held him, rocked him, and even sang to him when he was feeling poorly, and it had made him feel better. But now, he was ready to get up.

"Can I go see Lucky?"

"Not yet, dear. But you needn't worry, I've been taking good care of your pet." She brushed his hair with her fingers.

Tad pulled away with a grimace. It was all well and good to put up with a hug every so often, but he wasn't letting her treat him like a baby.

She gave him an understanding smile. "The doctor says you're well enough to travel. You should have something to eat first. I'll ask the cook if he can make up some of that broth you had earlier."

He wrinkled his nose. "Ugh, I'd rather eat cornbread and catfish."

"We'll try soup first." She headed for the door.

"Aunt Hallie, wait!" He'd almost forgotten. He had to find out what would please her so she would want to stay with him and Uncle Huck.

She turned around. "Yes?"

"What pleases you?"

She gave a soft laugh. "You want to know what pleases me?"

He nodded, eager to hear.

"Being with you pleases me, and going home."

Going home?

His smile fell away and his heart beat faster. "Are you leaving?"

"Not without you."

He chewed on his lip, not liking the sound of that either.

Aunt Hallie's eyes went all soft and kind, only now she seemed a little sorrowful. "I was waiting for the doctor to come and check on you before telling you. We're leaving today, to go home on the train."

"The train?" But his uncle had promised to keep him. He wasn't going home with Aunt Hallie, unless... "Is Uncle Huck coming with us?" he asked hopefully.

She went real still and her face got tight, like it did sometimes when he talked about his uncle. "No, he has to stay here. He has a job to do."

Tad shook his head. His uncle wouldn't go back on his vow, and he wouldn't let Aunt Hallie just up and leave. Not after the way he'd talked this morning, saying he wished he knew how to please her. She didn't understand or maybe nobody had told her yet. "But Uncle Huck said we could stay together."

"Did he now?" Her eyes narrowed.

Sure didn't look like *that* pleased her.

A SHORT TIME LATER, HALLIE MADE HER WAY TO THE STAIRS, carefully balancing a tray laden with a bowl of soup. Tad would need to eat before they left.

Not surprisingly, he'd gone back to talking about staying with his uncle. If Huck had changed his mind, he would have discussed this with her before they'd reached Sioux City. Tad had misunderstood or made it up. As soon as he finished eating, they would leave to catch the train.

Huck came thundering down the stairs.

Speak of the devil.

Hallie stepped to one side to avoid a collision.

He appeared surprised and darted a quick look past her. "Where's Tad?"

"Still in bed. I'm getting him something to eat before we leave."

"Ah, well, I need to talk to you about that." Huck's rueful smile ignited her suspicion.

"We have an agreement," she reminded him.

"That doc you met is a passenger." Huck went on as if he hadn't heard her. "He's traveling with us to St. Louis. He can keep an eye on Tad, so there's no need to take him off the boat."

"No need?" She tightened her grip on the tray, tempted to fling the contents into Huck's face. "He nearly *died.*"

"But he's feeling good now, and we got medical care aboard." Huck retreated a couple of steps. "No time to explain. We got to leave right away. Captain's orders."

He gave a wave before he ran back up the stairs.

Hallie marched to the next level, but he was already gone. It was pointless to follow him, might as well argue with a mule. Huck might not think he had to honor his agreement, but she would hold him to it. She would pack up and have Tad off this boat before it departed.

When she reached the room, Tad was sitting cross-legged on the bed, happily playing with a set of toy soldiers the captain had given him. She set the tray on the bed beside him. "Eat up, darling. We need to hurry."

Her hand hovered over the peg where she'd hung the gown Kate had given her. She sighed, resigned. Taking it wouldn't be right, considering she hadn't completed the mural.

She put on her frayed jacket and noticed Tad hadn't budged. "Why aren't you eating?"

Rather than picking up the spoon, Tad continued to play with one of the little soldiers mounted on a horse. "Uncle Huck said we'd stay here. Together."

Scolding would accomplish nothing. Tad's reluctance to leave was to be expected, and it wasn't the child's fault that Huck had gone back on his word.

She shook out her bedraggled bonnet. "He said that before you became so ill. Now he wants you to come home with me to recuperate."

"Nuh-uh." Tad shook his head. "He told me that when I was sick, and again this morning before you got here."

She jerked on the bonnet. *The dirty dog.* He'd never intended for them to leave and had only agreed to keep her quiet. This, after proposing a truce and no more deceptions.

The departure bell clanged. If they didn't leave now, they'd never make it.

"Forget the soup. Let's get you dressed."

"No!" Tad jumped out of the bed, spilling the tray. Hot soup splashed onto the floor.

She jumped back to avoid being scalded. "What's gotten into you?"

"He *promised*." Tad braced his feet, arms akimbo. He mimicked his uncle's belligerent stance—and personality—perfectly.

She resisted the urge to snatch him by the ear. "I am not arguing, young man. If you don't put your pants on, I'll take you out in your shirttails."

His face twisted into a disrespectful scowl, but he picked up his trousers and slowly pulled them on. Where were his suspenders?

She checked the top bunk and then peered under the bed.

The floor shook and the boat rumbled in readiness.

"No, no, not yet," she muttered.

Tad could go without suspenders. He could do without clothes, as far as she was concerned. She fumbled with the knob and threw open the door that led out to the upper deck.

The stage plank had been hauled up, and the boat was backing into the river. It was too late.

"Devil take the man!" She flung her bonnet down and stomped her foot.

Tad watched with wide eyes.

"Get back in bed," she said with forced calmness. "I'll get you something else to eat. Then I need to have a talk with your uncle."

AFTER HALLIE HAD GOTTEN TAD FED AND SETTLED AGAIN, SHE headed up to the pilothouse, still seething.

Huck stood in his usual position to the right of the big wheel, fully attentive to the river, like a man with a fascinating mistress.

She squelched a spurt of jealousy. Why should she care if he was in thrall? They were well suited to each other, both of them fickle and not to be trusted. "Might I have a word with you?"

He threw a glance over his shoulder. The wariness in his expression told her he'd rather not be in the same room. "Maybe we could talk later."

Oh no, he wasn't getting off that easy. Nor was she going to sit down and address his back. She wanted to see his face when she challenged his lies. "I know you can steer and talk at the same time. I've seen you do it."

He kept his gaze locked straight ahead. "How is Tad getting along?"

She fisted her hands at her sides, tempted to tear into him like an angry badger. Instead, she would give him a chance to tell her the truth *before* she bit his head off. "He is resting."

"What did the doc have to say?"

"Tad doesn't have pneumonia."

"That's good news."

"But he must remain quiet for the next few weeks."

"Hold on." Huck leaned forward to look at something out the window. "Let me get us past these snags then I'll be able to listen better."

She doubted he would be inclined to *listen better*, having shown no talent for it. However, to be on the safe side, she wouldn't interrupt him during a delicate maneuver.

The river did appear shallower here. Snags bristled alongside the boat. Her chest grew tight as anxiety resurfaced. Perhaps this wasn't the best time for a contentious conversation.

On the other hand, if she waited until he was off his shift, he would find some other way to avoid her, and she wanted to settle this before they made the next landing. If she couldn't persuade him to let her take Tad home, she would be forced into using the kind of tactics he favored—underhanded ones.

He turned the wheel, clearing the last of the snags. Now they would have a few minutes to converse before he became preoccupied with navigating an upcoming bend.

"When did you plan to tell me?" she asked in a smooth voice.

"Tell you what?"

"Cease pretending you don't know what I'm talking about. Tad repeated what you said about us staying together. I discerned your intentions easily enough."

"My...intentions?" His ruddy complexion darkened. He gripped the wheel and kept his eyes fixed straight ahead. If he weren't at the helm of a large steamboat, she would swear he was avoiding eye contact. "You think now is the right time to talk about that?"

She huffed at his obvious evasion. "No, the right time to discuss it would have been *before* we landed in Sioux City. Not after you forced my hand."

With a frown, he reached up and pulled a cord, clanging a bell that told the engineer to slow the boat. "I couldn't force you to do anything, even if I had divine powers. You decide for yourself what you want to do. I just thought this would work out for the best, so long as you don't mind coming along."

Dratted man. He was doing it again, twisting her words around to make it seem that she had somehow misunderstood.

"Of course, I mind, but what did you expect me to do? Swim to shore?"

The boat headed into a fast-flowing bend. Directly in front of them, a sandbar loomed.

Her heart jumped into her throat. "Watch out!"

A telltale scraping against the hull raised goose bumps on her arms. If he wouldn't turn them away, she would.

She grabbed the spokes.

"Hallie, let go." Huck wrestled to keep her from gaining control of the wheel.

"We'll run aground!" Panic made her voice shrill.

"Let *go*." He peeled her fingers off the spokes and shoved her away.

In a heart-stopping moment that seemed to stretch time, he nudged the bow slightly onto the sandbar, at the same time spinning the wheel to send the boat swinging around until the current caught it and pulled it stern-first into the roaring channel.

The boat strained against the current as he jerked on the bell cord, which brought on a harsh roar of pent-up steam. The engineer had thrown open the boiler's safety valves to release the pressure.

Hallie fisted her hands so hard her nails dug into her palms. Had Huck lost his mind?

With a firm grip on the spokes, he turned and peered out the rear window. She watched in amazement as the paddlewheel churned against the current, slowing the *Hesperia* enough for him to guide it *back* through the winding bend.

After he had cleared the tight curve, he rotated the wheel and brought the bow around, righting the boat.

She released a pent-up breath and nearly wept with relief. "Why did you do that?"

"It's safer. Fast as the current's traveling, if we were going forward, I'd have to keep her full steam or she'd run away from me. Backing her, I can take it slow around a bend without losing control."

It was an incredibly skillful maneuver. One she'd never seen. His explanation made perfect sense and proved he was careful, not reckless, as she'd surmised.

"I'm sorry. I shouldn't have grabbed the wheel."

"You need to trust me, Hallie."

Hadn't she trusted him before? Only to have her faith dashed against the rocks.

"I trust you to pilot this boat, but that is as far as it goes."

His lips tipped in a rueful smile that revealed a dimple and sent flutters into her chest. "You got to do better than that. For Tad's sake."

"For *Tad's* sake?" She recalled her purpose for seeking him out. "Is it for *his* sake you are keeping us hostage on this boat? Is it for *his* sake you want me to sign that ridiculous agreement to limit our relationship to two weeks out of every year? Am I to trust that you know how much time I should be allotted to love him?"

Huck looked at her as if she'd spouted nonsense. "I don't mean for you to sign that now. You can see him all you want if you stay with me."

"*Stay* with you?" She released a dark laugh. "I am *stuck* with you until we reach the next landing. Then I am taking Tad home on the train, as we agreed."

Confusion flickered in his eyes a moment before he smoothed his features into a neutral expression. "Reckon I misunderstood what you were talking about earlier. I thought you had it figured out."

"What am I supposed to have figured out?" she shot back, exasperated.

"I'm keeping Tad with me."

"Keeping Tad." She stared in stunned disbelief. "After what happened?"

He had the grace to look chagrined. "I'm not saying I didn't make a mistake. He's young and don't have all the knowledge he needs to survive. I'm going to fix that. Captain Kinney, he raised three boys on this river, and he's offered to show me how to do it right."

Almost losing Tad must have shaken Huck deeply if he would choose to alter his life and take on the responsibility of a child. She could respect him for it, but she couldn't agree to it. He couldn't raise a child alone.

Her heart skipped a beat. He didn't mean to do it alone. Hadn't he said something earlier about her staying with him? "Are you thinking of hiring me to take care of Tad?"

His eyes held hers. "Tad needs parents, not keepers. I want you to be my wife."

His wife?

Her emotions swung from exhilaration to pure terror. She had to clutch the side of the lazy bench to keep from collapsing. As it was, she had to sit down.

Had he proposed the night of the dance, she would've gladly accepted. But he'd made it crystal clear that he wasn't interested in a permanent relationship. Now, he was saying he'd changed his mind.

She sought confirmation. "You are certain you want to *marry* me?"

"I swore to Tad I'd keep him, and the only way I can do that is if I'm married."

The indifferent proposal sent a barb through her heart. No words of love or even affection. Huck wanted to give Tad a mother and wished to avoid an extended battle for custody. That he found her appealing enough to bed her was an added benefit. The man was eminently practical if nothing else. "That certainly takes care of your problem, doesn't it?"

He kept a hand on the wheel as he turned his head to glance in her direction. His frown indicated she'd reacted in some way that displeased him. "I understand how this might come as a surprise. Heck, I only worked it out today. But it makes sense if you think about it. You said you liked me, and I like you, and if we ain't fighting over Tad, we rub along well enough."

"Rub along?" That didn't sound very romantic. Then again, Huck wasn't much for flowery words. It wouldn't matter how he said it if she knew he loved her.

Was she really that foolish? Even if he came to care for her, he would never love her—or Tad—as much as he loved the river, and one day it would take him from them.

The wind whipped up foamy waves. Huck rang more bells, then came the creak of the wheel ropes. Still nervous, she got up to look out the front window. Her father had taught her a few things. Foremost being, not to depend on a riverboat pilot to change his ways.

"The channel is there." She pointed at high crests indicating where the water was deeper. "Veer to larboard."

Huck didn't turn the wheel. "Why do you say that?"

"The waves show the safest route."

"That's true—if the wind is coming upstream. But it's blowing downstream, which means the high waves are where the water is shoal. I'd ground her if I went over there."

His warning stirred up old memories, and with them, old fears. She had not recognized danger before. She would not make that mistake again. "Yes, you're right. I remember now. You were smart not to heed my advice."

The corner of his mouth curled up in a sympathetic smile.

"The signs are tricky. You might not recollect how to read 'em if you don't look at the river every day. But I can teach you—if you'll stay with me."

She couldn't deny, to herself at least, that she was tempted by his offer. Despite his trickery, Huck had many good qualities, and she was drawn to him with a powerful attraction. He had more than proven they would *rub along well enough* when it came to those matters.

As much as marriage would solve one problem, it would raise a host of others she wasn't prepared to handle. She would have to find another way to keep Tad with her. One that didn't require her to risk their lives or her heart. "I'm sorry, Huck. I cannot marry you."

CHAPTER TWENTY-EIGHT

Huck held his breath while he scraped his chin with the sharp blade. He rinsed it in the wash bowl and peered into the mirror, rubbing his fingers over the smooth skin. Yep, he'd gotten every whisker with nary a nick.

Setting the razor aside, he pulled a comb through his wet hair in an effort to tame it. Some of that Macassar oil might help, but he couldn't stand smelling like rotten fruit.

Now for the worst—blame stiff collar and tie. Might as well get haltered. But he'd put up with it, at least until he convinced Hallie to marry him. Preferably within the week.

He had accepted a permanent job on the *Hesperia*, which meant he needed to get hitched by the time they reached St. Louis. After a few days off, he'd take the boat back upriver with Tad and Hallie onboard. If the blasted woman would cooperate. After turning him down flat, she'd avoided him for the past four days.

Huck scratched a red spot on his neck. Blame it, she was giving him the hives. After fastening the buttons on his vest, he turned around and presented himself to his cabin mate. "So, how do I look?"

Mr. Lacey chuckled. "Like you's going courtin'. You got that skeered, worrisome look in yo' eyes."

"If I'm worried, it's that I'll choke before I can get up off my knees when I ask for her hand. Who thought up that nonsense anyway? What good does her hand do? I need all of her." He ran his finger beneath the collar. "Feels like a noose around my neck."

Still frowning, he shrugged on his coat. So many layers suffocated a body. The Indians were smart to wear next to nothing this time of year. Why couldn't white folks adopt the native fashions, instead of the other way around?

The steward motioned him over. "Lemme fix that tie."

Mr. Lacey fussed with it a bit then patted Huck's shoulder. "There now, you look real nice. Like a gentleman. 'Cept for that frown. You'll skeer that gal away if you grumble at her like a rain cloud."

"If I wanted to hear a funny man, I'd go to a circus show."

Mr. Lacey ripped out with a laugh. "Why Huck, you is gettin' as temperamental as my old lady."

His old lady? Now, there was an idea. Hallie would change her mind right quick about marrying him if she thought he'd worked out a way to keep Tad without her help. "Reckon your wife might be interested in coming along on the next trip? I'd pay her real good for watching Tad."

"No, suh. She got them plants she looks after all the spring and summer. She won't be leaving her garden to go traipsin' off on a steamboat." The steward's smile turned wise. "Besides, you hasn't tried hard enough to win that gal of your'n. You got to sweeten her up. Tell her how pretty she is, like a sunrise, and how you cain't get along without her no more than you can do without air. Women like to hear that kind of talk."

"Heck, I *showed* her how pretty I think she is—more than once —and she knows good and well I need her help."

Mr. Lacey gave a sad shake of his head like he was dealing with some fool. "You ain't listenin' to what I'm sayin'. Women don't wanna hear they's just good for watchin' over young'uns or keepin' a man satisfied. They got to feel appreciated, and petted. Treated more special than anything in the whole world. Give it a try, Huck. She'll come around lightnin'-fast once you start treating her like that."

The older man offered good advice. Sadly, those sweet words wouldn't sound half as natural coming out of Huck Finn's mouth, and he didn't have time to practice. He had to catch Hallie before she went downstairs to dinner.

Huck set off down the hall to where the officers were quartered. Most of the crew hadn't commented since he'd accepted that spare berth in the steward's cabin. But he knew some of them looked down on him for sharing a room with a Negro.

Did Hallie? The troublesome thought brought him up short. Then he shook his head. Nah, she'd praised him for how he'd handled things. Plus, the only person he'd seen her act uppity around was him, mostly because he annoyed her.

He stopped at the door to her room. Correction, *his* room. Maybe he ought to remind her how generous he'd been to allow her to have it. She would only remind him why she was there in the first place. He was out to make a good impression, not reinforce the bad one.

He yanked his vest down then rapped twice.

The door eased open a crack. "Huck?" Her eyebrows shot up like she was surprised to see him. Did she think he'd let her ignore him forever?

"Can I talk to you?"

As she opened the door, the sight of her stole his breath. She wore that soft green gown the captain's wife had given her, along with a pretty shawl, and had her hair done up in a mass of tempting curls. Without her spectacles, the light from overhead made her eyes sparkle.

"Yes? What can I do for you?"

For starters, she could invite him in so he could strip off her clothes. She'd never speak to him again if he suggested such a thing.

"You and Tad can join me for dinner tonight at the officers' table."

"I'm very sorry. We can't."

Her rejection set him back. It might be because he'd blurted it out like an order instead of taking the steward's advice.

He tugged at his collar and tried to smile. "You look most awful pretty." No, she looked more than pretty. She looked luscious enough to eat. But that wasn't something a woman would care to hear. "With your hair done up, and that flowy dress..."

Blame it. He was blabbering like a fool. He was in such a sweat he'd forgotten all about the present he'd bought for her. He dipped his hand into his coat pocket and pulled out the narrow box. "Here." He held it out. "I got you a present."

"A present?" She took the gift with a look of confusion.

"Thought you might want to paint some pictures in that book of yours." He rocked on his heels, excited for her to open it. "Those are watercolor paints."

He had known it was just the thing when he'd seen it yesterday after they docked in Kansas City and he went out to find her a gift. He'd thought of it himself with no prodding from Tad or Mr. Lacey.

She cracked the box open and her eyes got wide, then she pressed her lips tight.

His spirits sagged like a leaky balloon. "If you don't like it, I can get you something else."

Her eyes got shiny and bright. Oh hell, he'd made her cry. "No, it...it's a lovely present. Thank you."

Maybe it wasn't the gift she didn't like, but the giver.

"Never mind that," he muttered. "You *are* going to eat?"

"Yes, but..." Her smile turned apologetic. "Mr. Devol offered to escort me to dinner and I've already accepted."

Huck bit back a curse. He'd been trying to get her to talk to him for days. "So you can find time for that rascal but not for me?"

Her expression became guarded. "Dan isn't a rascal. He's been a gentleman."

"He's no more a *gentleman* than a skunk in a suit." Huck seethed with frustration. No matter what Dan wore or how he talked, he was still the same old cheat underneath. Why couldn't Hallie see it? She was acting worse than that fool woman Eve who'd listened to a snake, and look what happened to her.

"Where's Tad?"

She clutched the box of paints to her chest like she feared he might take it away even though she'd acted like she didn't want it. "I let him go to dinner with a friend he met earlier today. A little girl whose parents boarded at Sioux City. We're joining them at their table."

Even Tad had snagged a female.

Huck's face felt blistered. This was worse than when he was a boy and none of the girls would even look at him, except to laugh. He turned and stalked down the hall before he said something he would later regret.

Hallie's rejection ate at him all the way down to the dining hall. She was smart enough to figure out the most sensible thing would be to marry him, not encourage a bounder. Why was she making this so difficult?

You know why.

One little present wasn't going to make up for all the insults he'd dealt her. Plus, he hadn't exactly wooed her before he'd proposed. The old steward had it right. He was going about this the wrong way. Much as it rasped on him, he'd have to eat crow for a while. At least until he could get her off alone and talk sweet to her.

As Huck approached the officers' table, Captain Kinney peered past him. "Will Miss MacBride be joining us tonight?"

"No sir, she won't." Huck pretended he didn't notice the pitying looks he received. He wasn't about to admit she'd turned him down in favor of Dapper Dan. "Tad's got himself a gal, and they're sitting with her family tonight."

SILVER CLINKED ON CHINA AMIDST THE MURMUR OF CONVERSATION around the dinner table. Hallie dipped into a serving of strawberry shortcake the waiter had set in front of her. She took one bite and laid her spoon down. Even her favorite dish failed to tempt her. Not that it wasn't good. The entire dinner had been marvelous—an array of soups and cold dishes, followed by scallop of chicken with mushrooms, green corn, dumplings and potatoes. All in all, more food than she could think about eating. If she was hungry.

Dan leaned in from her right. "The shortcake is delicious."

"Yes, I tasted it. I don't believe I could eat another bite. There's so much food."

"Most of it you didn't touch."

How could she eat when her stomach was tied in knots?

She should have tried harder to talk Huck into a compromise before sending that telegram when they'd docked yesterday. What she had put into motion would surely destroy the fragile threads of trust between them.

On the other hand, he would not give up Tad and she refused to be forced into a bad marriage. It would be best if she gained custody of her nephew, then afterward negotiated with Huck about visitation rights. She couldn't allow him to drag their nephew all over creation and risk the child's life.

Dan spoke low, close to her ear. "Don't second guess yourself, if that's what you're doing. You were right to let the lawyer know about Tad's unfortunate accident. Finn is a decent enough fellow, but he's not considering your nephew's best interests."

"Yes, that's what I keep telling myself." And feeling less confident with every passing minute. She slid a furtive glance in the direction of the officers' table.

Huck looked so handsome in his new suit. He had combed his hair back and it gleamed like copper beneath the warm light from a chandelier overhead.

Over the past few days, he'd taken pains with his appearance, apparently trying to impress her. That precious gift of the watercolor paints had almost been her undoing. Other men would've bought her a fan or a broach. Huck knew her better than that. His gift had been perfect.

Which only proved what lengths he would go to to gain her cooperation. Hadn't she seen numerous times how crafty he could be when he was determined to get his way? This wasn't the first time he'd played on her heartstrings.

Across the table, Tad polished off his dessert with gusto. He launched into a harrowing account of his rescue while the yellow-haired girl at his side listened attentively. Even her parents appeared riveted.

It was an exciting story. Only, Tad left out the part where he almost died from a subsequent illness. He didn't tell them how his uncle had tricked his aunt into staying on the boat rather than keeping a promise to let her take him home where he could rest and not risk a relapse.

Tad couldn't see the chinks in his champion's armor. He hadn't yet experienced the bitter disappointment that came from believing in heroes.

She couldn't blame him. When she'd been Tad's age, her father could do no wrong. Only later, as the years passed and he stayed away for longer periods, did she realize what truly held his heart. The same lover held sway over Huck and she couldn't compete.

"Are you nervous about how Finn will react?" Dan whispered.

In hindsight, taking Dan into her confidence had been a mistake. She'd only done it because she was afraid to go to Kate for help, knowing the captain's wife would push her into Huck's arms. Also, Huck had been too watchful for her to get away. She'd needed someone who could easily leave the boat without rousing his suspicions.

Hallie put a hand on her churning stomach. "Forgive me. It was wrong to bring you into this when it is not your concern."

"*You* are my concern. That is why I offered to help."

She didn't *want* to be his concern. She had no intention of continuing their relationship past the time they were on this boat.

What a coward, to have used Dan as a shield so she wouldn't have to deal with Huck. There was only one solution—to stay away from *both* of them for the remainder of the journey.

She folded her napkin. "I'm feeling unwell. I believe I should retire to my room."

Dan scooted back in his chair. "We could step out to the promenade. Fresh air might help."

"Thank you, but no. I have to get Tad to bed."

"I don't want to go to bed." Tad's anxious gaze shifted over her shoulder and a huge grin split his face. "Hey, Uncle Huck."

"Hey yourself, Tadpole."

Hallie stiffened at the rumbling voice directly behind her. Great day, she hadn't heard Huck approach. Had he seen Dan whispering to her, or worse, heard them?

She stretched her lips into a smile and acted as if nothing were amiss. "Mr. Finn, how good of you to come over. Allow me to introduce you to Mr. and Mrs. Crowder." She nodded to the couple seated across the table. "And to Mary, their daughter. Mr. Finn is our pilot."

Huck rested his hand on her shoulder while he made small talk with the guests at the table. His warmth penetrated the thin dress and heated her face. He didn't take notice of her discomfort at his familiarity. Or was it a guilty conscience that made her want to squirm?

"Tad, you want to show your friend the pilothouse?" he asked.

"Would I! Let's go, Mary." Tad paused for a moment to pull out the chair for the little girl seated next to him.

Hallie smiled to acknowledge her nephew's good manners before twisting toward Huck, slipping his grasp without causing a scene. "How kind of you to offer to entertain the children."

His eyes lit with amusement. "You can thank the captain. It was him who offered to take them on a tour of the boat, and Miss Mary's folks, if they'd like."

"We would love to see the pilothouse." Mrs. Crowder beamed as if she'd been offered a tour of the Taj Mahal.

"Then it's done." Huck gestured to the door leading to the stairs. "Captain Kinney will meet you all over there."

Hallie stood as the party departed. Huck had arranged that tour to get Tad away from her. Why? She darted a worried glance at his face, but it told her nothing.

"Devol, you won't mind if I borrow Miss MacBride for a few minutes," he said, with less geniality than he'd used in addressing the other guests.

Dan tucked her hand in the crook of his arm. "Sorry, old man. She doesn't feel well."

"A walk outside might help. It's awful stuffy over here."

"We didn't notice the hot air until you showed up."

"Please, gentlemen, the air is fine." Hallie extracted her hand from Dan's grip. The last thing she needed was to have these two engaged in a very public dispute over her. "I will wait in the ladies' salon until Tad returns and we retire for the night."

Dan gave a reluctant nod before leaving her. She could tell he wasn't pleased with being dismissed.

Huck didn't take the cue and remained. "After you finish visiting with the ladies, we'll talk."

"What about?"

"You know." His lips curved in a half-smile that brought on an aggravating tingle.

Her defenses were not sufficient if he waged an all-out assault.

"Don't bother waiting around. I am certain I shall be occupied all evening."

CHAPTER TWENTY-NINE

An hour later, Huck stopped outside the frosted glass doors to the ladies' salon and sneaked another look to see whether Hallie was still inside. She was, and she appeared to be engaged in a lively conversation with Mrs. Kinney.

Women could go on like that for days. They'd had plenty of time to visit, so he ought to be able to interrupt. If he did, Hallie would accuse him of being ill-mannered. But wasn't she being downright rude by ignoring his request to speak with her? Still, making a fuss would work against him in his efforts to woo her.

He rubbed his forehead. All this arguing with himself was making his head hurt.

She intended to stay in there all night, hiding behind Mrs. Kinney's skirts. The captain's wife wasn't the problem. He wouldn't ever get Hallie alone as long as Dan kept hanging around. That pest had to go.

He sauntered to the other end of the main cabin where a thick layer of smoke marked the men's domain. Tonight, every table was occupied, and there sat Dan, right in the middle of the activity.

Huck ordered a whiskey and leaned his elbow on the bar,

watching while Dan laid out a hand. Odds were good that the gambler used the marked decks, but it was impossible to tell without touching the cards.

When a seat opened, Huck strolled over. "Mind if I join you fellows?"

"Not at all." Dan shuffled the deck. His smile seemed a mite strained.

Satisfied he'd guessed right, Huck waited as the cards were dealt and the ante set.

Excitement coursed through him when he turned up a red queen. He ran his fingers lightly along the edge and frowned. It wasn't marked.

He met Dan's steady gaze. A ghost of a smile appeared beneath the shiny mustache. The sneaky skunk knew precisely what was up and had started with a clean deck.

They played out the game. Dan won with a flush.

Huck called for another deck. The men around the table grumbled, but none objected too strongly, as it wasn't unusual for losers to question the cards.

The barkeep tossed over another pack.

With nary a glance across the table, Huck dumped out the cards and carefully checked them. They were clean, too. He shoved back his chair and strode to the bar, motioning for another deck. Then another. He checked every damn deck. They were all straight as an arrow. Not a marked card amongst them.

"Are you satisfied?" Dan drawled. "Or shall we needlessly delay our game further?"

Low chuckles circled the table.

Huck's face heated. Bad enough he looked like a poor loser, he wouldn't make it worse by accusing Dan of cheating without proof. He tossed the cards aside. "You fellows go on without me. These cards don't suit."

Dan leaned back with a smug smile. "Perhaps the problem isn't with the cards."

Loud guffaws broke out.

Huck came to a halt and flexed his fists. Every insult, every snide, snickering comment he'd put up with over his entire life, were rolled up into that one smart-ass remark.

Even if the scoundrel didn't cheat tonight, he would tomorrow or the next day. Why not do everybody a favor and heave the varmint into the river?

THE OTHER LADIES HAD LEFT THE SALON AND ONLY KATE REMAINED behind. Hallie had kept an eye on the door, half expecting Huck to barge in as he had on previous occasions. Hopefully, he'd given up waiting for her.

After Captain Kinney returned with Tad, she would take her nephew and retreat to their room. She couldn't face Huck. Not after what she'd done.

She joined her friend in front of the mural she'd completed the day before. "What do you think?"

"Your work is stunning," the captain's wife remarked. "Everyone was impressed."

True, the other guests had paid her compliments. One woman even went so far as to call it a masterpiece. But did Kate like the changes? She hadn't said.

Over the past week, Hallie reworked the scene based on Huck's descriptions and her ideas. Now the painting showed the *Hesperia* poised at the mouth of an oxbow bend, hemmed in by craggy bluffs on one side and a sandbar on the other. "I thought this setting more fitting, to show the way the Missouri twists and turns."

Kate touched her finger to her lips as she studied the mural. "Yes, I see that."

"I kept the sunset. I love the way it strikes the water and turns it to gold. But I added some of the dangers we encountered—the stampeding buffalo, a nest of snags, those whirlpools—to show the untamable nature of the river."

"Yes, you captured that perfectly."

"There *is* something you don't like. Is it the steamboat? I didn't make any changes, only to the scenery around it."

"I find it interesting how those things make such a difference. The boat looked so majestic before. Now, it looks...rather vulnerable."

Hallie tried to view the scene through Kate's eyes. "The elements of danger do make the river appear menacing. I meant to show the *Hesperia* bravely facing the elements, but I can make it appear larger."

Kate's responded with a slight smile. "The *Hesperia* isn't the only one who needs to find her courage."

Surprised, Hallie took a step back. "Are you saying I lack courage?"

"Since you own it so quickly, I suppose I am."

Kate was headed into another conversation about Huck. Hallie had no intention of getting drawn in.

She picked up her shawl. "I should go check on Tad."

"Captain Kinney will take good care of him. Come sit with me for a moment. I'm sorry if I came across as blunt. Having lived so long aboard boats, my social skills have become rusty."

"Your social skills are superior to mine and you know it."

Kate settled into an upholstered armchair. "Tell me why you refused Mr. Finn? I thought you would be thrilled."

Why was it not surprising that Kate knew about Huck's offer? He must have talked to the captain about it.

293

Hallie strayed to the sofa. She wouldn't avoid this conversation, so she might as well get it over with. "How thrilled can I be when he wants to marry me so he'll have a caretaker for Tad?"

"Is that what he said?"

"Essentially."

Kate sighed. "Men can be so unromantic."

"I wouldn't care about romance if I trusted he would eventually settle down. But he wants to drag us around with him. I won't subject Tad to that kind of life."

"Drag you?" Kate breathed a soft laugh. "You make it sound dreadful? It's not, you know. It's fun most of the time. Didn't you travel with your father? From what you've told me, you enjoyed it."

"I did—until he was blown to bits by an exploding boiler. After that, I didn't enjoy it so much."

Kate's gaze softened. "Oh, Hallie. I know how it feels to lose someone you love. We lost two sons in the war."

The gentle reminder put a vise on Hallie's heart. She wasn't the only person to have suffered great loss. "I'm so sorry. How did you bear it?"

"I don't want you to be sorry, dear. I want you to embrace life. It's fragile and far too brief. None of us know the time we'll be given. That's why we need to squeeze every drop of living out of every moment."

Hallie stared at the mural and its *vulnerable* boat. She hadn't always been so afraid. Once, she'd craved adventure and had even plotted to run away to find it. That was before her father had died and left her to care for a sickly mother and precocious sister. Before the man who had dared her to live had crushed her hopes. Being with Huck and Tad had reawakened her dreams, and it terrified her because she knew how easily dreams could be snatched away.

"Living it up isn't the point. Tad needs a home. If Huck isn't willing to give us that much, I can't believe he's ready to settle down, despite what he says."

Kate came to her side and wrapped an arm around her. "Tad doesn't care about where he lives. You're the one who wants security. But you won't find it by avoiding love."

"Love?" Hallie huffed, trying to sound disgusted but it came out more like a sob. "I'm not so foolish that I'd fall in love with a man whose heart is already taken, and I'm certain he isn't in love with me."

"Do you doubt he loves Tad?"

"No, but even that won't hold him. Mark my words. One day he will tire of having a family and he'll leave."

Kate hugged her. "Your fears are blinding you, my dear. Mr. Finn doesn't strike me as a man who would desert his family. Tell him how you feel. If he cares about you, and I believe he does, he will make concessions—"

A crash came from the other side of the thin wall, followed by shouts and the tinkling of glass breaking.

"What in heaven's name?" Kate started for the door.

Hallie followed.

As they exited the room, the noises grew louder. Down at the far end of the main cabin near the bar, men were yelling and cursing, all huddled around something—or someone. A table had been overturned, which accounted for the broken glasses.

"It's a brawl." Kate's disgust showed clearly on her face. She picked up her skirts and made a beeline for the chaos.

Hallie paused long enough to grab one of the poles used for opening the transom windows. It would make a decent weapon should one of those drunken idiots take a swing at the captain's wife.

"Stop!" Kate's shout had the effect of silencing the crowd.

Shamefaced, the onlookers parted, revealing two men rolling around on the floor. Huck and Dan. Fighting like schoolboys.

Kate marched to within inches of the dueling duo and propped her hands on her hips. "Mr. Finn! Mr. Devol! Cease this instant."

The sickening thwack of a fist on flesh made Hallie wince. She approached and lifted the metal pole. "Stop now or I will flog both of you!"

Huck twisted to look at her from where he sat astride his opponent. With a growl, Dan threw him off, then pounced, snarling like an enraged wolf.

Her arms trembled from holding the pole. Whom should she strike first?

Fiery curses rent the air. The first mate grabbed her arm and pulled her away, rescuing her from having to make a decision.

"That's enough, boys," Mr. Sullivan grumbled, as he stepped into the fray. The burly officer snagged Dan by the scruff and dragged him off. "If you two fools are aching to thrash each other, do it down on the boiler deck. Not up here where ladies are present."

Huck got to one knee before he stood. His face glowed red from exertion and the application of Dan's fists. He jerked at his coat, straightening it. One sleeve was torn, buttons were missing, and flecks of blood stained his shirtfront.

Hallie resisted the urge to rush to his side. It might give him the idea that she approved of his actions.

Dan staggered to his feet—heavens, he looked worse than Huck—and pointed an accusing finger at his opponent. "Finn started it. Laid hands on me for no reason." His words were slurred due to a swollen lip.

Kate's eyes blazed with righteous fury. "I don't care who started it. Both of you—" She surveyed the silent crowd. "Why, every *one* of you ought to know better."

The men standing around hung their heads like naughty boys.

Only Dan appeared unembarrassed. If anything, he acted offended.

He limped toward Hallie. "This isn't *my* fault. Ask the others, they'll tell you."

The others turned to leave, making it clear they had no dog in this fight.

Huck didn't refute the charge. Instead, he fisted his hands at his sides. If it weren't for Kate's rebuke, he likely would've resumed his attempt to pound Dan into the ground.

Unbelievable.

Why would Huck attack someone, even a man he disliked, without provocation? He wasn't given to explosive bursts of anger or confrontation. Something had set him off.

Hallie's conscience squirmed. She'd wounded Huck's pride when she rejected his proposal and then rubbed his face in his failure by spending time with a man he resented. Calling him out now would only shame him further.

"I am not taking sides," she told Dan firmly.

His mouth dropped open. A bead of blood glistened on his lower lip. "You don't believe me?"

Having no wish to embarrass him either, Hallie leaned closer and lowered her voice so only Dan could hear. "I am sorry if I led you to believe you are in competition with Mr. Finn. But I will not be drawn into a quarrel."

Dan's face, already mottled, darkened. He seemed to want to say something more, but whatever it was, he thought better of it. He turned and left the room, holding his spine straight as a spar.

"Show's over," the first mate announced. "Break it up."

As the remainder of the crowd dispersed, the kitchen staff ventured out and began to pick up the broken glass. Cards lay scattered across the parquet floor.

Huck cradled his side with one arm as he bent to right a table that had been overturned. The foolish man had likely re-injured his ribs in the scuffle.

"This is my fault," Hallie murmured.

Kate's hand came to rest on her shoulder. "They are grown men, Hallie. You bear no responsibility for their behavior. However, I advise you to stop avoiding Huck. You are only running from yourself."

CHAPTER THIRTY

Huck gave Hallie a headstart to the outside deck. *Now* she wanted to talk. He'd rather not. His face ached where Dan's knuckles had connected with his cheekbone, and his ribs burned like fire. Honestly, he just wanted to crawl into bed. But if he refused her request, she might not give him another chance. Thick-headed as he could be sometimes, even he could tell she was pretty well fed up with him.

Heaving a resigned sigh, he lumbered after her.

Outside, the mist rolled in off the river and cooled his abused face. Water lapped at the boat, and the summer locusts, invisible in the trees along the shore, droned a nighttime lullaby. The peaceful sounds calmed him like nothing else.

He'd need to be calm before he faced Hallie. She looked cross enough to club him with that pole. Since she hadn't brought it along with her, he reckoned he was safe.

He kept on her heels as they passed shuttered stateroom doors and continued around to a spot overlooking the forecastle.

First, he ought to apologize. Not that he was sorry for lighting into Dan. The scoundrel deserved it. He *was* sorry for the mess he'd made, and for disappointing her. Again.

She halted and turned to face him.

He longed to fold her in his arms and tell her everything would be all right, except he wasn't confident it could be. Not now that she'd seen the worst side of him.

Beneath an oil lamp dangling between the posts, her face appeared half in light and the other half in shadow, dividing her expression. Was her heart equally divided?

"What's going on between you and Dan?" she asked softly.

You. No, he couldn't say that. She'd only get angry again. There was plenty else between him and Dan, and it was time she found out what kind of scoundrel she'd taken up with.

"He was with me that day I got robbed."

Her lips parted in surprise. "I thought you were alone. You never mentioned him."

He hadn't mentioned it then because he'd felt so guilty, thinking all this time his friend had gotten killed in an attack he might've avoided if he'd been more careful. "Didn't see the need. I thought he was dead. That's why I was so surprised when he showed up. He told me he ran off because he was scared."

A crease appeared between her brows. Maybe she didn't believe the story or being yellow didn't rank high on her list of sins. There were more reasons for her to be wary.

Huck threaded his fingers through his hair to push it out of his face. "He's not just a coward, he's a cheat."

She gazed at him searchingly. "Why would you befriend a man like that?"

Why? Who else would have him? He'd taken up with Dan for the same reason he'd traveled with other shady characters.

"Pure lonesomeness, I guess. There aren't enough decent folks in the gold fields to fill a country church, and most men do worse than cheat at cards. Dan just happened to cheat the wrong folks, and we had to sneak out of the Territory. After I helped him get away, I reckoned he would stick by me. For all I know, he sold me out to those rascals. I can't prove it, but I don't trust him."

"That's why you picked a fight?" Using a lacy handkerchief, she dabbed at a cut on his lip. Her tender touch broke through his restraint and he caught her wrist. The mere thought of her wanting another man drove him crazy.

"I'm awful jealous, Hallie. There, that's the truth."

When she didn't pull away, he ventured to hold her. She didn't fight him. She wrapped her arms around his waist and tucked her head into the crook of his shoulder.

Huck heaved a relieved sigh. Maybe she wasn't done with him yet, and he still had a chance to convince her to marry him. He could tell her what he was feeling. Except what he felt was too confusing to put words around, and he'd already botched things up when he tried to propose before.

From the forecastle below, a fiddle scratched out a high-spirited tune. Soon, a voice drifted up.

> "As I was lumb'ring down the street, down
> the street, down the street, a han'some
> gal I chance to meet, oh she was fair to
> view…"

Now, the other hands joined in:

> "Buffalo gals won't you come out tonight,
> won't you come out tonight, won't you
> come out tonight. Buffalo gals won't you
> come out tonight and dance by the light
> of the moon."

The crew kept singing and clapping. When the thumping started up, Huck's feet itched to dance.

The last verse. That was how he could tell her the way he felt.

When the singers got to that part, he bent his head and crooned low in her ear.

> "I'd like to make that gal my wife, gal my
> wife, gal my wife. I'd be happy all my life
> if I had her by me..."

He buried his fingers in her hair. "Marry me, Hallie."

Her trembles shuddered through him. "I can't."

When she withdrew from his embrace, it left more than his arms empty.

"Is it because you prefer Dan?"

The lighted side of her face reflected anguish. "No, that's not the reason."

Her continued rejection set him adrift. What more could he say? He'd put his heart on a platter and offered it to her.

"Look, I know I'm not a gentleman, but I can try to act like one."

"Stop saying that."

"What?"

"Stop saying you aren't a gentleman, because you *are*." She placed her palm on his chest, right over his thumping heart. "Inside, where it counts."

Her declaration stunned him. He knew what he was, and it sure didn't add up to *gentleman*. But if she believed it, who was he to argue?

"If you're not pining for Dan, and you think I'm enough of a gentleman to suit you, what's stopping you from marrying me?"

She gazed out over the river and hugged her arms like she was trying to warm herself, even though the air wasn't cold. "If we were to marry, where would we live, Huck, when you don't have us out on a boat?"

"Where?" He hadn't thought beyond the next season. "I suppose we could live anywhere. We might go exploring out west. There are heaps of things to see, and you could paint 'em all. You'd like that, wouldn't you?"

She seemed to consider it before she shook her head. "We can't live like vagabonds. Tad needs proper schooling, more than what I can give him. He needs to have friends and to be around people he knows. He needs a home."

What was she saying? That she wanted to put down roots and live in some town? Just thinking about that kind of settled life put him in a sweat. He'd never be able to stand it. Why, it had taken nearly getting killed to keep him in one place for a few months. "I don't like being shut up in a house. Not since Pap locked me up in a cabin."

She looked horrified. "Good Lord. What kind of a man would do that?"

The kind that sired him.

"He got drunk and forgot I was out there." Huck wasn't sure why he felt the need to make an excuse for his sorry pap. Although his explanation didn't relieve her, based on her expression.

"I wasn't suggesting entrapment. I only meant we need a place to call home."

She meant a place that would suffocate him.

He opened his arms, gesturing to the wide-open spaces. "This boat makes a good place to live, and Tad has lots of friends. If you want, we can hire somebody to teach him."

"Huck, it's not just Tad. I need a home." She put her hand on his arm gently. "And a husband who wants to be there."

He gripped the rail, needing something to hold onto so he didn't break and run. She wanted him to be someone he wasn't cut out to be. A safe, settled fellow who didn't venture off his porch except to take a smoke. He wouldn't ever be that man. "I don't see why we got to plant ourselves in some town for the rest of our lives. You're plenty adventurous."

"Years ago perhaps, but not anymore." She sounded so sad it about broke his heart.

Growing desperate, he took hold of her arms. "You *are* adventurous. I don't reckon many gals would cross the country and do what you've done. You got more sand than any white woman I ever knew. Why, you took to living on that island like you were born to it. I can tell you love the river just by looking at those pictures you draw. And you're not near as stiff and prickly as you were when I first met you. This trip has done you good."

Sadness pulled at her features. "I've told you what I want. What do *you* want, Huck?"

The question threw him. What *did* he want? Before she and Tad turned up, he would have said he wanted to be left alone so he could live his life as he saw fit without having to answer to anybody. Only, that didn't appeal so much anymore. He got all shaky just thinking about going back to being that lonesome fellow he'd been all his life.

"I don't want to be alone," he confessed.

"Nor do I. But I cannot see how we will have a normal life if you aren't willing to give us a home and settle down."

"I'm a pilot, Hallie. That's how I earn my living. How can I support you and Tad if I don't go out on the river?" He shushed his ornery conscience when it reminded him that he'd learned plenty of other jobs, which didn't require being on a boat. None paid as well as piloting. "I'm not saying we won't ever put down roots, just not right off."

She reached up and stroked his cheek. He turned his face into her palm, couldn't help it. He craved the slightest touch. "Now you sound like my father."

Huck breathed easier. They were back on solid ground if she was comparing him to her esteemed father. She thought her pap hung the moon. "Well, you said he was a smart man."

"In some ways, yes, he was..." Her hand dropped away. "But when he married my mother, he swore that one day he would leave the river and spend more time with his family. She waited and waited, hoping he would keep his promise. But the years went by, and he always had some excuse. Over time, she became bitter. Her love turned into neediness. By then, I think he stayed away because he didn't want her to be clinging to him."

The story shook Huck more than he wanted to admit. If their marriage followed that path, their future looked bleak indeed.

He cupped his hands on her shoulders. "It doesn't have to be that way for us, don't you see? We can be together even if we don't stay in one place."

Tears glistened in her eyes. "I can't live like that, and I don't want to become like my mother."

He got so frustrated he gave her a little shake. "I understand you're scared. But shutting yourself up in some town won't make you happy."

"No, you don't understand, and you never will." She tried to pull away. He dragged her up against him, determined to hold on. If he let her go, she'd just run off and he'd have to chase her down again.

He'd always reckoned if he ever married it'd be because he got hogtied by a woman. Instead, he was trying to catch one—one who was greased up and running, at that.

When she continued to struggle, he folded her arms against his chest and held her tight enough to keep her still. She jerked a few more times, then sagged against him. "I can't fight you."

Huck's heart ached worse than his sore ribs. "I don't want to fight. I just want to—"

Love you.

He blinked, startled by the thought. He was getting married for Tad's sake. Falling in love wasn't in the cards. Why, he'd be a miserable fool. Hallie couldn't love him. Hell, he'd be lucky if she *liked* him in another year's time.

He tucked his finger underneath her chin and turned her face upward. Her cheeks were wet. Tender feelings welled up inside and his own eyes started to burn.

"Hallie, I..." He licked his lips and tried to form the words, but it was like trying to speak another language. There had to be some other way to get her to marry him, short of putting his heart on a spike.

He kissed her.

If she pushed him away, he'd let her go. What else could he do? He wouldn't force her.

But no. She came up on her toes and wrapped her arms around his neck and started kissing him like she was as eager for him as he was for her.

His heart pumped liquid fire. He longed to crush her against him, tear away everything that stood between them, even their clothes. If she'd let him, he'd show her just how well they fit and how they belonged together.

She made a mewling sound in the back of her throat. Maybe he *was* crushing her. Mauling her like she was a strumpet wasn't going to convince her he was marriage material.

He eased up and started over by pressing soft kisses against her mouth. Her lips were swollen and plump and downright luscious. Before, she'd liked it when he nibbled on them. He drew the lower one between his teeth and gently scored it.

She trembled like a leaf in a high wind.

He ventured sliding his tongue between her lips. She wasn't a bit timid about that and met him stroke for stroke. For a while, they dueled. He let her win the contest because it didn't matter whose tongue was in whose mouth so long as she kept kissing him.

Now, her fingers were in his hair, playing with it like she enjoyed touching it. Her nails scraped lightly over his scalp and pure want set him afire.

He dragged her against him, trailing kisses across her cheek until he reached her ear where he licked at the delicate curve. At her soft gasp, his body thrummed in response. Growing bolder, he plucked the pins from her hair and it spilled into his hands, all soft and springy, like nothing he'd ever felt. He wanted to wrap it around his fingers while he buried himself inside her. He needed what only she could give him. He was dead sure he'd never needed anything more. "Ah, Hallie," he groaned. "I want you something fierce."

She went rigid a half-second before she jerked away. "Are you trying to seduce me to change my mind?"

Her accusation made him feel lower than a snake. He hadn't been thinking past the moment. "No, I only meant...." He raised his hands in a plea for understanding. "I'm not trying to trick you. I...I just want to make you my wife."

Tears rained down her cheeks. "You don't want a wife, Huck. You want a caretaker for Tad—and a convenient bedfellow."

Her words ripped through his heart, leaving it torn and bleeding. Hadn't he tried every way he knew how to get across that he cared for her?

"That's not true, I..." The declaration died on his lips. Saying he loved her wouldn't make any difference. Hallie didn't want his love. She had a weakness for him, but that wasn't the same. She despised it, and she would despise him more than she already did if he pressed that advantage.

He had nothing left to bargain with, except for the one thing he knew she did want.

He dropped his hands to his sides, resigned. "I won't waste my breath trying to convince you about anything. If you want to be with Tad, you'll have to marry me—or you'd best get used to being without him."

CHAPTER THIRTY-ONE

The landing bell clanged, signaling the boat had docked in St. Louis. Hallie's sigh joined the hissing of steam through the pipes. They'd reached the end of the journey. In a few days, the boat would start another trip back upriver. But she would not on it. Nor, God willing, would her nephew.

Hallie peered into the small mirror on the wall to adjust her spectacles and secure the battered bonnet with the frayed ribbon, tied beneath her chin. She looked like she was on her way to a funeral.

One couldn't mourn something that had never been real, to begin with. Huck did not love her. He wished to bed her, and he was willing to make their relationship legal to have a caretaker for Tad.

Even if she could bear a loveless marriage, he refused to give up his adventuring ways. Her father had at least provided his family with a home he returned to a few months each year. Huck would not even grant her that. As much as she might wish things were different, he could not help who he was, and marriage would not change him.

A whining motor signaled the lowering of the boom. The passengers would soon disembark, and after the freight was unloaded, a small contingent crew would stay onboard to ready the boat for its next trip. Huck would be among them.

He had maintained a polite distance over the past four days. She'd tried, without success, to gain his agreement for Tad to live with her, except for a few weeks in the summers when he would join his uncle. Instead, Huck had informed her of his decision to remain with the *Hesperia* as a full-time pilot, and he planned to take Tad with him.

How could she prevent him from doing something that would lead to disaster? At this point, it would take a miracle.

A knock sounded at the door and her heart tripped. Perhaps Huck had changed his mind.

It was only the chambermaid.

"Pardon, miss. This came for you." The girl held out a letter.

After thanking her, Hallie closed the door and examined the envelope. How curious. Her name and the name of the boat were on the front, but there was no return address or postmark. She scanned the brief message written in a handsome script.

Miss MacBride,
I received your communique, and am willing to discuss your request for guardianship. If it pleases you to meet me, I will be at the brick warehouse adjacent to the wharf offices at eleven o'clock on the thirtieth. Bring the boy. Advise discretion.
Sincerely yours,
Ambrose Dubois.

Hallelujah! Her prayers had been answered.

Her hands shook as she reread the letter, slower. *Advise discretion.* Mr. Dubois wanted a private meeting. If so, why request that she bring Tad? He must intend to assign her guardianship immediately, without Huck's interference.

Her conscience niggled. She'd called a truce with Huck and had agreed to no more deceptions.

Their truce no longer applied. He had broken the agreement when he made a unilateral decision to keep Tad.

She reached for her watch before she recalled it was waterlogged and useless. The boat had just rung ten bells. If she hurried, they would make it on time.

Hallie swept her hand over the top bunk and stuffed the tin soldiers into a small sack. Her throat tightened when she picked up her box of watercolors. Huck only bought them to soften her heart. She could not fool herself into thinking he might settle down.

There was no earthly way a woman could tame a man like Huck Finn. He loved his mistress, the river, more than he could ever love a wife. And he valued his freedom above all.

She tucked the paints into the sack. Regardless of why he'd given them to her, she couldn't leave them behind.

Off she went to collect Tad.

Her nephew wasn't in the main cabin where he'd said he would be. He was with his goat or tagging along with Huck. She went out to the promenade deck and spotted him down on the forecastle.

Tad held his uncle's coat and hat while Huck helped one of the deckhands wrestle a barrel over to the stage plank.

Huck had spent the last two weeks teaching Tad how to live and work on a steamboat. What Huck could not teach their nephew was how to find his place in a world increasingly intolerant of slow-moving relics and uncivilized men.

By taking Tad away, she would destroy any chance they might have to become a family. But they could never truly be a family, as long as Huck had the itch to wander.

She cast an anxious glance at the bustling St. Louis wharf. The offices were beyond the last pier, and next to them, a brick building. It wouldn't take long to get there if she could lure Tad away.

Her stomach roiled at the prospect of practicing deceit.

Huck wouldn't think twice about doing the same to her.

She stopped one of the hands exiting the main cabin. "Would you kindly tell Mr. Finn that Captain Kinney wishes to speak with him? In the captain's quarters."

A few moments later, she saw Huck start toward the stairs. She hid until she saw him pass and then hurried down to the lower deck to where the animals were stabled.

Tad sat on a hay bale next to the goat's pen. A delighted smile lit his face when he saw her. "Hey, Aunt Hallie."

"I thought you might be here." She opened her arms and he ran to hug her.

As she folded him into her embrace, a fierce love consumed her. She'd left her home and traveled across the country for this child's sake. She would do whatever was necessary to give Tad the kind of life he deserved.

He wriggled out of her arms. "I'm teaching Lucky to count."

"Very impressive." She smiled to cover her nervousness. "I'll watch her do her trick later. Right now, I need you to come with me. There's someone I would like for you to meet, over at the wharf offices."

"I want to play with Lucky." Tad rubbed the goat's head, and the nanny butted him affectionately.

The goat rolled a pale eye in accusation.

Ridiculous. The creature couldn't know what she was up to.

"Your uncle said for us to meet him there. It is a surprise."

Oh, the lies.

Hallie threw a desperate glance over her shoulder. Confession could wait. She had no time for it now. She took a firm grip on her nephew's hand.

"Ow, that hurts." Tad pulled away and frowned at her.

"I'm sorry, I didn't mean to squeeze so hard." If she acted fretful, he might sense something was wrong. She gave him a playful nudge. "Why don't we race to the end of the stage plank?"

That fetched a smile. "All right. I'll count. One-two-THREE."

He took off at a dead run.

She lifted her skirts and followed as fast as the spool-heeled shoes would allow.

"I win!" he cried, jumping up and down as she reached him.

"How about giving me another chance? Race you to the offices, just over there." She pointed to the three-story brick warehouse and took a firm grip on the bag she carried with their few belongings.

Within a minute, she stumbled along, holding the hitch in her side. Tad had wings on his feet. That, or she was terribly out of practice. Not so many years ago, she'd bested the fastest boy in her village. "You win again," she gasped.

"How come Uncle Huck didn't want to race? Where is he? Does he know about the surprise?" Tad bounced on his toes and darted glances around her. "Hey, there's Lucky. She got out. We got to go catch her!"

Hallie threw a distracted look over her shoulder. Two men on the levee were chasing a loose pony next to an area where pens held a variety of animals, including goats and pigs. "I don't see Lucky."

"She was right over there," Tad insisted.

"Her pen was secure when we left. I'm sure there's more than one goat amongst all those animals." Hallie took her nephew's hand and walked up to the warehouse next to the wharf offices. This couldn't possibly be the place. Several windows had been broken out and it appeared to be abandoned.

Two gentlemen exited the offices next door and tipped their hats to her.

She acknowledged them with a nervous smile then darted another look over her shoulder at the *Hesperia*. Huck would've figured out by now that the captain wasn't on board. He'd be looking for Tad, and when he couldn't find the boy, he'd be looking for her. Even though he hadn't given in to her demands, he trusted her to deal with him honorably.

"Where's Uncle Huck?" Tad whined. "You said he'd be here."

"Maybe he's too busy." Hallie winced at the sharp prick of conscience. Tad would be devastated once he learned the truth. And how could she leave Huck with nothing? He'd only decided to keep Tad because he was so hungry for love. The child showered it on him unconditionally, something she couldn't bring herself to do.

She bit her lip and turned her back on the boat. This wasn't about her or Huck. It was about what was best for Tad, and living a wandering life with his uncle was not best.

As a concession, she would allow Huck to take Tad with him each summer as long as their nephew was back in time for school. Mr. Finn should be well satisfied with the arrangement, considering it was no less than he'd offered her.

HUCK TOOK THE STEPS TWO AT A TIME TO THE UPPERMOST DECK. HE waited in the captain's quarters for a few minutes then reckoned the mate had it wrong and Captain Kinney meant the pilothouse.

He wasn't there either.

Hadn't the captain said earlier that he and his wife had business in town? They might not be back yet. If so, why the message? Didn't make any sense.

Huck crossed to the edge of the top deck and stood with his

hands on his hips, surveying the wharf. Moored at an angle were six big packets, a far cry from the dozens of steamboats a few years back.

Cursed railroads. They were stealing all the passengers, and those ugly tugboats were taking the freight. Some called it the march of progress. He called it a damn shame.

Regardless, he'd work as a riverboat pilot for as long as he could. If necessary, he would find something else to do. He'd never had to be concerned with money before, but soon he would have a wife and family to support. Well, he hoped he would have a wife, preferably before the *Hesperia* started back upriver the day after tomorrow.

He threaded his fingers through his hair and muttered an oath. Hallie hadn't given an inch on her refusal to marry him. He hadn't budged on her request to let Tad live with her part-time. That would be the end of his hopes for giving the boy what he most wanted and needed—two parents.

You should've tried harder.

Why? He'd made his intentions clear and had shown her every way he knew how much he wanted to marry her. Heck, he didn't expect her to love him, but he hoped she would decide she could put up with him, if for no other reason than for Tad's sake.

He tromped down the stairs into the hall dividing the officers' quarters. He hadn't seen her outside. She might be in her room. Given that Tad was busy with his nanny goat, now was as good a time as any to get an answer out of her. They only had one day before the boat set out again. That was enough time to get married if she would just agree.

At the door to her room, he paused, and the thumping in his chest got harder.

What should he say?

Tell her you love her.

He'd do no such thing. Besides, it wouldn't help. She didn't want his worthless heart. She wanted a house.

Well then, give her one.

But *he'd* have to live there, too.

Huck stared at the door, debating his conscience. Just thinking about having to join civilized society made him itchy. He wasn't nearly as ignorant as he'd been when he ran off all those years ago. Still, he wasn't learned enough or polite enough or slicked up enough for most folks.

You don't care about most folks. You care about Tad and Hallie.

True enough. So what did they want from him? Tad was just a child, and he didn't ask for anything other than to be loved. But Hallie, well, she was a woman, and women were like birds. They needed nests.

Huck swallowed a lump that rose in his throat. He could stand settling somewhere for *part* of the year if that would make her happy. He wanted to please her. Maybe even more than he wanted to please himself. "All right then," he mumbled. "I'll do it."

He raised his hand to knock.

Something cracked against the back of his skull and he jerked at an explosion of pain.

CHAPTER THIRTY-TWO

"Why are we leaving? Isn't Uncle Huck supposed to be here? Where's the man you said we got to meet? What's the surprise?"

Hallie put a hand to her aching head. Honestly, how many questions could one child ask? Tad had kept up a steady stream since they'd left the boat. "It doesn't matter. We're going back."

She'd searched the wharf offices for Mr. Dubois, certain he hadn't meant for them to meet at an abandoned building. After checking every floor and wasting another thirty minutes, she decided she must've missed him.

What atrocious luck! Or was it the unfathomable hand of Providence? Either way, she couldn't live with the guilt eating at her insides.

No more deceptions. She would give Huck one last chance to see reason before advising him of her intentions to take him to court.

Still holding Tad's hand, she started back toward the dock.

"I want to live on a steamboat forever," Tad said with a dreamy longing. "Don't you?"

She rolled her eyes heavenward. *What next, a lightning bolt?* "Aunt Hallie!"

Her shoulders drew up at his shrill scream. When she looked in the direction Tad pointed, her heart stopped.

Flames shot up from the deck of the *Hesperia*, sending plumes of smoke rising into the blue sky.

"Uncle Huck! Lucky!" Tad yanked his hand free and shot off.

Hallie wrenched herself out of the horrified stupor and chased after her fleeing nephew. "Tad, stop!"

How could this have happened? All the fires had been extinguished so the boilers could be cleaned before the next trip. Had someone knocked over a lantern? Next to a boiler explosion fire was the most feared catastrophe. With all the wood and paint, it was like touching a match to straw.

She stumbled along the cobbled road, fighting to keep fear at bay. Certainly, Mr. Sullivan or Huck, acting in the captain's stead, had evacuated the boat. Only the crew had remained on board. Panting from exertion, she finally caught up with Tad just as he reached the edge of a crowd gathering along the levee. She caught hold of his hand. "You must not run from me."

"But where's Uncle Huck?"

"Your uncle is around here somewhere. We'll find him."

On the boat, the fire writhed like a living thing. Yellow-tipped fingers flung sparks into the air with every crackle and hiss. Two deckhands had a pump going, spraying a futile stream at the blazing inferno. The captain had returned and manned a second pump with Kate at his side.

Hallie bit back an anguished cry. Poor Kate and Captain Kinney. They'd put everything they had into that boat. Insurance might cover their losses, but it wouldn't make up for all the dreams they'd poured into her. And the mural, that was gone as well.

She pushed through the crowd, pulling Tad along, growing

increasingly fearful when she didn't spot Huck. He wasn't among the men fighting the fire with buckets either, including Mr. Lacey. He would know where Huck had gone.

With Tad in tow, she rushed down to where the old steward stood with a bucket in his hand. Soot covered his white service coat and tears coursed down his weathered cheeks.

"Mr. Lacey, where is Huck?" she gasped out.

He turned with a stunned expression. "H'ain't seen him. Thought he was with you."

With her? She'd sent him on a wild goose chase.

She shook her head, sucked in a deep breath, and found her voice. "No. He's not with us. He was on the boat the last time I saw him. On his way up to the captain's quarters."

"Lawd no." The steward's grizzled brows formed a distressed arch as he looked out at the fire. Fed by the brisk wind, it had gobbled up the first two decks and now feasted on the third.

Smoke billowed in great rolling clouds, drifting westward over the heads of the people who'd gathered to witness the spectacle.

Hallie shook her head. She refused to believe Huck was caught in that hellish blaze. He wouldn't be so careless.

She tightened her hold on Tad's hand. "Is it possible Mr. Finn went for more help?"

"I don't know for certain, but I found this." The steward bent to pick up Huck's hat and the buckskin coat. "Reckon he forgot 'cause he was in such a hurry to find you."

Fear closed her throat as she stared at Huck's belongings. He'd left those behind when he went to see the captain. He would've returned for them unless for some reason he couldn't reach them. "Where did the fire start?" she asked in a thin voice.

"On the main deck, we figure, but it sure did spread fast. We got lucky. Most folks had already got off the boat, except for deckhands."

And Huck. He would've gone looking for Tad—and her.

Dear God, what had she done?

Tad snatched Huck's coat and hat from the steward and took off running toward the boat.

"Tad!" she screamed.

He was halfway to the gangplank before she caught up with him. As she struggled with her squirming nephew, she broke into a drenching sweat. The air down here was hotter than on the worst summer day.

"You mustn't get close. It's too dangerous." She dragged him away from the dock and up the levee. Every step took all her effort due to the crushing weight of guilt combined with Tad fighting every inch of the way.

"What about Uncle Huck?" he screamed. "You can't just leave him there."

"He isn't..." She tried to force the denial past a knot in her throat, but her heart knew the truth. If Huck wasn't out here, he was on the boat.

SMOKE. HUCK SNIFFED. HAD HE LEFT HIS PIPE LIT? HE OPENED HIS eyes and blinked to clear his vision. Why was he lying on the floor? He lifted himself with his arms. Pain ricocheted off the inside of his skull.

He took deep breaths to keep his stomach from turning inside out. By moving slowly, he got his knees without vomiting. He touched the back of his head, wincing at a tender lump beneath slick, wet hair. His fingers came away coated with blood. "What the hell?"

Somebody had hit him. A thief? Even a ten-year-old pickpocket would know cash was kept in the clerk's office, not the officers' quarters.

Huck closed his eyes to ease the throbbing pain. He'd been

standing in front of the door to the cabin. Whoever had struck him had been strong enough to drag him inside.

He caught a second whiff of smoke and swung his head around, hissing at what felt like nails poking through the back of his eyes. He blinked until his vision cleared.

Tendrils of smoke snaked from beneath the door to the interior hallway.

The damn boat was on fire!

Huck scrambled to his feet with a curse. The room spun. He flung out his hands to grab the upper berth. Something poked his palm, one of Tad's toy soldiers. As he stared at it, panic blossomed in his chest.

Where were they?

He coughed uncontrollably as the smoke choked him and then dropped to the floor where clean air could be found.

The minute Hallie smelled the smoke, she would've grabbed Tad and hightailed it off the boat. She wouldn't let anything happen to that boy. She'd assume a grown man could fend for himself.

He crawled to the door and grabbed the knob. Someone had locked it. Where was the key? Not on the hook. He stared for another moment before his brain started to work again.

"You are thick as a post," he muttered.

He could get out through the transom window. Fighting nausea and the splitting headache, he pulled over a chair. Lifted the window off its hinges and set it aside. He squeezed through the opening and dropped onto the top deck.

Charcoal clouds filled the sky above his head. The air out here wasn't much fresher than on the inside.

An explosion of glass and flames shot out of the skylight. Huck scrambled to get out of the way.

That was a close one.

The fire blocked his only escape route, the outside stairway leading down. *Sweet Jesus*. He was trapped up here.

Sweat drenched his scalp as the lightheadedness returned. He had to get off this boat before he passed out.

From the direction of the levee came indistinct voices and the sound of water striking wood. He couldn't see anything behind the wall of smoke, but they sure as hell wouldn't get this fire out in time to save him. It was devouring the boat like a starving man at a picnic.

He stared with fear and fascination as yellow tongues tinged with black licked at the picketed rail. Even if he cleared the flames, it was a fifty-foot drop directly into a river filled with burning debris.

There ain't no other way, Hucky.

True enough. Though he'd never reckoned when the time came to pay his dues to the Almighty, he would willingly leap into hell.

He sucked in a deep breath and took a running jump.

CHAPTER THIRTY-THREE

An awful trembling spread through Hallie's arms and down her legs. She sank to her knees as her brain shut down, all except for the tiny part that told her to hold onto the child. If she let go, he'd run straight down to where the men were fighting the fire.

She locked Tad in her embrace, hardly noticing the discomfort from kneeling on the brick street near the levee. "If your uncle is... out there...we can't save him."

"No!" Tad's face bloomed poppy red. "Uncle Huck!" He reached out his hand, straining to get away. When she wouldn't release him, he turned on her, pummeling her with his fists. "Lemme go! Lemme go!"

She welcomed the painful blows—anything was better than this terrifying numbness.

Finally, he stopped struggling and sagged against her, weeping piteously.

An explosion and the sound of shattering glass came from the direction of the *Hesperia*. Several onlookers cried out in horror.

Crews from nearby boats worked furiously to drench their steamers so the boats wouldn't be set afire by wind-borne embers.

Hallie forced a breath into lungs that seemed to have shrunk three sizes. While she'd been sneaking away, intent on gaining control of her nephew, Huck had been searching for them, frantic with worry. He wouldn't have left the boat until he found Tad.

If Huck died, she would've killed him just as surely as if she'd set the fire.

She began to bargain with God. Spare Huck and she would never deceive him again. She would marry him, follow after him, do anything he asked, if only he could live.

Another explosion gave her the answer.

"Noooo," Tad moaned with his face buried in her shoulder.

Her arms felt wooden as she wrapped them around the inconsolable child. How could she hope to comfort him? He didn't want her. He wanted his uncle.

Huck loved Tad with a deep, abiding love. She needed love, too, but she'd been too bitter and scared to open her heart to the possibility. Huck had begged her to meet him halfway. She hadn't been willing to risk even that much.

"Hallie!"

At her name, she glanced behind her. She already knew from the voice that he was the wrong man.

Dan made his way through the crowd. He'd come by last night to bid her farewell and had gone on about how much he would miss her. She couldn't say the same to him and had felt guilty about allowing a relationship she knew would go nowhere. Dirt and ash marred his fine suit. Perhaps he'd been helping to fight the fire.

"Good grief. I've been looking all over for you." He rested his hand on her shoulder.

She shrugged off his touch, something she'd never wished for or invited, and twisted to look up at him. "Have you seen Huck?"

He shook his head and his expression turned worried. "No, I haven't seen him. I'm surprised he isn't fighting the fire."

"I want Uncle Huck," Tad cried.

Hallie held her nephew's head against her shoulder. Pieces of the steamboat broke off and fell away, blazing before they splashed into the river. Black smoke rolled like a wave across the levee, filling her nose and stinging her throat and eyes. She could taste it in her tears.

Dan bent down next to her. "My God, that fire got away fast. You think Finn is out there?"

She couldn't speak. All she could do was nod.

"I'm so sorry, Hallie. Finn and I had our differences, but I've always considered him a friend." Dan touched her shoulder again, triggering a wave of revulsion.

She pushed his hand away, unable to bear being comforted. Not only that, it felt wrong to take solace from this man, in particular.

"There's nothing you can do here," he said softly. "Come with me. I'll take you and Tad to shelter."

"Go away," she choked out. "We aren't leaving."

After a moment, Dan stood and gave a long sigh. "All right. If that's what you want."

Tad twisted in her arms to look at the burning wreckage. She wanted to tell him not to watch, yet she couldn't protect him from the pain of loss any more than she could save his uncle from a fiery death.

Dark water lapped at the hull. Broken pieces of the boat's blackened skeleton drifted on the surface. The *Hesperia* died in front of them, falling apart, piece-by-piece, along with her heart.

Fear and pride had brought her to this. If she'd stayed on board, she could've forced Huck to listen to her. Given him another chance. Given both of them a second chance.

There would be no more chances. She would never see Huck

again, never walk beside him or share a sunset, never hear his voice or touch him...or beg him to forgive her for being a coward.

Hallie screwed her eyes shut. She could bear no more.

"Look!" Tad cried out. "Between the boats. Something's moving."

"That is part of a stationary..." Her words died as a movement caught her eye. She squinted at the wreckage on the water. Was her mind playing tricks?

"Do you see it, Aunt Hallie?" The hope in Tad's voice tore at her.

Likely, it was only wreckage.

But there it was again, this time closer to the wharf.

She held her breath. Sweet Lord above, someone was in the water.

The swimmer crawled onto the dock and flopped face down like the effort had cost him all his energy. After a moment, he got on all fours. Then he stood, swaying.

"Uncle Huck!" Tad jerked away and dashed toward the soaked figure.

Hallie lurched to her feet, not certain it wasn't a daydream. She moved forward like a baby learning its first steps, walking, then running down the levee to meet him. By the time she reached him, tears streamed down her cheeks. She threw her arms around his neck, sandwiching Tad between them with a wet squish.

"Thank God, you're alive," she said against his shoulder.

He cradled her head with one big hand. The strong smoky smell that clung to his wet clothing bore testimony to how close he'd come to dying. She splayed her hands over his back, drawing comfort from how solid he felt.

Providence had brought him back to her, and she wouldn't waste another second running from him. Remaining together, as a family, was the only thing that mattered.

The fire blew its hot breath over them.

"We're too close." She tugged Huck's wrist to move him up the levee, out of danger.

He took a few unsteady steps. "Hold on. I can't walk that fast."

"Lean on me." She draped his arm over her shoulders.

"And me!" Tad took the other side.

Huck leaned on her as they made their way together to a safer location. "Sure is good to see you two. I wondered where you'd got off to."

Guilt singed Hallie's soul. He'd been worried about them while she had been intent on escaping him. "I'm sorry."

"What for?"

She noticed for the first time an alarming stain on his shirt collar. "You're bleeding. You must've hurt yourself getting off the boat."

As she reached up to find the injury, he caught her hand and drew back with a grimace. "Somebody put a dent in my head."

"Someone *struck* you?" she said, horrified. "Who would do such a thing?"

"I didn't see him. Reckon he was after money." Huck blinked and an odd blankness filled his eyes. She caught his arms to steady him. Heavens, he looked ready to topple over.

She turned to Tad. "Stay with your uncle while I go find a doctor."

Huck shook his head as if to clear it. Then he plodded in the direction of the crew manning the pumps. "Need to help put out the fire."

Tad followed. "I want to help too,"

She ran in front of them and held Huck in place. "There's nothing you can do. The boat is lost."

Seeing his face twist with anguish triggered her heartache. He hadn't just lost his job. He loved that boat. She loved it too. On *Hesperia*, she had found courage...and hope. But it was her, not the fire, who destroyed his dream. Could he forgive her?

"Here's your coat and hat, Uncle Huck." Tad held up the items like they were salvaged treasure.

Hallie patted Huck's arm. "Sit down and let me tend to that cut on your head."

"Stop fussin'," he grumbled. "T'ain a mortal wound." He put his hand behind him to find the ground and sat down awkwardly.

"If we don't stop that bleeding, you'll pass out." She lifted her skirt and ripped a lacy ruffle off the bottom of her petticoat.

Huck drew back with a frown. "Don't put that frilly thing around my head."

"It's only a bit of cloth. We'll get a proper bandage as soon as we find a doctor." Ignoring his protest, she tore the fabric into strips. Folding one, she pressed it against the injury and wound the other around his head to hold the makeshift bandage in place.

He held still and let her have her way.

"Look," Tad squealed. "It's Lucky!" The coat and hat dropped to the ground, forgotten, as he ran off up the levee and into the crowd.

Hallie rose to her feet. "Tad, come back here!"

"I gotta get Lucky," he called over his shoulder. "I'll be right back. I promise."

He ran past Mr. Lacey, who had stopped to talk to one of the chambermaids. Just beyond them, at the edge of the crowd, stood an older boy holding rope attached to a goat.

She hesitated, torn between going after Tad and staying with Huck. If she went after her nephew, Huck would try to follow. With that wound still bleeding, he'd drop to the ground, senseless. "It looks like one of the local lads found Lucky."

"Probably thinks he can sell it back to us. I'll go after 'em." Huck struggled to rise.

"No, don't get up." She put her hand on his shoulder. The fact that he didn't fight worried her all the more. "Tad will call for us if he doesn't get his goat. He won't stray far."

Her fingers trembled as she adjusted the bandage. "How are you feeling? Is your vision blurred?"

"No." Huck leaned back on his hands. "But my head feels like it got caught in the buckets."

"Here, let me look at you." She cupped his face and searched his eyes for signs of a more serious injury.

"What do you see?"

Her heart trembled, and she rubbed her thumb tenderly over his bristled cheek. "I see a fine, decent man I should not have run away from."

His teasing smile melted and confusion clouded his eyes.

With a deep breath, she gathered her courage. They could not make a life together with lies between them. "I was not on the boat when it caught fire. Tad and I were on our way to the wharf offices."

"How come you went there?"

She dug inside her reticule for the letter and handed it to him.

A moment later, he met her gaze with a scowl. "What is this?"

"A note I received this morning. It was in response to a telegram I sent while we were docked at Kansas City. I reported Tad's accident and asked Mr. Dubois to consider naming me as sole guardian. I didn't expect he'd contact me so soon, but..." This was the worst part. What she'd done could've ended in Huck's death. "I sent that man with the message from the captain to get you away from Tad. As it turns out, I couldn't find Mr. Dubois. I began to have grave reservations about my actions, and we were coming back to the boat when we saw the fire."

Her eyes burned with fresh tears. She couldn't have lived with herself if Huck had died.

Huck's leaden gaze sent despair plummeting to the pit of her stomach. "I asked you to marry me then you went off and—"

"Betrayed you? Yes." Her composure withered under a hailstorm of guilt and regret. She held her hands out, pleading.

"I'm so sorry, Huck. I shouldn't have contacted Mr. Dubois or gone to meet with him without talking to you first. I beg you to forgive me."

Unable to look him in the eye, she lifted her gaze over his head,

The boy with the goat had vanished.

She caught a sharp breath and anxiously scanned the crowd for any sight of her nephew. "Where is Tad?"

CHAPTER THIRTY-FOUR

The crowds and chaos on the levee made a search more difficult. Adding to the confusion, the big blaze drew the local boys like moths. If Tad was amongst them, Huck couldn't pick him out. Hallie suggested they split up to search a wider area. A child could easily get lost in the maze of buildings and piers that made up the busy wharf.

An hour dragged into two, then three.

Huck ended up back at the docks with his head pounding so hard it made him cross-eyed. He plopped down on a bench and pinched the bridge of his nose, wishing his head would either stop hurting or explode and be done with it.

Mr. Lacey sat down next to him and offered a flask. "This'll fix you up."

"Much obliged." Huck took a swig and then grimaced. "That's awful."

"The worse it tastes, the better it cures."

"I'll drink sludge if it'll make this headache go away," Huck muttered.

Nothing would cure the pain in his chest after Hallie had ripped out his heart.

"Have you found Tad?" he asked the steward.

Mr. Lacey shook his head. "Na suh. Cain't see why that boy would run off."

"Tad wouldn't have run if Hallie hadn't tricked him. She was desperate to get away from me, she lied to lure him off the boat."

"Is that so?" Mr. Lacey exclaimed.

"You don't believe me?"

"Well...I seen her while the fire was a-blazin'. She sho' was cut to pieces over you being on that boat. Cried like her heart was broke."

No amount of weeping and wailing would convince him she truly cared about him, as Mr. Lacey wanted him to believe.

"Guilt, is all."

"Mebbe. All I know is, she ain't in her right mind. She done told Miz Kinney she'll throw herself in the water iffen we don't find that boy."

Huck knew Hallie loved their nephew. She just couldn't love him, and she wouldn't marry a man she didn't love.

He put his hand to his head and touched the makeshift bandage. Hallie had fussed over him and wept, and begged him to forgive her. Why was he blaming her for something she couldn't help? He was as much at fault for pushing her too far. Now, Tad might pay the price for both of them being mulish.

The steward tucked the flask inside his coat. "I found that goat wandering around the other pier and got it tied up. I'll take good care of it 'til you find Tad."

If one of the local rowdies had lured Tad away, they would've kept the goat and peddled it for money. That it was wandering down near the boats triggered Huck's suspicion.

"You seen Devol?"

"Seen him talkin' to Miss MacBride a little bit afore you come climbin' outta the water like St. Peter. Ain't seen him since."

Huck's heart stumbled. For all he knew, it was another ruse. Hallie and Dan were long gone and had taken Tad with them. "They were together?"

Mr. Lacey frowned as if he'd read Huck's mind. "Together? Don't think so. She sho' didn't act happy to see him. I heard her tell him to go away."

Huck pushed himself to his feet and scanned the docks. Even if Hallie wasn't involved, that didn't mean Dan hadn't made off with Tad out of pure spite.

Or was there more to it?

What would spur the scoundrel to commit such a foul deed? The same thing that had tempted him to betray a friend and partner. He saw the opportunity to profit from it.

By dusk, Hallie had combed the wharf, visited other boats, knocked on doors, and even ventured into rough barrooms. She went to look for Huck, praying he had better luck. She spotted him coming out of the abandoned warehouse next to the wharf offices.

He strode up to her, flushed and swearing a blue streak, with a piece of paper crushed in his hand. "Damn us both to hell for not figuring it out sooner!"

Her chest tightened with dread. "Figuring what out?"

"Devol. That low-down son-of-a-mangy-mongrel snatched Tad."

Her mind screamed a denial, but her lungs couldn't take in enough air to voice it. Why would Dan do such a thing? Was it to get revenge on Huck or on her for spurning him?

"He tricked you, Hallie. I found this tacked to the wall in that warehouse where you were supposed to meet the lawyer.

Numb with shock, she took the crushed note he offered her and carefully opened it.

Bring ten thousand in gold to McDougal's cave tomorrow to exchange it for something of value.

Ten thousand in gold! An impossible amount. Where would either of them get that kind of money?

"It isn't signed," she said in a thin voice, still struggling to accept that she'd been so wrong about a man she had trusted.

"It doesn't have to be signed. I know his mark." Huck's lip curled in disgust. "Why didn't you tell me you were talking to him earlier?"

"I-I didn't have a chance before I realized Tad was gone." The thought had belatedly occurred to her that her persistent suitor might've taken Tad in some misguided effort to assist her. But when she hadn't been able to find either of them, she dismissed the idea. "He came up to us during the fire and tried to console me."

"I'll just bet he did." Huck reached out and grabbed her arm in a painful grip. "Let's go. You're coming with me."

"Yes, of course."

Her shock transformed into gut-wrenching guilt. Huck had warned her about Dan. He had also admitted his jealousy, so she'd taken what he said about the other man with a grain of salt.

Regardless, she should've seen through the fiend, especially after being fooled by a charmer once before. She hadn't fallen for Dan's flirtations, as Huck feared she might. She'd used the gambler as a shield—her first mistake—and had let him insinuate himself into her confidence because she'd been so determined to thwart Huck.

"I should've listened to you. If anything happens to Tad, I'll never forgive myself. I was a fool not to realize." She breathed hard as she attempted to keep pace with Huck.

Had Dan planned to take Tad all along to extort money from her? She had been so intent on her own goals she hadn't paid enough attention to Dan's interest in Tad. The two of them had spent time together on the boat. And she thought the biggest threat to Tad was picking up card tricks!

Was her nephew safe? Was he scared? What had Dan done with him?

Hallie's eyes burned. She would not burden Huck with more tears. "Why does Dan want us to come to McDougal's cave? That's miles upriver."

"It's remote. We both know where it is. And he has a sick sense of humor. I bet Tad showed off that gold coin he carries around, and bragged about me and Tom finding Injun Joe's treasure in that cave when we were kids."

"Treasure?" Hallie reflected on her conversations with Tad. She hadn't seen the gold coin and thought her imaginative nephew was making it up. "Tad tried to convince me you were rich. He might've told Dan the same thing."

Huck laughed. A harsh sound with no humor. "Too bad it ain't true. I gave up all that gold a long time ago. Being rich and responsible was too heavy a weight to bear. Plus, I feared my pap might murder me to get his claws on it. Devol knows all this 'cause I told him. Reckon he thinks I lied."

She gasped as the potential magnitude of Devol's evil sank in. "Do you think Dan was the one who hit you and set the boat on fire?"

"Wouldn't put it past him."

"Why would he do that if he thinks you have the gold?"

"Don't know. Don't care. We got to get Tad back." Huck dragged her along until they reached a corner and had to stop for a streetcar to pass.

She took the moment to catch her breath and gain her bearings. From where they stood, she could see the rail yard. "Are we going to the railway station?"

"Can't catch a boat in all that chaos. Looks like you'll get your train ride." His bitter reminder of her repeated request sent another shaft of guilt through her heart.

"How will we get our hands on that much gold by tomorrow?"

Huck met her gaze with a dark expression. "I'm thinking on it."

CHAPTER THIRTY-FIVE

A whistle shrieked before the floor lurched beneath Huck's feet. As the train groaned forward, he tightened his grip on Hallie's hand and led her through the crowded railcar to the only empty bench.

He slumped to find a comfortable position. Why a body would want to travel all cramped up like this was beyond him. Right now, time mattered more than comfort, and traveling by rail would get them to their destination in under two hours. It would take another day by steamboat. Longer, with all the confusion at the wharf on account of that fire. The confusion Dan must've counted on to aid him in his black-hearted plan.

Devol—damn his soul to hell—had given them less than twenty-four hours to round up more money than Huck had ever seen.

Ten thousand in gold. He hadn't mined that much after a whole summer digging in a stinking hole. What made Dan so sure he could come up with it?

Through the open window, dawn crept into the sky. They'd

already been delayed overnight while waiting for a train, and this one wasn't moving fast enough.

Huck bounced his leg. It wouldn't make the train move faster, but he couldn't sit still.

Hallie sat closest to the window, staring out at the sunrise. Whenever she got that far-away look, her mind was working on something. He should've known she was up to no good when she'd gone quiet that last day on the boat.

"I've been thinking," she murmured.

"Trouble always follows when you start thinkin'."

Instead of the usual spark of defiance, tears welled in her eyes.

His conscience set into him with a hickory stick. The pounding in his head wouldn't stop.

He snatched off the frilly bandage. "Never mind what I said. It ain't your fault. I gave that conniving snake the chance to snatch Tad. Should've pitched him overboard the minute he told me he was interested in you."

Hallie dabbed her eyes with a hankie. "He told you that?"

"Oh, he went on and on about how he was a changed man, and stopped using marked cards—the kind I recognized anyway. I wasn't convinced he could go straight. But I didn't reckon it might be Tad he was after." Huck huffed, disgusted with himself.

She reached out like she might touch him then dropped her hand in her lap. Leaving him wanting while at the same time hating himself for the weakness she inspired. "You couldn't have known Dan would do something like this. He can be very convincing."

Huck's boiler heated up. "What did that scoundrel *convince* you to do?"

Misery crept into her expression. "Not what you think. He gave a good impression of being a gentleman. I believed his friendship to be genuine."

Huck couldn't condemn her without damning himself. "You ain't the first person to make a mistake like that."

"After what happened with James Douglas, I thought I was immune to deception. I was wrong."

Her light touch on Huck's forearm sent a sizzling message to the part of his body that didn't have a lick of sense.

With a sigh, he leaned back and gave up trying to fight something he couldn't control. Even knowing she'd run off and left him, he still wanted her. But he wasn't so pathetic he'd give her another chance to break his heart.

The morning sun shone through the window, glinting off the gold rims of her spectacles and blinding him to the emotions reflected in her eyes.

Just as well. He couldn't stand seeing the hurt.

She lifted the lenses to wipe her eyes. "We need more people searching for Tad. I think we should go to the authorities as soon as we arrive in St. Petersburg."

Authorities? Hell no. They'd only mess things up.

"Told you before, if Dan thinks we've sicced the law on him, he'll disappear. God only knows what he'll do with Tad."

Her horrified expression made Huck wish he hadn't voiced his worst fears. He didn't think his old partner would harm a child. But Dan was a greedy rascal who didn't have a conscience. Or if he did, it wasn't a very active one.

"Dan saw his chance to make some money and took it. If he gets paid off, there's no good reason for him not to let Tad go. I sent Tom Sawyer a telegram. He'll help us get the money." Huck sure hoped his childhood friend would come through. There was no one else he could turn to. He had to depend on a man he hadn't laid eyes on in half a lifetime.

"If Mr. Sawyer won't help us, I have a small investment I could sell."

"No time for that."

She twisted the strings on a purse she'd been carrying around. He took the abused bag out of her hands. "What are you holding onto so tight?"

After he peeked inside, he wished he hadn't been so nosy. The box of watercolors he'd given her. Some of Tad's toys. Huck put his hand in his pocket and found the tin soldier he'd taken off the bunk. His throat closed up and it took a while before he could speak.

"Hallie, I'd call in the whole blamed army if I thought it would help." He put the toy in the bag, pulled the strings together, and returned it to her. "Trust me, the best thing to do is meet Dan's demands. Once we get Tad back—"

"*If* we get him back." Anguish twisted her features. "Huck, what if he's cold or hungry or scared? Do you think Dan cares? I'm not even certain Tad will make it to that cave."

Huck refused to consider the possibility. "Dan's got no reason to hurt him. He needs Tad alive to trade."

"But how on earth will we get ten thousand in gold by this afternoon?"

"Tom will help us." He sounded more confident than he felt.

Hallie sure didn't look convinced. Maybe he should've told her he'd given serious consideration to holding up a bank. He'd do whatever it took to get his nephew back. She knew that, so why couldn't she trust him?

You ain't exactly sowed the seeds for that kind of faith.

Huck squelched his conscience. "Even if Tom can't help us, I can talk somebody into loaning us that money." He'd sell his soul if he thought he could get anything for it, but it weren't worth two bits.

"I never should have let Tad out of my sight." Tears slipped from the corners of her eyes and trickled down her cheeks, made all the worse by the fact she seemed oblivious to them.

Huck fought against the tenderness pressing against the inside of his chest. She had no claim to those soft feelings after she'd run away from him.

You know why.

Hell yes, and he'd kicked himself for not speaking up sooner and offering what little she'd asked for. If he had, she might've reconsidered her plans and they would've worked things out.

He heaved a sigh. "When I got hit on the head, I was coming to tell you I'd buy you a house."

"A house?" She looked confused. "I already own a house."

That wasn't the response he'd expected.

"Well, you *said* that's what you wanted. Or was it just an excuse for turning me down? You were putting me off until you got a chance to meet with that lawyer."

"No, I didn't say that to put you off. You made it clear you would never settle down." She twisted the strings on the bag in her lap. "It was wrong to ask Dan to send that telegram for me. He knew I'd believe an answer, and how much I feared you would take Tad away."

So, there was more she hadn't told him. She'd trusted a lying, cheating scoundrel over him. That would've been the day he'd bought her them watercolors, around the time he reckoned he was making so much progress.

Huck's heart throbbed like a hurt toe. Dad-blamed fool. Whatever made him think he could just up and ask her to marry him and she would fall into his arms in a frenzy of gratitude? She hadn't wanted him then and didn't want him now. All this sweetness was just the result of feeling guilty.

He turned his face away rather than look at her and risk being unmanned. "He's got more schemes up his sleeve than a magician has rabbits."

"Huck, I never meant to hurt you. If only I'd handled things differently..." Her touch on his hand burned like a brand.

Wretched woman. She'd marked him, and there wasn't a

damned thing he could do about it. He had given her his protection, his promise, his loyalty, and she'd hove it overboard like it was slop not fit for pigs.

"It's a little too late for that," he rasped.

"No apology is enough. No excuse, I know," she continued in a ragged tone. "I feared the feelings you roused in me. I was terrified that you would leave one day and I'd never see you again."

"Don't get me confused with that rascal who mistreated you. You could've seen me all you wanted if you'd just been willing to put up with me."

"Put up with you? Huck, I—" her voice cracked.

If he didn't know better, he'd swear she was hurting as bad as him, but that couldn't be. Her pain came from a tortured conscience and fear for Tad.

She clutched his upper arm. "I would give anything to start over."

"Stop it, Hallie." He twisted his arm to break the connection so he couldn't feel her warmth. It wasn't real, and he was done with being a fool. "It's over."

"I understand," she said in a small voice. "I've given you no reason to trust me again." She went back to looking out the window and didn't say another word.

He fisted his hands, wanting to shake her and hold her at the same time. It wasn't Hallie's fault she couldn't love him or even trust him, and it wasn't Tad's fault that he was such a poor excuse for a father. Hell, it wasn't even *his* fault. It was just the way life made him. The sooner he accepted who and what he was, the better off everybody would be.

CHAPTER THIRTY-SIX

A wagon rumbled past, pulled by horses bobbing their heads in a lazy rhythm. The shouts of boys contesting a game of marbles mingled with a mother's admonitions to a wandering toddler.

From beneath the brim of her bonnet, Hallie observed the unhurried flow of life in St. Petersburg. The peaceful atmosphere of the old river town contrasted with her rapid steps and even more rapid pulse.

She hurried along behind Huck, unwilling to ask him to match his long strides to her shorter ones. The sooner they reached Mr. Sawyer's office, the better. Every minute wasted was a minute lost in their race to rescue Tad.

Huck had assured her that Dan would have no reason to harm their nephew if they came up with the money. Unfortunately, no amount of money would buy back time in order for her to correct her mistakes.

In hindsight, she should've accepted Huck's proposal and found a way to make the marriage work. Instead, she'd let fear and pride hold her back. Now, when it was too late, she realized what her mother had known all along. Running wouldn't cure her heart from loving.

Huck stopped so suddenly that she had to jerk to a halt to keep from slamming into him. He looked upward at a sign hanging perpendicular to a door.

Sawyer & Associates

"This here's Tom's office." Huck dropped a frowning glance over his shoulder that showed none of his earlier tenderness. "Let me do the talking."

Without a word, she followed him through the door.

A young man wearing a stiff white collar took Huck's hat and ushered them upstairs to a room that smelled of expensive cigars. "Have a seat. Mr. Sawyer will be right with you."

As the door clicked shut, Hallie glanced around. The furnishings included a simple desk, littered with papers, two well-used leather chairs for guests, and glassed bookcases packed tight with legal volumes. A faded brass knob, perhaps from an andiron, sat atop one shelf. An odd knickknack.

She prayed Mr. Sawyer was richer than this office made him appear or their time here would be wasted. They had less than a day to show up with the money to gain Tad's release.

Huck stood with his hands clasped behind his back staring at a clock on the mantle. The seconds ticked by. He hadn't expressed a hint of doubt about his friend's ability or willingness to help, but he was clearly anxious.

Well, that made both of them.

She approached him from behind. They were only inches apart, but it might as well be worlds. Yearning became a physical ache. She wrapped the cords on her bag tighter around her hand. Her consolation would have to be Tad's toys and Huck's gift. Those were all she had left to hold onto.

He turned his head and their eyes met. If he felt the inexorable pull, he didn't let on. Instead, he walked away.

Hallie blinked back tears. She couldn't expect him to forgive her after she'd destroyed his faith in her. By her own actions, she had killed whatever affection might've taken root in his heart. All her self-realizations—including the indisputable fact that she loved him—had come too late. This didn't stop her from worrying about him. "Are you all right?"

"Reckon I will be. Once we get that money." He threw a troubled glance at the door. "Wonder what's keeping Tom?"

Any number of things might demand the attention of a successful lawyer. But if Tom Sawyer was the man Huck believed him to be, he would not keep his friend waiting.

"I am sure he will not disappoint you."

Huck's stony mask crumbled and uncertainty leaked out onto his face. "He'll help us. If not for me, for Tad."

Huck placed a great deal of trust in his childhood friend. Sadly, he didn't have nearly the same faith in himself, and what she'd done had only reinforced his insecurities.

She wanted to tell him it was her heart she didn't trust. He hadn't failed her. Given what she'd learned about him, she should've known he never would. Oh, why did she always come to these important insights too late? The time for apologies and second chances had passed.

"If Mr. Sawyer doesn't help us, then we shall find someone else to loan us the money. You are a riverboat pilot. That certainly counts for something. And I shall vouch for your character."

Something flickered in his eyes that looked surprisingly like regret. "My character ain't worth ten thousand in gold."

Hallie drew herself up, looking him in the eye so he could see her unwavering faith. "No, it is worth far more."

· · ·

345

THE WORDS THAT POPPED OUT OF HALLIE'S MOUTH LEFT HUCK dumbfounded. She couldn't believe his character was worth even a penny or she wouldn't have deceived him and run off.

Before he could challenge her, the door opened and a black-haired gent done up in his Sunday best strolled into the room.

This well-heeled fellow didn't much resemble his rough-and-tumble friend. Not that he'd expect Tom to look the same, but he found the change astonishing.

"Uh, Tom?"

"Hey there, Huck." That cocky grin was familiar, even if the fancy clothes were not. Tom grabbed him in a bone-crushing embrace, then stepped back with a reproachful smile. "Didn't recognize me, eh? Well, I'd know you anywhere."

Huck looked down at his raggedy coat and grimaced. He looked like a bum, must be what Tom meant. Oh well. He didn't care if Tom thought he was as homeless as a stray cat. All he cared about was getting his hands on that gold. "Did you get my telegram?"

His old friend hesitated. Just a fraction, but enough for Huck to detect it. He'd been foolish to assume that a man he no longer knew would hand over a fortune to a fellow he hadn't seen in years.

Tom darted a questioning look at Hallie. Then the reason for his pause finally sank in.

Huck pulled Hallie up beside him—he wasn't just dressed like a bum, he acted like one too—and made the proper introductions. "This is Miss MacBride, Tad's aunt," he explained. "Hallie, this is Tom Sawyer."

Tom sketched a bow over her hand. "Miss MacBride. I'm pleased to make your acquaintance." He motioned to the chairs in front of the desk. "You two look tired. Sit down, please."

"Thank you." Hallie smoothed her skirt as she sat. Her rumpled black dress looked like something retrieved from a rag bag, but she wore it like was her best gown. She deserved the kind of man who could give her pretty dresses and a nice house and a settled life. No wonder she hadn't wanted to tie the knot with a wanderer.

Huck leaned forward in his chair. He supposed he should renew his acquaintance with his boyhood friend before asking him for money, but they were wasting valuable time.

He held out the note Devol had left for them. "We got to get our hands on ten thousand in gold. Take it to McDougal's cave no later than sunset. If we want to get Tad back from the rascally gambler who snatched him. Dan Devol."

Tom propped his hip on the corner of the desk and read the note. He looked pretty calm, considering the amount. "Dapper Dan, eh? He fleeced folks up and down the Mississippi River before he hightailed it out West. I won't ask how you got tangled up with him."

"Good. It's a waste of breath."

"Why McDougal's cave?"

What the hell did it matter? Or was this Tom's way of changing the subject so he didn't have to address the ransom right off? Huck wanted to say *pay up or shut up*, but he had come here with his hat in his hands. He had no right to demand anything.

"I'm sure Tad spouted off about our adventures and showed Dan that doubloon. Probably exaggerated how much gold we had. Dan grew up on the river. He knows about the cave...and the rumors that keep people away from it."

"You mean about it being haunted?" Tom folded the note and handed it to Huck. "It's also a good spot to stash Tad while he's waiting for you to collect the money. Difficult to know where to look for the boy without being told."

That cave had countless places where Dan might *stash* Tad. They might never find him if they didn't get the money.

Huck gripped the arms of the chair to keep from jumping up

and pacing. "I got an idea where to look. But I won't do anything that'll risk Tad. We need to give Devol the ransom first."

Tom's expression turned grim. "Would he harm a child?"

"I don't think so." Huck prayed he was right.

"Look what he did to you! And that fire, I'm sure he had a hand in it." Hallie held tight to her little bag and a tear slid down her cheek. "Nothing is beneath him. He's a devil."

"I won't argue that. But he doesn't see himself that way. My guess is, he set the fire to create a distraction, not to burn down the boat. If Dan intended to kill me outright, I'd be dead. He only knocked me out. It gave me a chance to escape. Kind of like what happened in Atchison. He set me up to be robbed then warned me not to go down that alley, even though he was pretty certain I wouldn't heed his warning."

She shook her head. "My God, are you defending him?"

"I'm just telling you how he thinks. I'm betting if he gets his money, he won't hurt Tad. There's no profit in it." Huck tightened his fingers into fists. If his bet didn't pay off, Dan was a dead man.

"Getting the money won't be a problem." Tom's assurance gave Huck hope for the first time since he'd walked into the office and seen a man he didn't recognize.

"You can loan us that much?"

"I don't know how you've managed to keep alive all these years, seeing as you are still a perfect sap head," Tom delivered the insult with a straight face. "You don't need a loan, Huck. You're a rich man."

Huck recalled his friend's penchant for pranks. "If this is your idea of a joke, it's not funny."

"Why would I joke about that?"

"Well, hell, I don't know. I got three hundred dollars to my name. I won't get paid until Captain Kinney settles his insurance claim, and probably not even then."

Tom crossed his arms over his chest. "You recall finding Injun Joe's treasure?"

"Sure I do, and I gave my part to Judge Thatcher years ago."

Tom shook his head again like he was dealing with a dimwit. "Huck, the judge didn't *keep* your money. He *invested* it for you. I reckoned you knew and would come home to claim it."

"Are you saying Huck has enough money to pay Tad's ransom?" Hallie didn't sound like she believed it either.

"He has more than enough," Tom said. "I gave Tad that gold coin and told him to remind you about the treasure. Sounds like he tried to tell you."

"I'll be danged," Huck whispered to himself. "He did remind me about it, but I thought that gold coin belonged to him."

Tom looked sympathetic. "If you hadn't shown up to claim it, all the gold would've gone to him, as well as the interest. That boy is your next of kin. The judge listed him as your beneficiary. Tad knows all this because I told him."

"And he told his *friend* Dan," Huck finished. "Ah, hell—"

Hallie grabbed his arm. "That's the part we've been missing. Dan courted me and wanted to help me gain custody, thinking he would end up as Tad's guardian, and take charge of his fortune. Oh, I could just..." She fisted her hands and her face got beet red.

"Strangle him?" Tom suggested.

"Yes! And to think he was out there on the levee, acting all concerned, cozying up to us, while poor Huck was trapped on a burning boat!"

Huck couldn't stay seated a minute longer. He got up and started to pace, disgusted with himself for befriending a rattlesnake in the first place. He didn't have any more common sense than God gave a gnat. "I wish Tad *had* got that money and stayed here where he was safe. I don't know why the widow sent him out to me."

Tom bowed his head, shaking it.

"What is it?" Huck demanded. "What haven't you told me?"

His friend leaned back, wearing a familiar expression. The same as when they were boys and Tom had done something that he knew Huck wouldn't like. "I was the one who suggested to Mrs. Douglas that she consider naming you as Tad's guardian."

"You did *what*?"

"When I received your letter, I was pleased to hear you were doing well. But I could tell you were lonely. I thought Tad would be good for you, and you'd be good for him. I knew you'd take to fathering an orphan like a fish takes to water. You know what it feels like to be left all alone in this world."

"You thought *I'd* be a good pap?" Huck dropped his jaw, disbelieving. "I was all set to give him to *you*."

Tom let out a laugh. "Oh no. I've got a houseful already."

"Huck *is* good with Tad," Hallie interjected. "He's wonderful, actually. The best father Tad could ever have."

Who had jumped into her body?

"You didn't feel that way when you took him." Huck regretted the resentful words as soon they landed. Like blows, if the stricken look on Hallie's face was any indication. He couldn't keep blaming her for his failures. "What I should've said is Miss MacBride wants Tad to have a real home. She knows I'm not keen on settling down. That's why she was trying to get custody of him."

Huck resumed pacing and forked his fingers through his hair, tempted to pull it out. From the start, he'd made one bad decision after another. "I can't imagine how you convinced the widow to give me that boy."

"I didn't have to convince her," Tom said solemnly. "She warmed to the idea right off. She always thought well of you, Huck. She believed in you."

"She's not the only one who believes in you," Hallie added. "Captain Kinney, Kate, Mr. Lacey, the whole crew, they all respect and trust you, and...I believe in you too. I made a mistake when I tried to take Tad away. But I didn't take him because I thought you weren't *capable* of being a good father."

Huck's neck grew warm as the two of them looked at him as if they expected him to agree. Tom hadn't seen him for years and had put his faith in an image he'd created in his mind. Hallie knew better. But now wasn't the time for ruminating over his qualities, good or bad.

"Where's my hat? I got to collect the money and get out to that cave."

Tom came off the edge of the desk. "Wait, we need a plan. You can't just hand over the ransom and expect Devol to lead you to Tad. He'll be looking for his chance to get away."

"I don't give a rip about the gold. I just want Tad to be safe."

"What's to keep the rascal from killing you the moment you show up?"

Huck had reasoned it out and had a good answer. "Avoiding a noose. He doesn't want his face on a *Wanted* poster for murder."

A knock came at the door. The young fellow who'd ushered them in stuck his head inside. "Mr. Sawyer? Someone just left this letter for you. It's marked as urgent."

Tom strode over and took the missive from his assistant. As he read the note, he frowned. "Huh, it's from Dapper Dan."

If they'd been dealing with anyone else, Huck might've been surprised.

Hallie came out of her chair. "Is he out there?"

"No one was out there except for the messenger, ma'am," Tom's assistant told her.

Tom handed Huck the note. "You aren't going to like this."

"He knew you'd come here first," Hallie mused.

"That ain't impressive. Any fool who knows me would be able to figure out where I'd go. He all but sent us here by telling us to meet at McDougal's Cave. He wants us to know he's in control."

Huck scanned the letter and swore. These extra demands put him in an impossible position and Dan knew it.

"What does he say?" Hallie reached for the note.

Huck saw no reason for her not to read it, though it wouldn't comfort her a bit. "He wants me to go to the cave to search for Tad while you bring the money and meet him at the path down by the river. He's crazy if he thinks I'll agree to that."

Her face went pale as milk. "We don't have a choice, Huck. He says right here *time is of the essence*. The way I read this, he's saying Tad may suffer, or even die if you don't get to him soon. And he's warned us against anyone else's involvement if we want to find Tad alive."

"I'll follow you and stay out of sight," Tom offered.

"No!" Hallie turned to Huck with a plea in her eyes. "You said we had to play this his way, and if we did, he would have no reason to hurt Tad. I'll take the money. You go to the cave. Mr. Sawyer has to stay away."

Huck flexed his fingers and imagined putting them around Dan's scrawny neck. "He's playing with us. Like a cat with a mouse."

"This isn't a game," Hallie said grimly.

"Not for the mouse, it isn't," Tom observed. He walked over to a map mounted on his wall, which showed the town and surrounding area. "Here's the cave," he pointed to the spot. "And this is where the path ends at the river. We'll load the gold in a skiff, as he asks, and have Hallie meet him here..."

Huck held his objection until Tom was finished.

"Downriver is that secret entrance I found when I was a boy. Huck, if you bring Tad out this way, I can meet you with some men. We'll go after Dapper Dan together. Follow him and nab him when the time is right."

Tom had mapped out a smart plan. Except for one thing.

"You ain't taking into consideration that he might snatch Hallie and use her as a shield."

"If he does, we'll take care not to spook him. She can distract him so he isn't onto us."

Tom loved to plot. If they had more time, he could lay out a plan that would likely work. He was one of the few men Huck knew who was smarter than Dan Devol. But they'd wasted too much time already.

Huck secured his hat. "Here's how we'll do it. I'll take the money and go look for Tad. You two stay here."

Hallie got in front of him. "You'll be begging him to kill you. He would just take Tad as insurance, along with the gold."

Anger made Huck's head throb worse. "I'll have Tom drop it off while I go to the cave."

Hallie shook her head. "Dan will assume we've betrayed him. If he insists on taking me along, I'll go. I have a better chance of escaping him than Tad does."

The mere thought of Hallie in Dan's clutches gave Huck the shivers. "No."

She got right up in his face. "Listen to me for once. We have to act fast, and we have the best chance of finding Tad if Dan thinks he's won. You said so yourself."

"To hell with what I said."

"She's right, Huck."

He turned on his friend. "You don't have a say!"

"I want to see Tad returned safely," Tom said calmly. "That means we have to be careful. Make Devol think we're following his instructions, but not let him get past us."

"It's a sound plan," Hallie added.

Huck looked between them, dead certain they'd both lost their minds. "It's a *crazy* plan. Tom, if it was you in my place, would you send Becky out there?"

"She'd be in that skiff before I could stop her." Tom went

around the desk and opened a drawer. He withdrew a pistol and offered it to Hallie. "We'll plan for all possible contingencies."

Huck intercepted her. If anything happened, he would never forgive himself. "Dan's slippery and he's smart. He won't let himself get caught."

"It's too dangerous not to do as he instructed," Hallie argued.

"I won't let you take the risk."

"It's *my* decision, Huck." She cupped her hand on his cheek. Her palm felt warm. He couldn't stop the awful thought that her skin would feel cold if he found her body washed up along the shore. "You know this is the only way. We can save Tad. If we work together."

CHAPTER THIRTY-SEVEN

"I t's awful dark in here." Tad groped his way through the cold cavern by keeping his hand on a rock shelf. Why had Mr. Devol picked *this* cave? Everybody knew it was haunted.

He stumbled over a ridge on the floor and the rope around his waist tightened so he could hardly breathe. "I don't like this place. I want out."

"You'll get out a lot sooner if you stop dragging your feet." The rope loosened as Mr. Devol drew closer. He set a lantern on the shelf. The light shined on his face and made it look scary.

Tad's skin went all prickly. He didn't know which was worse, Injun Joe's ghost or the bad man who'd taken him captive. "How come you brung me here?"

"I would think a boy as smart as you could figure that out. Your uncle knows where this cave is. It's not far from the town where he's got his gold in the bank. So it makes a good location for the exchange. Plus, I enjoy the irony." Mr. Devol drew a cigar stub from his coat pocket. "By the way, I never thanked you properly for telling me about your uncle's treasure."

Tad wished for all the world he hadn't told this bad man

anything. His uncle would be upset when he learned it was his own nephew who had given up his secret. "I didn't show you that dew-bloon so you could steal Uncle Huck's treasure."

"I am not stealing it. Your uncle doesn't care about gold. Therefore, he won't mind parting with it for the purpose of retrieving what he does value. I, on the other hand, appreciate wealth, so I deserve it. It's a good bargain. Finn should be grateful I can be trusted to keep my word."

Mr. Devol used the lantern to light his cigar and puffed away 'til he'd worked up a big cloud of smoke that made Tad cough. His uncle's pipe wasn't stinky like that cigar. It smelled sweet and warm and comforting.

While the villain who held the rope smoked, Tad chewed on the edge of a ragged nail, getting more worried by the minute. How deep were they going into this cave? He'd never been here before, despite his bragging. His granny hadn't let him. She'd told him it was too dangerous. He knew from listening to the other boys that there were twists and turns, and hundreds of avenues and forks, and caverns on top of caverns. Even Mr. Sawyer, who knew everything, had gotten lost in here when he was a boy.

Mr. Devol pulled a watch from his waistcoat and consulted it. "Your uncle should be arriving soon. We need to find a secure spot where you can wait, my young friend."

Tad sulked in silence. He weren't never going to be this man's friend again, although he wouldn't speak the thought out loud. He'd got into enough trouble already.

He'd been tricked by that older boy with the goat, and by the time he had realized what was going on, somebody had gagged him, tied him up, and stuck him in a barrel.

At first, Mr. Devol had talked nice and said he wouldn't get hurt if he just cooperated. He hadn't been about to mind a man taking him somewhere he didn't want to go, so Mr. Devol had dropped that friendly act real quick.

"You'll see your uncle again, as soon as I have my gold." He ground out the stub of the cigar on the ledge and grabbed the lantern. "Come on. Get going."

Tad moved slowly, fearful of what was in the inky darkness. "Injun Joe died in this cave. His spirit haunts it. He's looking for his treasure."

"If you meet him, be sure to tell him he's wasting his time, and reassure him I'll make good use of his gold."

Tad hoped Mr. Devol met the ghost instead of him. He shoved his hand into his coat pocket and twined his fingers around the strings of the worn leather bag. Would Injun Joe's ghost know about the dew-bloon? The other things were precious, too, but wouldn't be as interesting to a ghost. Uncle Huck had called the bag a *tallies-man*. He'd explained that all Indians had one to protect them from evil. So far, it hadn't worked very well.

"Can't you move any faster?" Mr. Devol grumbled.

"It's too dark. I can't see."

Light flickered over the rock walls as Mr. Devol moved out in front. "I'll lead the way. Stay close, or I'll drop you down a deep hole."

Earlier, he'd threatened drowning when Tad had bit him.

"You're a mean man."

"And you're a troublesome little brat."

Tad blinked back tears. He wouldn't cry like a baby. Soon, Uncle Huck would come and rescue him. That is, if his uncle could find him.

He kept his eyes on the man in front of him as he withdrew his bag and opened it. Digging around, he took out a marble and set it on the floor, being careful not to pull on the rope. After a while, he withdrew a rusty key and did the same. He had, by last count, at least a dozen different treasures, including the old coin. Better not drop that. With the way Mr. Devol was about gold, he'd notice the glint.

They walked along for what seemed like forever. Every so often, Tad left the clues he hoped his uncle would find: a Sunday School ticket, a piece of ribbon his mama had worn in her hair, his first tooth, a button from Papa's jacket, the handle off Granny's favorite teacup that he'd broke but didn't mean to.

A rustling noise came from the darkness above their heads. Tad trembled. Was it the ghost? He forced his feet to keep moving forward until all he had left was the gold coin.

They couldn't go no further or Uncle Huck wouldn't be able to track him.

"Look!" He pointed to a rippling rock formation that reminded him of a waterfall. He'd heard the older boys talk about hiding behind it. "There's a good place for me to wait."

Mr. Devol tugged Tad along, past the place indicated, and held his lantern over a dark hole in the floor. He tossed a rock. The clatter echoed as it fell.

Tad recalled the evil man's threat and took off running. Forgetting—until his feet flew out from under him—the rope around his middle. He hit the rock floor with a painful thud.

"Get back here," Mr. Devol growled, reeling him in.

"Don't put me down a hole!" Tad clawed at anything he could hold onto.

Mr. Devol took hold of his arms from behind, lifted him off his feet, and carried him, kicking and screaming. The horrid man snaked an arm around his neck, choking him. "Do you want me to strangle you before I throw you in?"

Tad went still so he could breathe.

Using the rope, Mr. Devol lowered Tad down the hole into the darkness.

"It's not far down." He was back to talking friendly. "Just deep enough you can't get out without help."

Terror squeezed the air out of Tad's lungs. His heart hammered so hard it felt like it would bust right out of his chest.

At last, his feet touched the ground. His relief was so great he nearly wet himself.

He groped in the dark along a cold, slippery wall. This was worse than when the big boys at school had locked him in the outhouse. "Mr. Devol? Please don't leave me down here. I'll be good, I promise."

Something dropped beside him. It was the other end of the rope tied around his waist.

"No!" His scream echoed and bounced around. Tad clawed at the rocky wall for something to hold onto, a way to climb out. His fingers stung so bad he had to stop. He cried great, gulping sobs.

A moment later, a light flickered from above and his tormenter stuck his head over the edge. "Cease with that caterwauling. I'm going to see if they've come with the money." He tossed something into the hole. "There you go, matches and a candle. You'll be all right."

Sniffling, Tad felt around on the damp floor. He hadn't heard anything when Mr. Devol threw down the candle and matches. A few feet out, the floor seemed to disappear.

He gasped. It wasn't a floor at all. He'd landed on a rocky shelf partway down a bottomless pit.

Shrinking against the wall, he shrieked. "Get me out! Please!"

Mr. Devol didn't reappear.

Tad hitched a sharp breath, then another. He had to be brave. His uncle would come soon and rescue him. He just had to wait a little while longer.

Darkness pressed in and something cold passed through him. Trembling, he slid into a cross-legged position on the ledge and twined the strings of the leather bag around his fingers. He'd do what his granny had told him to do whenever he was scared.

Pray.

CHAPTER THIRTY-EIGHT

The sun had already started its descent by the time Hallie dragged the skiff out of the water, pulling it through the reeds onto the bank. A feisty breeze rustled the leaves overhead, and the sound sent goosebumps over her arms. She didn't believe in the ghost stories, but out here it would be easy to fall prey to fear.

According to Huck, a footpath nearby led uphill to the cave, which was about a mile away. Too far for him to reach her should something go wrong.

Nothing would go wrong. Dan might bring Tad along to make the trade. If all went well, he would take the gold and leave, and she and Tad would go find Huck.

Thus far, nothing had gone well.

The rustling started up again, only louder, and coming from some bushes close to her.

"Have you got my gold?" Dan's low whisper sent a chill through her.

She darted a glance in the direction of the voice. The barrel of a handgun appeared through the bushes.

"Don't look over," he ordered. "Just tell me if you have it."

"We put the gold in a box in the skiff. You don't have to point that at me." She held out her hands. "As you can see, I'm not armed."

Her white lie could be forgiven. She'd tucked the small pistol Mr. Sawyer had given her beneath her garter.

"And Finn?"

"He went to the cave, as you directed, to search for Tad. I trust you left clues."

"If he's smart, he'll figure it out."

"I have no doubts about his intelligence. We've done everything you asked. Now tell me where you've put Tad."

"He's in a safe place until I get my gold."

"I told you. It's in a box under the rear bench. Ten thousand in twenty-dollar gold pieces. You can count it if you wish."

A moment later, Dan grabbed her arm. "You can count it later. Now give me your weapon."

Her heart fluttered up to her throat. "What do you mean?"

"Either give it to me or I'll look for it. Your choice. But you'd better hurry. I suspect Finn won't be able to resist coming down here. Or he might be foolish enough to send his friend. Either way, it would be a pity if I'm forced to kill them."

Hallie tamped down a surge of panic. "No one else is here. We followed your instructions."

"So you keep saying. I'm beginning to wonder." He pressed the gun barrel against her side, making it clear that he could easily kill her before she could get to her weapon.

Thus far, Dan had stayed a step ahead of them, having figured out their moves and how best to play the game.

"All right. Just a moment." She lifted her skirt and retrieved the pistol. It would go better if he thought he was in charge.

Dan snatched it out of her hand. "Thank you. Now get in the boat and take up the oars."

Hallie's knees shook. She'd suspected it might come to this and had prepared herself. "First, produce Tad. You promised an exchange."

His grip on her arm grew painful. "Get in the boat. Now."

Fear twisted her stomach into knots. "Just take the gold and send us word where to find Tad. We won't stop you."

Dan's breath brushed her cheek. "If you cooperate and I get safely away, I'll eventually release you unharmed. If you think to lead me into a trap, Finn will have to drag the river for your corpse."

AFTER HALLIE HAD SET OFF WITH THE GOLD FOR DEVOL, HUCK went to McDougal's Cave to search for Tad.

Eighteen years earlier, a solid oak door had been bolted to the entrance for the obvious purpose of shutting folks out. Now, the weathered door hung open and a rusty padlock lying in the dirt appeared to have been wrenched off the rotting wood.

Inside the chamber, chilly air seeped through Huck's sweat-dampened shirt. The cave felt like an icebox compared to the heat outside. By now, poor Tad would be cold and hungry—and scared.

Huck dug through the flour sack he'd brought along to hold supplies they'd need to make it out. He struck a match and wedged the lit taper into a candlestick made from a twisted spike. Light played across the damp walls and stone floor.

He couldn't track anybody's steps in here and didn't see any other clues. It would be just like that cowardly gambler to leave him to his own devices.

"Tad?" Huck's voice bounced around until it disappeared down the dark throat of the cave. Muttering curses, he started down a steep descent, using the steps Nature had carved.

Devol wouldn't make this easy. He wanted to give himself a head start.

Huck followed the narrow passage, which had been carved through layers of rock that looked like stacks of pancakes. Every so often, he passed a small chamber where a pool of water reflected the light. Underground rivers had formed this cave or so he'd heard. At one time, it had been a favorite spot for boys wanting to play pirates and robbers. He hadn't ever liked exploring it. Couldn't tell his direction, if he was up or down.

Considering how tight Tad's granny had tied him up in her apron strings, it was unlikely the boy had been down here. He could be wandering, lost, or might've fallen down a shaft.

"Tadpole? Where are you? Rip out so I can hear you." Huck's anxious shout echoed and dissolved. He held up the candle, searching for some hint as to Tad's whereabouts.

Soot marks on the walls marked the passage of earlier explorers. Some of them had written things. That writing looked like Tom's. He would've done it years ago to show the way to Injun Joe's treasure or the way out. Why hadn't he made it clear instead of marking an X?

Dan might've followed those marks, thinking they'd lead him to the place where the treasure had been dug up. It would amuse him to leave Tad there as a sick joke.

Passing through a cold spot made Huck's heart jump. Old Jim would've called that a *haint*. If so, it wasn't big. Just a little one. Roughly the size of a boy.

Huck braced his hand on the wall and took deep breaths. This creepy cave was getting to him. "I could use some help here," he muttered. "It ain't for my sake I'm askin'. It's for Tad."

He hadn't done enough praying to be in the Lord's good graces. But if it would help, he'd get down on his knees.

As he knelt, a sharp rock nicked him. He should've known

better than to start in praying at this late date, seeing as he hadn't kept up his end of any bargain he'd made with the Almighty.

Huck groped along until he came to a large chamber where ridged columns stretched from ceiling to floor. He recollected this place. He and Tom had passed through here on their way to find the treasure. Which passage did they take? He could see four possibilities, none of them marked. Curse Tom for not making it clearer. He'd put an X everywhere else.

A faint odor caught Huck's attention. He put his hand on a ledge and something fell to the floor. The stub of a cigar. He passed it under his nose. Smelled fresh, not old. His excitement lasted only a moment. This told him Devol had been here. Where he'd stashed Tad was still a mystery.

"Tad! Where are you?" Huck's voice scrambled around and circled back in an eerie chorus.

From a distance came a tiny squeak.

"Tadpole? Call out again." Huck strained to hear the slightest sound. He nearly wept when no call returned. He couldn't tell where that sound had come from, and it might only be a bat. He struck off down the tunnel nearest the cigar.

By now, Devol should've picked up his ransom.

Huck didn't trust that snake an inch. Devol wouldn't act honorably. He'd consider Hallie his ticket out and try to take her with him.

An awful suspicion wound its way into Huck's mind. What if Dan talked her into going along with his scheme? They could take the gold and Tad, slip past Tom and his friends and be somewhere laughing over how they'd played Huck for a fool.

You are a damn fool if you think that.

It was exactly what Dan wanted him to think. The scoundrel had played them both, and they'd lost far more than gold because of his schemes.

Only if you let him win.

Hallie didn't care about gold. She wouldn't run off with Dan. All she wanted was to get Tad back safe and sound.

And she trusts you to find him, Hucky.

That was one of the last things she'd told him. After everything had gone so wrong—most of it on account of his own stubbornness—she *believed* in him. That kind of faith was worth more than a house or ten thousand in gold or even the freedom he cherished so much.

By God, after this was over, once he found Tad and got Hallie back, he would buy her a house and live there with her, if that's what she wanted. He'd give her anything. Even his old worthless heart.

The candle flickered. He tipped it so the wax would drip away. As the flame swelled up, he saw something on the ground that looked like a bit of paper. He held it near the light to examine it. Weren't paper. Maybe an eggshell.

Hadn't Tad carried a blue eggshell in that little bag?

Huck's hope reignited. The smart little fellow must've dropped it. On purpose. He had kept his wits and trusted his uncle would recognize the clue.

Huck started off again with his eyes on the floor of the cave. Every so often, he'd see something and pick it up: part of a ticket, a bit of ribbon, a brass button. He followed the trail like a hound.

"Tad!" he kept calling.

"Uncle Huck?"

The child's voice drifted out of the darkness and Huck's hopes reignited.

"Tad? Call out again so I can find you!"

"I'm over here."

Huck took off in the direction he thought was right. It was impossible to know for sure because sounds slipped around and fooled a body.

"Past the waterfall."

Waterfall?

Huck turned in a circle, confused. The pools of water were deeper down and there weren't any...

Hold on. That rock formation some folks called Niagara wasn't far.

He sped to the spot. "Tad?"

"Over here. He put me down a hole."

Huck stretched out his arm, lighting the path in front of him. Just ahead, he noticed a dark spot, and as he drew closer, he spotted the vent on the floor.

"Uncle Huck!" Tad squealed.

The sound ricocheted.

Huck lowered the candle. He couldn't see but a few feet down, and couldn't make out his nephew at all. "Tad? Can you see me?"

"I can see you! I can see you! I'm down here on a ledge."

A ledge?

Huck's heart slammed to a stop. Tom had once told him that some of the vertical tunnels went right through the earth, all the way to China. Not likely. But they went deep enough that if Tad fell, he'd never be recovered.

"Don't move, Tad. Stay right there until I get a rope to you." Huck kept his tone easy and confident, despite his quivering innards. He wedged the candle into a crevice and rummaged through the sack.

"Watch out, I'm lowering a rope," he called, holding one end and feeding the rest through his hand. *Please let it be long enough.* "Do you see it yet?"

"Yes! I got it!"

"Good. Tie it around you, knot it tight, and when you're ready, give a tug and I'll pull you up. Be careful and hold on..." Huck kept up the chatter until he drew Tad out of the hole and set him on the ground.

When he knelt to remove the rope, Tad grabbed his neck so tight it almost choked him.

Huck didn't pull away. Instead, he clung to his nephew and buried his face in the boy's sweat-dampened hair. If he hadn't gotten lucky, hadn't seen the clues, he might not have found Tad before the child had died of exposure or thirst or fell down that godforsaken hole. He rubbed his hand up and down his nephew's small back, crooning reassurances for both of them. "It's all right, I got you. You're safe."

Tad sniffed. "I knew you'd come."

"Of course, I'd come after you. I'd never leave you here." Huck took hold of Tad's arms to release the stranglehold.

His nephew burrowed into his chest like a baby rabbit. "Don't let me go."

The plea fractured Huck's heart and cold rage bled out. What kind of monster would torture a child by sticking him in a dark, scary place all alone?

Your pap would have.

Well, yes. His pap had done that, and worse, but *he* wouldn't. He would never lock a boy in a cabin or put him in a closet or drop him down a hole. He wouldn't harm a child or a woman, and he wouldn't kill a man. Except for the cruel devil who'd done this to Tad.

By God, he would track the cur and give him a thrashing he'd never forget. And if Hallie was hurt, he'd rip Dan apart with his bare hands.

CHAPTER THIRTY-NINE

Hallie tightened her grip on the oars and pulled, sending the boat downriver. Dan had not only disarmed her. He'd put her to work.

He held a revolver in the hand resting on his knee, having tucked her pistol into the inside pocket of his coat. "You'll pardon me for assigning you a menial task, but I have to keep my hands free. I'm sure you understand."

The only thing she understood was the need to escape this madman. Until she had her chance, she would try to find out where Dan had left Tad. He wouldn't have made it easy on Huck to find their nephew.

"You've not upheld your end of the bargain," she reminded her captor.

Dan left off searching the shoreline and met her gaze. "But I did. I left Tad in exchange for the money. Finn is good at finding hidden treasure. He'll easily find this one—or hear him. The boy has a good set of lungs."

"You didn't gag him?"

Dan dared to look offended. "What kind of a fiend do you take me for?"

"The kind who would abduct a child and leave him stranded in a cave."

"Don't be dramatic, Hallie. It doesn't suit you. I left Tad in a safe spot near a well-known rock formation that looks like a waterfall. It's not so remote it can't be found."

Huck would find Tad. It was up to her to find a way back to them.

Bluffs dominated the western shoreline, the opposite side featured a low-lying swamp, and this part of the river was close to a mile wide. If she jumped overboard, she wouldn't be able to swim the distance. She'd get swept away in the current and could easily drown.

With patience, she would get her chance.

"How far are we going?"

"Are you afraid you'll have to row to New Orleans?" Dan asked, his tone wry.

Was that where he was headed? She might be able to put the authorities on his trail. If she made it back alive. His earlier threat niggled at the back of her mind.

"I suspect you have a larger boat tucked away somewhere downriver, or a wagon, or a horse and buggy."

"Something like that." Once again, he scanned the western shoreline. A slight frown was the most worry he'd shown thus far. Otherwise, he seemed confident with whatever plan he'd concocted.

As daylight faded to a pink glow behind the bluffs, their shadowy shapes slid across the river. Mr. Sawyer had said he would be waiting downriver, watching for them.

Hallie didn't see a ferry or small paddleboat. Perhaps it was hidden in a cove further on. Soon, it would be too dark for her rescuer to spot them. She guided the skiff closer to the western shore.

"Keep to the middle of the river," Dan commanded.

She pretended to struggle. "The current is strong."

He leaned forward and lifted the gun, reminding her he hadn't ruled out the possibility of doing away with her if she became troublesome. "I am not a fool like Finn. Best you remember that while you're looking for ways to outwit me."

Hallie guided the boat to the middle of the river.

"No, you are not a fool," she conceded with bitter regret. She, on the other hand, had made a perfect dupe, and would forever regret how blind she'd been. Huck, Tad, and her friends, the Kinneys, were suffering because of it. If she died out here, it was no more than she deserved.

"Why the sad face, Hallie?"

"I regret trusting you."

"Me? It is Finn's fault you are in this predicament. Had he helped me take care of those cutthroats in Montana rather than running, we would both still have our gold. I wouldn't need to go to these lengths to regain my fortune." Dan patted the box beneath his bench. "This should keep me for a while."

Ten thousand in gold would slip through a gambler's fingers as easily as sand. Huck, on the other hand, cared nothing for riches. Though he'd admitted to catching gold fever at one time. His near-brush with death, thanks to Dan's scheming, must've cured him of it.

"Do not try to make Huck your scapegoat. His only mistake was putting his faith in you."

"I'm surprised to hear you defend him, considering you couldn't wait to get away."

"I'm well aware of what I did wrong. But you tricked me into taking Tad off the boat."

"That was a nice touch, wasn't it?" Dan chuckled. "Getting Tad away from Finn was harder than peeling paint off a wall. I knew you'd figure out how to spirit the boy away. You're very resourceful."

He tucked the revolver into his waistband, apparently deciding she wasn't an immediate threat. "Have to say, though, you aren't good at following instructions. I waited for you at the warehouse. You went to the wrong place."

"I couldn't imagine Mr. Dubois would have us meet him at an abandoned building. I should've realized the note was forged."

"Don't be too hard on yourself. You have to admit, it was a clever scheme."

She rolled her eyes at his arrogance. "What was your plan, then? To knock me out?"

Again, he looked affronted. "I would never strike a lady. Or give up a valuable queen," he added with a gleam in his eyes.

"You intended to hold both of us for ransom?"

"I hoped to convince you of the wisdom of cooperating."

"At gunpoint, no doubt." She pulled the oars and looked longingly at the far-away shore. Having gotten ten thousand for Tad, he might ask for more to ensure her safe return. Huck would bankrupt himself to buy her freedom, even though she'd broken his heart.

"How can you live with yourself?" She might as well ask herself the same question. "You burned down the *Hesperia* and nearly killed Huck."

"If I'd wanted to kill Finn, I would've hit him harder."

Huck had said as much.

"As for your other accusation, I only paid that urchin to release the animals and start a small fire to create a distraction. I honestly thought they'd get the flames put out. It is a shame." He shrugged as if the terrible loss was not very important. "I'm not surprised Finn survived. He's lived through worse."

"If only *you* weren't so lucky," she muttered.

Dan's smile remained fixed. "When I was thirteen, my mother told me I'd been born under an auspicious sign. She said it meant I was destined for greatness." He continued without a smile. "That was a few months before she died of yellow fever and my father abandoned me. I suppose I deserve a little good luck. Don't you think?"

"You didn't deserve that ill fate, I'll grant. But Huck came from a similar background, and he didn't misplace his conscience along the way."

"Finn is far from a saint. You, of all people, know that. He lied to you and tricked you."

The barb penetrated a chink in her armor. Yes, she'd railed at Huck for misleading her while giving Dan, who was no better, the benefit of the doubt. "You are in no position to call the kettle black. Neither am I."

"Ah, then you admit, we deserve each other." The bounder's expression brightened. "It would've made this so much easier if you'd married me."

"What made you think I would consider it? I told you I had no interest in marriage."

"Women play coy all the time. You're just more difficult than most. I enjoy a challenge." Beneath the carefully groomed mustache, his firm lips curved into what she now recognized as a false smile.

She had missed other clues to his falseness because she'd been so intent on battling Huck. She had brushed off his warnings about Dan, and the rascal had worked both of them against each other.

In the encroaching darkness, Hallie's worry escalated. Dan couldn't intend for her to keep rowing much longer without being able to see where they were going. "We should put in somewhere soon."

"Not yet. We'll be there shortly, just around this bend. Then we can relax." His silky tone sent a chill down her spine. His idea of *relaxing* might be to lock her up somewhere and take advantage of her. He would probably call it *wooing*.

Selfish creature. He exhibited no remorse. He didn't appear to have the capacity for higher emotions. She wanted to hate him. Instead, she felt sorry for him. One who couldn't experience the depths of despair could never understand the heights of love.

Hallie started at a loud whistle that came from directly behind her. Twisting around, she gasped.

A row of lights winked like stars in the darkness. Lamps mounted on the guardrails of a steamboat crossing the river following the channel. The boat had come around the blind bend, and that whistle was meant to alert anyone who couldn't see them. The pilot would not see the skiff until it was too late to turn.

"Row!" Dan shouted.

Hallie dug in with the oars, but the current was too strong. It was pushing them into the channel, directly into the steamboat's path. Her heartbeat sounded in her ears like the slap-slap of a paddlewheel.

Dan stood and shouted at the steamboat. "Turn away!" He waved his arms. "Turn away!"

Another whistle screeched. Bells clanged in a cacophonous warning. They'd been spotted, but the pilot had no time to take action.

Fear skittered across Hallie's skin. They were too far out to attempt swimming, not to mention being dangerously close to the steamboat's massive paddlewheel. But if they stayed in this skiff they would surely die.

"It's too late!" she screamed. "Jump!"

Dan reached for the oars.

Hallie dove into the river.

CHAPTER FORTY

Using his memory as a guide, Huck led his nephew through the cave to the exit Tom had shown him years ago. He helped Tad climb up some rocks that had tumbled down.

The boy, being nimble and small, scrambled right out. Huck found it a tighter fit. He recalled being able to squeeze through a lot easier. Of course, that was when he was smaller and skinnier.

He dragged the flour sack out behind him and drew in a deep breath of relief. He'd never been so glad to get shy of a place in his life. Out here, living things croaked and buzzed and sang out to each other. The air smelled natural and stars twinkled in the clear sky.

"It's awful dark," Tad whined.

The boy hadn't shown any fear of the night before. But being stuck down a hold with no light would make a grown man go crazy. It'd be a long time before Tad would feel comfortable again with darkness—perhaps never.

Huck badly wanted to drop Dan down that shaft. His punishment would have to wait. They had to find Hallie first. By now, Tom had surely rescued her.

He dug out a second candle and lit it, then handed the candlestick to Tad. "Here, you carry the torch."

Tad guarded the tiny flame. It didn't shed much light, hardly enough to see a foot in front of them. "Where's Aunt Hallie?"

"With Mr. Sawyer, I reckon."

Tom had been hidden on a ferry behind a point reaching out in the river where it bent. He would've spotted the skiff and stopped Devol. Unless Hallie was in danger. Then, the plan called for him to sneak after them.

"How come Aunt Hallie didn't wait for us?"

A reasonable question. Tom would've taken his prisoner to the jail in town, but Hallie wouldn't have gone back with them. Not until she'd seen for herself that Tad was safe.

"She'll be here shortly."

A breeze blew out Tad's candle.

In the darkness, a flicker drew Huck's attention. Somebody was coming toward them, swinging a lantern.

"Look! Here she comes now." Relieved, Huck put his hand on Tad's shoulder and they started toward the light.

"Huck? Tad? Is that you?" Tom's voice came out of the darkness a moment before his face became visible.

"It's us, Mr. Sawyer! Uncle Huck found me!" Tad hugged Tom's waist. Tom squeezed the boy's shoulders and reached out to hug Huck.

Huck didn't see the person he wanted to hug. "Enough of that. Where's Hallie?"

"I'm sorry, Huck." Tom's solemn apology landed like an unexpected punch.

"Sorry for what? Where is she?" When he didn't get an answer, he snatched Tom by the lapels. "Devil take you! You were supposed to *rescue* her!"

Tom didn't resist or even push him away. "The skiff collided with a packet."

"Collided with a..." Huck released Tom's coat and took a step back, trying to wrap his mind around what his friend had said.

Tad tugged his coat sleeve. "Where's Aunt Hallie?"

Too stunned to speak, Huck stared out at the river, now shrouded in darkness, and a knot of fear lodged beneath his breastbone. When a steamer rammed into a small boat, the crew spent more time recovering bodies than survivors.

"You sure she was on that skiff?" he finally got out.

"Best as we can tell, she manned the oars," Tom answered. "It was close to dark by the time we saw the skiff coming downriver. We waited for it to pass to make sure we wouldn't spook him. Before we could set out after them, a big side-wheeler came around the bend. The skiff was right in its path, running without lights. One of the deckhands told us he thought he saw a woman dive into the water."

Tad yanked Huck's coat sleeve. "Was she Aunt Hallie? Did she swim away?"

Huck struggled to find his voice. "You know your aunt. She's brash as anything, and she knows this river. I bet we'll find her shortly."

Tom didn't shake his head but he might as well have. "The steamboat crew recovered Devol's body. It got hung up in the buckets. There was nothing left of the skiff, just floating lumber. We've been searching for the past hour. No sign of Miss MacBride."

Huck didn't need to hear more to know what conclusion his friend had drawn. Even if Hallie had survived being plowed over by a steamboat, she'd more than likely gotten pulled under by the current and drowned.

Anguish rolled over him in a hot wave. Why had he let her go meet Devol? He should've tied her to a chair.

"Uncle Huck? Are we goin' to get Aunt Hallie?"

Huck looked down at Tad's hopeful little face and his heart broke all to pieces. He hugged his nephew against him. No matter what it took, he would become the kind of man who deserved this boy's faith. "We're not giving up, Tadpole. We'll find her. I promise."

He took the lantern out of Tom's hand. "Let me borrow this. You ain't using it."

His friend's stoic expression melted into one of profound sympathy. "Won't do you much good. You won't find anything in the dark, Huck. Look here, I'll stay a little longer and keep searching while you take Tad back to my place. We can round up more men to start another search at dawn."

Huck's anger exploded, blasting away the numb unreality. "And leave Hallie out here by herself?" he shouted, furious at Tom, at God, but mostly with himself for letting her go in the first place. "Go back if you want or go straight to hell! I ain't leaving this river 'til I find her."

HOURS LATER, THE FERRY HAD SLOWED TO A CRAWL. THEY'D chugged downriver for miles, hugging the Missouri shoreline. At some point, they would cross over and comb the Illinois bank. The other men who'd fanned out to search earlier had headed home to their families, promising a fresh crew of volunteers at dawn. Only Tom had stayed, and he was with the pilot, giving instructions, as usual.

Huck peered at a black outline marking the shore and listened intently for the softest cry. Steam hissed. The paddlewheel struck the water with a steady thwack-thwack. Insects hidden in the thickets droned. Nothing else stirred. Even the birds had given up the day.

He would not give up. He'd scour this river from here to St. Louis and back. He wasn't quitting until he found Hallie.

The crew of the steamboat had confirmed what Tom reported. They'd rounded the bend and were on top of the skiff before they knew it.

Huck could imagine the scene too well. Upon seeing that packet bearing down, Hallie had known she stared death in the face and didn't have any choice except to jump out into the middle of a coursing river. The chance of making it to shore was slim for a strong swimmer. Less so for a woman wearing skirts that would drag her down.

Curse Devol's black soul. He'd known better than to run dark in the middle of the channel, especially around a bend. He must've been in a lather about being captured and had become careless. Huck wished the idiot had lived—so he could kill him!

Blazing light from torches mounted on the guards cast grotesque shadows over jagged bluffs looming above the river. As a boy, he'd imagined the craggy giants were ancient totems representing powerful river gods. The impartial deities watched over frail humans, so long as they treated the river with respect. Hallie's painting showed how much she loved and respected the river. Had the gods protected her?

Huck gripped the rail and leaned forward. Every shape along the shore that looked remotely human made his heart jump. Had he somehow missed a flash of pale skin or a hand waving? She was out there somewhere. She had to be alive because he couldn't bear to think otherwise.

"Looky there, Uncle Huck," Tad called out.

Huck turned his attention in the direction his nephew pointed. Disappointment rained down. "That's just a fox sniffin' around."

"What about that?" Tad sounded less sure.

Huck squinted as the light played across an inanimate object. "Looks like an old chair."

Anguish stabbed his heart. He refused to accept the very likely possibility that Hallie was dead. Yet, the image of her cold, lifeless body kept inserting itself into his mind, tormenting him.

All she'd wanted was to feel safe and secure. Why, she had come right out and asked him to settle down and stay with her. He hadn't been willing to do it. He'd chosen his damnable freedom.

Come to think of it, he'd been free all his life, but he hadn't ever *felt* free. Every time the restless feeling struck, he was off and running. Like a slave obeying the call of a master. His whole miserable existence didn't add up to anything more than a lifetime of aimless wandering. Oh, he'd worked jobs aplenty so nobody could call him a bum like his pap, yet the restlessness always drove him on. Except for over the past month when that itchy feeling hadn't bothered him so much. He felt downright peaceful ever since he'd decided to keep Tad and marry Hallie.

The truth burned into his soul. *They* were the secret to his peace of mind. It had come over him right about the time he'd started loving them, and he wouldn't ever feel truly free without them.

Huck squeezed his eyes shut. Tears escaped anyway.

Sap head. That's what Tom had teasingly called him but danged if it didn't fit. He *was* a perfect sap head. A fool who didn't know the value of the gift he'd been given until he lost it.

He wiped his eyes with the back of his sleeve, having misplaced his handkerchief. Hallie would scold such mean habits, but she never truly held it against him. She had accepted him for who he was, even told him he was a gentleman, inside, where it counted. He knew better, of course, but her encouragement had made him long to be worthy of her respect and deserving of her affection.

Like an idiot, he wasted his chance to win her love. Instead, he tricked and deceived her. He refused her pleas and caused her to lose faith in him. No wonder she hadn't wanted to marry him when he finally got around to asking.

If by some miracle they found her, he had to stop being selfish and do the right thing. Sign over the remainder of his money and give her guardianship of Tad. She didn't have to marry him to get it. He wouldn't force her hand. He loved her too much to bind her to a man she couldn't love in return.

Sensing his nephew's silent presence next to him, Huck put his arm around the boy's shoulders. Lord, he loved this child, but he hadn't done right by him. Just look at what happened. His nephew had nearly got killed—twice.

The best thing for Tad would be to make sure he had a home with someone who'd do right by him. If Hallie was alive, she would be the best mother Tad could ever hope for. Tom could help her out until she found a husband she could well and truly love.

But Hucky, you promised you'd stay.

His chest ached as regret squeezed out the last of his pride. He would find something to keep him close enough to see Tad regularly, until the boy didn't need him anymore. He could force himself to smile and act pleased when Hallie found a man who deserved her.

Tad reached up and patted his back, comforting him.

Huck got so choked up he couldn't speak. He held Tad close and tried to come up with something reassuring. When nothing came to mind, he squeezed the boy's shoulder.

"Uncle Huck? I see something over there." Tad's voice didn't ring with its usual optimism.

Huck braced himself, not wanting to get his hopes up, considering his nephew had pointed out every piece of trash along the way. "Looks like timber caught up in the brush."

He leaned over the railing to get a better view. Among the broken branches were large pieces of lumber. Part of that broken-up boat had gotten snagged and piled up. At one end, he saw something on top. It looked almost like a pile of rags...that *moved*.

His heart went from a standstill to a gallop.

"Starb'd!" he yelled, motioning frantically to Tom and the pilot. "There she is!"

CHAPTER FORTY-ONE

A WEEK LATER

Hallie leaned back against feather pillows propped against the headboard and raised a china cup to her lips. She finished the tea, sweetened with honey, just the way she liked it. "You are spoiling me."

The bed shifted as Huck sat next to her. "Are you complaining?"

"Not a bit." She put the empty cup on the side table. No one, least of all her, could criticize his attentiveness in the week since he had pulled her out of the river.

Upon returning to St. Petersburg, Huck brought her to a grand old house once belonging to Mrs. Douglas. He tucked her into a soft bed and tended her through a bout of fever, waiting on her hand and foot while she recuperated. He even came into her room in the wee hours to hold her when she cried out whilst in the grip of nightmares.

Her smile fell away when she recalled those awful dreams. Dan had risen up out of the river. His decaying, dripping corpse had come after her, accusing her of stealing his treasure.

Huck told her they had mounted a search for the box of gold

coins. She half wished they would leave it at the bottom of the river. It was cursed.

"Have you found the gold?" she asked.

"Not yet. For all I care, Dan can take it to hell with him." Huck gently rubbed her fingers.

He'd taken every chance to hold her hand, touch her face, her hair. She welcomed his attentions and hoped it meant he'd forgiven her.

"If we do find that gold, I'm giving it to Captain Kinney. Even if we don't find it, I still got enough left to put toward building him a new boat. I bet Kate would like for you to paint that river scene again. That was the best I've ever seen on any steamboat."

Hallie curled her fingers around his hand and squeezed to let him know she understood his heartbreak and sense of guilt. "I'd be happy to do it. Though nothing I can give them will truly replace what they lost." She heaved a regretful sigh. "If I hadn't fallen for Dan's tricks, none of this would've happened."

"He would've found some other way to get to you and Tad." Huck released her hand and ran his fingers through his mussed hair. He hadn't shaved lately. If the circles under his eyes were any indication, he hadn't slept much either. "I've been kicking myself for letting you go to meet him alone. That wasn't a good idea, no matter what you and Tom thought."

She drew the covers aside and scooted closer. "You couldn't predict what would happen. We both did what we thought best, and I'd do it again in a heartbeat."

"You won't get that chance. I ain't letting you out of this bed. Not until you agree to mind me." Huck cupped her face with his hand and brushed his thumb over her cheek in a gesture so tender it brought tears to her eyes.

"Agreed." She turned her face and kissed his palm.

He put his lips against her hair and smiled. "That was too easy. You ain't never been easy."

"No, I haven't." She sorely regretted how difficult she'd made it for both of them. "Do you forgive me?"

"For not minding?"

"For not trusting you."

He turned her face up and looked deep into her eyes. "You had good reason not to trust me to take care of you and Tad. I was being pig-headed."

"I misjudged you."

"Misjudged *me*?" His mouth kicked up on one side. "Oh, I think you had me pegged. Remember, I mistook you for a dried-up old maid." He trailed his fingers through her hair and the heated look he gave her sent shivers across her skin. "There's nothing old or dried up about you."

"There you're wrong. When I met you, I was as dry as an ancient well. Bitter, judgmental, distrustful. All those things you called me. You were right."

She touched a button on his shirtfront and recalled the day she'd seen him working the docks bare-chested, and the passion he'd awakened in her without even trying. "That other woman is dead. She drowned in the river, and I intend to leave her there. Along with her spectacles."

"You don't need them?"

"When I read or paint, I do. Otherwise, I see just fine."

With his fingertip, he traced her eyebrow. "You got the prettiest eyes. I noticed that right off, even behind them goggles."

"Mr. Finn, you have a gift for flattery."

He was, as usual, without a coat, his shirtsleeves rolled up, utterly unpretentious. She admired the fact that he was comfortable in his own skin. There were other things she admired as well, and she intended to tell him. Better yet, show him.

She pulled at his arm to make it easier to curl her other hand around his nape and bring his mouth closer to initiate a kiss. He groaned, a sound somewhere between pleasure and torment. As much as she wished to be bold, her shyness reasserted itself and broke the spell.

He sat back, his face flushed and his breathing ragged. "What...what was that for?"

She fiddled with the lacy neckline of the borrowed night rail. "Is it not obvious?"

"That's not what I meant when I said you got to mind me."

She smiled.

He didn't.

Perhaps he thought she'd been too forward.

"I didn't mean anything improper—"

He put his forefinger to her lips, stopping her apology. "You couldn't be improper if you tried. What I wanted to tell you... For some crazy reason, the widow left this house to me. It's a nice place for you and Tad to live. I mean to give it to you."

"Give it to me? Why? What about you? You'll live here, too, won't you?"

Instead of reassuring her, he shifted his attention to the window. "I let you down, Hallie, and I'm awful sorry. You don't have to marry me—or do anything else—to get a house or money."

Her heart lodged in her throat. "You did *not* let me down. *I* was the one who ran. I should never have betrayed you."

Perhaps he had some worry about finances after losing a fortune in gold.

"I have a house. If we need extra money, we can sell it."

"You don't have to sell it. There's plenty of money left to support you and Tad. What I'm trying to say, is..." His throat worked as he swallowed. "You don't have to marry me. I've decided to give you custody of Tad. I want you to raise him."

His blunt admission upset her so much she couldn't appreciate the irony. Finally, when he gave her exactly what she wanted, she no longer desired it. Raising Tad alone wasn't enough. She longed for a husband and a family, and she'd found both with Huck. God forbid him from leaving. Not now. Not when she finally knew for certain they were meant to be together.

"You can't just walk away." Desperation made her tone strident.

He got up and paced to the window, perhaps to prove that he could do as he liked. "I didn't say I'd walk away. But I can't keep pretending I have what it takes to be a good husband and father. Tad nearly got killed—twice—because of me."

"No!" Her shout got his attention. "Neither of those incidents was your fault. Forgive me if anything I said made you think that. You're no more to blame than I am. We can only do our best to keep him safe. But I know for a fact he'll be safer if we're raising him together."

She threw back the covers, ready to go after the stubborn man if she must. The moment she put her feet on the floor, Huck returned to the bed.

"Stay put. Doctor's orders."

"I will not *stay put*. Not if you leave." Hallie gulped a deep breath. *Remain calm. Convince him.* Even if he didn't love her now, that didn't mean he couldn't in the future. If he would just give them a chance.

She reached for his hands but he didn't let her hold them. "Huck, please. You're the best father Tad could ever hope for. He loves you, and he needs you."

Huck picked up her legs, put her back into bed, then stood and propped his fists on his hips. "You promised to mind."

He only frowned like that when he pretended to be angry.

"I will." She could reach his sleeve to tug it. "If you'll sit next to me."

He sank down with a sigh. "That ain't minding. That's bargaining."

Bargain. Barter. She would do anything to keep him beside her.

Without him, she would die inside. She took his hand in both of hers. "I won't let you leave."

"You're not hearing me. I didn't say I won't be around." He looked down to where she'd clasped his hand. Slowly, deliberately, he peeled her fingers open and withdrew from her grip. "I'll find work somewhere in town so I can be close enough to spend time with Tad, just like I promised. But I won't force you to marry a man you don't love."

He hadn't been listening or paying attention, or maybe she hadn't been clear enough.

"Huck, I *do* love you." Her voice wavered. "I *love* you," she repeated, this time more firmly. "Not for your money or because you'd give me a house or even for Tad's sake. I love you because you're...you."

His expression reflected utter astonishment.

She had tried to show him with that kiss. Obviously, she needed more practice. "Do you doubt my word?"

"No, I don't doubt you. I just never thought you could... Well, I would've settled for you *liking* me."

He didn't see it. All the wonderful things that made him who he was. She would have to remind him.

"Do you remember telling me what I need in a man? You said he has to be good as wheat about caring for his family, someone respectable, but middling fun so I won't get bored. He will listen to me speak my mind, but have the gumption not to let me walk all over him."

"I recall saying something like that," he mumbled.

"You described yourself, Huck. You are the man I've been looking for all my life. I love you so much I can't bear the thought of being without you." Her restraint snapped and she threw her arms around his neck and pressed a fervent kiss against his mouth.

His startled stillness lasted only a moment before he returned the kiss with a passion that took her breath away.

How could he imagine she didn't love him? Couldn't he feel it in her kiss, and in the way she trembled at his touch? He'd brought her back to life and vanquished her shame. He understood her fears, knew her flaws, and wanted her anyway. She'd never loved anyone more.

His kiss became soft, lingering. Then he rested his forehead against hers and held her head between his hands. "Ah, Hallie. I vow you make me want to put down roots."

She stroked his bristly face. "I do believe that's the second sweetest thing you've ever said to me."

He sat back, appearing puzzled. "What's the first?"

At his continued confusion, she gave a soft laugh. "Oh, for Heaven's sake, sir. Ask me to marry you."

"This time you got to stay put, so I can catch you," he quipped. He put his hand over hers. "Miss MacBride, I'd be honored if you'd be my wife. You reckon you can put up with a low-down, ornery fellow like me?"

"I would be honored, Mr. Finn. You can be aggravating, but you have never been low-down. And, as I told you before, you are a gentleman in every way that counts."

"The widow would be awful pleased to hear you say that. She worked hard to turn me into one. It was something nobody reckoned could be done." His smile straightened into a solemn line. "I wish I could thank her for giving me Tad—and you."

"I'm not certain she intended the latter. She was the kindest and most cordial of souls. But after I neglected my sister and nephew for so long... Well, Mrs. Douglas could not have been very fond of me."

"Don't be so sure. Before she died, she told Mr. Dubois she had a feeling I'd soon be meeting my future wife."

It seemed unbelievable that Tad's grandmother had predicted

the future. Whether or not that was the case, Hallie wanted to thank the good woman, too.

Huck lifted her hand and kissed her knuckles. "Live here with me, Hallie. Let's have more young'uns. Grow old and crabby together."

Love filled her to overflowing and the tears spilled out. "That would fulfill my fondest dreams. Will you pilot on the Mississippi, then?"

"Oh, I don't need to go on the river. Even without what I gave for ransom, I got enough treasure to loll around here, lazy as I please. I don't have to work at all if I don't want to. Pap would be proud."

The enormity of what he offered astounded her. It was what she'd asked for, but it wasn't what her heart truly wanted for him, or for their family, for that matter.

"I don't want you to give up piloting. The river is part of you. You wouldn't be *you* without it. Tad and I can go along during the months when he's out of school. You can take time off in between."

Huck regarded her with a look of wonder. "You'd do that for me?"

"Yes, I would do that for you. For us."

The door slammed open with a bang.

Startled, she jerked back as Tad shot into the room and jumped on the bed.

He bounced, excitedly. "That's bully, Aunt Hallie. When are we leaving?"

"You little sneak." Huck snagged his arm. "How long were you spying on us?"

Tad's face took on the sorrow of a penitent. "I just wanted to see Aunt Hallie."

"We'll let it slip this once." Huck's tone remained stern, then he winked at Hallie. "Reckon we ought to see about getting a lock for that door."

"Can we go out on the river again, can we?" Tad begged. "Mr. Lacey brought Lucky back, and he says he'd be glad to go with us."

"Not this season. Me and your aunt are getting married. We'll need some time to settle in." Huck drew her into a protective embrace.

She leaned her head against his shoulder, basking in his affection, and reached for their nephew's hand. "We shall have plenty of opportunities for adventure, dearest. I promise."

Tad's expression turned solemn. "I'm sorry you lost your treasure, Uncle Huck."

With a smile, he pulled Tad into their circle of love. "I got all the treasure I could ever want. Right here."

EPILOGUE

MARCH 2, 1871, ST. PETERSBURG, MISSOURI

D awn tiptoed in, bringing with it just enough light to let the birds outside know it was morning. Their happy songs made Huck want to break out singing. He resisted the urge. His bellowing would scare Hallie and wake her up.

Smiling, he snuggled his wife's warm body. They fit together like two spoons in a silver drawer. He'd never imagined marriage could make a man so content.

He ran his hand over her slim curves. Well, she was mostly slim, except for a little bump right beneath her middle. Every time he touched her there, he grinned like a fool. If folks had told him a year ago he'd be this excited about being a father, he would have laughed right in their face. Now he felt like laughing for a whole different reason.

Shhh. Don't wake Hallie. She needed her sleep, especially after last night.

What could it hurt to give her one little kiss? Right here on this ticklish spot beneath her ear. He put his lips on her smooth skin and inhaled her soft, womanly scent. Never failed to arouse him.

"Mm," she murmured. "Do you have something in mind?"

"Might."

She twisted around and circled his neck with her arms before dropping a kiss on his chin. "Bristly."

"Think I ought to shave?"

"I don't mind the whiskers. They give you a certain roguish appeal." She stroked her fingers over his cheek with a touch that sent a sizzling telegram straight to his lower parts. "Did I ever tell you, with a beard you look like a pirate?"

"What? You never met Finn the Red-handed?" He slid his leg between hers and tried to look dangerous. "When he takes you prisoner, he won't let you go 'til you pay a ransom."

"Perhaps *he* will be the one who pays." Her clever hands found him, and pretty soon he didn't care who paid the durn ransom.

Afterward, he held her draped over his body, both of them sweaty, spent, and well-pleased with the outcome of their negotiations.

He nuzzled her hair. "I like playing pirates with you. Don't tell Tadpole, though. He reckons pirates isn't a game for girls."

Hallie propped her arms on his chest and smiled down at him. "You know, Tad will soon get to an age when that nickname embarrasses him. I'm surprised he still lets you use it."

"Tadpole? It's a good handle."

She arched her eyebrow at him. "This from a man named after a berry."

"I am not named after a berry." Huck huffed, mildly offended. "When I was born, Pap took one look at me and said, 'Danged if that boy ain't a huckleberry above a persimmon.' And the name stuck."

Her eyes widened. "So that's where it came from. Now, it makes sense. Your father thought you were extraordinary."

Embarrassment worked its way up Huck's neck into his face. Why had he told her that silly story? He'd always thought it was just a foolish excuse Pap made up because he'd been drunk when he named his son. "I reckon he forgot he ever said it."

"I won't forget. You are special. One of a kind."

"Well, there's a good thing. Don't know as the world could handle *another* Huckleberry Finn."

She leaned over and kissed him. "I agree. One is enough for me."

He ran his hands over her buttocks and gave her a wicked smile. "You feeling up to another game of pirates?"

A knock came at the door. "Aunt Hallie? Are we going to give Uncle Huck his surprise?"

"Oh, dear! What time is it?" She scrambled out of bed before he could restrain her.

"I don't know. Does it matter?" Huck admired the view as she rushed around, picking up her nightgown and robe from the floor where he had tossed the unnecessary articles last night.

Good thing the door was locked. He was in no hurry to see her cover up that lovely body. She was still slender, yet filling out ever so nicely.

He crossed his arms behind his head. "What's the surprise?"

A smile curved her lips. "Get dressed and you'll find out."

An hour later, they were headed down to the wharf. By this time, Huck was eaten alive with curiosity. He had asked and asked about the surprise, but all she would say was that some ship had come in.

Up the river?

He hadn't ever seen a full-fledged ship like the kind they took out onto the ocean. That would be quite a sight.

They strolled down to the wharf where a few boats had put in, but he didn't see anything bigger than a packet.

"Where's the ship." He turned to Hallie. "Is it a clipper or a whaler?"

Tad snorted with laughter. "It's neither, Uncle Huck." He cast a sly glance at his aunt. "Can I tell him?"

Hallie nodded.

Huck looked from one smiling face to the other. He braced his hands on his hips, more than a little annoyed at all the secrecy. "Tell me what?"

"Look there, behind you." Tad pointed.

Huck turned around. Why, that wasn't a ship at all. It was a steamboat, and a new one by the look of it. A fine stern-wheeler with a duck-billed bow, like the mountain boats he'd worked on. He walked to the front so he could see her name, painted in bold black letters below the pilothouse window.

Huckleberry Finn.

Surprise took his breath. *His ship*, they'd said. *His* ship had come in.

He turned to Hallie. "Is this?"

"Your boat? Yes, it is." She smiled proudly.

Huck's jaw dropped. How on earth had she managed it? After he'd donated the lion's share of his gold for Captain Kinney to have a new boat, he wasn't poor, but— "We don't have enough money to outright *buy* a steamboat."

She slipped her arm through his. "Do you recall what I said about having a small inheritance from my grandmother? I invested it in the railroad. My investment paid off rather handsomely. Along with the money from the sale of my house, I was able to purchase this lovely steamboat."

His heart swelled to bursting. Then it hit him. "We can't just up and leave. Why you...you're..." He gestured to her stomach where the telltale roundness would soon begin to show.

"I'll be fine." She flicked her wrist, putting on like she'd lived her whole life on a steamboat. "If we can manage to make it back to ensure our child will be born on land, I'd be most appreciative."

"Hooray! We're going!" Tad took a running leap onto the deck and ran to the stairs that led up three stories to the pilothouse. He would not be left behind.

Hallie seemed to have no problem with it either. All the more unbelievable.

Huck gazed upon the *Huckleberry Finn*, and a sense of awe came over him. The woman who never wanted to get back on a steamboat had bought him one. She even planned to set out with him and Tad.

Turning to his wife, he lifted her on her toes and kissed her in front of God and everybody. "I love you, Mrs. Finn."

"And I you, Mr. Finn." She smiled as she slid down his body.

"Hey, you two," Tad called from the upper deck. "Stop kissin' and let's go!"

Huck grinned at his nephew. He had to be the luckiest man alive. He didn't warrant it, but that was the backward way of Providence to lavish blessings on the undeserving.

His heart beat like a tom-tom as he paced the length of the boat, absorbing every detail. What grand adventures they would have, taking this fine steamer up the Missouri River. All the way to the headwaters. There were so many astonishing sights he wanted to show his family. Adventures he longed to share.

Excitement as heady as a strong drink surged through him, along with a feeling that had been with him for as long as he could remember...the pull of the river.

It was waiting.

ALSO BY E.E. BURKE

The New Adventures

Tom Sawyer Returns

Taming Huck Finn

Steam! Romance and Rails Series

Her Bodyguard

Kate's Outlaw

A Dangerous Passion

Fugitive Hearts

Lawless Hearts

The Bride Train Series

Valentine's Rose

Patrick's Charm

Tempting Prudence

Seducing Susannah

American Mail-Order Brides

Victoria Bride of Kansas

Santa's Mail-Order Bride

The Brides of Noelle

Twelve Days of Christmas Mail-Order Brides

Jolie, A Valentine's Day Bride

The Drum (Twelve Days of Christmas Mail-Order Brides)

ABOUT THE AUTHOR

E.E. Burke weaves a potent blend of adventure, romance and suspense in award-winning historical fiction. Her newest collection envisions Mark Twain's youthful characters as adults, engaged in adventures connected to American life and its spirit. *Tom Sawyer Returns* won international recognition, taking the Grand Prize in the 2021 Laramie Awards (part of the Chanticleer International Book Awards). In addition, her work has been featured by the Mark Twain House & Museum.

Over the years, she's been a disc jockey, a journalist, and an advertising executive, before finally getting around to living the dream--writing stories readers can get lost in.

Find out more about her books at her website: www.eeburke.com.

TOM SAWYER RETURNS

Chapter 1
August 15, 1864, St. Petersburg, Missouri

Poets and dreamers possessed the right words to explain love. Ordinary people were left to work it out one difficult decision at a time.

Becky Thatcher considered herself quite ordinary, despite what she'd been led to believe as a petted and pampered child. While stirring a pot of beans on the stovetop, she mulled over the only marriage proposal she'd received over the course of her life. The only one that counted because the man who'd issued it could be depended on to honor his word.

Was she in love with Alfred? The right question might be, did it matter? Passion, ardor, *amour*, or whatever one might call that fleeting, ephemeral force, had given her nothing more than a broken heart. Alfred offered her a path to safety and security, which was far more than her previous beau had ever promised, much less delivered.

In present circumstances, she should count herself fortunate that a childhood friend wished to honor her with marriage. Other women in her situation would simply end up on the trash heap of failed dreams as desperate soiled doves or embittered old maids.

A faint scratching sounded at the kitchen door.

Becky stopped stirring and held motionless. Surely her cousin knew better than to come around for handouts and risk being seen by the commander of the military police.

More scratching, followed by a faint yowl.

Jeff wouldn't carry on like that. It had to be the old stray that turned up with some regularity.

Setting aside the spoon, she went to the door and opened it. A scruffy tabby sat on the stoop, regarding her with a green-eyed stare that bespoke expectations.

"So, it's you again. Is the army rationing mice now?"

The rangy tom flicked its torn ear then stepped over the threshold and wound around her ankles, purring loudly. She considered shooing it away, but relented and returned to the stove to spoon out a fragrant bit of pork from the bone she'd used to season the beans.

She bent down to offer the treat to her uninvited guest. "Here you go. That's all I can spare."

The cat sniffed at the offering before taking it.

"You do know we're in the midst of a war? Beggars can't be picky." Becky wiped her fingers on her apron and waited for the cat to finish eating.

Afterwards, she opened the back door. "Go on now. I happen to know there are vermin aplenty in the carriage house."

Upon hearing the news, the predator raced into the dusky eve across the back yard toward a building that had once housed a pair of fine horses, confiscated by Union soldiers over a year ago. She was lucky to have kept an old milk cow.

Standing on the stoop, she gazed up at the first faint twinkles in the sky. Later in the night, the Little Dipper might be visible and she could find the North Star. That is, if she went back out to look for it, which she wouldn't do because civilians weren't allowed outside after dark. Even if she could locate the right star, she wouldn't make a wish on it. Wishes were for dreamers, and she could no longer afford to be one.

Once, long ago, she had fancied herself in love. But Tom, like that unpredictable stray, would never settle for permanence. When adventure beckoned, he'd left her behind with nothing more than lofty promises, which turned out to be as worthless as Confederate currency.

No one in town had a clue about what happened to him, and most believed, for good reason, that he had come to a bad end. After clinging to hope for seven long years, she'd finally accepted reality. She would never meet Tom Sawyer again this side of eternity. Not even long enough to dispatch him to the next world by putting a bullet through his worthless hide.

Becky put her hand into the apron pocket where she'd tucked Alfred's letter. His ardent proposal held far more value than Tom's useless vows.

She sniffed. *Something's burning...*

"Oh no! She rushed inside and opened the oven door, nearly crying when she pulled out the scorched cornbread. They'd have to eat it anyway. Given her father's unemployed situation, they couldn't afford to waste food.

She set the bread and beans on the table and called down the hall. "Papa, dinner's ready!"

No response came from the front of the house. The judge must not have heard her or perhaps he had gotten absorbed in a book.

Taking a lit tallow lamp, she made her way down the hall without stopping to light the candle in the wall sconce. *Waste not, want not.*

"Papa? Time to wash up." Becky paused at the entrance to the study and frowned at the empty chair behind the desk, where he typically sat this time of day, reading a book or the newspaper.

He hadn't come home yet. What could be keeping him this late?

A brisk wind swirled through the room and sent a pile of newspapers stacked on the desk fluttering to the floor. She crossed to the open window, but before closing it leaned outside, peering the direction her father usually took home.

In the soft twilight, a dark figure, his shape as familiar as his methodical pace, made his way up the cobbled street.

"Hurry!" she whispered, despite knowing he couldn't hear her. Calling out would draw too much attention. The provost marshal lived right across from them in the same house where he and Tom had grown up. Stodgy Sid wouldn't hesitate to lock up a civilian who violated the curfew.

Her father strode past their picket fence. When he opened the gate, the rusty hinge squeaked, causing her to heart to trip.

She rushed to the front door and flung it open. As soon as he stepped onto the porch, she grabbed his arm and hauled him inside. "What on earth! Did you forget the curfew?"

"There's nothing wrong with my memory," her father grumbled. "We had to finish putting out the newspaper."

Granted, the hours he spent helping his friend, the publisher, kept his mind off his own troubles.

"Mr. Stearns ought to be mindful of the time and not take advantage," she scolded.

"My tardiness isn't his fault." Her father hung his hat on the hall tree. The light she held reflected off his white hair, which not that long ago had been flaxen. On his face were grief lines carved by loss upon loss. His beloved wife, his brother, his position, his reputation—everything had been taken from him. If that weren't bad enough, his only nephew had cast his lot with rebels and would be hunted down like an animal.

Come to think of it, perhaps the newspaper was only an excuse for a more dangerous errand.

"After you put the paper to bed, did you stop off on another errand?"

"I don't know what you're talking about." The judge brushed past her on his way into the study. He stopped to pick up one of the newspapers that had been blown onto the floor.

Becky followed, collecting loose pages along the way. "You know precisely what I'm talking about. You left something else for Jeff, didn't you? The brand-new quilt our sewing circle just finished is missing."

"I don't know what you're talking about. Jeff is gone.

"That's what we tell everyone. You and I know better." She folded the gathered pages and placed them on the corner of the desk.

Her father arranged it into a neat stack before retrieving his pipe from its stand. As he lit it, the bowl glowed and the room filled with fragrant smoke, a smell she had once associated with comfort and security, but tonight it made her eyes water.

"Papa, I understand why you want to help him and I sympathize, I do. But you cannot continue to supply Jeff with food or bedding or anything. It only encourages him to remain here. You know Sid is itching to arrest you after you refused to declare your loyalty to the Union."

Her father straightened to his full height, looking every inch *the judge*, which was what everyone still called him even though he no longer presided over the county court. "I *have* declared my loyalty."

God give her patience. How many times had they argued about this?

"Verbal declarations mean nothing until you sign that piece of paper. Why won't you just put your name to the blessed oath and be done with it?"

"My principles won't allow me to sign a vow I can't uphold."

"Principles will do you little good should they put a rope around your neck."

"A man who acts without honor isn't worthy to be called a man."

"If that's true then this country is populated by animals."

"Rebecca..." The judge only used her full name when he rebuked her or wanted to hug her. He opened his arms.

She longed to run to his embrace, regress to the little girl whose father could fix anything. Except escaping into fantasy wouldn't save either of them. "Please don't lecture me on honor and family loyalty."

"I won't lecture you on something you understand as well as I do."

The judge set his pipe aside and pulled her into his arms. The soothing backrub might work if she was ten. "I know you're frightened, my dear," he murmured. "You don't have to remain here. Go to Illinois and stay with your cousins."

Another ploy to prevent her from doing something that might actually help.

She broke away to remain stalwart against his tender attack. "My plans don't include a trip to Illinois. You know that. Alfred has asked me to move to St. Louis and marry him. I want you to come along."

"He hasn't proposed to me," came the glib reply.

"Don't be silly. He wants you to be safe." She gripped the loose sides of her father's coat with dismay. "Look at you! You don't eat enough as it is. If I leave, who will fix your meals? Come with me to St. Louis and you won't have to fend for yourself."

He gathered her hands with a paternal smile. "I will manage fine on my own."

"Will you? If you insist on staying here to sneak food to Jeff, you'll end up in jail, and Alfred can't help you."

The softness in her father's expression vanished behind the judge's stern demeanor. "Is that why you're so anxious to tie the knot? For my sake?

Pride wouldn't allow him to accept such an arrangement and it wasn't the only reason. Ever since they'd reconnected, quite by accident, Alfred had written to her without fail every week.

"Of course not. Alfred is devoted and very attentive."

"So is a dog."

Becky clamped down on her exasperation. This was precisely his intention, to fluster her and make her doubt her judgment. "Why on earth would you object to Captain Temple? He's wealthy, well educated, from a distinguished family. He's everything you could want in a son-in-law. You know how Mama prayed for the day I'd chose a man like him."

"Is that why you want to marry him? Because your mother would approve?"

He had switched to fighting dirty by attempting to stir up resentment at her overprotective mother, who had been dead for four years and had nothing to do with this decision.

"I'm only pointing out that she would be happy for me, as you should be."

"And I would be, if Alfred Temple were the right man for you." Her father sank into his desk chair, regarding her with that infuriating matter-of-fact expression.

Was it any wonder she remained unmarried? No man could be the paragon her father sought for his only daughter. Tom had left rather than try.

She propped her hands on her hips in a gesture her mother had used successfully to face down the judge. "Alfred is a Union captain, and he has the influence and means, not to mention the desire, to protect and provide for me. Who can meet your high standards if not someone like him? Pray tell, who can be *right* enough?"

The judge lifted the pipe to his lips, cradling the meerschaum bowl between thumb and forefinger, puffing placidly. "Are you in love with Captain Temple?

The question put a knot in her throat. What did *love* have to do with this? It had taken her seven years to purge the malady from her system and the process had nearly killed her. She wasn't even certain it was unrequited love. Perhaps her suffering had more to do with an unquenchable thirst for meaning and significance. Regardless, it was a distraction she could little afford in the midst of the chaos that had descended on them over the past three years. Her only concern was survival—hers and her father's.

"Rest assured, I have a deep affection for Alfred. He and I are well suited. You'll see. Once you get to know him, I am sure you will come to appreciate his finer qualities."

"Which are, other than penning romantic letters?"

A crash resounded from the back of the house.

She whirled around. "What was that?"

"The wind blew the kitchen door open?"

"And heaved a boulder through it?"

Her father had already stood and retrieved a pistol from a drawer. He clearly didn't believe it was the wind and only said as much to avoid sending her into a panic.

"It might be Sid's men," she whispered. "Don't let them see your gun. They'll shoot without giving you a chance to explain."

She crept after him down the hall to the doorway leading into the kitchen. When he came to a stop, she had to jerk to a halt to avoid running into him. "What is it?"

He gestured with the pistol.

Just inside the back door, a man was sprawled face down on the floor. He had his right arm stretched out, as if pleading for help. Or had he been reaching for the sack and rifle he'd dropped? He didn't wear a uniform, which meant he could be anyone, a robber or a raider, or possibly one of Jeff's unsavory friends.

The judge approached the still figure, whose lean, powerful body reminded her of a panther, and nudged the larger man with the toe of his shoe.

She ventured closer. "Is he—?" Her mouth went dry and she had to wet her lips. "Dead?"

"Hard to tell." The judge knelt and rolled the unconscious intruder onto his back.

Beneath a crisscrossed ammunition belt, the rise and fall of the stranger's broad chest confirmed he still breathed—for the time being. Blood matted his dark, tousled hair and collected in the curve of his ear and in a thick, black beard. Even senseless and wounded, he appeared fierce, dangerous.

As she bent to peer at his face, her heart pounded. His eyes remained closed. But a small, worried voice whispered that if he opened them, they would be forest brown with flecks of green and gold.

No, it wasn't possible. It couldn't be...

"Tom?"

Read the rest of *Tom Sawyer Returns*.
On sale now at all major online retailers.